TIDE OF SHADOWS

BOOK TWO OF THE SHADOWS AND SHINERS TRILOGY
CHRISTINA CROTHERS

Tide of Shadows by Christina Crothers

Published by Between the Pines Publishing LLC

ChristinaCrothers.com

Copyright © 2025 Christina Crothers

All rights reserved. No portion of this book may be reproduced in any form without permission from the publisher, except as permitted by U.S. copyright law.

The characters and events in this book are fictitious. Any similarity to real persons, living or dead, is coincidental and not intended by the author.

Cover by GetCovers

ISBN: 979-8-9869024-2-5

For Jenny,
Who has been capturing imaginary people and worlds in written
stories since we were kids and who inspired me to give it a try

A cacophony of chaos woke me from sleep. The noises follow me to my desk, where I try to untangle them on paper. From my right, I hear crashing waves and the screams of the lost. From my left, I hear the sparkle of wild flowers and harmonies dancing on strings. When I look straight, all the sounds clash and yet . . . there is something more. A drip, drip, drip, that relentlessly carries me towards the chaos.

~Gwyneth Webb

Day 172 since The Annapolis Magic Containment Breach

One

Zach
Thursday afternoon
Guard HQ, Washington, DC

"If my life was a graphic novel, these walls would be made of stone," Zach said. The office chair squeaked as he leaned back to survey the sterile white walls. Yellowing papers, old books, and meticulous notes buried the stainless-steel table he was working at. Reaching his arms over his head, he stretched his lanky frame.

Sadie looked up from the seventeenth-century journal she was translating. "What?"

Oops, I actually said that out loud. Zach shrugged and picked up the 5B pencil he'd been using to sketch in the margin of his notes. "I was just thinking how we could all be characters in a graphic novel. Our lives sound cool enough on paper." Because Sadie looked bemused and he was stuck on the translation of a grammatically impossible sentence, he elaborated.

"Here we are, in a hidden basement under the headquarters of a secret organization. Our current mission is to clean up a magic containment breach before the rest of the world knows what's happening or it starts a cascade of breaches that lead to a mass extinction event. If I drew the novel, these walls would be made of craggy gray stone."

Sadie looked around the modestly sized manuscript-restoration lab and frowned. "The climate control wouldn't work," she said in her light Scottish burr. "The books would be damaged."

Zach fought back a smile. "But it would look cooler."

With a dismissive snort, she bent her head to her work. Research time was precious. The first few weeks after The Annapolis Magic Containment Breach, TAMCoB for short, they'd worked themselves practically into zombies trying to figure out how to clean it up. Once it became clear that the process would be a marathon, not a sprint, they'd had to shift to sustainable hours.

Sadie looked up again. "And calling us a secret organization makes us sound bigger than we are."

Crossing out the nonsensical sentence he'd just written, Zach frowned. *I'm being distracting instead of helpful, again.*

"True," he said. Though he loved the extravagant language used to describe everything Guard related, Sadie wasn't wrong. For most of his life, "the Guard" had meant a handful of families and friends using an old legend as an excuse for get-togethers and to sit on the board of a tiny manuscript restoration and antique business—a far, far cry from J's Men in Black or Potter's Ministry of Magic. The fact that the board called itself a Council didn't change that.

It had been a hell of a shock when TAMCoB happened. As of six months ago, magic had been safely trapped in inert knots for centuries, apart from a few relatively minor incidents. No loose magic meant enchanted artifacts didn't work, spells couldn't be crafted, and no one developed magical abilities, like Shadows and Shiners.

A large organization would have had almost nothing to do, and the more people who knew about magic, the greater the risk was that someone would get it into their head to cut a knot, turning the stable tangle into fabric-of-reality-altering, monster-spawning chaos.

Since TAMCoB, though, Zach and Alexis had developed Shadow abilities, allowing them to see snippets of the past, present, and future in shadows. Brian had developed Shiner abilities; he could manipulate the strands connecting the world around him. Sadie, who, like the rest of the Guard, hadn't shown signs of any innate magical ability, had taken charge of crafting spells to help keep magic a secret while it was present. And any Guard members who could put their lives on hold had found ways to help, especially if they could assist from outside the 150-mile radius of the magic contamination zone.

Zach was doing his best to enjoy every minute of being in the thick of it. Soon, Merlin willing, the breach would be sealed, all the magic safely back in its knot, and he'd go back to figuring out what he was supposed to do with his life. The Guard couldn't afford to pay him a living wage in restoration or antique sales, even if he'd had an interest, especially after sinking so much money into sealing this breach. He'd go back to marking the yearly picnic on his calendar, swinging by any time he happened to be in DC, and grabbing a meal with random Guard members when their paths crossed.

Your mind is wandering. He sighed and tried to focus on rechecking his translation of the journal in front of him.

His sigh must have been louder than he'd intended, because Sadie cleared her throat.

Zach looked up.

She touched the right side of her forehead. "You have a smudge of something. Graphite?"

Giving an amused shrug, he rubbed his forehead. His fair skin did nothing to hide smudges from his fingertips, discolored from sketching.

She nodded to let him know he'd gotten it, or at least smeared it out of visibility.

Sadie's blonde hair was in a neat bun, and her business casual outfit wrinkle free. Whereas, after several hours of trying to help with the translation, Zach's wavy, auburn hair was sticking out in odd directions. His blue jeans and black surrealist T-shirt looked like he'd picked them off his floor, which wasn't far from the truth.

Twirling a pencil between his fingers, he tried to refocus on the work in front of him. The mirage spell they'd found hidden in a rambling story about mist wasn't working. Being able to hide one's intentions from enemy Shadows would be invaluable, but it was written in a creative gibberish that was supposed to be Latin; it fell so far short it was closer to pig Latin or Tolkien's Orcish.

"I don't believe a graphic novel could do this justice." Sadie tapped her pen thoughtfully on her notebook.

"Why not?"

"It would be difficult to capture how engrossing it is. Sorting through old legal documents, journals, and travel books, searching for the tiniest scraps and clues to understand something our predecessors worked so hard to remove from the history books. I don't think the thrill could be captured in a drawing."

Torn between laughing and putting his head down on the desk in defeat, Zach settled for stretching. "Sadie, I admire your enthusiasm. I, however, need more caffeine."

Rolling back his chair, he got up and walked over to the thermos on the other table. Zach had serious doubts about the people-won't-misuse-magic-if they-don't-believe-it's-real plan his long-ago ancestors had concocted. Destroying all evidence that magic existed worked great until something went wrong; the answers they needed to clean up a breach were erased, too. The few surviving sources of information about magic were in lost volumes almost exclusively written in dead languages and often in some kind of code.

Leaning his hip against the spare table, Zach sipped the lukewarm, bitter coffee. Endless rabbit holes, red herrings, and no new magic breaches had dulled his panic. Less helpful, it had also dulled his motivation. *I'm lucky to be here*, he reminded himself, and gulped down the rest of the caffeine so he could return to translating.

"Coffee?" he asked, setting down his mug with a grin.

She shot him the expected frown. She'd fought having beverages in the lab, but since she refused to let the spellbooks and magic-related papers out of the lab, Zach, Brian, and Russel won that battle. Sadie was so enthusiastic about security, even her cute, bioengineering girlfriend had no idea what Sadie was really doing at work. It had been a weird staff holiday party.

Still smiling to himself, he returned to his squeaky chair and dug back into the journal. Progress was slow and painstaking, but he was absorbed by the work when the door to the stairs opened with a beep.

"Hey," Terra said as she entered, followed by Brian and Alexis. "We just received time-sensitive intel. We need a field bag."

If there was a graphic novel about the Guard, Terra would be the one handing out the missions and doing the debriefings. One day,

Zach was going to capture the contradiction between her real-life appearance and her shadow. On the DC streets she passed as an average white woman in a suit, but the shadow at her feet was painted in vibrant acrylics, sharpened by analytical lines and a touch of glitter.

Zach stood up and went to the supply shelf to triple-check the field bag was in order, per protocol.

"Where's Russel?" Sadie asked. Russel was the spellcaster on the field team. His specialties were mechanical instruments and collecting measurements.

"He and Elliot are testing a magic barometer," Terra said. "They took the shadow hounds as an excuse to be dog walking in case someone started asking questions, but that's not why we're sending out the field team. Nick reached out ten minutes ago."

"I still think he should be in prison," Sadie muttered, like she did every time Nick's name came up.

Mentally, Zach agreed, but it wasn't *his* family that had been held hostage, and despite causing TAMCoB, Nick had been useful since.

If anyone had reason to object, it was the guy trying to pull a stray pen off the floor with an invisible strand of magic. With Brian's relaxed, easy smile, jock build, and dark wavy hair, he looked like a person who'd had life easy, not the kind who'd risked everything to save his family. Brian gave an amused shrug when Zach met his eyes and still managed to catch the pen as it jumped into the air. He started to throw it to Zach, but Terra frowned at them and Brian placed the pen sheepishly on the closest table.

Alexis, a pretty, petite brunette, slid her hand into Brian's free one, warmly drawing his attention back to the conversation. Matching magic-bracelets stood out like emerald tattoos against their white skin; the physical manifestation of them being tied. On the magical plane their individual magics wove together in a way that made both of them more powerful. In the graphic novel version of the Guard, they'd be the lead heroes.

Terra ignored Sadie's comment and Brian's frivolous use of magic. "Nick says there's a possible knot in Potomac, Maryland. It's a long shot, but Searcha agents are on their way from Richmond. That gives us a head start if we act now."

All graphic novels needed an antagonist; if the Guard's job was to protect humanity by keeping the world magic free, the Searcha idiots wanted to unleash that toxic nightmare.

"Potomac, Maryland, is a pretty good-sized place. Did Nick give us anything else to work with?" Alexis asked.

Zach was glad Alexis was such a nice person; it'd made it wonderfully easy to get over his initial resentment. When they'd first met she'd already been better than him at deciphering the disorganized images their new abilities showed them in the shadows, but after tying with Brian, she'd gone from an outsider who'd never heard of the Guard to arguably its most magically powerful member—over a long weekend.

Just as well, since when it came to real life he'd always preferred the role of helpful and supportive secondary character. Contributing, without the weight of making all the hard decisions, was far more comfortable than some imagined world where he was the World's Best Shadow and lead hero. As a bonus, his Latin and Ancient Greek were good; they were invaluable languages for the bulk of the translation work.

Terra double-checked her notes. "Within eight miles of Great Falls Park."

"That narrows it down," Brian said. "The compass should get us the rest of the way."

Sadie straightened a stack of papers louder than necessary. "The field team is one short without Russel. Two, if you count a shadow hound. I can see how this is time sensitive. Do you need me to go?" She looked about as thrilled as if she was proposing they eat dripping barbecue sandwiches at the translation table.

"I don't like sending the team without a spellcaster, but it's a long-shot mission, and I know how valuable your time in the lab is," Terra said.

Sadie breathed out a small sigh of relief. "But someone should go. A full team is in the guidelines we established at the last Council meeting."

Zach hid his smile as he slid the first-aid kit back in the backpack he was checking. Everyone in the room had been at that meeting.

Terra frowned. "I'm not up to speed yet on spell casting."

"You've been busy. And didn't you say you have three more virtual meetings this afternoon?" Alexis said.

Crafting spells is like being asked to make a souffle from a crumbling, well-used cookbook written in old-fashioned cursive, Zach mused as he zipped up the backpack. *The book's missing pages and some of the ingredients are long-gone name-brand items, and sometimes the dessert falls flat for no apparent reason.* No innate magic was required, but it wasn't a job for most people. Terra was too valuable in her role for her to be wasting time trying to keep up with the spellcasters.

Zach offered the backpack, fully stocked for the field mission. Brian nodded thanks and shouldered it. Giving him a thumbs-up in return, Zach slipped back towards the translation table.

"I do. I could move them, but . . . Zach!" Terra's eyes alighted on him before he could sit down. "You're up to speed on spellcraft."

"Sure." He shrugged casually, one hand on the back of his chair, but excitement crackled in his stomach. Field missions tended to be wild-goose chases, but a valid excuse to take a break from translations was irresistible.

"Perfect," Sadie said.

Brian grinned. "Great, we're ready then?"

"Alexis?" Terra asked.

Alexis frowned at the floor as if trying to burn a hole in it. "The future has a wavy, undeveloped edge."

Zach tried to see what she was talking about, but the harsh shadows cast by the bright, artificial light in the lab were only giving him a peek at the present. A sketch in red crayon of a lopsided clock silently ticked away in Terra's shadow, probably indicating her worry that their head start on the Searcha agents was shrinking as they spoke.

"Wavy, undeveloped?" Sadie asked. "Maybe you're seeing the mirage spell Zach is working on."

Alexis rubbed her temple. "Maybe. Can we pack it too?"

"Can't guarantee it'll work, but I'll get it." Zach plucked the nickel-sized quartz crystal off the shelf of neatly labeled spells. After hours or weeks of steeping, brewing, and chanting, sometimes the spells worked, sometimes they didn't. Spell rocks were only good for one use, so testing them meant starting the whole process over again, no matter the outcome. The mirage spell, in particular, had felt like an exercise in insanity, but Zach unzipped the pouch on the field bag Brian was wearing and added it.

"I'm sorry I can't see more," Alexis said.

Terra smiled reassuringly. "We're all doing our best. You all should get moving."

Alexis gave herself a little shake. Gratitude bloomed in Zach's chest; he didn't envy the weight of being the most skilled at seeing the future. Even when the shadows were at their clearest, they held too much back.

"Let's go," Alexis said, and gave everyone a smile.

Out a security door, up a flight of stairs, and through the hidden door, they wound their way out of HQ. Alexis led the way to Terra's Corolla parked on the street. The car was an unremarkable tan and a year younger than Zach's twenty-two.

"You want to drive?" Alexis asked.

"Nah." Zach opened the rear door. "You know I prefer the back. Thanks, though."

Brian was the navigator, using Merlin's Compass and the GPS on his phone, so he took the front passenger seat while Alexis slid behind the wheel.

Enjoying the graphic novel idea, Zach settled into the back seat, pulled out his sketchpad, and experimented with ideas for the vehicle he'd take if he drew this mission. A Batmobile style would be too obvious.

"Anyone want a strawberry toaster pastry?" he offered, digging in his messenger bag.

"I'm good, thanks," Alexis said, sounding relaxed, but her shadow had a pea-green color to it. "Dinner will be ready when we get back."

"Sure, thanks," Brian said, putting out a hand.

Shrugging off the unusual shade of green, Zach passed up the silvery foil packet, and then opened his own.

He took a large bite of strawberry and sugar as a motorcycle vroomed past, slipping between the two lanes of traffic. The pastry would have been better toasted, but he'd had too much coffee on an empty stomach and needed something to settle it.

He twirled his pencil. A motorcycle would be cool, weaving in and out of traffic, racing to beat Searcha to dangerous artifacts. *Yes.* With a few quick lines, he sketched himself riding a Ducati, wearing a cool black leather jacket.

Amused, he chewed the last of the toaster pastry, ignoring his twisting stomach, and started sketching. A larger-than-life version of the seven Guard members currently living at HQ was an interesting challenge.

"Zach?" Alexis asked.

He looked up and met her eyes in the rearview mirror.

"Something seem off with the shadows to you? I'd think I was getting carsick, but I'm driving."

"Oh." Zach frowned. The last time the shadows had made him feel physically ill, the Baltimore Knot had almost been cut. "I feel off, but the shadows aren't showing me any clear warnings."

"Me neither. Weird. Maybe it's not related?"

No idea. But Zach found the shadows baffling more often than not.

"It wasn't what we had for lunch. I feel good," Brian said.

Zach shrugged. "I have a few pieces of ginger candy. Would you like one?"

Alexis nodded. "Thanks."

Zach passed up the teal-wrapped candy and opened one for himself. Glad Alexis was on the shadows, he ignored his stomach and focused on his sketch pad. The figures practically drew themselves, the ideas flowed so easily.

"Shit!" Brian said. The wire of a compass glowed above the palm of his hand. "Nick's info *is* good. There's a knot nearby."

Zach's pencil slipped out of his hand and rolled under the front seat. *Shit*, was too mild an expletive. *Not a wild-goose chase.* His uneasy stomach wasn't a coincidence. *But why aren't the shadows showing a warning?*

Two

Kayla whooped as the tiny sailboat caught the Chesapeake breeze and heeled, tipping sideways and nearly dumping her into the bay. Leaning as far back as she could on the high side of the deck, she tried to balance the boat, Kayla against the wind-filled sail. Adrenaline sang in her veins. Waves against the bow sent water droplets dancing into the air. She laughed.

Learning how to sail was the best perk of her new job—not what she expected when she'd been recruited as an agent for the super-secret organization working to free magic. Of course, she'd been expecting to learn actual magic, which, a month into training, still hadn't happened. Maybe learning to manipulate strands of energy would be cooler than sailing, but Kayla wasn't counting on it.

Hannah, on the other sunfish, waved Kayla over.

Don't tell me it's time to go in already? Frowning, Kayla came about. Pointing her boat towards Hannah's, she ignored how the chilly breeze tugged a strand of her long blonde hair free from her

French braid and raised goosebumps on her fair skin. The wetsuit and PFD—life jacket—were awesome protection from the cold, but even they couldn't prevent the sun from flirting with the horizon. Still, being chilly on a sailboat was better than working through the stack of Latin translations that was due tomorrow.

If hell existed, it would include being forced to research and write papers on long-dead people and memorize Latin declensions.

Kayla maneuvered her sunfish into a comfortable shouting distance. "Thanks again for teaching me sailing!"

"I'm glad you're enjoying it. Hopefully, clearing your head will make your translations easier to finish."

Kayla gritted her teeth. She was going to spend her whole evening fighting to meet deadlines. Hannah would work with her, saying she was getting ahead on her own assignments, but really she'd be there to make sure Kayla stayed on track.

Kayla tried to be grateful to have such a helpful roommate. She really did.

Hannah's world revolved around the assigned busy work and her devotion to freeing all magic. Born and raised in the South, she'd kept the accent and little else when she'd reinvented herself in California as an indie musician. She'd been touring with her band in Richmond when Searcha freed the First Knot. Developing Shadow abilities, Hannah was discovered by Dr. Caligo and recruited by Searcha. Having been at Tidal Water just shy of six months, she was the most experienced trainee. A dubious honor, in Kayla's opinion, since an entire class of alchemists had arrived and graduated in that time.

Kayla winced. *If I'm not lucky, I'll be here just as long.* Alchemists, the bulk of the trainees, were clearly on an expedited schedule compared to those with innate magic.

"Can we sail over there?" Kayla asked, pointing to a spit of land as far away as she thought she could get away with.

Hannah shook her head and opened her mouth to speak, but a gust of cool air from across the bay jibed Kayla's sail to the other side. She fought to sort her lines after the prevailing wind shift of 180 degrees.

"What was that?" she called.

Her roommate was staring out over the bay, a deep frown marring her pretty features.

Kayla shivered. Maybe the cold was getting to her. "Hannah?"

Hannah shook herself. "Something was weird about that gust of wind. I'm feeling kinda nauseous." She shrugged. "I'm probably just hungry. If we head back now, we'll have just enough time to clean up before dinner. You'll want a shower too."

Kayla brightened at the thought of food. Hannah wasn't wrong about a shower, either. Hannah looked like something off a Hollywood set; her brunette updo looking expertly windblown, her make-up natural and perfectly applied, and her fair skin had a pretty pink warmth from the cold. Whereas Kayla had capsized twice. It would take half a bottle of conditioner to sort out her hair. "Race you to the beach?"

Hannah hesitated.

Kayla immediately regretted her words. She'd meant it as a fun way to get back quickly, but Hannah took everything seriously and was set in her belief that she was better at everything Tidal Water related. Hannah would probably win, so it was fine.

"See you at the beach," Hannah answered. "Ready? Three, two, one, go." She tightened her sail, and her sunfish took off.

Mentally kicking herself, Kayla followed. Hannah would be way more fun the whole evening, or at least more tolerable, if she was in a good mood. She'd know if Kayla tried to throw the race, too, and that would make things worse.

Kayla wiggled her jaw to loosen the tension building there and gave up thinking. Trusting her gut to calculate wind and angles, Kayla's sunfish flew towards the shore. Laughter bubbled up, and she leaned further over the high side of the deck. What her tall, slim build lacked in curves it made up for in athleticism.

A gust shook the boat. Pulling into the wind, Kayla narrowly escaped capsizing. She lost momentum and zigzagged. Channeling her adrenaline boost, she fought to get the wind back. Savoring each second, Kayla coaxed every bit of speed out of the tiny boat. The biting breeze sang by.

She was almost beside Hannah's boat as they passed the jetty. *Crap, I might actually win. Maybe Hannah will be delighted by how good of a teacher she is.* Kayla snorted. *Why couldn't I have any other trainee as a roommate?*

Kayla was underwater before she realized what'd happened. Cold water saturated her wetsuit. She hadn't seen the gust coming. Her PFD popped her right back to the surface. Sputtering, she wiped water off her face *That's what I get for being overconfident. Hannah's still the better sailor.* Kayla hooted with laughter before taking stock. Hannah, well on her way to shore, waved cheerfully.

Grinning, Kayla waved back and turned her attention to the sunfish. It was drifting off, completely upside down. *Turtled* was the term, and that was rather what it looked like, except for the drag board, sticking up like a shark fin. Swimming over, she uncleated the mainsheet from the deck and then climbed onto the upside-down hull. Grabbing the top of the drag board, she stood at the very edge of the hull and leaned back. Leverage and body weight pulled the little boat over until it was upright. Hauling herself onto the deck with a big kick, Kayla took the bucket tied to the stern for just this sort of thing and bailed the water out, again.

Even with the wetsuit for protection, the beds of Kayla's fingernails were turning blue by the time she got underway. Keeping a closer eye on the waves and wind, she headed back to shore. Her stomach was growling, but the idea of warm, dry clothes was as appealing as tacos. Still, she was grinning ear to ear when she arrived at the beach. Definitely her new favorite sport.

"Nice job." Hannah jumped into the waist-deep water to pull her sunfish onto shore. "Like Captain Fitzroy always says, if you're not capsizing now and again, you're doing something wrong."

Kayla laughed. "I don't think he meant three times in one afternoon."

"Nah, you're doing really great."

Kayla stopped herself from rolling her eyes. Hannah meant well, even if she sounded patronizing. With an elaborate bow, she said, "Thanks."

Hannah smiled and sent Kayla to the boathouse, while she started putting away the sailing equipment.

See, she can be perfectly lovely. I don't know why I worry, Kayla thought as she peeled off her dripping wetsuit and swimsuit. Quickly, she slid into dry leggings, an athletic tank top, and her favorite russet zip-up hoodie. Hair still dripping, she was back in time to help hang the sails.

"What's that tune you're humming?" Kayla asked as they put away the ropes. The minor key and upbeat tempo sounded familiar, but she couldn't place it.

Hannah looked down, pink embarrassment staining her cheeks. "Sorry. No idea. The shadows have been all stirred up since that weird gust hit us. At first I heard the theme song to *Jaws* and that was a *little* creepy. It played over a swelling, discordant symphony that finally faded." She shook her head and looked up. "Now I've got this random piece of folky music stuck in my head, made extra weird by a synthetic sound that all the shadows are reflecting at the moment."

Hannah heard all sorts of musical things in the shadows. Sometimes it meant she knew more about what Kayla was thinking or feeling than Kayla did. It *always* meant she *thought* she knew more than anyone else around her. She kept what she saw to herself, though, except in her weekly reports to Miranda and when she was pointing out how Kayla could do things better. Hannah could hear Kayla's mind wandering from her studies on the other side of the two-bedroom they shared.

"Synthesized means possible future information?" Kayla asked, to show off that she did sometimes pay attention to Hannah's explanations of what magic was like for her.

"Yes." Hannah gave her a smile. "I'm so looking forward to being tied. I'll finally have a clearer idea what the shadows are trying to tell me."

Kayla didn't want to hear that speech again. "I feel like I know the tune you were humming, but you know I don't have an ear for music." Hannah pointed it out at least once a day.

Hannah hummed it more clearly, tapping out the rhythm with her fingers on the metal shelves as Kayla closed the last of the supplies away in the cabinet.

A clear memory hit Kayla; she could almost taste the baking bread. "I think it's a Russian folk song. About a woman waiting for her man to return from war."

"Weird. How would I have gotten that in my head? It could have something to do with your shadow. Where do you know it from?"

"It's from my past, though, not my future. My great-aunt, Sonya, used to sing it, especially when she was in the kitchen. I never learned Russian, so I don't know the words, but that's what she said it was about."

Hannah frowned at the ground as they started walking back towards their cabin. "Have you been thinking about your great-aunt lately?"

It was tempting to jog ahead and jump into a hot shower, but Kayla shortened her stride to match Hannah's. "I don't think so. She died in my senior year of high school."

"Sorry," Hannah said, but she sounded more focused on the shadows than on empathy.

Kayla shrugged. Thinking about Aunt Sonya's death still made her chest ache a bit. Kayla bounced a few steps and tried to push away the feeling. "She was old, and her mind was going." Those basic facts didn't help.

Kayla's favorite run had taken her by the nursing home, so she'd often stopped in for a chat and a snack. Aunt Sonya had always enjoyed hearing about adventures and problems, while never seeming to mind Kayla's short attention span for her own. After Aunt Sonya died, Kayla wished she'd worked harder to pay attention.

Kayla bounced a few more steps. Nothing she could do about it now. Heaving a sigh, she kept her pace snail slow.

The Tidal Water property encompassed two hundred acres, tucked in the middle of nowhere between two creeks and a wide river, just off the bay. With a scattered hodgepodge of buildings, it was about an even distribution of forest to fields. Kayla and Hannah's small two-bedroom house was nestled in the pine forest on the eastern side of the property. It would have been a ten-minute walk if Kayla had been alone.

Kayla hopped up the porch steps and held the screen door for Hannah.

Her gaze glued to the ground, Hannah didn't seem to notice. "You sure that's where you know the song from?" But she still caught the door so it wouldn't slam.

"I guess." Kayla started for the shower.

Hannah snagged her arm, but her eyes stayed on the ground. "This is important. Why would the shadows bring up your dead great-aunt and indicate it's about the future?"

Tearing her eyes away from the bathroom door wasn't easy, but Kayla managed. "I don't know. She was great."

"In what way?"

Kayla groaned, but it wasn't a hard question. A smile tugged at her lips. "Gave the best advice and enjoyed being outrageous. Left me her taxidermied possum when she died. You should have seen it! I shrieked when I opened the box and saw all those teeth snarling at me. Aunt Sonya was probably laughing from her grave. Though I should have recognized the monstrosity right away. Her name was Nellie." Kayla had no regrets about donating Nellie to a dumpster.

She did regret not being there for her aunt as she had faded. She'd wanted to be anywhere else as Aunt Sonya's cheerful conversations slid into terrified warnings. Absurd fears about monsters, a government conspiracy, and Great Uncle Yerik, her husband and the love of her life, who'd died before Kayla was born. Kayla wished she'd been strong enough to sit by her side and be present for her, even when Aunt Sonya kept asking where Yerik was.

Kayla's thoughts jarred like a jibing sail.

"What?" Hannah squeezed her arm tighter.

Kayla shook Hannah's grip off. "Just a sec." Hannah got a clearer reading on someone when touching physically, but Kayla didn't need her to explain what was going on. She moved into her room and dug through her plastic bin. She found what she was looking for under a University of Maryland T-shirt. The bound journal was peeking out between a book on mindfulness from her little brother that she'd never read and a stack of photos her mom had packed with her. It was a memento of home and family Kayla had added on impulse, faded orange with grid paper, the kind engineers and scientists might make notes in.

Pulling it out gently, Kayla examined the journal with fresh interest. Aunt Sonya's ramblings about magic and Merlin didn't sound so far-fetched now. She opened it gently. The strange scribbles looked like a mashup of gibberish and the scrawl of a mad scientist, but for the first time, Kayla recognized a few of the words as Latin.

"What is that?" Hannah asked quietly. "Its power is filling the room."

"Aunt Sonya left it to me." Reluctantly, Kayla offered her the book.

Hannah took it reverently. Gingerly, she flipped through the pages. "It's a grimoire, but I've never seen one like it. This is what the shadows were trying to tell me. We need to take this to Miranda, now."

Kayla took a quick step back. "Just let me get a quick shower." Her skin was sticky from the brackish water and a damp spot on her lower back was spreading as her braid dripped.

"Later!" Hannah was half a head shorter than Kayla's five ten, but she dragged Kayla by the arm out of her room. "This is important. It would be a huge find any day, so few grimoires have survived the Guard's purging, but there has to be a reason the shadows are demanding we find it now. We have to go!"

Groaning, Kayla forced herself to give in and be towed along.

Three

Zach
Thursday afternoon
MacArthur Boulevard, MD

Zach reached under the car seat in front of him to retrieve his fallen pencil, hoping to collect his calm along with it. Finding the former, he sat up without the latter. Out the window, oversized houses passed by, crowded into the spaces between park land, just as they had two minutes ago, but now Zach knew everyone here was in danger.

A knot was like an unknown nuclear bomb. They wouldn't know how big it was until they found it, but even a small one was bad. The First Knot was the smallest on record, about the size of a lime. Cutting it had caused TAMCoB and spawned a unicorn. The two knots in the Guard's vault, each the size of grapefruit, would spawn far-more-deadly-and-dangerous golems and magic if cut.

Brian, riding shotgun, shifted his hand, but the wire stayed floating in the same direction. "It's still up ahead."

Zach tried to read anything helpful in the shadows; they were smudged to charcoal gray.

"I didn't accuse Nick of anything," Brian said.

Zach glanced up. *What'd I miss?*

"You're thinking it," Alexis said.

Brian sighed.

Zach rolled his eyes. *They're communicating silently again.*

Brian grinned and pulled a piece of magic the size of a pea out of his pocket. "Might as well join the conversation."

Zach's nose wrinkled. "Is that necessary?" Molded from magical clay, the earbuds transmitted projected thoughts to those connected to it. It was the difference between speaking out loud and in your head, only subtler, and trickier to tell when you'd accidentally thought louder than you meant to. It did have the advantage of being able to discuss magic in public without worrying about being overheard, but you could also just be discreet.

"Better to be prepared if Searcha catches up to us," Alexis said. "If we have to split up."

Red paint splattered on Brian's shadow—a memory, but a vivid one.

"You don't need to remind me of the stakes," Zach said, before Brian could share. They'd all been in Baltimore last fall. "What about some unicorn backup?" As far as nightmare-inducing, mythological-creature golems went, Storm had been a useful ally so far.

Brian closed his eyes. "Let's see."

Zach could see the shadows, like smeared lines, as the Shiner touched the different strands around him. Oil pastels added color when he touched the lines connecting him to his family and then thundercloud-gray watercolors when he found the strand he was looking for.

Brian opened his eyes. "Storm is a long way off, almost to the southern edge of the contamination zone." He pushed his hair out of his face. "That's good, right? If there was impending doom, she'd be closer?"

Alexis frowned. "Something about the shadows isn't right. It's as if I'm looking at them with the wrong focal length."

Zach's stomach dropped. Alexis's magic was the best they had. "I thought that was just me. The shadows looked extra smudged today."

"If you're both having trouble, maybe something is off with the magic," Brian said.

Alexis's frown deepened. "Maybe it's blocking some of Storm's abilities as well."

"Do you think Searcha is doing something like the mirage spell you're working on?" Alexis asked.

"Is that even possible?" Brian asked.

"That spell is only meant to hide the shadow of one person, not all of this." Zach played with his pencil. "But we've barely scratched the surface of what magic can do."

"Wait. The Compass changed directions. The knot is behind us and to the left." Brian turned to look, but there were just trees.

"This doesn't look like a safe place to leave the car. We passed a parking lot not far back." Alexis used a side road to pull a U-ey.

It felt like ten minutes before they reached the uneven gravel lot, but it might have been three. The car bounced as Alexis navigated the potholes. She pulled into the first spot they saw, between a dusty red Jeep with a kayak on top and a navy-blue BMW with a bike rack.

"Earbud," Alexis reminded him.

Zach made a face at the lump of green magic. Gingerly, he slid it into his ear. Alexis had gotten good at molding them, and, once they'd dried, they didn't zap, so it was a comfortable fit.

"*You're our acting spellcaster, want to carry the bag?*" Brian asked in Zach's head as they got out of the car.

"*Of course,*" Zach thought back and accepted the bag. "*I hope we don't need it.*"

"*Agreed. If Nick bought us enough time, we can be in and out before Searcha gets here,*" Alexis replied.

Zach winced—he'd hadn't meant to think that part loud enough to be heard.

"This way." Brian pointed towards the trailhead and hid the compass in his jacket.

Zach dug his hands into his pockets as they walked down a steep hill to the trail map.

"The compass isn't specific enough to tell us which trail will get us there the fastest," Brian said.

Alexis traced several of the lines on the map, which showed a stretch of interconnected parks on the Maryland side of the Potomac. "I'm getting an image of an old whitewashed house. I think that's what we're looking for." She lifted her hand from the map and massaged her forehead.

"You okay?" Brian asked.

"The distortion in the shadows isn't fun, and my stomach still isn't happy, but I'll be fine." Alexis shrugged. "This should be the path."

They turned away from the bridge that crossed to the busier towpath and set a brisk pace on the quieter walk on their side of the canal, which was tucked into the hill.

Brian took Alexis's hand. Zach looked away when he saw a green spark play around their interlaced fingers. Seeing the intimacy between them in their shadow could feel like he'd walked in on them making out. Zach gave his shoulders a shake and looked anywhere else.

The trail was wide enough to walk three abreast, but Zach fell in step behind, lengthening his stride to keep up. Taking a deep breath, he tried to ignore the itchy feeling of time slipping away and instead sink into the moment. To connect with his surroundings. To connect more deeply with magic. To bring the shadows to life around him, illuminating possible dangers.

The promise of summer was in the air, but only a few spring-green leaves had unfurled on the sleepy tree branches and many were heavy with orange or yellow pollen. The half-drained canal reflected the blue sky, and a pair of mallards floated among the weeds on the edge. The air was bright and heavy with the scent of damp leaves and growing earth.

I'm seeing it in my mind, but not feeling it. Why is this taking so long? Zach noted the impatient thoughts, but let them drift by. Absorbed for a moment by the warmth of the sunlight baking into his black T-shirt, something in Zach shifted. Color bloomed in the surrounding shadows, as if a pencil sketch was being turned into a watercolor. *There!* A smile tugged at his lips. He could be a spellcaster and a Shadow.

Pale-blue paint splashed across the shadows. Air caught in Zach's throat. Hands on his knees, he gasped for breath. Around him, ice crept into the shadows, turning them monochrome blue. His vision darkened around the edges.

"What the hell!" Alexis gasped, doubling over as if punched in the gut.

Brian put an arm around her. "That bad?"

Zach rode the wave of panic, pain, and fear crashing down on him, breathing his way through it until he could straighten up and swallow back the nausea. Opening and closing his hands, he tried to be curious about when they'd stop shaking.

Alexis leaned heavily on Brian. "There is definitely a knot, and it's in danger of being cut."

"We're almost there," Zach said. Now he could see the white-washed house in the monochrome shadows. It was two stories tall, with boarded-up windows.

Brian took Alexis's hand and picked up the pace.

When they rounded a corner, ahead of them was the house from the shadows. It had no driveway and belonged to an older era. Beyond it were the huge, overgrown beams of a lock.

Alexis snapped a few quick pictures to center herself as Brian consulted his compass.

"What's a knot doing in an old lockhouse?" Alexis asked. "Never mind. Get the knot now. History research when we get back to HQ."

"My kind of plan." Brian grinned and jumped over the waist-high gate at the top of a long row of stairs.

Alexis hesitated before following. "Zach, can you stand lookout?"

Zach gave the house a curious glance before digging in the field bag. "Of course. Here's the magic-containment box." He handed over the lead-lined cedar container.

"Thanks." Alexis took it and accepted Brian's help over the gate.

Zach leaned with exaggerated casualness against the metal pole railing, wishing they had a shadow hound or two with them. The large Newfoundland mixes could see or smell the magical plane, making them invaluable additions to the field team. *How would they look in graphic novel form?* Zach yanked his focus back to the prickly shadows.

Searcha had to be close, but he couldn't see any sign of them. The blue leaked out of the shadows as he squinted at them.

Rubbing the gooseflesh rising on his skin, he checked the sky for clouds. None, but the color was dissolving out of the sky. Shadow fog rolled in. *What the hell? Is it me or the magic?*

"Alexis!" he mentally called. *"Something's wrong!"*

A jogger in an orange T-shirt, damp with a V of sweat, came towards him up the path. Zach reached into the field bag, but he couldn't see the shadows clearly enough to know which rock contained which spell without pulling them out to look.

The jogger barely glanced at him as he went past.

The gray and fog grew darker.

"Alexis!"

Static, like blood pounding in his ears, filled his mind.

"Zach, I can barely hear you. We've almost got the knot. It's a big one." Alexis's thoughts were distant and scratchy, like a dusty record being played on the other end of a long tunnel.

Zach tried to keep the expletives in his own head.

Two women in their early twenties, emphatically complaining about beltway traffic, came into view. They seemed oblivious to the haze, so thick now that Zach could barely see them despite one of them wearing a fuchsia-pink tank top.

Zach shook his head. Thinking was slow, but his heart raced.

The women and their loud conversation walked past.

Leaning heavily on the railing, Zach turned to look for more people.

A strand of invisible magic yanked Zach off his feet. Gravel dug into his knees and palms. Rolling free, he pushed to his feet. The one with the fuchsia tank top glowed with neon-pink geometric patterns on her exposed skin. The other was sunken into the black hoodie she wore. Their black cargo pants and boots matched. Zach had never seen them before, couldn't read their shadows through the haze, and wouldn't have noticed they were identical twins if he hadn't realized who they were.

"Searcha's tied team is here!" Hopefully, Alexis could hear him through the interference.

Zach caught a flicker of movement, a slight distortion, like a snake swimming through water. He jumped; the strand flicked by.

"How did they get here before us?" the Searcha Shiner asked her sister. The pink highlights in her short ponytail matched her markings.

"That crappy cloaking potion works both ways," the Searcha Shadow muttered. "Get him out of the way."

Fuchsia Shiner and Shadow Raven, that's what I'd call them in my comic. "That is definitely a shitty spell," Zach said with a smirk, hoping to buy time.

He saw the strand in time to sidestep it. Pride bubbled up.

Shit! He dove, barely escaping as the ball of crackling pink magic flew over him. The gravel was sharp, but better than twitching on the ground like he'd been tasered. He rolled to his feet. Brushing pebbles off his grazed palms, he watched for the next attack, cursing himself for getting overly confident.

"It's two against one," Fuchsia said. "Just get out of the way."

"Actually, it's three against two," Brian said, taking the steps up the hill two at a time. Deep-green Shiner's markings bloomed on his skin. "Why don't you get out of the way?"

Alexis followed almost as quickly, but didn't draw attention.

"Why would we do that?" Fuchsia asked. "So you can lock another helpless entity in your vault? After connecting with magic, how can you want to hold it captive?"

Alexis stood behind Zach and slid a heavy object into his bag.

Brian laughed without humor.

Zach tried not to think about Alexis or his bag. He focused on Brian's reply, trying to hide his shadow with the fog lifting.

"Clearly your abilities weren't developed last fall, or you'd know how dangerous this shit is," Brian taunted with the truth.

Alexis slid something small out of the pack into his hand. A spell. *The mirage spell!* If he could hide his shadow, they wouldn't know what was in the field bag. *Fingers crossed, the spell works this time.* Maybe he could help it along.

It was Fuchsia's turn to laugh.

"They're stalling." Alexis said. *"Zach, move. We'll give you a head start."*

Anger helped hide shadows. *When was I really angry? Fifteen!* Zach dug into his memories of being angry and misunderstood in a world where everyone else had important stuff going on and his own desires seemed so unimportant and so impossible that he'd forgotten how to dream them outside of his sketchbook. He dropped the piece of quartz. It cracked. *Please, let the spell work!* Edging down the path, letting anger wash through him, he couldn't tell if his shadow was hidden.

Raven pointed at Zach. "Where are you going?"

Brian used the opening and sent a ball of green magic clay at the Searcha team.

Raven ducked in time. The ball hit the end of a magical strand and bounced back like a yo-yo, hitting Fuchsia. She went down twitching. Raven crouched beside her sister.

Zach bolted. The shadows were clearing; without looking back he could see that Alexis and Brian were on his heels. The Searcha team was between them and the car, but Zach was pretty sure the map said the path would meet up with one that would get them back. There was a steep trail up the hill to the right that might work.

"She's calling for backup." Alexis's thoughts sounded breathless. *"That bridge!"*

Easier than the steep path. Zach raced forward. The bridge spanned high over the canal.

On the far side he leaped down the steps four at a time, stopping for a moment on the towpath to get his bearings. Hikers, joggers, bikes, and dogs on long, trippable leashes clogged the path. *Which way to go?*

"There!" someone shouted.

Zach spun to see a man on a bike pointing to him. *Shit, shit, shit!* A Searcha spellcaster, or *alchemist* as they called them. He and three bikers behind him were wearing the same black cargo pants as the tied team.

"This is no place for a magical battle." Alexis's thoughts gave shape to the crimson splash in the shadows.

Zach bolted for the nearest side path. *"This way!"* It was further up the canal, away from the car, but the path was narrow, marred by roots and large rocks—their pursuers couldn't follow on their bicycles.

Alexis and Brian stayed close. Zach tried not to think about how all the people they were racing around were in danger if Searcha caught up to him.

There was a crash as the alchemists dropped their bikes to follow.

Around a bend, Zach skidded by gray boulders and onto a cliff overlooking the raging river far below. The Potomac. It was like stumbling into an epic movie. Zach dodged around hikers. The shadows warned him that the alchemists were close behind.

Zach reached into the bag. The spell to cover tracks would come in handy.

"Yowch!" Pain bit into his hand. The knot had fallen out of the box, and he'd touched it. Images of raging waves stormed his mind; the stench of rotting fish filled his mouth. His legs gave out; rocks cut his knees

Brian yanked him up by the arm.

"Thanks," Zach managed, zipping the bag shut. Gulping clean air, he pushed forward again. He'd return the black tangle of stinging magic to the box later.

Brian and Alexis fell in behind, protecting the knot and Zach.

"*What the hell is wrong with that knot?*" Zach asked.

"*I don't know. It's twisted and dangerous. Even more dangerous than the Baltimore Knot,*" Alexis replied. "*What is Searcha thinking, wanting to release something like this?!*"

"*More running, less thinking.*" Brian glanced over his shoulder. "*Bloody hell, they're gaining on us.*"

Zach kept both hands out wide as he jumped from rock to rock, following the sky-blue trail blazes.

They started to pull ahead of the Searcha agents—broken ankles seemed to be a concern for them. *A valid one*, Zach conceded, as he slipped and nearly twisted his own in a gap between two rocks.

Scrambling over boulders, Zach remembered the awful team-building trips Terra would take his generation on. If not for those, he'd be looking like the hikers they had just passed, slowly picking their way along on all fours.

"We're going to have to thank Terra for those trips when we get back." Brian's thoughts bubbled with laughter.

Zach wanted to rip the ear bud out, but maybe he and Brian were just thinking along the same lines. "Definitely," he panted.

They'd almost gained enough ground on the alchemists. All Zach needed was a fork in the path, and he could use the track-covering spell in the bag.

They stopped short at the base of a cliff.

"What the hell kinda trail is this?!" Zach hadn't meant to think loudly, but *Shit!*

A handful of hikers inched their way down a slim ledge that cut diagonally up the wall of gray rock. Half-a-dozen people in front of him waited patiently for their turn.

Zach grinned at the tirade of colorful expletives Brian was mentally shouting. "Couldn't have said it better myself."

Brian grinned sheepishly.

Zach's smile widened. It was nice to know he wasn't the only one who struggled with the earbuds.

"We got to go," Alexis said.

Glancing back, Zach could see the alchemists closing the distance.

"Excuse me, sorry." Zach nudged hikers out of the way when he couldn't go around them.

"We're coming down!" a woman on the cliff shouted.

"Sorry!" Zach kept going. When he reached the hikers, he held his breath and moved to climb around. The sole of his sneaker slid. Each inch brought him closer to the deadly river and sharp rocks. Cursing, he shifted his weight and held on with his fingertips.

Searcha agents burst into the clearing.

Angry shouts indicated the hikers had had enough bad manners for one day.

"Get down here now!" the lead alchemist called.

"Come and get me," Zach shouted back, because, *seriously?*

"Watch out!" Alexis yelled.

Zach tried to duck. His shoes slipped. He grabbed a hiker next to him. The woman shrieked and flailed her arms.

Thud.

The dagger missed Zach. His pack wasn't so lucky.

Shit, I should have kept my mouth shut. Zach found his footing.

Burning, frigid liquid bit into his right hip. Pain slithered down his leg, attacking his thigh and calf like fire ants.

The alchemists were coming up after them.

Fighting pain, Zach focused on scrambling to the top.

Sinking to a rock, gasping for breath, he yanked the pack open. The dagger was lodged inside. It had hit one of the spell rocks and nullified the magic, but that was the least of it. The knot had fallen out of the box, as he'd noticed earlier, and the dagger had nicked the dark coating on the tangled strand. The coating streamed off, turning into invisible magic, which dripped to the rocky ground, leaving a bone-white knot in its wake. Pins and needles bloomed in his leg. A magic leak.

No time.

He braced himself to touch the knot. The wave of shadow images and pain wasn't as bad when he was prepared. A quick check showed the thread of the knot was intact. Not a full breach then. The dripping coating would spawn a damaged version of the knot's golem, given enough time, but with the knot itself intact and inert, the monster couldn't spring up fully formed the way Storm had. *Immediate problem first!*

Zach crammed it back into the box, as he should have when he first realized it was loose. Taking the gauze from the first-aid kit, he wrapped it around the box to keep it closed and tied it off. Next time, they'd add a latch to the box. He shoved everything back into his bag as Alexis and Brian made it to him.

"They're gaining again," Brian gasped.

Zach nodded. Running as best as he could on a mostly numb leg, he led the way. At last, they came to a split in the path. He tossed the spell to cover tracks into the intersection.

"Please, Merlin, let that spell work," Alexis said, breathing as hard as Zach was.

Quickly, before they lost all of their lead, Zach took the left fork. The sign said it would take them back to the towpath. The shadows said it would take them to the car and then HQ. *"Elliot will know how to fix the knot, right? Stop the golem before it forms?"*

"I don't know," Alexis said.

Limping heavily, Zach forced himself to run.

Four

As Hannah towed her towards the main camp, Kayla's curiosity warred with her annoyance. "What do you think it means—that you saw it now?"

Hannah brandished the slim orange volume. "Something must have shifted with that gust of wind. Something important. Something to do with the future."

"And it can't wait until after I've had a shower? Or, better yet, a shower and dinner?" Still, it would be interesting to see Hannah seek out Miranda, the head of the training facility. Kayla had only talked with her twice; other than that, she just saw her across the dining room one or two meals a day.

"You shower fast, you'll still have time before dinner."

An icy gust bit through Kayla's sweatshirt and pricked her skin like static. The local flock of crows fussed indignantly from the grove of buffeted pines that Hannah was dragging her past. Kayla glanced at the sky for signs of rain being blown in, but the scattering of wispy clouds looked harmless.

Hannah tripped, but caught herself. "Stupid stomach," she muttered.

"You okay?" Kayla asked.

Hannah gave herself a shake and straightened up taller. "We're almost there."

Kayla blinked in surprise. She had no idea Hannah could walk this fast.

Xander was coming into sight. Officially, *Alexander Hall*. A sweeping, mansion-like building, with a fresh coat of white paint on its three-story colonial structure, flanked by wide, two-story wings. It might have been a hotel before Searcha bought it—Kayla hadn't really listened to most of the tour on her first day. She'd been waiting to learn more about magic, which had been a waste of time. No one would tell her more than what she'd learned during her recruitment. Xander held the communal dining room, kitchen, offices, study rooms, workout room, and so on. Most of the trainees' bedrooms were on the second floor. Jason, Miranda's right hand, had the third floor to himself.

Kayla smiled reluctantly. *At least I'm warming up from the pace.*

Hannah led the way past the guest house, just behind Xander, that Miranda used as her residence. Kayla was pulled through the patio, pretentiously called Freedom Square. Then she followed Hannah up the grand back steps of Xander, across the wide porch, through the backdoor, and down the hallway to Miranda's office. Hannah hesitated at the entrance and then passed it to go to Jason's office.

"It's open," Jason called at her knock. He was a couple of years older than Kayla and Hannah's twenty-two and the only innate on staff. Kayla had hoped that because he was a Shiner like her, they'd be friends, but he was a professional and didn't socialize with the trainees.

Hannah opened the door and peeked in. "Ah, Miranda. I was hoping we could have a minute of your time, if you have one. Hi, Jason, you probably want to hear this too."

Kayla looked over Hannah's head into the brightly lit office, where Jason was sitting behind the desk. The walls were the same shade of buttercup yellow as his Shiner markings when he glowed. Kayla couldn't tell if it was a color he liked or if he was bragging. His fair skin was tanned, his blond hair boringly cut, his jeans and flannel shirt looked like he'd copied them from the cover of an outdoor lifestyle magazine, and his boots looked awful to run in.

Miranda sat across from him. She was athletic, with stylish, short gray hair, and the energy of someone thirty years younger than her fifty-odd years. Today she wore white pants and a black blouse, with an artistic white-and-gray slash across the left shoulder and arm. Everything, from her pearl pendant to her shoes, looked understated and designer quality. Her makeup was subtle daywear, highlighting her Mediterranean skin tone and features.

"What's on your mind?" Miranda asked.

Hannah pulled Kayla the rest of the way into the office and handed Miranda Aunt Sonya's journal. "We found this." She turned to Kayla. "Tell them."

Kayla shrugged. "My great-aunt left it to me."

Miranda opened the book and flipped through a few pages. Her expression shifted from polite interest to shock to avid curiosity in a moment.

"It's a grimoire, isn't it?" Hannah asked.

Miranda handed the book to Jason without taking her eyes off Kayla. "Who was your great-aunt?"

Aren't you going to answer Hannah's question? "Sonya Gause." The silence stretched. Kayla shifted from foot to foot. "She was my grandmother's sister. After her husband died, she moved in with my grandparents when my mom was a kid."

"Is *Gause* Russian?" Miranda asked.

"Yes, she and my grandmother emigrated to the US shortly after World War Two with their parents." Kayla resisted the urge to follow that up with how the rest of her family came to the US. Her dad's side included a grandmother from Nova Scotia and a grandfather who traced his roots back to Scottish immigrants in the mid-1700s.

"Do you think the grimoire was originally your great-aunt's?" Miranda asked.

Kayla shrugged. "I think maybe it belonged to her husband, my great-uncle."

"Who was your great-uncle?" Miranda asked, not quite managing to hide her impatience.

"Yerik Gause. Also Russian," Kayla added before Miranda could ask. *Though, why does it matter?* Kayla couldn't guess. It wasn't about food. Warm, savory dinner that would melt in her mouth, fill her complaining stomach, and thaw her toes.

"He died in 1979?"

Kayla started. "What?"

"Yerik Gause. He died in 1979?"

Kayla stared up at the ceiling for patience and answers. "I'm not sure. I could ask my mom." She wasn't going to try to do the math, even if she knew how old her mom was when Aunt Sonya moved in.

"That is the year listed on the inside cover," Jason said. "What makes you say it's a grimoire, Hannah? I've never seen anything like it."

"It sounds like one." Hannah blushed, but kept her head up. "Its shadow, I mean."

Good for her. Hannah had a habit of stumbling over her words in front of her crush. Kayla didn't think Jason was worth it, but she found crushes uncomfortable nuisances, so she was probably biased.

Jason nodded pensively at her answer.

"We should have Ara look at it. There's Russian mixed in with the Latin and Greek, and I've never seen one laid out this way. It's a really significant find, Kayla. You're going to go great places with Searcha."

Anger overtook hunger for the moment. Hannah'd had her powers as long as Jason, but the leadership treated her like she was barely there. "I didn't do anything. Hannah saw something in the shadows and kept pushing until I remembered the journal. As soon as I dug it out of my stuff, she brought me here to show you. If it was up to me, I'd be getting cleaned up for dinner right now. And I'd like my great-aunt's journal back when you are done."

"Interesting." Miranda looked directly at Hannah for the first time since they'd walked into the office. She nodded almost imperceptibly before turning back to Kayla. "You said you dug it out? You didn't just get it?"

"No, I've had it for years."

"It's been in your room the whole time you've been here?"

Kayla tried to take a calming breath. "Hannah saw something when we were sailing. The wind was weird."

"You've been out sailing?"

Kayla gritted her teeth so she wouldn't scream.

Hannah started, as if the shadows had just informed her of something. She placed a light hand on Kayla's arm before saying to Miranda, "We had Captain's permission. I've been teaching Kayla to sail the sunfish. We just wanted to bring this to your attention immediately, but can we please continue the questions after dinner?"

Miranda exchanged an excited look with Jason. "I'm sorry my tone came off accusatory. I just wanted to be sure. It sounds like you two are becoming tied. That's why your powers are growing, Hannah. I'm so thrilled for you both!"

"What?" Hannah said with a puzzled frown.

"Wait . . . I thought it was the wind." Kayla's stomach lurched. Being stuck with Hannah as a roommate was bad enough, but as her teammate for all her missions as a field agent, too? Kayla would almost rather be told to master Latin like a first language.

"I know it's a lot to take in," Miranda said, saving Kayla from saying something rude. Though Hannah could probably hear her horror in her shadow. "We've been hoping for this since you joined us, Kayla. Hannah is overdue for graduating. We just had to wait for magic to send us you. I'll let you get cleaned up for dinner. We'll talk afterwards about your new schedule. You'll start magic lessons as soon as possible."

"Wonderful!" Hannah said, collecting herself quickly and then dragging Kayla out of the room. They were free of Xander and walking towards their house before she spoke firmly. "You're hangry. That's perfectly reasonable. This will look brighter after you've eaten." Hannah's voice filled with enthusiasm. "Magic lessons! I know you've been looking forward to those."

Kayla's hunger evaporated.

"I thought you said something changed in the shadows when that wind hit us, and that's why you saw the grimoire?" Kayla protested.

Hannah shrugged. "I guess I was wrong. It was our future the shadows were trying to show us. A tied team!"

Kayla shook her head. "I wonder if there's a stomach bug going around."

Hannah frowned at the shadows, her tone growing uncomfortably happy. "You'll feel better as soon as you eat. This means you'll graduate soon. That'll mean no more Latin translations. Coming fully into your power means you'll be safe in the outside world. No risk of being poked and prodded by doctors and scientists who want to know why your skin glows sometimes. And being an agent means full protection for your friends and family during the Unavoidable Upheaval as we continue to free imprisoned magic entities. Things in the world will of course get worse before they will get so much better, and it'll be good to keep your loved ones sheltered during the transition."

Kayla gritted her teeth. *How indoctrinated does she have to be to go on like that?*

"Sorry. I don't mean to go on." Hannah gave Kayla's arm a squeeze.

Get out of my head! Kayla choked the words back, but pulled her arm free. Hannah generally kept the requisite three feet from everyone except Kayla. It had never bothered Kayla before, but maybe it should.

Hannah tried to hide her hurt. "I promise this is a good thing. A wonderful thing."

Kayla clenched her jaw to keep from screaming. Just thinking about a career with no privacy and endless slow walking made her shudder.

"I'm going to run to the cabin." She took off without looking back.

Five

Zach
Day 0 of the Lockhouse Knot Leak
Thursday, early evening
Guard HQ, DC

"How the hell could this happen?" Elliot's brown skin paled as he glared at the box on the conference table tied closed with gauze.

Zach looked at the wooden floor, unable to voice any of the hollow excuses that rose to his lips.

Unhelpful papers and dead-end leads littered the conference room. Terra and Sadie had decided it was safer to keep the leaking knot out of the restoration lab for now, in case the magic reacted badly with any of the artifacts down there. Breaking protocol, Sadie had brought up everything that might be useful, so they could scour it for clues while monitoring the box.

Zach wasn't sure how watching it would help; it wasn't like the box was one of Doctor Who's Weeping Angels, who couldn't move while being observed, but it did make him feel better.

Prince and Nobel, the younger shadow hounds, growled softly at the box from the doorway. Their older relative, Duchess, snuffled and snarled in her sleep under the reception desk on the other side of the wall.

When no one answered him, Elliot continued. "The last magic leak like this was in 1979, and eight people died. How can this be happening again?"

"It could have been far worse. We could be facing a full breach," Alexis said gently. "Perhaps a better question would be, how do we fix it?"

The silence stretched and stretched. Each moment without an answer felt like it added more weight to Zach's shoulders. *If I'd seen the dagger coming a few seconds earlier or not taunted that stupid alchemist, we wouldn't be facing our second magic disaster in six months. Better yet, I could have passed the bag off to Alexis.* She'd seen the dagger coming.

"I don't know how to fix it," Elliot said.

Zach's head jerked up. In his graphic novel version of the Guard, Elliot was an African American cross between Gandalf and an Italian mob boss. A robust man in his seventies, Elliot channeled his rare fears into anger, but this time his voice was so bleak it hurt.

"How'd you fix it last time?" Alexis asked, radiating calm and patience. Her shadow was the only hint she understood just how bad things were. Brian moved closer to her side and put an arm around her waist.

The box on the table vibrated, like the low snarl of some terrible monster.

Prince barked. Nobel's growl intensified, showing her teeth.

"Well, that was creepy." Brian said dryly.

Zach stifled a laugh.

"The knot growled," Alexis explained to the people in the room who didn't have innate magic and therefore couldn't hear it.

"Fun," Russel said with deep sarcasm.

Zach slapped a hand over his mouth. Laughter had to be better than panic, but Elliot didn't look amused.

"We're still trying to figure out how to fix the full containment breach from last fall," Alexis said, as if working through the facts out loud would help bring answers into existence. "But this is only a leak, the knot is still intact. It's just the coating that's damaged. We can fix it the same way you did last time?"

Elliot sank into a chair that had been pushed against the wall. "As you know, I joined the Guard during the 1979 leak. What I play down in my retellings is that I was in way over my head.

"I did help the team that repaired the knot, but I only knew my part. It was Petrov's friend who had the plan and the spell we needed, but Petrov and his friend . . . Yerik, that was it, Yerik Gause. But Petrov and Yerik were two of the eight people killed by the leak. The remaining team tried to track down Yerik's notes afterwards, but in all the chaos, we weren't able to find any of it. And his widow wanted nothing to do with us."

"The box is leaking only minute traces now," Russel said, fiddling with a magic barometer. It was no surprise he'd quit his office job to become a spellcaster when TAMCoB happened. As a kid, he'd been the one to sneak away from group activities and into the vault, where he'd play with the artifacts—before they'd upped security. He'd gotten a mechanical engineering degree with a minor in archaeology. At twenty-six, he was average in height and build, with a thoughtful smile, brown skin, and an unparalleled understanding of magical gadgets. In a graphic novel, he'd be a tech-wizard detective. Just like in real life, his character would store his pencil behind his left ear and wear three watches, only one of which told the time.

"Do you have a read yet on how far the magic leaked?" Elliot asked.

"There was a big ripple that my sensors on the coast picked up nineteen minutes ago. But I think it was a reaction from the magic already there rather than new magic spreading." Russel looked up from his watches to see if he was making sense. "Like a pebble being dropped in a bucket of water, the ripple was noticeable, but the water level didn't rise significantly. The box is holding for now, and I have some ideas to reinforce it, but they're not long-term solutions. From our research, the coating stabilizes the knot. Without it, the knot will start to slide and untangle, eventually untying on its own, even without the assistance of the golem. The box won't hold *that*." Russel chuckled at his epic understatement.

"How long do we have to find a long-term solution?" Terra asked.

Elliot frowned. "Last time, it took several days for the magic to coalesce into a golem and a few weeks before the monster grew large enough to start eating people. We have an exact timeline in the records. As confused as the military was about what had happened, thank Merlin, they worked so diligently to cover the whole thing up."

"I'll review the file again." Russel consulted his gadgets and sketched a quick graph in his notebook. "But I doubt I can give an exact answer. We don't know if all the knots function the same way. If you need me to guess? Maybe a month, if we're lucky. But I wouldn't count on more than three weeks."

Silence fell heavy on the room, like oppressive summer humidity that made it hard to breathe.

Terra collected herself and shifted her gaze to Alexis. "Can you see Searcha's next move?"

Alexis shook her head. "I don't see them trying to storm HQ yet, but short of that, the shadows aren't shedding any light."

Zach wished they'd continue to focus on the leaking knot and not Searcha. Three weeks wasn't enough time. They'd already scoured every source they could find for information about retying knots—repairing a damaged knot would have been something they'd have noted.

The shadows flickered in front of him, like faded pamphlets blown in the wind. He followed them to Elliot. "Where haven't you thought to look? For the spellbook."

The others stopped to listen.

Elliot blew out a long breath. "I don't like it, but if anyone might know, it would be Nick Steele. He's Petrov's grandson."

Elliot's shadow shifted at his words. There was a glimpse of an athletic blonde woman holding a faded orange book. She laughed and glowed with a deep-red amber. The image held for a heartbeat. Then she disappeared below the water, pulled down by teeth. A puddle of ink swallowed the image. Goosebumps prickled Zach's arms, indicating a possible future. *But whose possible future and why am I seeing it?*

Shuddering, Zach looked at Alexis for clarification.

Her frown deepened before she looked up from the shadows. "I think asking Nick is a very good idea."

Elliot grumbled, but Terra opened her laptop.

"I'll contact him now," she said. "Elliot and Sadie, we need alternative options if this doesn't work. Alexis, Brian, Zach, and Russel,

I want a workable plan for security for that leaking knot before dinner."

"I'm getting a second magic source, weaker than the first?" Russel frowned at his barometer. He shifted until he stood in front of Zach.

"Oh? Well, some of the energy from the damaged knot splashed on me earlier. I might still be dripping." Zach shrugged. He'd been ignoring the pins-and-needles feeling in his leg all afternoon.

"Wait, what?" Alexis turned her scrutiny of shadows towards him. "Are you okay? I thought you sprained an ankle. I should have seen it earlier. Your whole right leg is glowing blue in your shadow."

Zach shook his head and rolled up his pant leg. He'd checked it earlier when he'd cleaned up his skinned knees. His leg looked normal. Underneath the skin, his muscles and bones were numb and prickly, as if they'd been submerged in a frozen sea and just starting to thaw. Wishing away the feeling hadn't worked.

"There's a thick strand, here." Brian brushed magic Zach couldn't see, but he felt the twang on his leg, like a hair being tugged. The box on the table rumbled darkly.

Elliot waved a dismissive hand. "You'll be fine."

Zach exhaled roughly. Worry that he'd ignored to the point of forgetting about seeped out of his body.

"Just a bit of magic scalding," Elliot said. "Happened last time. Without the magic of the strands to bind to, the coating is radicalized. Splattered three of the scientists in the lab last time. The men weren't innate, so they didn't see what happened, but they had some bad numbing for a few days. They thought it might be poisonous gas. While they were chasing their tails trying to figure it out, the Guard made its move. Magic scalding saved the world back then. Probably not an enjoyable feeling, though."

Zach grinned. "No, it's not, but it's good to hear I won't lose the leg."

Brian and Russel laughed, but Alexis fixed him with a hard look, seeing through his joke.

Elliot smiled, then softly said, "Magic isn't a game. If we don't fix that knot before the coating forms a monster, losing limbs will be the least of our worries."

"Terra's right, though, we need to secure the knot before we deal with repairing it," Alexis said. "If—no, *when*—Searcha realizes we have it, they're going to come for it."

Zach shifted to the edge of the room, put his hands in his pockets, and slouched against the wall. He had nothing to add that the others didn't already know. Concentrating on the shadows, he tried to sort through the images they offered him; most looked like they'd been trampled in the mud, but just maybe, in the chaos, he could find a way to help fix his mistake.

Alexis shifted to the wall beside him, her eyes on the shadows on the ground.

"Are you mad?" Her voice was so soft, Zach touched his ear to make sure he hadn't forgotten to take the earbud out.

"Mad? At myself, some." But it shouldn't have been enough to draw her attention.

"You're radiating anger." She rubbed her temple, her brow deeply furrowed. "That's why I didn't notice your leg at first. It was a layer below the emotion. But the rage is a hair out of focus, like it was photoshopped in. What's going on?"

"Huh?" Zach asked. "I don't know. I don't feel angry. How long has it looked like that?"

"Maybe during the fight with the Twins? Could it be a lingering effect of their mist spell?"

"Oh!" It couldn't have been clearer if a lightbulb had gone off over his head. "The mirage spell. I used it at the same time I was drawing on my old teenage anger to hide my shadow. Hoped it would give it an extra boost."

"That's what we were missing!" Sadie said.

Zach looked up and realized everyone was watching them. He forced himself to stand up, away from the wall, and take his hands out of his pockets. "That would explain why it worked this time and didn't before, even though we didn't do anything different to the spell itself. The conditions upon release were different."

"How long is it supposed to last?" Alexis asked.

Zach looked to Sadie.

Sadie put her palms up. "I don't know. This is the first time it's worked."

Brian laughed. "Got to love spellcasting."

Groaning, Elliot's head sank to his hands. "If Searcha doesn't end the world with magic, you guys will."

"Well, let's try not to do that. But it's what we've got until you find a better way to stop magic without using it ourselves. I'll add 'determining the length of effects of a mirage spell' to the list." Terra said, making a note. "Everyone can bring their updates to dinner."

Zach added 'unknown side effects of a mirage spell' to his mental list of things he didn't have time to worry about as he followed Brian outside to do a perimeter check.

Six

Kayla
Day 1 of the Lockhouse Knot Leak
Friday afternoon
Tidal Water, MD

"I'm going to quit," Kayla announced with a great sigh, and flopped into the cushy navy-blue couch in the West Study.

Ben and Jade, in the matching easy chairs on the other side of the coffee table, looked up.

Ben gave a sympathetic smile. "Bad morning?"

"Hannah giving you the silent treatment again?" Jade asked.

"Yes! How the hell are we supposed to resolve anything if she won't talk to me?" Kayla sat up a bit. She'd hoped to find the newbie alchemists here. They'd started a week before her and hadn't drunk as much of the Kool-Aid as the rest of the trainees.

"I thought you were the conquering heroes last night?" Ben said. Tall and athletic, he was often up to kick a soccer ball around or shoot some hoops, and there was always laughter when he was on kitchen duty. It horrified Kayla that anyone, but especially such a nice guy, could have stories of being harassed during the early days of the pandemic for being Asian. It would have been idiotic even if his ancestors hadn't been in the US longer than most of Kayla's.

"That's the problem. Miranda and Jason think we're getting tied. It's making Hannah's mothering even worse. I push back, and she gets upset. Makes me want to climb the walls." *And vent.*

"We finally have a preliminary version of this potion we need to try, so we have to go to Newton. Why don't you come with and tell us about it?" Jade said. She was quiet and empathetic, which made her a great listener when she wasn't hiding in a game on her phone. Her light skin freckled instead of tanned, and she was almost as tall as Kayla, but the way she carried herself made her look short. Her best feature were her green eyes, but she obscured them with choppy, dark-brown bangs. Even when she pulled her hair into a ponytail, as she did today, her bangs were still in her face.

Kayla jumped up. "Sure." She wasn't allowed in the Newton Lab without an invite from an alchemist. Another stupid rule.

"What do you think Hannah is mad about this time?" Jade asked, pulling on her rain jacket.

"It's so annoying! I was lacing up my sneakers to go for a run, and Hannah tells me I should go to yoga with her instead." Kayla held open the door for Jade and Ben.

Ben pulled up his hood against the biting drizzle. "I'd rather jog five miles in a downpour than go back to Dahlia's class, no offense to Dahlia, of course."

"Exactly!" Kayla pulled up her hood and followed. Her rain boots splashed with a satisfying squelch through the puddles. "I enjoy a yoga flow. Lots of movement. But Dahlia's class is all about pretzeling into uncomfortable poses and holding it forever."

"Two to five minutes," Jade said. "That's yin yoga. It can be very meditative, but I can see how that doesn't work for you."

"My brain and body just scream at me the whole time. I started mentally reciting song lyrics just to get through it." Kayla shrugged. "So I told Hannah, 'Thanks, but I'm going for a run,' and she had like a total meltdown about how it was cold and raining and I'd catch a chill and we needed to do more stuff together."

"What'd you say?" Ben asked.

"I said I'd run in far worse weather, and I know how to take care of myself. And you know what she says?" Kayla waited a beat. "She says it's her job to look after me now, and it's not safe for me to go running."

"Ouch," Jade said. The understanding in her eyes was visible, even beneath her bangs and hood.

"Exactly!" Kayla threw her hands in the air. *See?* She wasn't over-reacting. They got it. "And then, I needed a run even more! I asked her if she read that in my shadow. Maybe I was going to slip or twist my ankle or something. It wouldn't be the first time. And she said, 'No, it's common sense.' Like I don't have common sense, like I'm not a fully functional adult, like I don't know how to dress for the weather!"

Taking a deep breath of wet air laced with wood smoke, Kayla tried to dislodge the anger that was building all over again. Ahead, built of gray stone, Newton looked squat and rectangular. Three of its sides were originally a U-shaped stable, with stalls that opened to a courtyard in the middle. The final side was a single wall that had been added to close off the courtyard when it was renovated into a lab.

"That really sucks," Jade said.

"Yeah, if she doesn't respect you, how are you supposed to be a team?" Ben held the steel-reinforced oak door.

"Right?!" Kayla stepped into the entryway, which had been converted from the old tack room.

Jade waved cheerily to the camera that no one, as far as Kayla knew, monitored, and then punched in the code to the security door that cut the room in half. Kayla and Ben waved, too, because it was funny. Ara, the most tenured alchemy trainee, taught everyone to do it, a tongue-in-cheek nod to spy movies.

The second half of the entryway was open to the gravel courtyard. When it wasn't raining, the two picnic tables were loaded with equipment and notes. There would be a fire in the fire pit, and another charcoal grill or two going. Today, Ara, with her lava-red bob curling in the rain, was using a wood burner under the edge of the open, communal lab. She was stirring a big steel pot that was resting in the fire. Ara was practically staff, but, as she put it, she didn't want to leave the fun table; there was more freedom to experiment with potions while in training than as an agent at the main lab.

"Hey, Ara," Ben said.

Ara waved her free hand. "Eighty-seven, eight-eight."

"Got it, counting," Ben said.

Jade nodded, as if that was a perfectly reasonable thing to say.

Kayla followed Jade and Ben across the courtyard to their lab, one of the converted stalls. Another code was needed. Kayla added remembering the weekly changing codes to her reasons she was glad she wasn't an alchemist.

"If we use Sterno, maybe we can settle for opening the window," Ben said.

Jade hung her coat on a hook by the door. "We have to get all the ingredients ready first. Maybe the rain will have stopped by then."

Kayla hung her coat as well. It was chilly, but at least this way she wasn't dripping everywhere.

"So did you go for a run?" Ben asked.

"Yes, I had to. I got so frustrated that Hannah wouldn't listen, I started to glow! Running was the only way to calm down. I tried to make it up to her when I got back and spent lunch with her, but she gave me the silent treatment." Kayla threw her hands in the air.

"And she thinks *you* act like a child." Ben snorted with amusement.

Kayla laughed, feeling marginally better. "You've got a point. What potion are you working on?"

"We're trying to make this crystal glow, so it can be used like a flashlight-glow-stick thing," Ben said.

"Why not just use a flashlight?" Kayla asked.

"But that wouldn't be magic," Jade said, her eyes laughing.

Ben shrugged. "It would be a whole lot easier."

"Has any potion been done yet that does something we can't do with science?" Kayla asked.

"Ara was up all night trying to decipher your grimoire. She thinks it has a potion she's been looking for, a way to hatch a fire salamander," Ben said.

"And Ben made a really cool spell that hides people's shadows. The field team tested it yesterday," Jade said, selecting jars off the shelf that lined two walls and putting them on the folding table in the middle of the room.

"They had notes, a lot of them," Ben muttered. "I wouldn't call it a success."

Usually Kayla would have questions about the field team, but . . . "Like an actual living salamander?"

"Yep. It'll be cool if she can pull it off. She tried to explain it earlier, but it's way over my head," Ben said. He checked the list Jade was using. "We need orange peels dried in the summer sun, smoked moon jelly, and pine-tar crystals from the storage room?"

"Yes, and we're low on rainwater cleansed by firelight." Jade swished the quarter-full glass jar.

"Got it," Ben said, and pulled his hood back up before leaving.

"I don't really understand tying. What is it?" Jade asked, pouring dried herbs from a jar into a stone mortar and grinding it with the pestle.

Kayla rocked from the balls of her feet to her heels and back. "Honestly, I don't really get it either. Some kind of magical bond that makes both our magics stronger. Practically, I guess it means we work together, like cop partners, for all our missions. Hannah seems to think it gives her the right to run my life."

"So you're quitting?"

Kayla shrugged. "It's weird hearing the words out loud, but I haven't been able to get them out of my head since I woke up this morning. Hannah will be happier with a different Shiner. I was skimming the notes and journals Miranda gave me last night. They're full of poems I don't understand and quotes from people who died ages ago. How is any of that supposed to teach me to use my magic?"

Jade made an understanding sound as she worked, so Kayla continued.

"I understand poetry about as well as I understand Latin. So I asked Nathan. You know, figured as a Shiner he'll have some helpful thoughts, but he just quoted more poetry at me, as if that explained anything. I don't think I'm cut out to be a Shiner. Which is fine. So far it hasn't been anything like Dr. Caligo made it sound. Now that I know what's going on, I won't end up in another CT scanner or psychologist's office. I don't glow often, and like today, even when I do, it's not bright. Only another innate would notice."

Kayla wandered over to a shelf of ingredients, trying to shove away the memories her words had dredged up. If she never became a proper member of Searcha, she'd still be grateful they'd recruited her. Knowing the magic she was seeing wasn't just in her head was worth far more than memorizing her share of Latin declensions.

One of the most haunting moments had come less than half an hour before she learned the truth. Kayla had been in Dr. Caligo's waiting room, when a dark-haired woman in her early twenties with a weird vibe had sat down next to her. The woman had acted like they were old friends and told Kayla all about the voices in her head, including the one that said Kayla would meet a tall, handsome man with eyes the color of magic. It should have been funny, but it wasn't, especially when the woman asked for help and then waltzed off as if she did that kind of thing all the time. Kayla had been terrified that she was becoming equally bonkers.

"What about Searcha's protection for your friends and family?" Jade asked, yanking Kayla back to the present.

Kayla sighed and poked at one of the glass jars with rocks in it. "Protection from what? Unavoidable Upheaval? What does that even mean? The world is a shit show. How much more dangerous could it be to add a bit of magic to the equation? Potions are cool and all, but even that fire-starting one Ara showed off the other day was only impressive cuz it was magic. A lighter or a firecracker would have been just as useful, and a lot less work. And it'll be great for innates. A wider access to magic literacy means Shadows and Shiners will have a chance to understand what's happening when they start developing their abilities without waiting for it to be explained by a member of Searcha."

Kayla picked up a wooden box. Jade didn't protest, so she peeked inside as she talked. "Shadows telling people's futures or pasts? Sure, I guess it's got some advantages, but I doubt Hannah can predict the lottery or anything."

The box held dirt. Kayla returned it to the shelf. "My magic? Ha! Jason makes it look cool enough, but I don't think the world is in danger from someone being able to pull objects to them, and the magic clay is less useful than a taser, cuz a taser you can just recharge—or do they run on batteries?" Kayla tilted her head to the side, considering. She'd never seen one used in real life, but her point stood. Sure, some people would freak out, and some would be loud about it, but most would be too busy with their lives to spare time or energy getting involved until it was integrated into everyday life.

"You're not worried about Ara's fire salamander or the unicorn, or whatever else spawns next?"

Kayla laughed and stepped away from the shelves before she could pick anything else up. "Ara better not be hatching a critter unless it's benevolent, and if the other mythological creatures are as cuddly as a unicorn . . ."

"But they're not," Hannah said.

Kayla jumped. Herbs spilled from Jade's pestle.

"She called over for me to let her in," Ben said, not meeting their eyes.

Kayla sighed. In practice Shadows outranked alchemists, so it wasn't Ben's fault.

Hannah walked into the lab with a gallon-size Ziplock bag of papers under her arm. "I got permission from Miranda to show you what Jason found out about your grimoire."

"So *now* you're talking to me?" Kayla asked.

Hannah took a deep breath. "Just because I'm excited about our future together doesn't mean it's fair of me to rush you. I'm sorry."

Kayla waited for the other shoe to drop. When it wasn't forthcoming, she relented. "Thanks. I'm sorry I yelled." She was, but she wasn't sorry about going for a run. She'd been so angry it hadn't cleared her head the way she'd hoped, but it was better than nothing.

Hannah nodded graciously. "I gather you're struggling with why Searcha's mission is so important?"

Kayla crossed her arms. *Does she really want to have this argument in front of Jade and Ben? Fine.* "I get why it's important. There are tons of trapped magical entities. It's awful, but there's plenty of other injustices in the world to fight too. I can't fix them all, and, clearly, I'm not cut out to deal with this one, so I'll leave it to people like you." Kayla had never been one for fighting injustice, anyway. The problems felt too huge and too complicated for her to make a difference.

Hannah gave Kayla a condescending smile. "Would you like to know the history of that grimoire you found yesterday?"

"I have phone time." Kayla checked the wall clock, looking for any excuse to get out of there. *Damn.* "In an hour. I still don't get why we have allotted time on the landline or why they built a camp where there is absolutely no cell service." Withdrawal from social media and the ability to call and text whenever she wanted had been no joke for the first two weeks. She still caught herself checking her phone for notifications. Now all it did was play music. Hannah had strongly encouraged her to delete her few offline games—something Kayla still resented her for. So what if she had more time to translate Latin now?

"The story won't take an hour," Hannah said, with that grating patience of hers.

"Fine." Kayla shrugged. *Why is it so hard not to act like the child Hannah thinks I am?*

Hannah took another deep breath before starting. "During the Cold War, a Russian defector named Petrov promised to help unravel the mysteries of magic for the US. The government was trying almost everything to get ahead of the Russians. Maybe you've heard about them trying to use psychics and other absurd stuff?"

Kayla shook her head.

Ben and Jade snuck curious glances in Hannah's direction, clearly listening as they worked on their spell.

"Well, they did." Hannah unzipped her bag and pulled out a manila folder. "Petrov was at a military base in Maryland in the late 1970s. He had a knot, but he couldn't figure out how to untie it. Hitting a wall in his research, he reached out to an emigrant family, who like him, had ties with the magical community back home. Your great-uncle, Yerik Gause, joined forces with him."

Hannah pulled a paper out of the manila folder and laid it on the plastic table in front of Kayla. Two serious men in lab coats stared back at her from the copy of an old photograph. The lanky one on the right looked like the overjoyed man from her great-aunt's wedding photo.

"Now we have made dozens of daggers enchanted to cut knots, but back then, without Alexander's grimoire, they didn't have an easy shortcut, but still managed to cut the outer coating of the knot. The coating contains the knot's guardian. Then the Guard got involved."

Hannah placed another paper in front of Kayla. The image was grainy, but showed a mud hill with four legs, a tail, and arching white lightning coming out of its snarling mouth as it engulfed an old-fashioned car. Kayla shuddered.

"That poor creature, lashing out in terror, unable to find its knot, should have been this." Instead of a photo, Hannah put down a digital drawing. It was a gorgeous, eagle-like bird, with lightning coming off its face and wings.

"The Thunderbird," she continued, "was said to eat evil spirits and was revered by many Native American tribes. Had Gause and Petrov been able to untie the knot, that bird would now be happy and thriving in our world, helping to keep evil at bay.

"But the Guard killed them and resealed the knot. That glorious creature is trapped in a knot in the Guard's vault."

Kayla gaped at Hannah. "The Guard killed my great-uncle?"

"Yes."

Kayla shook her head, trying to make that fit with what she knew about her family's history.

"What about the person in the car?" Jade asked.

"What?" Hannah said.

Jade shifted the picture of the thunderbird and pointed to the car being eaten by the mud-hill monster. The image was grainy and lit by spider-webbing lightning, but it looked like there was a person in the driver's seat.

Hannah shook her head slightly. "A few innocent people were probably hurt in the conflict, but that's the Guard's fault. Had they let Kayla's great-uncle and his friend untie the knot instead of killing them, no one would have been harmed. You certainly can't blame the creature. It was terrified and couldn't fly away to safety. See these people with guns shooting at it?"

The soldiers seemed to outrage Hannah, but if Kayla had been a bystander watching a monster eating a car with people in it, she would have attacked it, too, or run for her life.

"My point is," Hannah said, collecting her papers, "your great-uncle gave his life to free magic. You are exactly the kind of person Searcha needs."

"Is Searcha going to release more creatures like that?" Jade asked.

"If we release the guardian and all the magic trapped inside at the same time, the mythological creatures will spawn fully formed, not broken like this poor beast. They'll have no reason to lash out against anyone or anything," Hannah said. "Of course, we're going to release them. We're going to release them all."

"And if the Guard tries to stop us?" Kayla asked. "Or kill us?"

"We're better prepared. Of course there will be Unavoidable Upheaval as society is reshaped for the better by magic and the guardians. Healing can be painful. Metaphorically, badly set bones will have to be rebroken and aligned properly so they can heal. Shortsighted, ignorant fools like the Guard will try to stop us, and there will be conflict. It's not going to be easy, but if we don't heal our world, broken because magic has been removed, then humanity will destroy itself and take the planet down with it." Hannah shook her head sadly and then smiled. "But we're going to be successful. Magic will be free, and can you imagine how amazing it's going to be? Magical birds the size of planes flying in the sky, and so many more incredible beings living among us."

Amazing wasn't the first word that popped into Kayla's mind. *Are the birds going to file flight plans?*

An explosion rattled the dishes on the table. Red light streaked angrily through one wall and out the other.

Kayla and the others rushed outside, forgetting their jackets.

"Sorry!" Ara called between coughing fits. "I guess I stirred it too many times. Stupid potion." She was covered in black ash, and the front edge of her coat looked singed. The rainy air held a twirling plume of sulfur-scented smoke.

"You okay?" Hannah called.

"Yeah." Ara coughed several more times. "It's not the first time I've had a potion blow up in my face, and I could only read every other word of the directions for this one."

"It's going to be an interesting time to be alive," Ben said with a laugh. "I'd better see if she needs some help cleaning up."

Kayla stood in the rain, more shell-shocked than Ara.

"Alchemy might not be much yet, but it's still in its infancy," Hannah said quietly at her side. "It's going to be an interesting world when anyone can brew a potion in their garage. Your family will be a lot safer with Searcha's protection. And you don't have to worry about the other injustices. When magic balances the world again, they won't be a problem."

Kayla swallowed hard. *Magic is powerful enough to fix all problems? What are we playing with?* Hannah expected her to not only help save magic, but the world? Jason had said something along those lines on her first day, but she'd thought he was exaggerating—when she'd been listening at all.

"Don't miss your phone time," Hannah said sweetly. She handed Kayla her rain jacket.

Kayla gave Jade a 'well, that-was-interesting' look as she swished on her jacket.

Paler than usual, Jade managed to nod in acknowledgement.

Rain boots sinking deeply into the mud, Kayla walked back towards Xander.

Shit! Shit! Shit!

The evil Guard had killed the love of Aunt Sonya's life. Kayla shook her head, jaw aching. If the Guard interfered again, there could be more hills that ate cars. The ability for anyone to brew not only explosions, but living creatures in their garages or kitchens. Was it possible to right all the world's wrongs? How would the government react? Or big business or the billionaires? The Unavoidable Upheaval wasn't a throwaway term used by the staff after all. They meant it.

She had been wrong. This wasn't playing at being a secret agent. It wasn't just a cool job or an interesting career like she'd assumed.

Kayla had been given the chance to protect her friends and family from what was to come. *What kind of horrible person walks away from that?* She hunched deeper into her rain jacket.

Noah. She'd call her brother first. He was sane and steady and got her. She couldn't tell him most of it, but he'd help it make sense. Maybe with all his psychology classes, he'd even have some advice for getting along with Hannah.

The rain pattered relentlessly against her hood as Kayla ran through every expletive she knew.

"If quitting isn't an option, I'll just have to make the best of it," she muttered. She tried to find her smile. Jaw tight, she pushed inside, swearing to herself that she'd be nicer to Hannah at dinner.

Seven

Zach
Day 1 of the Lockhouse Knot Leak
Friday afternoon
Washington, DC

The gray drizzle turned downtown DC into a sea of black umbrellas floating between the hills of white marble buildings. Locals walked briskly, with worlds to change, high cost of living to contend with, and daily trips to the gym, leaving them without enough hours in the day. Tourists tried to navigate between landmarks, clogging streets and crosswalks. Zach itched to capture the image in India ink as he walked half a block behind Alexis.

Traveling in scatter formation required two shadows, so Alexis took point and Zach took the rear. In between, Brian walked Prince while Terra pretended to talk on her cellphone. No one acknowledged anyone else in the group except through magic earbuds. On sunny days, he and the other members would spread out, making them harder to spot and allowing them to take in more shadow information. Rain blurred images and softened the light, forcing them to close ranks so Searcha agents didn't slip through unnoticed.

It was good to be in the back, easier for Zach to downplay his lingering limp. The needles of numbness were making it hard to concentrate on the shadows, which shifted and swayed as if they were projected on sand under a foot of clear ocean.

He'd never seen shadows do that before. The rolling waves were more inclined to make him motion sick than to share their secrets. *Am I picking up on a flood?* A future one, he guessed, based on the prickle of gooseflesh on his arms. Whatever it was, it was annoying as hell. No matter how hard he tried to push away or still the water, the waves kept washing back. Zach shivered. The whitecaps had teeth.

Alexis had seen no sign of Searcha agents when they were preparing to leave. Scatter formation might be a bit over-the-top, but they weren't taking chances with Nick's cover.

Searcha had made a few attempts to stake out HQ over the winter, but the shadow hounds spotted them right away, and the Guard had developed an arsenal of discreet and creative ways to drive them off. One time Brian's youngest sister even called the cops on a Searcha agent. Em did a very convincing scared middle schooler when she put her mind to it. She'd tried to leverage her success to stay at HQ, but even if her parents hadn't overruled her, the Council would have.

The itchiness in his leg was a reminder why the Council had pushed so hard to evacuate all nonessential Guard members from the containment area. No one knew what the effects of long-term exposure might be, and they didn't want to risk any of the young people developing innate abilities. Elliot admitted he still had nightmares from when he had Shadow abilities during the Fort Meade leak. He was loudly relieved he wasn't showing symptoms this time round and had fought the hardest to send Zach back to school. Despite his scalded leg, Zach was grateful Elliot had lost that debate.

Grad school had been a bad fit, to put it politely. His advisor had been a narcissistic, neurotic micromanager, and his lab had been a political and competitive nightmare. Getting the call from Terra to "Please drop everything and drive straight to DC" had felt like a miracle. Citing a family emergency, he'd thrown a few belongings in the car and escaped.

Crossing into the magic contamination zone had proved he was a Shadow, a childhood dream he'd thought he'd packed away with his worn-out action figures. When Alexis and Brian returned to their respective schools to finish their bachelor's, Zach had successfully argued HQ needed a Shadow to help protect it. By the time they finished in December, the Council had agreed to let Zach stay in DC for the rest of the breach. He'd only gone back to Florida long enough to tie up loose ends and get the rest of his stuff.

It was good to be an active Guard member, but Elliot was right, the nightmares sucked. In the early hours before dawn that morning, Zach had given up on sleep and filled page after page with dark water and a physical manifestation of rage that wasn't his. His pencil captured how the cloud of furious golem magic morphed into one monster after another, as if trying to find the deadliest form. It had been a relief when his alarm went off and Zach had an excuse to get up.

Four cups of coffee hadn't banished his nightmares—it only made him jittery. Maybe the magic scalding hadn't had long-term side effects in 1979 because that knot had been fixed and retied. Maybe Zach was turning into Knot Man.

He chuckled to himself. It was easy to picture the image he'd draw in a graphic novel, a comic, evil version of himself with his head turned into a knot.

I should have ducked in time. Zach's smile slipped. *Or better yet, handed off the pack to Brian.* A long exhalation helped bring him back to the present. *I'm going to miss something if I'm too in my head.* He breathed in a fresh lungful of damp city air, full of fried and spicy aromas from a line of food trucks. He'd already analyzed what he could learn from his mistakes. Letting go was easier said than done, but it was time he tried.

Rain pattered on his umbrella. The sidewalk was solid beneath him, with a few cracks he could feel through the soles of his damp sneakers. His core muscles added lift, his chest opened, and his shoulder blades slid back and down. Fluffy white-and-pink cherry blossoms hugged two of the trees ahead like magical clouds. Goosebumps prickled his forearms.

The shadows sharpened. All the waves had teeth as they crested and crashed. They devoured the shadow of a mounted police woman as a future version of her tried to stand against them. The waves pulled the shadow of a little girl in a rainbow raincoat away from her parents.

Zach's heartbeat drowned out the sound of the rain. Shallow breaths refused to press against his diaphragm.

"Zach," Alexis's thoughts in his head yanked him back to the present. *"you okay?"*

"Sorry. I think the magic scalding is messing with me. All I'm seeing are waves with teeth," Zach answered.

"Maybe try using your regular vision instead? You know what all of the Searcha field agents look like," Alexis said.

"Thanks. Good idea." Tuning out the shadows and lifting his eyes off the ground, Zach got his breathing to even out. *"I can do that."* There were only about a dozen Searcha agents field certified at present, and thanks to Nick, the Guard had profiles on all of them.

Umbrellas and rain jackets made it hard to pick faces out of the crowd, but Zach tried.

The wide marble steps of the Lincoln Memorial were coming up fast. It was just the right amount of busy to shelter a clandestine meeting. It would make a spectacular spread in a graphic novel. In reality, the conversations from tourists and the rain echoed off the hard surfaces, making it far louder inside than was ideal.

Alexis walked around under the roof with her camera, hiding an earbud in the designated spot while taking her time lining up shots. Terra wandered around the inside, reading signs and munching on a cheese Danish she'd brought with her. Dogs weren't allowed, but Prince obliged Brian by thoroughly sniffing everything just outside.

Zach took a spot leaning against a pillar looking out over the Mall. Pulling his small sketch pad out of his inside pocket, he tried to capture the waves. Maybe giving them his attention would help calm them.

"He's on his way." Alexis's thoughts came through clearly despite the noise.

Zach shifted slightly and, using his peripheral vision, spotted the double agent's shadow first. Charcoal gray and smudged worse than usual by the rain, it shouldn't have stood out so clearly, and yet it gave almost nothing away. In contrast, the tall, blond man was all sharp lines, only softened by the curve of his black umbrella. In his dark business suit and expensive black jacket, Nick could have passed for a super villain or a highly paid lobbyist.

Zach stayed facing the mall. Keeping an eye out for Searcha agents, he drew a quick sketch of Nick falling into a puddle; it would make Brian smile.

There was a note of static in Zach's ear. Nick found and put in his earbud.

"Here," Nick thought.

No duh. Zach flinched. He was pretty sure he'd kept the thought in his own head.

"Thanks for coming," Terra responded. *"Report?"*

"Good news or the bad news?"

"Start with the good," she replied.

"Searcha doesn't realize the new knot is leaking, and I located the spellbook."

Zach released his breath. *It's all going to be alright after all.*

"And the bad news?" Terra asked.

Zach's pencil slipped, marring his sketch. He flipped the page, and as he tried to focus on scanning the crowd for Searcha faces, Nick came into view in his peripheral vision.

The double agent seemed to be fully focused on his phone. *"The current owner of the spellbook was recruited by Searcha a month ago and is in their training camp."*

Terra frowned at the last half of her pastry. *"Do you know where the spellbook is being kept?"*

"No, as a field agent, I can't be too curious about the training facility. The camp just had a group of graduates, as I informed you in a recent report, so it's fairly empty until they recruit more. Maybe you could send a strike force in to retrieve it."

Zach snorted. The Guard was a step away from being a student-run lab crossed with his mom's book club.

Terra shook her head. *"Our people aren't trained for military maneuvers."*

"I'd recommend you some hired guns, but they tend to panic like cockroaches when faced with something as benign as a unicorn." Nick's dry humor vibrated in his thoughts before he turned serious. *"Maybe it's time you train your people for war. Searcha is."*

Zach shivered.

"People die in wars. We're trying to stop this before it gets that far."

"The only life you're willing to risk is mine?" The coldness in Nick's thoughts bit deeper than the breeze.

Zach glanced over. There was a flicker of blue on Nick's skin, faint enough not to register on the visible spectrum. *Why's he so angry?* Surely Searcha would kick Nick out if they caught him, not kill him.

"Is it worth blowing my cover for? I think I can get it," Nick said.

A group of tourists walked by, their cacophonous banter making it hard for Zach to hear.

"No." Terra caught herself shaking her head this time and stopped. *"Your reports are far too valuable in the long term, and I doubt this is the last immediate crisis we'll face before magic is secured. We'll find another way."*

"You said they're recruiting? Could we send someone undercover as a spellcaster, uh, alchemist?" Brian asked.

Nick went back to looking at his phone. *"Caligo handpicks each alchemist recruit."*

Zach had read Nick's report on the subject. Caligo selected recent college graduates, usually with degrees in language, who had ended up in customer-service jobs struggling to pay back their student loans. She looked for specific psych and personality profiles of people who would see Searcha's mission as the answer to their search for purpose, and who would respect leadership and not ask too many questions. More stable than your average cult recruit, but still with minimal ties to the outside world. The report had concluded with a sarcastic note: *between their standard personalities and field uniforms it's exceedingly difficult to tell them apart.*

Nick continued. *"I'm not sure how you'd get one of your people in front of her, and they'd need a serious cover ID if it was someone from a Guard family. Besides, there's a Shadow in training. Even untied, she'll be hard to fool for long."*

"Sending a spellcaster is too risky then," Alexis agreed.

"What about sending a Shadow or a Shiner? Would they be a valuable-enough addition to not be looked at too closely?" Terra asked.

"You have a spare one of those laying around?" Nick snorted.

Zach fought to tune out a lively child who'd started reading aloud the Gettysburg Address, which was written on the wall.

Terra said, *"We don't know for sure—"*

"No, Vicky might have come up as a Shadow on her personality test, but she's still in high school," Brian interrupted.

"You're right. You're right. Maybe Sadie and Russel will have found another way while we've been out," Terra said.

Waves with teeth that Zach had absentmindedly doodled snarled up at him from his pad. He knew the manuscripts and books at HQ backwards and forwards; there were no answers for how to stop the leaking knot. Sadie and Russel were spellcasters, not magicians. They couldn't pull a rabbit out of a hat or a spell out of thin air. The Guard did, however, have a spare Shadow lying around.

"You said field agents and trainees don't mingle?" Zach asked.

"Yes. I'm invited to the facility only occasionally to do presentations to the students about what it's like in the field." Nick said.

"No one at the training camp would be someone I'd have run across?" Zach said.

"No, they probably wouldn't have even read Searcha's file on you. Searcha shares info on a need-to-know basis only."

"Alexis?" Zach asked.

There was a long pause, Alexis's frustration palpable.

"This stupid rain," she answered at last. *"It makes it so hard to read anything. You're right about the waves, though, Zach. Now that I'm looking for them, they're everywhere. They're reflecting the golem the knot coating is becoming. It'll be a truly dangerous and bloodthirsty monster. We need to fix the knot as soon as possible. I think we need multiple plans in play, backups for the backups."*

A shiver of dread skittered down Zach's spine. *Shit.* He wasn't hallucinating.

"So you think it's a good idea? To send Zach undercover? That's what you're suggesting, Zach?" Terra asked.

"If Alexis thinks it could help, then yes," Zach said. He prayed volunteering wasn't taking a spot from someone else who could do it better, and, hopefully, Alexis could see that.

Alexis frowned at the ground. *"Your shadow is still hard to read, Zach. It has the same blurred filter Nick's has since he started wearing that family ring."*

"You noticed?" Nick asked, sounding curious rather than defensive.

"Of course. I saw your Shadow from before," Alexis thought.

"He's hiding his shadow from you?" Terra asked sharply.

Alexis pretended to use her camera again. *"Blurring it a bit, it's fine. It keeps him safe when dealing with Searcha. It makes it hard for me to protect him, but that's his choice. If the mechanics are the same as the spell on Zach's shadow, it would be hard for the Searcha Shadow to read. But I can't get a clear reading on his future. There are too many variables at play."*

"With no room for error, we could use as many backup plans in place as possible. Zach, are you sure about this?" Terra asked.

Hell no! He was nuts, but the knot had been under his care when he taunted an armed alchemist. If he could make up for that by fixing it, if they couldn't find anyone else who could do it better, then, *"Yes. I'm sure."* His inner child cheered. He was finally going to get to do something badass.

"Okay. But only as a backup. As soon as Russel and Sadie find another way, I'm pulling you," Terra said.

Zach nodded a little numbly. *"Sounds good."*

"I'll get the ball rolling then. We'll need an excellent story, and Zach will need a different last name and some kind of digital footprint," Nick said.

Zach leaned heavily against the pillar beside him as a quick plan was drawn up. The cold rain picked up. Heavy drops splattered off the marble and sank into his sneakers.

It took him a moment to realize they'd finished the preliminary planning and Nick was talking to him.

"Then I'll pick you up at the New Carrollton Metro on Monday."

"See you there," Zach replied.

Alexis took one more photo of Lincoln before stepping out into the rain. Turning to follow the others in their staggered formation, Zach caught himself before he could nod to Nick in acknowledgement. The double agent would leave in the opposite direction in his own time.

What the hell did I volunteer to do? Opening his umbrella, Zach stepped into the downpour. Excitement warred with fear in his chest.

Eight

Kayla
Day 4 of the Lockhouse Knot Leak
Monday morning
Tidal Water, MD

Kayla bounced on the balls of her feet, waiting. *Jason said the back porch of Xander, didn't he? Maybe he said the front porch?* More likely she was just early.

Too wired to eat breakfast, especially after surviving yoga, she'd left for magic class early. To appease Hannah's nagging, Kayla had wrapped up a peanut butter sandwich and a banana, but she'd tossed them into her bag as soon as she was out of sight of the house. She would throw up if she tried to eat now. She was finally going to learn how to use magic and secure protection for her family and friends. *If Jason would just get here already!* And maybe, if she could prove she was good at magic, Hannah would stop worrying about her so much.

Kayla leaned over the railing to look around. There was a grove of tall pine trees rising out of the far side of the lawn like a mountain range, a host of crows playing in the branches. To the right of the trunks, the bay sparkled in spring sunshine. Jason was nowhere in sight.

"It would have been a perfect morning for a run," Kayla muttered.

A crow hopped out of a pine and glided down, alighting on the railing a few yards from Kayla. One of his toes was crooked, as if it had been broken and healed wrong, but his black feathers looked glossy and healthy, and his eyes were curious. He tilted his head and looked Kayla over before cawing at her.

Kayla tossed her palms up, waist high. "What?"

The crow tipped his beak down and made a woop-woop sound.

"You agree with me? It's a perfect day for a run!" Kayla asked, laughing at herself.

Woop-woop.

"Exactly! I tried to go last night, but Hannah was like, 'You've already run once today, and it's raining, and it's dark, and don't you want to watch another episode of my favorite tv show?'" Kayla said.

The crow tilted his head as if listening.

"It's not a bad show. It's full of backstabbing politicians and bright-eyed werewolves, but they got all mixed up in my nightmares." Kayla dug the banana out of her pack. The worst part of her nightmares was when the mud monster hunted down and ate her whole family, including her three-year-old niece and infant nephew, but it felt dangerous to voice that part. Tempting fate. Besides, it was stupid. Searcha was saving the world with magic. If magic lashed out at people, it would be the Guard's fault, like with the thunderbird.

"Sure, I know it's terrible to feed wildlife, but I've seen you crows eating out of the trash pile behind Newton, and you're being such a good listener."

She put a small piece of banana on the railing and backed away. When she was two yards from the banana, the crow hopped over and gave it an experimental poke before swallowing it in a gulp.

Woop-Woop.

"Glad you like it," Kayla said. "Of course, since I slept badly, I didn't get up in time to run before yoga, and of course I couldn't skip yoga and miss my daily dose of torture. This time, I started tearing up for absolutely no reason. Had to wipe away tears before I could get out of pigeon pose. Luckily, no one noticed, but how embarrassing! I don't know what's wrong with me."

The crow cawed. Kayla took it as sympathy, but in case it was a demand for more food, she tossed another piece his way. He caught it out of the air.

"Noah, one of my brothers, gave me a few good phrases to help me deal with Hannah. He said I need to work on my boundary setting, but when she looks so sad, how am I supposed to stay strong? And she's going to be my Shadow. I don't know if normal boundary setting applies."

A second crow, with several white flight feathers, landed on the railing beside the first. There were half-a-dozen partial albino crows in the flock. Ara assured Kayla they were that way before they'd started eating leftover potion ingredients.

The white-tipped crow cawed.

"See, this is one of the many reasons it's bad to feed wildlife," Kayla told the birds, tossing a bit of banana to the new bird. This bird was more suspicious, holding it with her feet and pecking at it, but she ate it when the crooked-toe crow hopped her way.

"Noah would love seeing this. He'd give me grief for feeding wildlife, but he'd find y'all fascinating." Kayla tossed another bit of banana to each of them. "He'd probably name you after those crows Odin was supposed to have had." Her brow furrowed. "Right, Hugin and Munin."

Hugin, the crow with the crooked toe, cawed.

Munin, the white-tipped crow, looked down the porch, and then they both took off for the trees.

The back door opened. Nathan came out.

Kayla folded up the banana peel and quickly tucked it back in her bag.

"Morning." Kayla bounced over to Nathan. He was a bit taller than her, with a triangular torso and athletic build he'd maintained from his competitive swimming days. Kayla was a tad jealous of his gorgeous teal Shiner glow, which looked amazing against his brown skin.

"Good morning," Nathan said, zipping up his black windbreaker.

"Good morning. Where's Jason? Are you here to help with my lesson, too?" Kayla asked.

"Yes. Learning magic is a long road. You're going to have to work on your patience," Nathan said gently.

Kayla groaned. "Isn't it supposed to come naturally?"

"That just means the magic comes from within, not from the outside, like the alchemist. It's like learning to swim. The not-drowning-in-calm-water part can be learned easily, but mastering the breath, style, and techniques required takes years of training and practice."

Kayla raised her hand to hide a yawn.

Nathan frowned.

Kayla tried to shake her sleepiness and plopped into one of the wooden rocking chairs that lined the porch. "I thought the goal was to get us through training fast, so we can help in the field."

"That's the goal for the alchemists. I was here three months before they started my Shiner training, and I still have a ways to go. It's vital that we have a basic understanding of history and alchemy. It'll make us more effective in the field. Besides, we're a lot more powerful, so we need to be more careful."

It was tempting to roll her eyes. Ara's accidental explosion had packed more punch than anything Kayla had seen Jason or Nathan do. She managed to nod.

"We are fighting against the Guard. Our magic has to be stronger and faster if we're going to right their wrongs."

"So we should get started. Where's Jason?" Kayla hopped up and tried another rocking chair. It was just as comfortable as the first. *Would Nathan scold if I stood on the railing?* It looked wide enough to walk on like a balance beam. Not that she'd lasted more than five weeks in gymnastic classes. She'd been six, the pull-up bar had been too hard, and her BFF had started playing basketball, and that looked fun instead.

Nathan shrugged and walked over to hold the door for Dahlia, who was carrying three gray yoga mats. Dahlia, besides leading yoga classes every morning, was the maintenance manager and non-magic supply manager for Tidal Water along with her husband, Captain Fitzroy. Her purple leggings and paisley handkerchief shirt showed a curvy figure. Her graying, curly chestnut hair was pulled back in a messy bun, and at the moment she had on enough hippy jewelry to supply a table at a farmer's market, but she was just as likely to have swapped them out for a tool belt and wide-brim hat that seemed to do nothing from keeping her fair skin from tanning to a bronze.

"Thanks," Dahlia said to Nathan, letting him take one of the yoga mats. "Sorry, Kayla. Jason has to finish preparing for a new trainee who's arriving this afternoon, but since he didn't want to postpone your first lesson, I'll be helping you."

"A new alchemist?" Nathan asked.

"A Shadow. Exciting, right?" Dahlia said.

Kayla stilled in the rocking chair, hope fluttering in her chest. "Female?" Maybe there'd be someone besides Hannah she could tie with.

Dahlia shook her head. "His name is Zach . . . something."

Kayla jumped up from the rocking chair, hope vanishing as quick as it came. Searcha had a policy that you couldn't tie with anyone you might develop a romantic relationship with. So Kayla was only allowed to tie with an equally straight female. Kayla had asked what would have happened if she was bi or ace, but Miranda had neatly sidestepped the question and moved onto the next topic.

"So, magic class?" Kayla asked.

"Normally, the first lesson is in the yoga room, but I thought we'd take advantage of the weather and set up on the beach," Dahlia said.

"Great!" Nathan said.

Kayla frowned as she took a mat from Dahlia. "What do yoga mats have to do with learning magic?"

"Don't worry, you've had your dose of yoga for the morning," Dahlia said, leading the way towards the beach. "It's common for emotions trapped in muscles to be released when you allow the muscle to stretch, by the way."

Crap, she noticed. Kayla ignored the heat rising in her cheeks.

Dahlia turned to Nathan. "When I sat in on your introductory class, Jason talked for a while. Would you like to summarize?"

"Ah, sure. Magic connects everything within its range in a complicated web of . . . connections," Nathan said, as if trying to teach a topic he barely understood himself. "It's like that quote from John Muir about how if you try to pick out one thing in nature, you find it's connected to everything in the universe. It's like these rocks and trees and air."

Kayla nodded, as if she had any clue what he was rambling on about. She hissed in pain as the toe of her shoe caught on a rock; she had to hop to stay upright. The rock wasn't connected to the tree roots next to it in any way she could see, beyond proximity. And neither of them had anything to do with her except as trip hazards, but theory had never been Kayla's strong suit. She had to just nod her way through to the doing, where she was usually fine.

"Shiner magic allows us to see and utilize those connections. The other part of our magic is this." Nathan stopped and pointed to the air about two feet off the ground.

"What am I looking at?" Kayla asked.

"Can you see how it glitters and shimmers in the sunlight?" he said reverently.

Kayla squinted, moved closer, and frowned deeper. Finally, she leaned back on her heels and feigned nonchalance. "Nope. I see air."

"With practice, you'll be able to see them." Nathan plucked a bit of air, about an inch wide.

As he pulled it loose from something unseen, it solidified into a glittering, teal-colored, chickpea-sized orb. A whiff of ocean spray tickled Kayla's nose.

"Wow! What is it?" Kayla reached out to touch it.

Nathan drew his hand back. "Careful, until it's dried, it'll zap you. If you'd picked it, you could hold it and I'd be zapped if I tried. Nothing serious with a bit this small, but still not comfortable."

Kayla swung her hands around to interlace her fingers behind her back. "What is it?"

Nathan shrugged. "We're not exactly sure. The strands of magic seem to excrete it like sap. It's handy. With a big-enough lump, you can use it like a taser on someone. When it's fresh, a Shadow can manipulate it into shapes that will come in handy when we figure out what to use them for."

So you don't actually know anything. "Well, it's pretty." Kayla wished Jason was here. He must do a better job explaining. *Why'd the new Shadow have to choose today to arrive?* Kayla skipped a step to shake off her annoyance.

Ahead of them, the boulders separating water from land turned abruptly away from shore, forming a jetty. Beyond that was the beach. A swath of silty, pebbly sand stretched to another jetty, beyond which was marshland. Kayla jumped onto one of the rugged, granite boulders and hopped to the next before skipping back to the grass.

"Kayla, you need to focus," Nathan said.

On what? You aren't saying anything useful. "Sorry. Magic sap that zaps. I'm following."

Nathan let out a long breath before continuing. "It's secreted from the vine, like offshoots from the strings of connection."

"Okay," Kayla said, so he knew she was listening. There was a particularly flat boulder she wanted to jump onto, but one glance at Nathan's serious face, and she forced herself to walk past it.

"It's more than just understanding how things are connected, it's being able to feel it so strongly you can make that connection solid. Can you see the strands now?" Nathan asked.

Kayla's brow furrowed, trying to figure out what answer he wanted. "You mean the glowy white lines that look like a cross between snowflakes and spiderwebs?"

"Yes!" Nathan smiled warmly.

"Not at the moment."

His face fell, but he caught himself before his disappointment turned into a frown. "Still, you get what I'm talking about?"

Kayla shrugged. "Sure." She'd seen the weird lines a couple of times since last fall. The first time she'd thought she'd fallen and hit her head too hard and was seeing stars, only she couldn't remember falling, and the weird lines didn't dance around her. The second time, her doctor decided she needed a CAT scan. Kayla swallowed hard against the memories. It had been a relief to not have a brain tumor, but the psychiatry path they'd sent her down next had been equally filled with sleepless nights. Luckily, Dr. Caligo found her and explained what was actually going on.

"Have you ever meditated before?" Dahlia asked.

"What?" Kayla asked. "Not really, no."

"It makes seeing and connecting with the strings of magic much easier," Nathan said.

Kayla raised her disbelieving eyebrows. "Meditation?"

"Scientists have proven that it helps increase focus and awareness and reduce stress," Dahlia said as they reached the steep slope down to the beach. "Those're all things that help connect Shiners and Shadows to their magic."

Shit! Hannah is going to expect me to join her for her predinner meditation class. That was time Kayla usually spent shooting hoops or kicking a ball around with the alchemists. The monster from the photo Hannah showed her snarled through Kayla's thoughts. Gritting her teeth, she nodded. She could do this for her family.

Dahlia and Nathan rolled out their mats on the sand, and Kayla followed their example.

Nathan took a seat on his mat and pulled his feet up so each was on top of the opposite thigh. "I noticed the difference after a few days. Now I see the strands all the time, but I meditate for an hour every morning on my own and then forty-five minutes in the afternoon with the class."

Dahlia sat in a cross-legged pose that looked more reasonable, so Kayla tried that. It wasn't comfortable to sit up straight, but whatever.

"It takes practice to build up to an hour, so we'll start with ten minutes," Dahlia said.

Kayla was still thinking about the meditation class that was going to be added to her day; it took her a moment to catch up. "I thought this was a magic lesson."

"We start every magic lesson with a short meditation," Nathan said. "It clears the mind and makes it easier to connect with the strands. Ninety percent of our magic is about connecting to and learning to manipulate those strings."

"But I can't see the strings!" Kayla's chest rose and fell with rapid breaths. She should have gone for a run that morning.

"I told you, magic takes patience." Nathan rested his hands palms up on his knees and closed his eyes.

"You'll get comfortable seeing the strings in your own time," Dahlia said. "Now, we're going to focus on our breathing. Feel your belly expand as you inhale. Close your eyes, feel your shoulders melt down your back as you exhale."

Kayla scrunched her eyes shut. *Ten minutes, I can do this.* Clenching her jaw, she tried to sit up straighter. Dahlia's voice was slow and mellow. Kayla tried to follow along, but she kept missing bits. *How do shoulders melt, anyway? Am I even doing this right?*

"Relax your face," Dahlia said.

Kayla peeked to see if Dahlia was watching, but the woman was upright and comfortable, eyes closed. *How'd she know my face isn't relaxed? Maybe I'll blow off working on that stupid research paper and go for a run after lunch.*

The breeze pushed a strand of hair into her face. Kayla frowned, ignoring it. Three breaths later, she shoved it behind her ear.

What if I can't see the strings? Kayla gritted her teeth. She hadn't seen them in weeks. A couple of months, maybe. *Can I learn magic if I can't see them?* Jason would have done a much better job explaining things. *Stupid Shadow showing up today!* The tension in her jaw creeped up to her temples, nudging her towards a headache.

"Feel the energy rising up your spine," Dahlia said.

What energy? It was more of the woo-woo crap Kayla didn't get in Dahlia's yoga class.

Kayla's right leg was going numb, and a knot was forming behind her left shoulder blade. She rolled her neck, trying to loosen it.

Seriously, who has this much discipline? They must miss out on all the fun in life!

It's ten minutes. Just sit still!

Kayla tried to melt her shoulder blades again. That stupid knot behind her left one was getting bigger.

Sit still! You're terrible at this, you're going to suck at magic too! Kayla growled at her inner voice. *That's a horribly judgmental thought. Just shut up and sit still!* Dahlia's reminder to check in with her breath slid between Kayla's thoughts. Shallow breathing was the opposite of slow, deep breaths. Kayla forced air deeper. The more her mind spiraled in increasingly critical circles, the more she wanted to climb out of her own skin.

This had to be the longest ten minutes in the entire history of the world! She hadn't seen Dahlia set a timer. Maybe she'd lost track of time. Kayla tried to wait it out.

"Kayla," Dahlia said, with attention-getting energy. "Are you breathing?"

"Oops, nope, holding my breath," Kayla realized. "Hasn't it been more than ten minutes?"

Dahlia checked her watch. "Seven."

Kayla bit back a scream of frustration.

"You're glowing," Nathan said with a smile. "Then you can see the strands?"

Kayla could barely focus on the burnt-orange patterns glowing faintly on her hands or anything else. If she didn't get up now, she was going to lose it.

"I can't," Kayla managed to say.

"That's probably enough meditation to start with," Dahlia said.

Kayla jumped up, shook the pins and needles out of her legs, and tried to roll the knot out of her shoulder blades.

Concern furrowed Dahlia's brow.

Nathan rubbed the back of his neck before smiling reassuringly. "Don't worry, it's like those flat images you stare at and a 3D image seems to pop out. Once you learn to see them, it's a lot easier."

"I can't see her glowing, so a low-level glow from an emotional response?" Dahlia asked.

Nathan nodded. "That would be my evaluation."

"I've never glowed bright enough for people without magic to see it. Are you sure I'm a Shiner?" Kayla asked, a bit of hope blossoming. She'd never been able to see those 3D images either.

"Of course!" Dahlia said.

At the same moment, Nathan said, "Yes."

Kayla bounced on the soles of her feet. "But I have such a loud personality, you'd think my magic would be louder."

"That's nice and self-aware. Once you get the hang of it, you'll be excellent at meditation," Dahlia said.

It's not self-awareness, I've just been told so, a lot. Kayla managed not to roll her eyes. "So what's next?

"I applaud your enthusiasm. Do you have questions about the poems you were assigned to read? I'd be happy to break them down with you," Nathan said.

Kayla shook her head. She was too lost to have questions.

"Then I don't think there's anything else we can do right now," Nathan said.

Dahlia nodded. "I'll get permission from Miranda, and we can download a bunch of meditations so you can practice. I'm going to recommend that you work on your own and in your magic class, but that, until you work your way up to forty-five minutes, you skip the afternoon group class."

Kayla's stomach flopped like a landed fish. She didn't want to go to the meditation class, but if she was too incompetent to attend, what did that mean for her graduation?

"So, that's my first lesson in magic?"

"Yes." Nathan rubbed the back of his neck again. "It's a good start. I'll take the mats back."

Kayla almost believed he meant it.

"You could always use this time to memorize a few poems or work on one of your research papers," Dahlia said, rolling up her mat and handing it to Nathan. "We'll see you tomorrow, same time and place. Jason will have the Introduction to Magic class to teach the new guy, but he should be able to teach you the day after."

Kayla growled in frustration. Memorization was a punishment, not a perk. She handed her mat to Nathan, too. "I'm going for a run. Thanks!"

Kayla didn't wait for a response. Taking off towards the marsh trail, she yanked her earbuds out of her pocket. Picking a hip-hop playlist on her phone, she turned it up two clicks louder than usual and pushed herself hard before dropping into a maintainable jog.

It's Hannah's fault for not letting me jog before my lesson. If I hadn't had nightmares, I would have been better rested. Stupid Shadow had to pick today to show up and monopolize Jason's time. And it's Jason's fault I didn't learn any magic, because he chose the new Shadow over me. If Nathan had explained it better, I totally could have learned something.

Pushing her legs harder, Kayla tried to outrun her inaccurate, lying thoughts.

Eventually Kayla's energy flagged. *Shit, shit, shit, it's my own fault. Not any of theirs. If I'd paid more attention, if I'd been able to sit still.*

Breathing was hard, but she pushed herself until the stitch in her side screamed. *Magic sucks!* But unlike every other time she'd been bad at something, she couldn't switch classes, sweet-talk her teacher into giving her extra credit, quit, or walk away. There was no outrunning the changes magic was going to bring to the world.

Kayla put her hands on her thighs and leaned heavily. "What the hell am I going to do?"

The crooked-toed crow, Hugin, landed on the ground a few yards away and cawed at her.

"What! I suck at magic!"

Caw caw.

Kayla groaned, but the interruption to her flow of thoughts made it easier to breathe.

"I can't do magic," she muttered.

Hugin cawed at her, as if calling out the word *can't.*

"You're right. Can't isn't a helpful word. Noah would say I have a . . . what is it? A fixed mindset, and I would be better served with a flexible one. He can be so annoying!"

Woop woop.

"Fine. You want me to lie? I'm a Shiner, I learn magic."

Caw caw.

"I know that's clearly bullshit. I haven't learned any magic. I should have gotten it today."

Hugin tilted his head sideways, as if waiting for her to try again.

Kayla groaned. Noah called her out when she used the word *should.* "Fine, how about: As a Shiner, I'm capable of learning magic. Are you happy?"

Woop woop. Hugin dipped his beak then lifted it up, tilting his head sideways and looking at her with curious eyes.

Kayla burst out laughing. "Here I am talking to you about my problems as if you can understand, while you just want more banana."

Tension washed away, leaving her drained. She wiped tears that had to be from laughter out of the corners of her eyes.

The banana was browning and mushy after being jostled around in her bag, but Kayla tossed the crow another bit of it and wiped the slime off on her pants.

Hugin snatched the piece and flew off.

"Thank you!" Kayla called after him. This whole flexible mindset thing probably didn't work on her. There were some things in life she just simply sucked at and some things she was good at. *Noah would call bullshit if I said that out loud.* Since no other inspiration struck it was worth a try. Picking up a brisk walk to cool down, Kayla headed for the house to clean up before lunch, muttering her new mantra under her breath.

"As a Shiner, I'm capable of learning magic."

Nine

Zach
Day 4 of the Lockhouse Knot Leak
Monday morning
New Carrollton, MD

Zach was standing in bright sunlight on the sidewalk outside of the New Carrollton Metro Station when a black Porsche purred to the curb. The window slid down, and Nick gave Zach a condescending once-over.

"What are you supposed to be, a James Dean wannabe?" Nick scoffed.

Annoyance pushed Zach's shoulders back. His chest inflated into the jacket, owning it fully for the first time since he'd tried it on yesterday. "Says the guy driving a car that must have been in a Bond movie."

Nick smirked. "If it was, then this is a newer model. Bag in the trunk, we have a schedule to keep."

Shaking his head, Zach walked to the trunk and tossed in his duffle bag. His messenger bag went at his feet in the small, low front seat. As the smell of new car wrapped around him and the plush leather cushioned his body, Zach gave himself a moment to wonder if it was jealousy that made him resent the car. *Nah.*

Nick sent the car zooming out of the pickup zone. It was Nick's blatant and casual display of wealth that annoyed Zach. There had to be a better use for money than this flashy conveyance. Especially since Nick seemed to have more cars than Tony Stark.

Fine, maybe I'm a little jealous of his wealth. But Nick had inherited it or been given it by his father, and from the little Zach knew about Nick's family, Zach wouldn't trade his family for Nick's for all the money in the world. Zach smiled slightly and relaxed into the seat.

Nick stopped the car for a red light and glanced over. "Where'd you get that jacket? A dumpster?"

Zach crossed his arms. "A thrift store. It's part of my cover. Zach Ryder has had this jacket forever, part of his angry-at-the-world-and-authority vibe he's got going." Plus, it had an added mirage enchantment on it, a magic earbud in a secret pocket, and a button steeped in a distress spell, like a flare, in case he was caught.

"Where'd you pull the name Ryder?" The light turned green, and the Porsche rumbled forward.

It was easy to ignore Nick's derisive tone; Zach had lucked out with a name that sounded like a comic book character's. There had been several less interesting options.

"I went to school with Zachary Ryder. Alexis's best friend is a social media expert, and Mia's boyfriend is a tech guy. Eric asked Ryder if he could borrow his social media for his thesis project. Superficially, his stuff looks like mine now." It had been a scramble, and there were a couple of false starts, but Alexis's friends had proved their worth to the Guard—Zach's cover had been sorted out. Borrowing someone else's identity had been easier than building one from scratch. The cover was only skin-deep and wasn't good enough to land him a real job, but Searcha wasn't asking for his Social Security number or passport. The cover only had to hold up for a few days, a week or two at most.

"The Guard members are like children playing with fire," Nick muttered.

Zach shrugged. It was an exaggeration, but not by a lot. No one in the Guard had been prepared for magic to come back in their lifetime. Except Elliot, but everyone had assumed he was growing a bit paranoid with age.

Zach slouched back, looking for a change of topic. "What does this car say about Nick the Searcha agent?"

Nick's smirk grew. "If you want to get deep, I could say wealth and a secret agent's abilities are directly tied in people's subconscious. It's an interesting commentary on mass media and our capitalist culture. Personally, though, I picked it because Terra asked that I leave a car for you that's flashy and has an automatic transmission. One more escape route for you as part of one of her backup plans."

"You're leaving this car with *me*?"

Nick shrugged. "It's not one of my favorites, and I expect you're a competent enough driver to get it back to me in one piece. Trainees aren't allowed to keep their own vehicles on the property. Easiest way to keep people from leaving midtraining. If you have to make an emergency getaway and blow your cover, I can be more upset that you 'stole' my father's car than that you're a traitor, that'll help protect my cover. I can say my father has the info for activating the security features when stolen, he's notoriously hard to reach. I assume it was Alexis's idea—that woman elevates shadow reading to an art."

Zach's shoulders tightened at the implied dig at his own abilities. *I'm being overly sensitive.* He rolled his shoulders to loosen them and dug his sketchpad out of his messenger bag.

"Thank you. I appreciate having a way out."

Nick passed him a spare key. "Just following orders. Terra also had me leave you a few supplies, including a prepaid cell in the glove box and another in the first-aid kit in the trunk. There's no cell service on property, and if anyone catches you with them, I will disavow any knowledge of them."

Zach rolled his eyes as he tucked the spare key into an inside jacket pocket. "I won't blow your cover."

Nick shot Zach a dangerous look. "My cover isn't just important to the Guard. It protects my brother."

Zach opened his mouth to ask what the heck Searcha could do to Nick's little brother, but the shadows flickered with images of a blond teenager locked in a windowless room being starved and manipulated until he used his Shadow abilities to help Searcha.

It was probably Nick projecting his fears, not an actual possible future, but a shiver ran down Zach's spine. *Is that the fate that awaits me if I get caught?* He shook himself and dug his pencil case out of his bag. *Absurd.* Shadows saw so much truth it would be hard to manipulate them into doing anything they didn't want to, and the Guard would find a way to save one of their own, eventually. At least, now that Alexis was a leading member. Zach swallowed hard, trying not to think of how the Guard had reacted when Brian's family had been kidnapped.

"There is another spare key hidden in the rear passenger-side wheel well. Try not to lose them," Nick said coldly.

Zach let it slide by. "Thanks."

Amusement cracked Nick's frown. "You don't make a very convincing angry young man."

Surprise pulled a laugh from Zach's chest. "I didn't realize I had to be yet."

Nick's smile dissolved. "Unless you can flip a switch and be someone you're clearly not, you should get started." Nick put on a podcast without asking.

Zach put in his headphones and pulled up one of the angry playlists the team had helped him make. Groaning, he selected a black gel pen out of his pencil case. Ryder would not be a comfortable person to be, but his anger was useful. The mirage spell faded nuance and sharpened primal emotions and was overlaid with anger from his initial use of it, but the more Zach could give the spell to work with, the better.

It had been decided, mostly on information gained from fiction because there'd been so little time for research, that building the Ryder identity as close to Zach's as possible would be best.

As Zach sketched himself in his new leather jacket, leaning against a motorcycle, arms crossed, he dug back to what it felt like when he'd been fifteen. Back when he was angry with the world and society. He'd been sure no one understood him and that he'd never belong anywhere but on the outside. It came easier now, after all the practice of the last few days.

Saturday, he'd spent hours trying to work on his new persona. It had been weird going through old notebooks. It had been harder sketching himself in those angry, teenage days, digging down, finding he'd not let go of as much as he'd thought. But Alexis had said it was necessary, and it had been as educational as it had been uncomfortable.

Saturday afternoon, when Zach had as clear a picture as he could of who he'd been, he sat down with the team. Alexis brought her Shadow abilities, Terra brought her years of working with youth, and Brian backed him up with a male perspective. They'd helped Zach craft the story of an aged-up, imaginary version of that angry kid. As if his life had split, and he'd not taken the path that made him who he was today, but a path that would lead to being recruited by Searcha. Zach talked about the character in the third person, giving himself space to see more clearly.

Ryder didn't have wonderful parents and sisters who loved him unconditionally, even when they'd not fully understood him. Ryder didn't have the support and community of the Guard to treat him like family. Terra also wanted to cut out the mentor who'd taught Zach tai chi and qigong, but Alexis had argued against it. She pointed out confidence would make it easier for Ryder to build the trust he'd need to get the spellbook, and martial arts training made it believable. Zach was grateful; the grounding of his practice would help him stay sane while under cover. To help conceal Zach's dislike of Searcha, they'd given Ryder a simmering and universal dislike of authority. They'd rounded out the character by agreeing that much of the youthful rage had backed into cynical humor, giving Ryder a way to show and vent anger without constantly losing his temper.

Sunday, Alexis went thrift-store shopping with Zach, hunting for the leather jacket to help sell the persona.

It had all sounded great on paper, but now, zooming towards enemy lines, Zach had to stop thinking about Ryder in the third person and be him. Gut twisting, he sketched Ryder, himself, riding away on the motorcycle from a family that had their backs turned on him. Another of him standing alone on a cliff overlooking a turbulent sea. The waves had teeth. Zach set down his pen and interlaced his fingers, pressing the palms away, dissipating some of the tension rising in him. Picking up his pen, he sketched himself with a smirk, flipping off faceless authority. Zach chuckled under his breath. Humor wouldn't help hide his shadow, but it helped everything else.

Zach fiddled with the cylindrical, five-and-a-half inches long, wood-and-bronze pendant he wore on a brown leather cord around his neck—a gift from Sadie and Russel. It was really a small pen that used magic ink. It would allow him to brainstorm and clarify shadows, but keep them hidden in case Searcha searched his stuff. His normal art supplies were adequate for everything else.

Nick glanced over. *Is he trying to see my sketchbook?*

Zach flipped him off.

Nick snorted in amusement and turned his eyes back to the road.

Zach hid his smile and looked out the window. The curved bridge over the Chesapeake Bay seemed to have them driving into the air. Morning sunlight sparkled off a wide expanse of wind-rippled water. Boats moved below, and birds flew above. Breath expanded Zach's rib cage, warmth spread, and tension melted. The beauty caught in his chest. A large, dark shape swam towards the bridge. Zach leaned his forehead against the cold glass of the window. It wasn't a fish or a whale; it was a shadow of something longer than the tugboat the shadow was gliding under. The future, the prickling on his forearms warned. Before Zach could see more, they were on the other side of the bridge.

Boats were docked in the marinas on both sides of the road. Zach watched for more flickers of shadows, but nothing besides the persistent waves was out of the ordinary. The land embraced flatness. Flipping the page of his sketchbook, Zach made a few efforts to capture the lines of trees and farmland, but they turned into sketches of floods and teeth.

Sighing, he flipped to a new page and returned to sketching himself into being Ryder. In a series of panels, he captured the backstory of how he was supposed to have met Nick and been recruited. Carefully, he pictured as many details as possible, blending in reality and fiction so he could show as much of the story as possible in his shadow. Redrawing frames over and over until he could almost believe them himself.

"Do you ever wonder if being undercover is changing your memories?" Zach asked.

Nick raised an eyebrow at him.

Zach flushed. "Because we're supposed to remember our memories when we think of them, and that can change them, by remembering my memories wrong. I'd just wondered."

As the silence stretched, Zach started sketching again. It had been a stupid question. Well, not stupid. It seemed a decent hypothesis based on what he'd learned about the brain in college, but he hadn't realized how personal it could be until he'd said it.

Nick did speak eventually, though. "I don't know. Be glad you're only undercover for a short while. Just long enough to clean up your leaking knot mess before it goes nuclear."

Part of Zach flinched at the truth of the words. Another part wondered if it was a shield against his question. *What's Nick hiding?* But then he remembered he was Ryder. Zach gave Nick's shadow a slow inspection, blatantly reading it in a power move the Guard would consider rude. Nick's shadow crystalized into the sharp lines, black ink on white paper, of a true Searcha believer.

Feeling like a bucket of water had crashed over his head, Zach yanked his gaze up to Nick's face.

"What? See something that scares you?" Nick smirked.

Gone were the charcoal smudges Zach always associated with Nick's shadow. "How do you do that?"

It seemed for a moment like Nick would play dumb, but he glanced ahead at the cream-and-blue sign that read *Tidal Water Retreat Center* and sighed quietly. "In a perfect world, magic would be a gift beyond imagination. When I speak with Searcha, I remember that. I can feel and taste that world. When I speak with the Guard, I remember we live in a deeply flawed reality, and the price everyone is paying and might pay for the mistakes I've made. My ring hides the nuances and my flickers of doubt. You, the Guard, and your cover are in no danger from me. Now, pick your jaw off the floor and own that inane jacket."

Zach closed his mouth and his eyes. The car rumbled softly through the soles of his combat boots. Digging into the lonely, angry life of Ryder, Zach opened his eyes. Ignoring the pine forest they were driving through on a blacktop road that was barely a lane and a half, he put away his sketchpad and pen. If he could hide his shadow in this crystal-clear sunlight, then he'd have a chance of getting away with the spellbook.

Slouching casually back in the seat and crossing his arms, Zach Ryder heaved a heavy sigh. "Are we there yet?" he asked in a deeply sarcastic tone.

Nick shot him a glance that might have held respect, but Zach only saw it out of the corner of his eye and wasn't sure.

Ahead, beyond a gravel lot, stood an old-fashioned, three-story, white manor with two wings stretching back diagonally and a deep porch. A handful of crows were perched on the roof, adding a sinister air.

"We're here." Nick parked the car at the edge of the lot. "And so is the welcome party."

Two of the Searcha leaders, both marked *dangerous* in the Guard's files, walked down the wide steps. Zach took in as much of their shadows as he could. Miranda was a true believer, her faith even more clear than Nick's ring-enhanced shadow. Jason believed in magic and projected a confidence that wasn't fully reflected in his shadow. Zach frowned as he looked harder. Jason thought Zach might be a possible Shadow for him and was trying to be hopeful, but he was lying to himself about something. Zach didn't have time to dig deeper. Miranda was leading. She was greedy to add another Shadow to Searcha's ranks, but she didn't trust him. Neither of them did.

Zach swallowed back the panic rising in the back of his throat. *Do they suspect something?*

Nick opened his door and got out.

The clear sunlight was warm on Zach's skin through the window. They didn't trust him because he could see past their words and faces. He would see their secrets and know their lies. They didn't suspect where he came from. The insecure edges of their egos feared his judgment, but more powerfully, they feared they couldn't control him. They couldn't predict everything he'd see or how he'd react to it. Control and being respected were important to Miranda and vital to Searcha's mission.

Cynical smile on his face, Zach Ryder opened the car door and stepped onto the crunching gravel.

With a barely visible swallow, Miranda pushed away her flicker of doubt. She had every intention of making him a productive member of Searcha.

"Welcome to Tidal Water." She smiled at him with a warmth that didn't reach her eyes and didn't offer a hand to shake.

"Looks like it'll be an interesting time," Ryder said with a smirk. His mission had begun.

Ten

Kayla
Day 4 of the Lockhouse Knot Leak
Monday, midday
Tidal Water, MD

Kayla's feet dragged as she approached Xander. Mondays, the group meal was lunch. Her stomach and Hannah would never forgive her if she missed it, but surely someone would ask about her magic lesson. If ten minutes with the maintenance manager and a fellow trainee could be called a lesson.

Hannah, Ara, and Ben had their heads together by the side door. *Crap, did my failure already reach them?* Tidal Water had a grapevine that surpassed that of her high school, but Kayla had hoped Nathan and Dahlia wouldn't say anything.

Bracing her shoulders for scorn, Kayla danced forward, a bright smile engaging her cheek muscles. Cheerfulness was both her favorite shield and weapon.

"Kayla!" Hannah waved her over. "How was your first magic lesson?"

Kayla stretched her smile wider and shrugged. "Educational. I've got a lot to learn."

"I'm so excited for you! I'm sure you'll pick it up quickly. Guess what?" Hannah grinned, as if she couldn't wait to share.

Relieved, Kayla's forced smile relaxed into a real one. "They've canceled all research papers?"

Hannah frowned, and the others laughed. "A car we don't recognize just pulled up."

Ara tossed a lock of her fire-engine red hair off her forehead. "You sure it's not just someone wanting to check out the retreat center?"

"In that car?" Ben nodded to the black Porsche parked at the far edge of the gravel lot.

"Whoever it is has magical power. Two people, I think," Hannah said, tilting her head, as if listening hard.

Kayla shrugged. "Oh, it's probably just the new Shadow and whoever drove him out here."

"Just? That's huge!" Ara said. "We only have like seven innates in the whole of Searcha."

"How do you know he's a Shadow?" Hannah asked.

"Jason passed my lesson on to Nathan and Dahlia because he had to help prep for the new guy's arrival," Kayla said casually. It was delightful being the person who knew something for once.

"That's quite a get. Who do you think is escorting the Shadow? That's not Dr. Caligo's car," Ara said.

Ben gave Hannah a friendly punch on the arm. "You're going to have some competition."

Hannah frowned at him, then turned back to see the two men who were getting out of the car. "Oh, Nick Steele. That explains it."

"Nick who? Sounds like the alter ego of a superhero," Kayla said. The name was familiar, some Searcha member, but Kayla couldn't remember anything about him. She'd asked more to enjoy the look of predictable horror on Hannah's face than out of curiosity.

"Nick Steele! The man who freed the First Knot, our first victory in the magical revolution! He's a Shiner. Have we taught you nothing?" Hannah said indignantly.

Kayla fought back her spreading grin. It was too easy. "Oh?"

Ben laughed, then tipped his head towards the men. "Which is which?"

The two men talking with Miranda and Jason were similar only in height.

"The blond is Steele," Ara said.

Even from a distance, the name-brand, business-casual clothes showed off the figure of a man who spent time on his appearance and at the gym to good effect. Kayla enjoyed the view, even as she sized him up as too rigid to be interesting or fun. He shook hands with Miranda and Jason and introduced the other man.

Kayla frowned at the guy who'd kept Jason from her lessons, but it faded as she took him in. He had a wiry frame made more obvious by his large, well-loved leather jacket. His auburn curls had a touch of gel, giving them a deliciously casual look. His jeans were tight, showing off his height, and his combat boots were more practical than showy. *He looks like the best kind of trouble.* The thought was confirmed when he kept his hands deep in his pockets and smirked through his introduction to Miranda and Jason.

"Yep, leather jacket guy is a Shadow," Ara said. "That's the only reason Miranda and Jason wouldn't shake hands with someone."

"Because he'd be able to read them more clearly?" Ben asked.

"Yep, which is why you should think twice before you punch Hannah in the arm again. She might tell you something about yourself you'd rather not know," Ara said.

Ben laughed, but edged away from Hannah. "Right, the three foot rule, sorry."

Hannah snorted with derision or maybe amusement. Ara shrugged an unapologetic shoulder.

Not caring enough to guess what that was about, Kayla looked over at the new Shadow and found his eyes on her.

A shiver of heat raced up Kayla's spine, and butterflies bloomed in her stomach. *Trouble indeed.* His gaze shifted, as if he was staring off into space. Maybe he hadn't been looking at her at all.

Kayla looked away. "Who's hungry? Isn't it lunchtime?"

"Definitely." Ben opened the door for the rest of them.

Kayla smiled thanks and skipped inside. Food would settle her stomach, probably. She needed a clear head for meditation practice this afternoon.

Ara followed, but looked back at Hannah. "Do you think they'll pair him with Nathan?"

"Maybe." Hannah studied the wood floor. "Though they're hoping Nathan's younger cousin will develop Shadow abilities and they can be paired." Her frown deepened. "Maybe with Jason, but whatever they do, they'll want to get to know him better first."

Ben sat at the white folding table for trainees. "Do you think Steele will stay for lunch?"

"I don't know. We don't see him often," Ara said, taking the seat next to him.

"I still think it's annoying he got to skip training, just because he's the one who released magic," Hannah grumbled as she took a seat.

Kayla tapped the back of her usual chair beside Hannah's, reluctant to sit. "Where's his Shadow then?"

"He's powerful enough, he doesn't need one," Ara said. "Kinda like Jason."

"Nick's brother is going to be his Shadow, and Jason is still here looking for his," Hannah said.

"I thought you had to be tied to leave training," Kayla said.

"There's more leeway for the powerful Shiners," Ara said.

"It only looks that way," Hannah said.

It is more than looks if Nick is out doing cool stuff on his own. Kayla bounced over to help Samantha with the dinner trays. Samantha was a round-faced alchemist with beautiful box braids, who collected eyeglasses the way Kayla collected shoes. Today Samantha was wearing a pair of rainbow-colored cat-eye glasses.

Kayla's mind was too busy dancing for her body to sit yet. There was a way to complete training without being tied to Hannah after all.

Crafting a mental plan to spend every free moment studying magic and meditating, Kayla didn't notice Steele join the staff table or the new Shadow join the trainee table until she carried out a bowl of salad. *Great.* Leather Jacket Guy took the seat next to her empty one. *I'm going to have to be nice to the guy who ruined my first magic lesson.*

Brightening her smile, she sat down. "Hi, I'm Kayla." Trying to ignore the overfriendly note in her voice, she offered her hand.

There was an audible gasp around the table.

Kayla gritted her teeth. *Shit. That's what I get for not paying attention.* But it felt rude to drop her hand now.

Amusement lit the Shadow's russet-amber eyes, but he shook her hand. "Zach Ryder." A shock jumped between them as his large hand closed over hers.

Kayla started and pulled back. "Sorry, I must have picked up some static." She gave an embarrassed laugh.

"Kayla," Hannah hissed, pulling her further away. "You don't touch Shadows."

Zach smirked. "Says the Shadow with her hand on your arm."

Hannah let go as if Kayla had burned her.

Laughing didn't quite dislodge the queasiness in Kayla's stomach. "I'm an open book. As you both might have noticed, I'm hungry. Please pass the rolls."

Zach tipped his head to her, like a little salute, and handed her the wicker basket of steaming bread.

"How'd you find out you were a Shadow?" Ara asked.

Kayla shot her a grateful look, then focused on serving herself spaghetti and salad as they were passed around the table.

"I was driving up from Florida to visit some friends when I started seeing trippy shit. Three in the morning is the best time to be on the road, but it can get dicey when the caffeine wears thin and the sugar overloads, so I blamed that at first."

"Last fall?" Hannah asked.

Zach shook his head and swirled his waterglass for a moment. "Friday—well, technically, Saturday morning."

"Why hadn't you noticed magic before that?" Ben asked.

"Florida is outside magic's current range," Nathan said. His Shiner markings glowed ever so softly teal. "Are you going to let him finish?"

Ben gave a grumpy sigh, but motioned Zach to continue.

Kayla wondered if Nathan was glowing on purpose; if so, it was an impressive flex. She'd have to learn to control her abilities that well. She added it to her mental list of things to master.

Shrugging, Zach started buttering a roll. "I pulled off at a rest stop between Richmond and DC and tried to take a power nap. When I woke up, it was worse. There was a freaking unicorn standing outside my car staring at me. I decided as long as I was hallucinating at that level, I shouldn't drive. Blamed the brownies my roommate had given me. Figured he'd accidentally switched the regular with his experimental ones. By afternoon, sick of eating vending machine crap, I tried to shoo the unicorn away. Nick had been watching the unicorn watch me. Something about it being out of sync with the solid world." Zach put down his roll and twirled a bit of spaghetti on his fork tines. "Anyway, when he saw me interacting with it, he knew I was a Shadow or a Shiner. He approached me and let me in on what the hell was going on."

"And he just brought you here?" Hannah asked.

Zach finished chewing a mouthful of spaghetti. "Had to sort everything out with the friends I was supposed to be visiting and my entanglements back home, but yeah, basically. How'd you know you were a Shadow?"

"I was in Richmond when the First Knot was cut. The emergence of my abilities led me to seek a medical professional. Dr. Caligo, a member of the Searcha leadership, is on the lookout for innates. She has spent years positioning herself in the medical community there and found me almost immediately," Hannah said, giving the condensed version.

Zach nodded, finishing a mouthful before asking about how her Shadow magic worked.

Hannah gave cryptic answers, her frown deepening as he focused on the table and asked uneducated follow-ups. It didn't take him long to give up and ask the next person how they got to Tidal Water. Kayla figured he was asking questions more so he could eat than out of curiosity.

Eyeing the wicker basket, Kayla weighed whether it was too early in the meal for thirds. Everyone else was still on their first serving.

Zach picked up the basket and offered it to her with a wink.

With a surprised chuckle, Kayla snagged another. "Thanks."

"Show-off," Hannah muttered.

Annoyed, Kayla turned to her. "Because I have a high metabolism?" It wasn't her fault Hannah counted carbs.

"Not you, him." Hannah was so quiet, Kayla wasn't sure she'd heard right.

Scrunching her face, she gave Hannah a confused look.

Hannah waved a hand at Zach.

He glanced up from the table with a mischievous grin before turning to ask Ara how she'd been recruited.

Oh. Kayla realized as she spread a nice layer of butter on her roll. *He isn't tuning them out, he's watching the table the way Hannah does when she's using her magic.* Kayla grinned and took a bite of the soft bread. At least there was little on her mind she wasn't happy to say out loud, except when she was being polite, so few reasons to fear her shadow being read.

"Your turn, Kayla," Ben said.

Having heard everyone else's stories of finding out about magic before, she'd zoned out. With an embarrassed smile, Kayla quickly chewed and swallowed the last of her roll. "It's not very interesting," she hedged.

Especially after Nathan's story of glowing, bright teal while swimming laps in a public pool. He'd been rushed off to the emergency room while the pool was shut down so it could be tested for toxic chemicals. A Searcha field team had to go in and do an elaborate cover-up while Dr. Caligo intercepted Nathan at the hospital and brought him safely into the fold.

"I could see occasional flashes of stuff." Kayla shrugged. "The strings of magic, my skin glowing, but no one else could. So I went to the doctor, who sent me to a specialist, who sent me to someone else, and so on." Kayla had gone on more runs and partied harder in that month and a half than she had in her first semester at college. She was still grateful for all the hand-holding two of her best friends and her mom had done—it had gotten her through. "Finally, I got sent to Richmond and Dr. Caligo."

Zach nodded, a small line between his auburn brows as he studied the table.

Kayla frowned. *He can't possibly see how horrid that time was for me, can he? Why is he still looking?*

"And now we're here." Hannah raised her water glass in a toast. Everyone joined in, and then the talk shifted to the latest book series being passed around camp. This one was a miserable-sounding dystopian sci-fi; Kayla couldn't bring herself to read it.

The wicker basket caught Kayla's eye again. The rolls really weren't that big.

Zach nudged the basket further away, not looking up from the table. She swatted his shoulder with a laugh. Grinning, he looked up from the shadows. Laughter dancing in his eyes, he passed the basket.

"Anyone mind if I have the last roll?" Kayla asked, ignoring Hannah's scowl.

When no one objected, she buttered the fluffy bread and savored the first bite. Zach was forgiven for ruining her first magic lesson. He was fading to the background at the table, the way Hannah did, but unlike her, he had a sense of humor Kayla was going to enjoy. Kayla reached for another bite of her roll, but she'd already finished it.

Sighing, she looked around for something else. She really didn't need more pasta. The salad was pretty good, so she served herself more of that. As she chewed a forkful of romaine lettuce liberally coated in ranch dressing, she made a mental list of what she needed to do to excel at magic so she could get out of training without being tied. If Jason and Nick could do it, she could too.

Most important thing on her list: learn how to meditate. *How hard can it be?*

She pushed a carrot bit around her plate, appetite evaporating. Realizing the talk on the other side of Hannah had shifted to basketball brackets, Kayla jumped eagerly into the conversation. She finished her salad between laughter and teasing about different players and teams.

Eleven

Zach
Day 4 of the Lockhouse Knot Leak
Monday, midday
Tidal Water, MD

Zach watched the shadows flicker across the table, playing up his abilities, but he gained more insights from his peripheral vision. The lighting was weak, old-school fluorescence, creating smeared shadows with little depth. Why hadn't Hannah or the Shadow Twin complained about it? Alexis would have gotten it fixed if it was this bad at HQ, if only because it was headache inducing and distracting to catch glimpses of distorted images.

Noticing the direction of his thoughts, Zach pulled himself back to the table. Hannah was his biggest threat. Luckily, in this light, he doubted she was getting a better read on him than he was on her. He wasn't looking forward to stepping into the sun. Hannah's shadow abilities were a problem, but they were compounded by her possessiveness towards the owner of the spellbook.

Kayla's reflection on the table kept tugging at him. *It's because she's the owner of the book I need.* Not because it was the most beautiful shadow he'd ever seen. Even in the terrible lighting, it swirled with energy and reflected her thoughts, like an impressionist painting in oil pastels. It was mesmerizing, begging him to guess what was going on in her head. Delight bubbled up in his chest when he could pass her the rolls unasked and give her a cheeky wink.

He grinned at Hannah's outrage, but his mind fought to find a solution for hiding his shadow.

Most of the spellcasters . . . *alchemists. Shit, Zach, get the vernacular straight!* That'd give him away faster than his shadow. Zach took a moment to ground himself in the hard plastic-and-metal folding chair before bringing his focus back to the origin stories being told around the table. Most of the alchemists' stories of having language degrees and being recruited from customer-service jobs matched Nick's summary report. The Shiners and Shadow, though, made his skin crawl.

The Guard had dropped the ball. *If Searcha hadn't been there to cover up why Nathan was glowing in the pool . . .* Zach tried to keep his shudder on the inside. Even Kayla's casual few sentences about finding out she was a Shiner glossed over a deep well of pain. The terror that he could guess at from her tone and posture were reflected in dark mud and ink smears in her shadow. *How many more Shiners and Shadows are lost, without answers? How many accidental uses of innate magic risk the world finding out the fabric of reality has been damaged?* Like in Nathan's case.

The Guard had assumed there wouldn't be many Shadows or Shiners in range, that magic would be so short-term it wouldn't matter, and that there weren't enough resources to spare on more wild-goose chases. As the echoes of Kayla's pain faded from her shadow and Zach clinked his glass with the others for Hannah's toast, he resolved that the Guard would do more. They didn't have a well-placed psychiatrist, but there had to be other ways.

He couldn't help teasing Kayla with the bread basket again, but otherwise forced himself to look away from her.

As soon as there was a break in the conversation about an overly angsty sounding sci-fi series, Zach turned to Ben and asked, "Alchemy sounds kinda cool. What are you working on?"

"Mostly, I'm still learning and doing reports, analysis, and prep work. Though I finally got to do a whole potion myself. It creates this cool mist that blocks a Shadow's abilities."

"Problem is, it worked on our Shadow as well as the Guard's," a green-eyed alchemist said, half hiding behind her choppy dark bangs. Jade, that was her name.

"Yeah." Ben used his fork to play with the spaghetti on his plate. "It got tested in the field last week."

Zach pushed a mushroom around his own plate, hoping his hatred of the weird-ass vegetable that wasn't even a plant would hide that he knew exactly what that spell looked like in use.

"It worked though," Ara said. "The report you sent with it was clear and concise. The field agents didn't think through how they used it. Not your fault." Ara turned to Zach, pushing a strand of her fire-engine-red hair behind her ear. "The field agents are always complaining."

"You only say that because you're jealous—they're out there and you're still here," Nathan said affectionately. "She's been here longer than anyone except Hannah."

"I'm here by choice!" Ara said. "I enjoy helping the next batch of recruits learn what they're doing."

"But you said all the good grimoires are at the Agent Lab," teased Samantha.

Ara grinned. "They *were*."

Zach got an image of a small, slim scientific notebook. He tried to look closer, but a wave crested over the orange cover and swallowed it into the depths.

"Ara is better off here with us anyway," Ben said, "where her potions can explode without calling in the fire department."

All the alchemists and Kayla laughed. Though Zach wasn't sure how it was funny.

"I got the hang of that fireball potion before I did any real damage!" Ara protested with a laugh. "I'll get the hang of this next project too."

The girl hiding behind her bangs frowned. Zach looked closer at her shadow. *Jade doesn't like the new project, or is it something else? Might she be an ally?*

"Looks like Steele is leaving," Ben said.

Nick was up and shaking hands around the staff table. Jason stood up to walk him out.

Zach swallowed his bite of bread without fully chewing it. Dry and scratchy, it slid down his throat. As much as he disliked Nick, part of him wasn't ready to be left behind enemy lines without someone familiar. *This is what I signed up for.*

"You sure you don't want to stay and give a presentation about what you've accomplished?" Jason asked as they walked towards the trainees.

Nick gave him a look of deep derision.

Zach fought the grin tugging at his lips. Nick's expression was amusing when it was not aimed at him.

"I'll leave the teaching to you," Nick said. "I've got knots and artifacts to hunt."

Hannah frowned and stabbed a cherry tomato hard enough to squirt juice across her sleeve.

"Do you have any good leads?" Ben asked, missing Nick's dig.

Nick's derision shifted into a bland smile. "I had a promising lead crop up this morning, but I won't know if it's a good one until I follow it. Ryder, you want to get your stuff out of my car?"

Zach slid his chair back and stood up.

"How'd you recognize the First Knot when you saw it?" Ara asked.

"It was obvious," Nick said.

"Because of the shape of the knot? Or information in your grandfather's records?" Ben asked.

Nick gazed at him in amused dismissal. "The Guard woman responsible for it was wearing it around her neck, like an amulet. Old records and descriptions of artifacts mean very little in the field."

Zach started to suppress his amusement, but it fit his dislike of authority, so he let himself enjoy Nick's snark.

"If old records aren't helpful in the field, why are we spending so much time with them? Would there be a faster way to learn?" Kayla asked at the same time Ben started a question about how Nick had tracked down the knot.

Nick sighed. "If you want to walk with me to my car, I'll answer questions along the way."

Any hope Zach had of asking Nick how he was going to leave the car vanished as Kayla and Ben jumped up and the others followed.

Nick started for the door. "We had an inside man who provided invaluable intel for finding the First Knot."

"Such a shame his cover was blown, and you didn't help keep him out of prison," Jason said, clearly enjoying the chance to return the earlier dig.

Nick shrugged. "Coming up against a tied team was incalculably bad luck. The good doctor was going to prison either way. Publicly turning against him kept me free to continue his mission. Seth understood, and his pleading guilty kept the police from asking too many questions." Nick sounded like he was bored with repeating himself.

Zach dug for an emotion that would hide the truth of what had happened that night in Baltimore. There was no reason to get mad. What other basic emotion could he feel?

"You're not tied, though, so Shiners don't need a Shadow?" Kayla asked, bouncing a step, but then playing with the end of her braid when Nick turned his cold eyes on her.

Desire worked as well as anger to hide thoughts. Zach had seen that in Brian and Alexis's shadows way too often for comfort. It was easy to picture unbraiding Kayla's hair and running his hands through the long, blonde strands. Too easy to imagine pulling her close and feeling her athletic body pressed against his. He could get lost in the blue of her eyes. His blood heated distractingly, but it was worth it. His shadow would show only desire.

Nick opened the front door, leaving Jason to hold it open. "My younger brother has all the markings of being a Shadow. He should be coming into his magic soon. We'll make a good team."

Golden, watercolor paint warmed Nick's shadow, not just from the sunshine hitting him, but from his deep love of his brother. It was the only thing Zach ever fully believed in Nick's shadow. Siding with the Guard would give his brother the best chance at a safe future.

Zach cringed at the direction of his thoughts. Luckily, Hannah was focused on Nick's shadow. Hastily, Zach turned his attention back to Kayla. The luminescent color in her shadow caught his breath; it was like seeing a spectacular sunrise from the top of a mountain vista.

"But you're managing just fine now?" Kayla asked.

"My record speaks for itself." Nick beeped his car unlocked.

"You already said you had help locating the First Knot, what have you done since then?" Hannah challenged.

Nick smirked at her. "That's above your clearance." He pulled a strand; the car door unlatched and opened for him.

Zach mentally admitted it was an impressive mastery of magic as he opened the trunk and retrieved his duffle. *Maybe Nick changed his mind about leaving the car?*

Hannah crossed her arms. "But still, with a Shadow—"

"A Shadow is a glorified reader of body language," Nick said coldly. "You see things in shifting sand and speak in riddles. I, on the other hand, can locate a string of magic connected to an artifact, and then all I have to do is follow it. My recovery record is better than the Twins'."

Zach froze for a second, stopping himself from turning to look. Quietly, he closed the trunk. He didn't know what Terra, Alexis, and Nick were doing to protect his cover. He might well be bringing Searcha artifacts. Hopefully broken ones. But that was the last thing he needed to be thinking about.

Hannah was still glaring at Nick. *Thank Merlin!*

"You said you have a promising lead?" Ara asked.

Nick stood by his open car door, ready to get in, but he found his polished smile. "Several. Soon there will be enough magic loose that there will be no turning back the tide." It would have been a stylish parting line if there wasn't a rumble like thunder.

"What's that?" Kayla asked, looking up at the blue sky.

"What's what?" Ben asked.

Nathan looked towards the left. "Did it come from those trees?"

"I didn't hear anything," Ara said.

Nick closed the car door and propped his hip against it. "Wonder what trail she's found?"

Zach dug his hands into his pockets to keep himself still. There was a rumble again, closer this time. She'd helped the Guard, but he didn't trust her. And what would it do to his cover story if she ignored him like usual?

"She who?" Ben asked.

"Oh, wow," Kayla said in awe.

"Only innates can see and hear her when she's in the magic plane," Nick said, as the storm-gray unicorn cantered out of the woods. "I wonder if there is a potion that could change that."

Zach didn't take his eyes off the approaching unicorn. *Why is Nick giving Searcha helpful ideas?*

With a whinny of thunder, Storm slowed to a walk a few yards from the car. Tossing her head, she shimmered into solid reality, like a mirage made manifest.

"*Wow* is right," Ara breathed.

Storm nickered to Zach like a wave breaking on the shore.

He blinked in surprise, but collected himself and gave a flat-hand-over-fist bow of respect, like he would at the end of a tai chi session. It probably wasn't quite right, but Storm nickered again, amusement brightening the sound like added chimes.

She shifted her dark-eyed attention to Nick, passing close enough by Zach he could have reached out and touched her. The scent of fresh rain wafted back to him.

"Hello, darling." Nick offered her his hand. She sniffed it and let him rub her nose.

Lion-like tail swishing, she turned her head, snorting at Jason and pinning her ears. The Shiner took back the step forward he'd taken.

Dangerous humor lurked in Nick's eyes. "Might want to give her space. Magic creatures may look huggable, but they are entities unto themselves."

Storm turned her head back to Nick, her ears flicking forward. She bit his sleeve and tugged. Nick beeped the car locked.

"Looks like she's found a trail for me to follow. I'll come back for my car later." Nick jumped on her back with the help of her magic. "Keep up the important work."

Zach gaped with the rest of the trainees. *Did Alexis and Nick plan this?* Nick'd been the one to release the First Knot; surely that created some kind of bond with the unicorn, but did Storm give him rides often? *Flashy excuse to leave the car though.* A smile warmed his cheeks.

Storm cantered towards the woods and miraged into the magic plane, taking Nick with her.

The trainees watched, jaws hanging. The unicorn's strides covered more distance than a horse's or a deer's. In moments, she and Nick had disappeared out of sight.

"That man knows how to make an exit," Zach remarked dryly.

Ben hooted in agreement. "Did he just dissolve into thin air?"

Laughter rippled around the group, and Ara began explaining the theory of mythological creatures.

Zach was inclined to join their amusement, but Hannah had turned her probing gaze on his shadow. He was alone now, behind enemy lines. There was no room for error. Pulling his simmering anger, dislike for authority, and lust for Kayla around him, he prayed he was ready for the battle ahead.

Twelve

"Today would have been more fun if they'd asked me to beat my way through a brick wall with my head," Kayla declared, more to the living room than to Hannah. Sighing, she shook pins and needles out of her legs. The meditation pillow Dahlia had given her at dinner wasn't working. She scowled at the small space. "And there's nowhere to practice."

Hannah glanced up from her notebook. "You're being dramatic."

Kayla shrugged and tried to stand. "Life's more fun that way." Her legs held, so she tried rubbing the numbness and soreness out of her butt.

"For you, maybe, not for the people around you," Hannah muttered.

Kayla wasn't sure she was supposed to have heard, so she concentrated on getting her kinked muscles to work. Jumping several times made her feel better, but earned her another judgmental look from Hannah. She tried to dig for patience as she reached for the ceiling to loosen the knots building in her upper back. It wasn't Hannah's fault that meditation sucked.

"Sorry. I know you're trying to get your report done."

"It's alright." Hannah didn't look up from her notebook. "It's taking longer than usual since the shadows are all stirred up with Steele's visit and that new Shadow arriving. I'm having trouble clarifying what I magically heard today. What do you think of the new Shadow?"

Kayla picked up the meditation pillow, alternatively squashing and tugging it like a stiff accordion. "Nice not to be the new person anymore."

"You know that's not what I asked."

Kayla turned away and tossed her pillow to the couch to hide her annoyance. "Honestly, I haven't given him much thought. Trying to write up an analysis of the Shiner reports was a waste of time. There is no logic to them. When I was over fighting with that, I started trying and failing spectacularly to meditate." Sure, Zach was amusing and attractive, but that just made him a distraction. Kayla had even less time than usual for that. Mastering magic well enough to be more valuable in the field than she was in training, without being tied, was going to take all her attention.

Hannah gave Kayla a long, speculative look before shrugging. "I'll be done in a minute. Do you want me to go over your analysis with you and help write your paper?"

Kayla bounced several times on the balls of her feet. *Seriously? I'm an adult. I can do my own work.* "Thanks, but it's fine."

"You want it better than fine, though, right? It shouldn't take long."

Kayla gritted her teeth. Hannah was just trying to be helpful. *Right?* The room felt like it was shrinking. Her daily reserve of self-control had already been spent trying to sit still and get her brain to shut up. Fleeing from Hannah was the kindest thing she could do at the moment.

"I can't now. I'm going for a jog." Three long strides and Kayla was at the door and yanking on her right sneaker.

Hannah's brow creased. "It's cold and dark. And don't you have the last of your Latin translations to finish? After that, you won't have to do another, now that you're learning magic. It'll be nice to have them done and behind you."

"Thank you, but my head would explode if I tried to do Latin tonight." Kayla shoved her left foot into her other sneaker. *Jacket. I need my jacket.* "After trying to sit for"—Kayla checked the wall clock—"an hour and a half." Luckily, Hannah had just gotten home, because, to be fair, Kayla had spent most of that time rearranging her own desk and bed and trying to find the perfect spot.

"Did you try a guided meditation?"

"Yes, several. Now I need a run. And upside, you can focus without my fidgeting." Snagging her black windbreaker off the hook by the door, she stepped outside without looking back. She barely caught the screen door before it slammed behind her. If she had to redo her whole analysis paper with Hannah micromanaging every word, she was going to scream. That was fact, not hyperbole.

Pausing only to tie her shoes, Kayla was halfway across the property, cold mist sinking into her skin, before she remembered she'd already been for a run that morning. Experience had taught her that overdoing it would cost her tomorrow, but she was craving escape. Slowing to an easy lope, she circled around to the water. Stopping at the edge, she pulled her jacket closer against the biting breeze. The expanse of dark water was highlighted by waves reflecting the silver light of the half-moon. The clear, cold sky was filled with stars, reminding Kayla of how small and alone she was. Shivering, she dug her hands into her pockets, wishing she hadn't forgotten her gloves.

This was a stupid idea. Kayla bounced on the balls of her feet, trying to stave off the slow circling of depressing thoughts and warm her toes. Frowning toward the cabin, it was easy to imagine Hannah's I-told-you-so attitude if she returned now. Groaning, Kayla wandered along the shore. *To hell with my complaining toes.* But her critical thoughts were harder to ignore. Hunching in her jacket, Kayla stepped onto one of the boulders that stood guard over the beach and kept the land from washing away. Small waves lapped on the sand seven or eight yards away. Empty. This cove was as isolated as she felt.

Kayla reached for her phone. *Stupid habit.* It offered no escape.

It was a waste of time, but Kayla hopped down to the sand, anyway. *Just around the point.* She began to bargain with herself: maybe if she walked slowly enough back, she'd have been gone long enough to plead tiredness. Crawling into bed, she could watch some mindless TV that she'd talked Dahlia into downloading onto her laptop along with the meditations.

Rounding the point, Kayla hesitated. Someone else had braved the cold. A he, from the wiry, masculine build silhouetted against the silvery water. Not Nathan. One of the alchemists? *Is he doing yoga?* But that wasn't right. It was some kind of martial art. One form glided into another like a slow motion dance.

Kayla had tried kung fu once. It had looked fun, but then she'd learned in the first class it was all about self-control and doing the same thing over and over, like a million times. She'd told her parents she preferred soccer and had never looked back. But something in the man's movements called to her.

It seemed polite to turn around and leave him to the beach and the night breeze, but Kayla burned with curiosity. He was out in the open; surely he didn't mind if he was seen, even if he was all the way out here at night. She settled on a smooth rock, her back against a rough boulder that sheltered her from some of the wind. Mesmerized, Kayla tried to memorize what he was doing. Her dark thoughts and taunting failures of the day faded.

All too soon, he stilled, facing the water. He bowed to the bay and then spoke. "What do you think?"

Kayla squinted at the water. After seeing a unicorn today, she wouldn't be shocked if merpeople were a thing. Her eyes had adjusted to the moonlight, but the waves looked normal.

He turned and grinned at her. The new guy.

Kayla's stomach flipped. She scrambled to her feet, barely catching herself before she apologized for spying. *That's not what I was doing.* "I didn't want to interrupt. That looked really cool. What is it?"

"Tai chi." He looked her over thoughtfully. "Want to try?"

Kayla hesitated. Tidal Water was a small place, and she'd carefully friend-zoned the guys, treating them like brothers and teammates. Finding any of them on a dark beach wouldn't have given her a second thought. *But—what's his name—Zach?* He didn't know her. Might he read something more in her curiosity than there was? It wouldn't be the first time her open and friendly personality had been interpreted as sexual interest. It didn't help that he radiated a delicious masculinity.

"It looks complicated," she hedged.

He shrugged. "The basics aren't bad." He tilted his head to the right. A grin tugged at his lips, attractive even in the moonlight. "I could show you another time. Maybe when the sun is out?"

An answering grin warmed Kayla's cheeks. "That sounds like a dare." If she had any sense, she'd agree on tomorrow and go back to Hannah and Latin homework. Kayla almost laughed out loud. It was a simple decision.

"Take it how you like." His smile was inviting.

She forced herself to do a quick gut check. Her hesitation was because he was attractive, not because she sensed any threat from him. Besides, her athleticism and self-defense classes gave her confidence that she'd be fine if her read was off.

She skipped towards him and the water. "How do I start?"

He nodded, but didn't comment on her choice. "Feet together."

Kayla picked a spot three yards from him and followed closely as he demonstrated. Soon she was through the warm-ups and Brushing the Horse's Mane. Working her way through the next few forms with reasonable accuracy, she could sense or at least imagined she could sense the energy Zach kept talking about. It sounded less woo-woo coming from him than from Dahlia. Each movement was tied to a breath and flowed with a power unlike anything Kayla had ever experienced. Every bit of her body required her attention, from the direction of her toes, to the shift of her weight, to where her hands were in her peripheral vision. A grin spread across her face. The exertion of slow precision had warmed her; she unzipped her jacket and rolled up her sleeves. When her focus slipped, Zach would gently remind her to exhale with that movement, or make that step more of a crescent instead of a straight line.

Making mental notes, but with no space to hold on to thoughts or follow them as they wandered off, Kayla was engrossed. Tension drained from her neck and shoulders. The ball of anxiety in her chest untangled and melted, but she was too focused on where her feet and hands were to do more than yawn and smile wider.

Kayla had no sense of the time when Zach led her through the closing. She returned his bow.

"You're glowing a bit." He smiled warmly as he straightened up.

Startled, Kayla looked at her hands. Reddish-amber light, in geometric designs, glowed softly on her skin, tracing the veins in her wrists and twirling around her fingers. Excitement spiking in her blood, she looked around. Fine white strands laced through the world around her.

"I can see them. The strings of magic!" But even as she spoke, the strands faded like the afterglow of a bright flash, and her markings evaporated, leaving her skin pale in the moonlight.

"Easy," Zach said, as if she were a spooked animal.

"What the hell happened?" Kayla spun in a circle, searching, but the magic was gone.

"For a moment there, you looked like an enchanting firefly." The warm smile in his voice drew Kayla's frantic gaze, inviting her to share in his amusement.

Kayla's shoulders sagged. "I hate magic. Wait"—amusement bubbled up—"did you just call me a bug?"

He nodded earnestly. "An enchanting bug." His lips twitched.

Kayla broke first. Zach only lasted a second longer before joining her in wild laughter.

"I don't know why that's so funny," Kayla grasped, trying for sanity, before giving up. Placing her hands on her thighs helped keep her on her feet.

No more able to stop than her, Zach sank to the sand. "No idea."

The ground looked like a good idea, so Kayla joined him. Slowly their hysterical laughter faded, leaving the sound of the waves.

"I needed that," Zach said at last, leaning back on his arms.

"Me too. What a shitty day." Kayla wiped the wetness under her eyes away. "Present excluded."

"Happy to be excluded." He held out his right hand, palm up. "May I?"

Not sure what he wanted, Kayla offered her right hand. Her skin was glowing again, but she was too wrung out to fight with magic now. Static leapt between them, warmer and less jolting than a normal shock. His hand closed around hers. The glow on the back of her hand and wrist intensified. With his left index finger, he traced one of the hexagonal-edged swirls on her wrist. A shiver of awareness that had nothing to do with magic danced up her spine.

"I never would have expected such a deep color. I would have thought you'd be sunshine or flowers, but that'd be washed out compared to this deep fire glow." His voice was reverent. The smile in his eyes was warm, lit now by the gilded glow of her magic more than the cold moonlight.

"It does look cool in the dark," Kayla admitted, though she was having trouble looking away from his face.

"Gently, on an exhale, can you see the strands of magic woven across the sand between us?"

Closing her eyes, Kayla breathed in. She opened them on an exhale and looked. Like gossamer spiderwebs shimmering with dew, the strands clung to the sand between them. The warmth of awe bloomed in her chest.

"Don't force them, keep breathing," Zach said, in the same quiet, nonjudgmental tone he'd taught her tai chi. "Can you feel one of them?"

With her free hand, Kayla tentatively traced one. "Yes?" She gasped. Understanding resonated deep in her, like the bass from a great speaker. "Yes. Not so much with my finger, but in my gut. This strand echoes my joy at building a sand fort with my brothers, it connects me to these bits of sand. In this strand"—she touched another—"I can hear echoes of my niece's laughter. I can feel her with me?"

He nodded slowly, as if he understood her to her core.

Kayla let go of his hand and leaned back on hers, putting a little distance between them.

"You are a Shiner. It's just one aspect of who you are. It gives you the gift of having the ability to learn to feel those connections, and many more, in a way specific to your magic type. Saying it's innate does us a disservice. It doesn't give us the room we need to experiment and make mistakes. But we have to learn how to use our abilities just as much as the sp—the alchemists." Zach cleared his throat, pulled his knees up, and looped his arms loosely over them. "I see the heart of the same thing you do, but in shadows. The closest analogy I've come up with so far is stardust."

Kayla leaned closer. When he studied her face instead of elaborating, she asked, "Stardust?"

"You know, how when you break things down chemically, we're all stardust, or elements created from stardust." His face lit with enthusiasm. "You, me, everything on this beach, those stars in the sky, all made of the same stuff. Our choices, our existence, are woven into the fabric of reality. I feel it to my core, even as the logical explanation falls so short of the wonder."

Goosebumps pricked Kayla's arms; the glow of her markings intensified.

"I'm not sure I'm making much sense." Zach sighed.

"No, you are. Way more sense than anyone else has," Kayla said with a wry grin. "How'd you figure this all out so fast?"

Zach shifted to look out over the water. "I guess I've always believed we're more deeply and intrinsically connected than science has yet been able to prove or model, in something bigger than myself. My magic, at its heart, for me, simply illustrates that fact. As if confirming what I've always believed. Parsing past, present, and future in all this chaos, on the other hand, is a nightmare." He chuckled.

A light breeze ruffled strands of Kayla's hair. Was it her imagination, or could she feel how it brought with it traces of where it had been and would add traces of her to where it was going? The earth beneath her, the moon above—she was so close, she could almost feel all the strands of connection around her.

Zach gave her a smile so intimate that Kayla felt the power of it as deeply as the strands of magic around them.

She turned to look at the water. The breeze ruffled the bay's surface, making the moonlight dance. With a shiver, she pulled her jacket closer.

Trying to collect herself, she said, "They gave me all this poetry and crap to read. I think that's what it was getting at, but I didn't get it."

"I don't think it can work intellectually. I think it has to be felt."

Kayla nodded, but her eyes slipped back to the water as she tried to swallow a rising tangle of feelings and thoughts.

Waves splashed softly against the shore.

"Probably late." Zach got up and dusted himself off before offering her a hand.

Kayla took it and let him tug her up. *Is the intimacy between us just because you helped me connect with my magic, or is it something more?* She didn't step back. *We've only just met. I don't need to complicate my life more.*

So much thinking! All she'd done today was think. She was over it.

He didn't step back. The firelight of the magic swirls on her face lit the planes of his. The warmth and laughter in his amber eyes shifted to something that made her body hum with more than magic. *Is this just me?*

Kayla lifted a hand, traced the lapel of his jacket, and held her breath, searching for a way to ask.

Thirteen

Zach
Day 4 of the Lockhouse Knot Leak
Monday evening
Tidal Water, MD

Magic radiated off Kayla's skin as Zach helped her up. There was a russet swirl on her left cheekbone; it flirted with her ear, made a node at her jaw, and played down her neck, all the way to where it disappeared below her jacket. Every molecule in his body yearned to trace that path, first with his fingers, then with his mouth. He took an uneven breath, unable to step back.

Her light touch on his lapel was like a spark on kindling. It took all his strength not to wrap his arms around her and pull her close. *Does she want my mouth on hers as much as I do, or is that wishful thinking?*

"I do love this jacket."

Her words crashed over his head like an icy wave. Stepping back, he took a ragged breath. The jacket was a lie. Everything about his being at Tidal Water was a lie. He was going to betray everyone here. Especially her. He was going to steal her family spellbook. None of that could be helped if he was going to stop the magic leak and save the world from the teeth that haunted the shadows. But this, whatever this crackling energy between them was, he could help. Or at least not act upon it. If that was the most he could do for her, it was also the very least.

Firelight magic faded from her skin, leaving the night darker. Hurt lined her face in the ashen moonlight.

Scrubbing his face with his hands, he tried to find his footing. His mind raced over what he'd seen in her shadow so far, trying to come up with some excuse she'd resonate with and not take personally. After a deep, steadying breath, he could finally look her in the eyes.

"Our magic is complementary. Shadows and Shiners are meant to feel connected. It clouds judgment. At least it apparently does mine." He tried for a what-can-you-do shrug and smile. "Doesn't help that you're as beautiful as a fire nymph." A ghost of a self-deprecating laugh helped with the vulnerability of the truth. "But I'm new. I can't afford to play with this kind of fire. I can't risk us tying. Not only is it against the rules, but I'm pretty sure Hannah would gut me like a fish." He forced himself to stop talking. Maybe he'd assumed too much. Maybe her hurt had been at the strength of his retreat from her friendly or joking comment. He dug his hands into his pockets and tried to keep his shoulders from rounding forward.

Kayla gave an uncomfortable laugh. "So let me get this straight. You feel this attraction, too, but you're afraid it's only the product of our magic and might get us tied?"

Zach nodded. He had no freaking idea how it worked. He'd never asked exactly how Brian and Alexis got themselves tied. It hadn't seemed important to know, since Brian was the Guard's only Shiner.

Kayla put her hands on her hips. "Like we're drunk at a frat party, and you want to be a gentleman?"

Zach burst out laughing. Kayla's straight face slipped, and she joined him; tension evaporated.

He collected himself. "Exactly. I do want to be friends. I don't want to mess that up by impulsively asking to kiss you while 'drunk' on magic." She fascinated him, but more importantly, being her friend was his best chance at getting that grimoire. It was an awful, sobering thought, but the truth. "And I have no idea how tying works, but it goes well with your frat-party analogy. Such a weird form of magic."

Kayla snorted with laughter. "I'm glad you're not as impulsive as I am. I'll like you more for it in the morning. Friends, then?"

Zach hesitated only a moment before taking her hand. At some point, he was going to have to warn her how much he could see when she did that, even in the surrealist moonlight, but not tonight. He could tell that her pride was a bit bruised, but she didn't like the emotions that went along with romantic *anything* and, now that the sexual tension had faded, was already glad he'd stopped whatever it was. Her self-control had been badly eroded by the day. She was telling the truth; she'd like him more for his restraint.

They walked back up the beach, and Zach asked general questions about the training center and what he should expect in his first few days. Things that would help him and make Kayla feel like she was the veteran trainee, which she clearly enjoyed. The crackling energy had faded, leaving a barrier; Zach tried not to regret the loss of intimacy. He'd been an idiot for letting things get as far as they had.

Zach glanced back at Newton Lab, the gray stone alchemy building they'd just passed, trying to think of a way to ask about it. Jason had pointed it out, but not offered a tour. Zach started to ask if she'd seen inside, when he realized she'd stopped.

"I'm going this way." She nodded toward the trees.

"And I have to go back up to Xander." Zach frowned at the sprawling white building, ghostly beyond the formal garden and wide, ironically named patio.

"Be glad you're still staying up there. It means they haven't picked someone for you to tie with yet." There was wistfulness beneath her bright smile. "There's a spare bedroom on Jason's floor and in Nathan's cabin."

Zach studied her until he realized his scrutiny was making her shift from foot to foot.

"I don't understand a lot of what I see in the shadows yet," he said. It was too late to take back what he'd already shared, but he was supposed to be brand new to his powers, and they both needed to remember that. "But I can see that only you and the person you tie with can make that decision. Miranda and the others can encourage and facilitate, but they can't force that choice." Zach's gut told him he was speaking the truth, but the intensity in his voice surprised him. *Am I being an idiot, trying to help her connect with her magic and encouraging her to find a suitable partner?* If she never got a hang of her magic and tied with an unsuitable person, the Guard would be better off.

"Thank you." Kayla laced her fingers behind her back. "For everything tonight, really, thanks."

Zach swallowed hard and gave a nod of acknowledgement. "See you tomorrow."

With a last sparkling grin, she turned and wandered off along the rocks guarding the water.

Zach watched her for a minute, then shook himself and turned towards the manor. Miranda's home, converted from a pool house, was just to the right of the square. To the left was a tennis/basketball court. Zach took that route.

Walking slowly, he mulled over Kayla and their encounter. The day had sapped his body and emotions, leaving him hollow. Expanding his vision to include the peripheral softened his shoulders and deepened his breath. But when he brought his thoughts to Kayla, he couldn't get past his stupidity for almost kissing her. *I don't have time to beat myself up over that.* What he needed was some mental distance.

"If this was in a graphic novel," Zach muttered under his breath, "what kind would it be?"

Superheroes were too flashy and overemphasized magic. Pulling a pencil out of his pocket, he twirled it between his fingers. Star-crossed lovers? *Nah.* Too melodramatic and not his style. He was an undercover spy. Not a dashing James Bond or a gritty Jason Bourne, where stuff was exploding around every corner. *It better not be!* More like an old-fashioned Cold War movie. That thought resonated in his chest and echoed in the dreamscape shadows.

If this was a spy novel, what might happen next? *How can I get the secret documents and not betray the enemy agent I'm growing to like?* He almost laughed out loud. It was too obvious. Kayla could defect. If he could convince her to come over to the Guard, he'd save her from Searcha, and she'd bring the grimoire willingly. Maybe, just maybe, if they were both in the Guard, it would be worth asking Brian how he and Alexis became tied.

Zach stepped through the manor's far left-side door. It was dark, but there was enough moonlight coming through the big windows to not bump into any of the coffee tables or cozy couches or chairs in the West Study. *How would it look lit by Kayla's glow?* Zach shook the thought and carefully opened the door to the hallway. It was empty, except for the scent of curry still hanging in the air from a microwavable dinner. Mouth watering, Zach was tempted by a midnight snack. There was a load of communal sandwich fixings, but it was late, and he wanted to sketch out his brilliant plan before bed.

He took the steps two at a time. No one was in the common room, but there was still a light on under Ben's door as Zach slipped down the guys' side hallway. *Is it always this easy to move unnoticed around the property at night?* He contemplated the advantages of that as he headed for the room at the end of the hall, apparently the biggest on their side. Being a Shadow seemed to rank him both above the alchemists and off to the side. Because Shadows could see how dangerous magic was, Searcha wanted him reasonably isolated until he was fully indoctrinated.

He flipped the light switch, and sharp fluorescent light drowned out the moonlit graphite sketches and blue watercolor. He blinked as his night vision dissolved and ink black, teeth-capped waves swamped the shadows. He switched on the bedside lamp, then backtracked to turn off the harsh ceiling light. The lamp shade, which depicted a ship sketched on parchment-colored fabric, gave off a yellow glow and softened the sharp edges of the shadow's art. Zach breathed a sigh of relief and pulled off his leather jacket. Giving his vision and the waves a chance to settle, he hung the jacket over the back of the uncomfortable wooden chair, nautical themed like everything in the room. *Because all I need is more water in my life.*

Zach snorted and got ready for bed, pointedly ignoring the waves and teeth.

Yawning, he finally settled down on the bed, his back against the mock driftwood headboard, with his pencil box and sketchbook. Lavender laundry detergent wafted up as he pushed the blue-and-white pillows around until he was comfortable enough. He picked a 6B pencil that would smear across the paper. He let his pencil explore lines and shapes, trying to let what he was seeing in the shadows take shape.

His gut lurched when he took in the whole picture, yanking him to full alertness. Hannah. She glared distrustfully out from the paper.

Rubbing his forehead with his free hand, Zach took a deep breath. *Don't beat yourself up for not seeing it sooner. That's why you're sketching it out before you jump.* He'd wanted it to be easy so badly that he'd missed the glaring hole right in front of him. Hannah considered Kayla *her* Shiner and was already planning their future as Searcha agents. She would scrutinize every move Zach made. For his plan to work, he'd not only have to convince Kayla to switch sides, but he'd have to do it without her would-be Shadow noticing. Zach groaned and let his head sink into his hands. That had about as much chance of happening as Captain America being corrupted into a Sith Lord.

Back to plan A. He'd have to steal the book from Kayla. At least he'd managed not to kiss her, but he really shouldn't have helped her connect with her magic. He'd almost given away that he knew more about magic than a newbie, and he wasn't here to strengthen Searcha's Shiners.

Lifting his head, he flipped to the next page. An image of Kayla doing tai chi practically drew itself on paper. *How the hell am I supposed to think of her as my enemy?* His sketch depicted her athletic figure and her energy, but didn't give him any insights into his next move. He yearned to learn her hopes, dreams, fears, and passions, but that had nothing to do with getting her grimoire.

Get a grip! Flipping to the next page, he filled it with waves and teeth. Frustrated, he checked the time. *Shit.* It was getting late. He needed a full night's sleep if he was going to be at his best for more training sessions tomorrow.

Jason's tour, along with what Zach was mentally calling Magical Indoctrination 101, had been both horrifying and oddly fascinating, like a train that had jumped the tracks and was rolling downhill towards everything he knew and loved. With charisma and attention to detail, Jason had retold the stories Zach knew from both history books and Guard legends and warped them into a whole new creation. With unnerving skill, Jason laid the groundwork to make Zach a contributing member of Searcha, while also preparing him for the uncomfortable realities of the Unavoidable Upheaval. The leadership needed Shadows on their side, but were afraid of how they'd react when they saw the truth of what was to come. Jason had done his homework on Zach Ryder, expertly threading the needle of making a compelling case for magic despite what it would cost.

A hard shake of Zach's head helped clear it.

The Guard would want notes on what Searcha was telling their recruits, but Zach would have to make it look like something else. His invisible pen didn't have unlimited ink, so he would use it sparingly, and there was always a chance someone would snoop through his stuff or figure out he was using it.

Zach quickly sketched out the lines for the panels he could almost see in his mind. Tapping the back of his pencil several times, he decided not to overthink. To save time coming up with a character, and because it fit, he sketched a dark-haired version of Jason in an ancient Greek tunic. It probably wasn't historically accurate, but neither was Jason's version of Alexander the Great, or to be fair, history's. The early Guard had meticulously doctored the records to obscure the truth. Zach drew the conqueror with his hands on his hips, looking out over all he surveyed with wisdom and a noble spirit, or some such thing. It wasn't easy; Zach itched to depict him as a villain. Or at least as a heedless conqueror who wanted glory and didn't care about the destruction he would leave in his wake. But this was Jason's story—Searcha's version of events.

Below the sketch he wrote: *Alex G. Visionary and brave sage.*

Zach sketched a quick figure of Alex G. coming upon the First Knot, aka the Gordian Knot, recognizing it from his teacher's lessons. Zach sketched the knot larger than life to get the point across and hide the fact that he'd seen it in person.

The panel he captioned: *Alex G. saw a knot of magic. He understood that small-minded people will always fear and try to destroy what they can't understand. He saw past his own fears to the scared, trapped being locked inside.*

With the side of his pencil, Zach smudged an abused horse-like creature in the knot's shadow, stretching across the desert sand, head low in defeat and misery. *Was there even sand there?* Zach reached for his phone to check, but of course there was no signal. *You're just procrastinating, anyway.*

Zach pursed his lips and breathed out a long, controlled breath, trying to wrangle his attention back to the paper.

As distractions slid away, it was harder for Zach to ignore the itchy, uncomfortable sensation between his shoulder blades. Seeing in graphite what Jason had said aloud crystalized why Zach hated Searcha's introduction to magic. Jason's shadow had shown no hint of doubt as he painted the Guard as bigoted, closed-minded monsters who abused magic, burned books, and buried the truth out of fear and hatred. It was impossible to recognize the secret organization Jason railed against as the warm, kind-hearted, dedicated, and brilliant people that were Zach's second family. Everything, except the plain facts, were wildly different. Jason's absolute belief in the injustice done to magic was an inverted mirror to Elliot's understanding that, given the slightest chance, magic would rage unchecked, more destructive than a nuclear winter.

Even if Searcha was right, even if magic was alive somehow, did it matter? *Yes.* It made it so much worse. Because there was no place in the modern world for magic. Zach's stomach turned at the memory of the horror filling the shadows when the Baltimore Knot had almost been cut.

Am I refusing to acknowledge that magic might be alive because it's too uncomfortable a thought? Or because it's bullshit?

Zach tapped his pencil against the paper. *I'm too tired for this. Please stop stalling.* Sitting up straighter, he tried the next panel.

He sketched Alex G. cutting the First Knot with his dagger. Better if it's a sword. Makes it look like I wasn't quite paying attention. *Oops.* With a few quick lines, Zach added the sword to the last two panels, hanging from Alex G.'s belt.

The next showed the mighty unicorn golem, Bucephalus, springing free of the knot. The unicorn looked like a larger, darker version of Storm. They circled in the next panel, taking the measure of the other. The final panel filled with Alex G. on Bucephalus, charging forward to release more magic. All of magic. To right the wrongs of humankind and bring the world back to balance. AKA, conquer the world.

Zach stared at his sketches, sad that the character he'd depicted would be murdered many adventures later to stop such noble ideals and deeds.

"Thank God, that's not the way it happened." Saying so out loud helped ease the ache between his shoulder blades. He closed his sketchbook with a snap of his wrist and shoved it into his bag.

At least he'd made friends with Kayla. Maybe he'd be able to get the spellbook, grimoire, tomorrow, or at least by the end of the week, and get the hell out of here. With that heartening thought, he settled down in the bed and tried to find sleep.

Fourteen

"Your shadow sounds like you're torturing yourself instead of meditating," Hannah said.

Kayla jerked around, her knotted, pins-and-needles muscles protesting. She'd been so wrapped up in her internal arguing that she hadn't heard Hannah come home.

"There's a difference?" Kayla asked. It was supposed to sound like a joke, but it came out frustrated. All the progress she'd made on the beach last night had faded to the point she was wondering if she'd dreamed the tai chi lesson.

Hannah gave her a sympathetic smile that almost managed to not be condescending. "At least you can take a break now."

"I don't have time for a break."

Hannah beamed. "I'm glad you're finally taking this seriously. But our computer lab time is scheduled at the top of the hour, and a break will do you good."

Sitting in front of an old computer researching a report Kayla didn't want to write about Shiners long since dead wasn't her idea of a break. It was part of her training, though. Skipping assignments wouldn't help her build a case that she was capable enough to be in the field alone.

Sighing, she climbed to her unsteady feet. "Right, thanks."

"I've got your back. I realized you'd forgotten in plenty of time to come get you."

Your own fault for not checking your calendar! Kayla mentally growled at herself as she stepped out of the house. Now Hannah had another excuse to manage her. Though Kayla probably hadn't updated the calendar with the computer lab time, anyway. *Hannah isn't that bad. She's trying so hard.* Kayla really wished she wouldn't, but it wasn't Hannah's fault they'd make a terrible team. And it was big of Hannah not to mention the tai chi lesson, considering it probably showed in Kayla's shadow.

Every muscle in Kayla's legs begged her to outrun the endless, unhelpful tangle of tumbling thoughts in her mind. *Running off and leaving Hannah to make the walk herself would be extremely rude after she walked all this way to get me.* Kayla settled for a few skipping steps.

"Have you picked a historical magic user for this report?" Hannah asked.

"Ugh, I was thinking maybe Aristotle. He taught Alexander the Great about magic, didn't he?"

"Yes, he's a big-deal historical figure, but you're going to have trouble finding anything new to say about him."

Kayla frowned. "I mostly picked him because at least I'd heard of him." And Jason had mentioned him several times on her first-day tour, so Kayla was sure he was magic.

"There are a lot of other interesting magic users. I'm sure you've heard of a bunch of them. I'm putting together a report of known or suspected ones in the American colonial era. It's an overview, so there'd be no conflict if you wanted to write an in-depth report on any of them."

"Oh?" It wouldn't hurt to get ideas, even if they were from Hannah.

"A lot of settlers trapped magic, hunted species to extinction, and made a mess of the land, but not all of them were evil. Some worked on the side of good."

"Any you're enjoying in particular?"

"Well, I'm trying to see if Anne Hutchison has any ties to magic, and I've got pages and pages on the Salem Witch Trials. Research is difficult, though, because of how much the historical records have been tampered with. Besides what the Guard did to magic, they're monsters for the amount of ancient knowledge and history they've destroyed or corrupted."

Kayla tried to pull Hannah back before she dove down that rabbit hole. "Not sure I'd be great at wading through a bunch of altered documents looking for the truth, so maybe not the witch trials?" And she had no idea who Anne Hutchison was. "Anyone else?"

"Tons, I've only scratched the surface in my own research, but let's see . . ." Hannah opened the folder she was carrying and flipped through as they walked. "Lewis and Clark were a tied Shadow/Shiner team, and Sacajawea definitely understood magic, probably an alchemist. And, yeah, Captain John Smith, the guy who helped found Jamestown, he was a Shiner."

"Wait, what? From the movie *Pocahontas*?" Kayla asked.

"Historically inaccurate travesty of a movie." Hannah waved her hand in dismissal. Something caught her attention in Kayla's shadow, though, and she blatantly studied it.

"I loved that movie growing up," Kayla protested. Pocahontas had long hair like Kayla and a yearning for adventure instead of a conventional, safe life. Plus, her animal sidekicks were great.

Kayla's thoughts were pulled up short at Hannah's frown. "Though, if you think it's a bad idea," she said, "I could pick Lewis and Clark. Explorers are interesting."

Hannah's intense gaze didn't waver, and it pulled her and Kayla to a stop. Kayla shifted uneasily from foot to foot. Her backbone shifted, as if her spinal cord had been replaced by a worm. Fighting to stand still while being silently observed was an uneasy reminder of her time with psychiatrists and psychologists. She'd seen several of both types when she'd started seeing magic. *What the hell is Hannah looking for?*

Hannah threw her hands in the air and started walking again. "Training isn't meant to be torture. It's a way to help you better understand magic and its history, while also building up Searcha's resources. Here. Apparently the shadows like Smith as much as you do." She pulled out a file from her folder and offered it to Kayla as they approached the building. "I've got too much information on him for my report. He's a glory-seeking chauvinist. I didn't do much research, but with a modicum of digging on top of my notes, you should be able to write a passable profile. His early days as a merchant and pirate seem like they'd be interesting to you. And you can see for yourself all the ways the movie was crap. There are a decent number of primary sources for your research."

It would only encourage Hannah if Kayla welcomed help, but when the alternative was getting lost in a maze of internet searches for a pointless paper . . . Kayla accepted the folder. "Thank you."

"Glad the research I did is good for something. He's barely getting a paragraph in my report."

With a laugh, Kayla held the back door open. "Happy to help."

They walked through the common area, past Miranda's and Jason's offices, to the computer lab. It was a small, windowless room that looked like it'd once been a spacious storage closet. There was a desk for a staff member, an old printer, and four computers set up on a rectangular folding table in the middle of the room with two cheap metal chairs on each long side. It had to be the most depressing room at Tidal Water. At least today it smelled like fresh-cut grass. Dahlia's sturdy work pants were coated in clippings from the knees down.

"Hey Dahlia, we're checking in for our brain-melting time," Kayla said.

Dahlia looked up from a doorstop-sized historical novel with a smile. "Welcome. Let's see." She consulted the list on the desk. "Here you are." She glanced at the square clock on the wall. "A few minutes early, but I'll put you down for the top of the hour."

"Thanks," Hannah said. "I didn't want to be late. I have a lot of work to do."

Kayla sighed, and Dahlia smiled sympathetically before returning to her book.

Jade, hiding behind her bangs and facing their way, shifted her attention away from the monitor for a moment to nod.

Ben, on the opposite side, twisted around to see them. "Sorry, Dahlia, almost done."

Dahlia didn't look up from her book. "Mmph."

"You've still got six minutes." Hannah unpacked her notebooks and reference material in the space at the computer beside Ben.

"They ask us for reports, but the library doesn't have enough resources yet, and we have so little computer time," he complained, while tapping at the keyboard.

"I don't get why they're so antitechnology," Kayla agreed. "What are you working on?" She leaned lightly against the end of the desk, not ready to sit.

Ben groaned. "Researching characteristics of tree species. The one used in the original potion appears to be extinct. Not sure a substitution will work, but worth a try." He scribbled a quick note. "I can't take any more of this today." He hit the print button and started collecting his stuff. "Overall, I love alchemy, but some of this really sucks."

"I get it!" Kayla was grateful she was an innate. After training, she wouldn't have to write another research report.

"Jade, you coming?" Ben asked.

"Yeah, in a minute." Jade looked up from her screen. "Actually, I might go back to the lab. I need to double-check something."

Ben shrugged. "Good luck," he said to the room in general. Thanking Dahlia, he picked up his papers from the printer and left.

Kayla took the vacated seat on Hannah's side and opened the folder on Smith. Chauvinistic or not, he sounded like the most interesting magic user she'd heard about so far. Pirate, explorer, love interest for Pocahontas, though the last part was a fabrication, according to Hannah's detailed summary on the first page. A good thing, Kayla admitted when she saw the age gap. The entire file was meticulously organized. It was practically a full report, plus sources.

Kayla ignored the handwritten table of contents and eagerly flipped through the file. The primary sources seemed to be gibberish, written before modern grammar, spelling, or capitalizations practices. The secondary sources were promising, though. Bouncing lightly in her seat, she sketched out a timeline for his life. After skimming what Hannah had collected, Kayla opened a browser and searched for resources to round out the report.

Once in a while, Kayla would look over to share her enthusiasm with Hannah, but her roommate was especially focused on frowning at her computer or staring into space. Kayla looked over at Jade, but she was rushing to finish up. A glance at the time showed that Kayla's almost-two hours on the computer were half up. She needed to focus and stop pulling on strands that led her down paths that wouldn't help with her report. Watching a video of a hot shirtless guy explain how Native Americans made dugout canoes wasn't actually relevant.

Three minutes later, Kayla looked over at Hannah again, itching to share. Smith, according to a source she'd found, made up the bit about Pocahontas saving his life around the time the Native American princess came to England. It was just a theory, but Kayla liked it.

Hannah caught her glance. "Find something interesting?"

Kayla grinned and started explaining.

Hannah got up, as if to look at Kayla's research, and placed a hand on her shoulder.

"See," Kayla said, "it might not have been a brag about his attractiveness on Smith's part, but a ploy to help her be treated better at court—as a royal princess who'd saved his life. And there was an actual incident with a compass, nothing like the movie, though that had a compass, too, but it made me wonder if he had a compass like Merlin did?"

"Interesting," Hannah said, clearly not hearing a word. Her grip tightened on Kayla's shoulder. "I need to run out real quick. Can you watch my notes, please?"

Kayla turned to look at Hannah. She opened her mouth to ask if something was wrong, but Hannah gave her a warning look.

"Sure, no problem," Kayla said with a shrug.

"Thanks." Not looking at anyone, Hannah slipped from the room.

Kayla shook her head and redoubled her focus on the computer.

She ran into several dead ends and more of the same information. The metal chair was making her butt numb. Finding a good secondary source for in-depth details of Smith's early years without a lot of extra info was turning out to be a pain. Maybe Hannah would know where to look. Kayla glanced at the empty chair. Twenty-six minutes. *Was Hannah abducted by aliens?* She was missing her computer time. Kayla should have gone with her. Stretching her legs for half an hour would do Kayla a world of good, but that would be the end of her computer time this week.

Kayla rolled her shoulder. Interlacing her fingers, palms facing out, she lifted them above her head. Better. She could do this. Tabling Smith's early years, she doubled back to his time in the Chesapeake. He probably passed right by Tidal Water, and might have even stopped here at some point. There was a trail named after him, and a place called Stingray Point in honor of where he'd been stung by a ray. Maybe Kayla could talk Miranda into letting her go on a field trip. It would be awesome to get off property, even for a little while.

How can Jade sit here this long? Maybe she'd been late to her computer time. Cuz if she'd been there her whole allotted two hours, plus an hour and a half of Kayla and Hannah's time—*I can't even binge watch a TV show for that long.*

Dahlia didn't seem to have noticed, but that wasn't a surprise. Everyone knew if you needed a few more minutes of computer time, Dahlia was the staff member you wanted on duty. *But an hour and a half extra?* More power to Jade for having that kind of focus.

Kayla started printing files she thought might be useful. Surely, she had plenty of information now for her report. If only Hannah would come back for her notes. Maybe she should collect them and take them with her, but if Hannah got back and her notes were gone, and she lost what little remained on her computer time, she'd be sulky for hours, possibly days.

The door opened. *Thank heavens.*

Kayla turned, but it was Miranda walking in the door, her white-and-cream suit ensemble stylish as always. Jason followed, his red flannel shirt matching the inlay in his cowboy boots; his skin glowed with the softest hint of yellow Shiner markings. Hannah came in last, hugging the wall.

What the hell?

Dahlia looked up from her book. "Shift change already?" She checked the clock, brow furrowing in confusion.

Miranda, standing ramrod straight, shook her head. "We have a problem."

Kayla followed her dark gaze to Jade. The alchemist's face was white behind her dark bangs.

"What problem?" Dahlia asked. "Oh, Jade stayed a little past time, but with all the research y'all assign . . ." She looked at Miranda and Jason, bafflement written on her kind face.

Miranda waved her away. "Jade, were you aware that everything you do on the computer can be seen from my office? It's an admin thing, allows me to remotely access the computers to fix them, but it also means I can see exactly what you are doing."

Jade inhaled sharply. Her voice trembled. "It's not what you think!"

Kayla froze in her seat. *Shit, I'm never peeking at a social media site again.*

Miranda crossed her arms. "Oh? How isn't it what I think?"

"I was just experimenting with different perspectives to better understand the potion I'm working on."

"Then you won't mind us looking through your room?"

"What about privacy?" The panicked squeak in Jade's voice belied her attempted indignation.

Kayla moved her seat back to stand up and defend Jade. Clearly, there was some serious misunderstanding. But Hannah put a firm hand on her shoulder, pushing her to stay down.

"You violated your NDA. That violates our privacy. Can't begrudge us returning the favor, can you?" Miranda's smile made Kayla's skin crawl. "Jason, please bring Jade along. Kayla, I want you with Hannah. Hold her arm, please."

"What's going on?" Kayla asked, trying to gather up her papers.

"Not now," Hannah hissed. She grabbed Kayla's arm and started tugging her, then her head jerked up. "Jason, in the bottom pocket of Jade's bag. Be careful."

Jason put out a silent hand.

Jade pulled her bag close to her chest. "This is absurd!"

Kayla agreed and started to say so, but Hannah's fingers bit into her arm. Frowning, Kayla closed her mouth, but it hurt to see Jade so upset.

"You're on private property, and we're not the police. We don't need a warrant to search your bag. Hand it over," Miranda said.

"Or what? You'll kick me out? Fine!" Jade said.

"Please, just hand it over," Hannah pleaded, looking almost as pale as Jade.

"I was just doing some research," Jade protested, but let Jason take her bag.

He placed it on the table and carefully dug down to the bottom pocket. Gingerly, he pulled out a small canvas bag.

"I didn't mean any harm," Jade pleaded.

Jason undid the drawstring and tugged open the bag, revealing a cloudy white crystal about two inches long. The only thing that distinguished it from something sold in a shop was the slight glow on the magical plane that showed it was potion infused.

"It's a fire enchantment," Hannah said.

Jason returned it to the bag and handed it over to Miranda, who tucked it away into a pocket in her tailored suit jacket.

"I know I'm not supposed to take it out of the lab without permission, but I was doing some research," Jade protested.

"Enough with the lies!" Miranda glared at the alchemist until Jade dropped her gaze to the ground. "Hannah, anything else here?"

Hannah shook her head.

"Let's go check her room, then." Miranda held the door open, a professional smile falling into place. "Dahlia, I'm canceling computer time for the rest of the week. I want everyone in Freedom Square in twenty minutes. Please get the word out."

Hannah stumbled over her own feet as they left the computer lab, but Kayla caught her by the elbow. Hannah nodded thanks, but her troubled gaze was on Jade's shadow.

"What did Jade do?" Kayla muttered.

There was fear in Hannah's eyes when they met Kayla. "I should have seen it earlier."

Not an answer. "Why do I have to come with?"

"Because your magic makes it easier for me to get answers."

A shiver spiderwebbed down Kayla's spine. Not just because Jade must have done something awful and was being led like a prisoner, but also because Kayla and Hannah were being treated like a tied team.

Fifteen

Zach
Day 5 of the Lockhouse Knot Leak
Tuesday afternoon
Tidal Water, MD

Sitting in the cozy West Study, Zach frowned at the photocopied page of Latin scrawl he was supposed to be translating. It had to be from a grimoire, but with only one page from the middle of a set of instructions, he couldn't figure out what the spell was supposed to do. If he'd been as new to all this as he was pretending, he wouldn't have even known it was a spell . . . potion. *Need to get the vocab straight!* It looked like a piece of badly written poetry.

Zach tapped the end of his pen slowly. *Are they still checking for competency?* Since his required reports on what he was seeing in the shadows were something he was going to fudge, he had to be decent at something or they'd get suspicious. There were four semesters of Latin in the college transcript Miranda had asked for, so Zach had faithfully translated the section from the Gallic Wars he was assigned. But translating something written by Julius Caesar wasn't the same as translating a possibly dangerous potion. If they hadn't assigned him one yet, they would.

The sooner he gained Kayla's trust and her book, the better. He'd already made her a more formidable enemy by helping her connect with her magic, and now he was considering translating an unknown potion. *What next? Helping invade HQ?*

Increasing the force of his tapping pen, Zach read through the page again. Stirring rainwater, collected in summer, and chanting about the combustibility of dried grass, twigs, logs, and torches. *Some kind of fire spell?* His pen picked up the rhythm as he mentally said the words of the chant in his head. It was the only well-written bit of the entire poem, probably because it was the bit meant to be spoken, or maybe because it had come from an earlier source. Sadie would like it; she'd have the patience to sit and say the words over and over again from the recommended sunrise to noon.

Groaning, Zach let his head fall to the table. *How dangerous is this spell?* If it was a torch that would be as useful as a flashlight, he'd have no qualms. If it was for some kind of explosion, and a Guard member could get hurt because of his work, then it would be better to mangle key parts of the translation now. However, if Searcha had already translated it and was still checking his skills, they wouldn't believe a full-fledged mistranslation, and targeted mistakes would give him away. Lifting his head, he scanned the carpeted floor. The shadows around him were extra stirred up in waves and . . . *fire? It is a fire spell?* Frowning, Zach held the paper up to the sunlight coming in through the window and examined the rectangular shadow it cast. No, the fire wasn't coming from the page.

"You are absolutely no help," Zach muttered to the shadows, and let his head sink back to the table.

"Zach!"

His head jerked up, bracing himself to complain about the tediousness of this assignment, when he saw Ara and her cherry-red hair in the doorway to the outside.

"Something big is happening in the square. We're all supposed to gather there." She tilted her head for him to follow and disappeared out the door.

Curiosity warring with relief, Zach shoved the papers into his messenger bag before following. Stepping into the clear sunshine, he pulled his thoughts and emotions closer. There were no clues in the shadows for him to guess at what was happening, just waves.

Ben exited the library and jogged a few steps to catch up with Zach. "Any idea what's going on?"

Zach shook his head. "This isn't normal?"

"Not that I've seen."

Unease itched Zach between the shoulder blades. Trying to shake it, he focused on Ben. "Whatcha working on?"

"Potion Assessment Report." Ben gave a *meh* shrug.

Zach raised his eyebrows.

Ben grinned. "You're such a noob. We take the translated directions and make lists of the ingredients, time required, and turn it into a shorthand, step-by-step guide. Then we summarize how useful we think it is and give our evaluation on the first page."

"Sounds repetitive. Why not just work from the directions directly instead of breaking it down into—what, a recipe?"

"That's a good word for it. Yeah, it's a pain in the ass to do, and if I did the original translation, it's boring as can be, but most of the time a different person does each step. The spell I'm working on was translated by someone who graduated before I started. Ideally, soon, we'll have a catalog of Assessment Reports. They're great to work from, clear and easy, just follow the steps. Usually the lab already has all the ingredients on hand, since Ara uses the reports as a guideline for what we stock. You just need the time."

Zach fought to keep his shudder on the inside. Sadie and Russel would have the know-how and intimate knowledge of the nuances of any spell they'd already done, but they were just two people. If the Searcha's model worked as well as Ben thought, they could make potions by production line.

Ben picked up the pace. "What the hell?"

It looked like every person on Tidal Water property had gathered on the patio area behind the main house. Zach didn't need to read the shadows to sense the anger and agitation radiating from the group.

Kayla was near the center. Zach fought the urge to go to her side. Hannah was already there, along with Miranda and Jason. Zach picked a spot on the periphery, where no one tall was blocking his view and he could lean nonchalantly against the split-rail fence that marked one edge.

Ben climbed onto the bottom rung, putting a hand on Zach's shoulder to steady himself.

Zach fought back a laugh, not that he could get a read on Ben with the crowd and the fire-tipped waves, but it was entertaining how much of Jason's lessons were spent drilling personal space into him. *Can't have me accidentally reading more than I should.* Three days ago, he wouldn't have thought twice about offering a shoulder for balance.

"Miranda, Jason, and Jade are in the middle. Hannah and Kayla are close, but everyone else is giving them space," Ben murmured.

With his height and the small crowd, he could see most of that. Samantha, directly in front of Zach, shifted, giving him a better view.

His stomach twisted uneasily. "Is Jade in trouble?" Jason had her by the arm in a way that didn't look friendly.

"I don't know," Ben said.

Samantha joined Zach against the rail. Her octagonal, forest-green glasses contrasted sharply with the flames in the shadows.

"I think so," Samantha murmured. "Miranda and Jason pulled her room apart, dragging Hannah and Kayla with them."

"Hannah saw something in Jade's shadow?" Ben asked.

Samantha gave a helpless shrug. "I guess so?"

Jason finished a quiet conversation with Miranda over Jade's head and turned to the crowd. "Hello, everyone."

"Hello, Jason," said everyone who'd been paying attention, silencing the rest, like they were in grade school.

"We have some devastating news." Jason's face was grim. He swept his free hand, leaving the floor to Miranda.

Jade looked like a trapped mouse. The shadows were too jumbled and crowded for Zach to even guess at an interpretation.

Miranda took a deep breath, allowing the silence to gain weight before speaking. "I've heard some of you ask why Merlin and Arthur started tying magic. The answer is simple. Fear. You've heard about this in the abstract. How they thought humanity would be selfish and greedy and corrupt with such power. I've always believed they were wrong about the majority of humanity, and for the rest? Magic makes it tangibly clear that we are all one unified whole. How can we hurt each other when we'd be so clearly hurting ourselves? The answer is more magic, not less."

Zach shivered. Despite the warmth of the afternoon sunlight, he pulled his collar up. The logic in Miranda's words was chilling.

"I know the majority of people are braver and smarter than Merlin gave them credit for," Miranda continued, her voice reaching everyone in the small crowd without effort, "that if we free magic and nurture it, we'll lead the world into a harmonious future." She looked down. When she looked back up, vulnerability and pain were etched on her face. "I still believe that, but today I've been reminded that we still have a long way to go. Greed and fear still dominate so many minds."

Jason shoved Jade to the pavers in front of them.

"Jade has been caught red-handed selling secrets about magic."

Zach gasped. Images of being rounded up and treated like science experiments by masked government officials flitted through the shadows. No prickle on his forearms was warning of the future—it was just something imagined by someone in the crowd—but fear was sour on the back of his tongue.

"You're playing with forces you clearly don't understand! People are going to die!" Jade protested.

"You're not worried about lives! You sold the story to a blogger!" Jason thundered.

"The police wouldn't listen. Someone has to listen!"

"You got paid. And that wasn't enough for you. No! You were going to smuggle out enchanted crystals as proof, for a thousand dollars," Miranda said, her voice as deadly as an icy road.

Jade scooted back. "I needed them to take me seriously."

Fingers numb, Zach cursed himself for not seeing any sign of any of that in the shadows. If magic was revealed to the government and believed, maybe the current Searcha members could be stopped, but

Guard members would get caught in the crossfire, and there'd be no way of keeping magic safely locked away. Zach was never going to make fun of Sadie's security measures again.

"We are dangerous only to those who are greedy and treacherous like you," Miranda said, her words soft but still reaching Zach's ears clearly.

Jade's eyes hardened. She looked like she'd hit the end of cowering and her spine stiffened. Standing up, she pushed her bangs out of her eyes. "This is a farce! What are you going to do? File a charge of corporate espionage? The police will laugh, or maybe take me seriously! Call me a ride, and I'll happily get the hell out of here."

"Shut up," Hannah hissed.

"You tell her, Hannah!" Ben shouted. Others agreed.

Something black and inky darkened the shadows, extinguishing the last traces of fire. *Hannah is trying to protect Jade, but from what? What could Miranda actually do?*

Miranda lifted a hand to silence the angry crowd before addressing Jade. "Magic is in the infancy of its return. It can't protect itself. You betrayed it. You betrayed us. And you have betrayed the world. Your actions could have led to a billionaire sending his private army to beat down our doors, taking our people and using their skills as tools for their own greedy ends. Our Alchemists forced to give them more power. Our Shiners pulled apart to see how they work. Our Shadows enslaved to tell the future. In my youth, I worked for the wealthy. You have no idea of their power and greed."

Zach frowned, curiosity stemming his fear. *What billionaire?* Miranda was playing on the prejudices and fears of the jaded and indebted youths against an easy villain.

Jade rolled her eyes. "Yet another pretty speech."

"Shut up," Zach muttered under his breath.

Miranda smiled dangerously at Jade. Zach crossed his arms instinctively to protect against the wave of ice and poison he could feel all the way from the fence.

"Ara," Miranda said.

The crowd shifted to let the alchemist through.

Only the barest hint of warmth softened Miranda's smile as she turned to Ara. "Please, retrieve the memory potion from high-security storage."

Ara blanched. "We haven't tested it."

"Now is a perfect time. This is exactly the kind of situation that potion was made for. Jade can leave us as soon as her memory is wiped."

"You can't be serious!" Jade said. Suddenly, she bolted, not waiting for an answer.

Jason looped a strand of magic and yanked her back. Grabbing her by the arm, he pulled her to the center of the square.

Miranda drew a roll of duct tape out of her pocket and used a piece to seal Jade's protesting lips, then bind her flailing hands. The shadows gave him no hints of how he might help her without blowing his own cover.

"If anyone comes around asking questions," Miranda said, as if binding and gagging were a perfectly normal way of dealing with a former trainee. "tell them Jade left Tidal Water after an argument with me, though you don't know why. I'll deal with them. You haven't seen her since lunch today. Now, I'm sure you all have things you need to be doing."

Miranda and Jason marched Jade off towards the house.

Ben jumped off the wall. "Yikes!"

"Yeah." Zach shuddered. The memory-altering spell Sadie had found had a warning three pages long. For once, he hoped Searcha's potion was of a better design. Getting the authorities involved in magic would have been a disaster, but Jade's fears were completely valid and he'd seen too late to help her.

"I can't believe Jade is a traitor," Samantha whispered, adjusting her glasses. "Did you suspect anything, Ben?"

Ben shook his head vigorously. Fear flared yellow in his shadow. "I had no idea!"

"It's okay." Zach clasped his hand on the other man's shoulder. "No one is accusing you of anything. I didn't suspect anything either."

"Sorry! I didn't mean it to come across that way," Samantha said. "I just—you started on the same day, so you were closer."

Ben heaved a sigh. "She didn't tell me anything." The yellow haze eased some from his shadow, but it flickered through the rest of the trainees', settling low around them like a mist of distrust. A traitor had come out of nowhere. People were wondering if there might be others.

"I'll see you at dinner," Zach said. He gave Hannah a wide berth as he headed for his room. He had a segment of a potion directions to translate perfectly, to hell with the consequences down the road. Get the grimoire and get out before what was happening to Jade happened to him.

Sixteen

Kayla
Day 5 of the Lockhouse Knot Leak
Tuesday evening
Tidal Water, MD

Kayla was tempted to skip the communal dinner, skip having to deal with the day's events, but her stomach wasn't inclined to cooperate. When Hannah knocked on her door, saying it was time to go, Kayla grumbled her assent and pulled herself away from her Captain Smith report.

Tugging on her jacket as she left the house, Kayla automatically slowed her pace to fall into step with Hannah. It was a beautiful evening. Gold and pink highlighted the fluffy white clouds, the beginnings of a beautiful sunset they would miss at the dinner table. The air was crisp, with a light, briny breeze that lifted a strand of hair off Kayla's forehead. If only she could follow the dancing air and see where it took her.

"Do you want to talk about it?" Hannah asked.

Kayla hunched into her fuzzy jacket, trying to zip it up. "Which part?"

Hannah sighed. "Whichever part is bothering you."

"Can't you see that in my shadow?" Kayla hated that her words made her sound like a petulant four-year-old. Her stupid zipper wouldn't catch.

Hannah groaned. "I've used a ton of magic today. I've got a terrible headache. Even if I tried to read your shadow right now, I doubt I'd be able to understand any of it. But it doesn't take magic to see you're upset. Are you mad I went to Miranda about Jade? What else was I supposed to do?"

Kayla's neck unkinked a notch. She should be used to Hannah reading her all the time, but it was a weight off her shoulders to hear it wasn't happening at the moment. "Of course, you had to go to Miranda. Can you imagine what would have happened if you didn't? I can't imagine being locked in a lab! I'd literally start bouncing off the walls."

Amusement softened Hannah's face.

Kayla's zipper teeth caught, and her jacket closed with a satisfying zip.

"Some people are going to be uncomfortable around me now. They'll be afraid I can read their minds and might draw the wrong conclusions," Hannah said, with a casualness Kayla didn't buy. "But reading shadows isn't at all like that. Hell, it took me a dangerously long time to realize something was up with Jade. Too much longer, and we would all have been in danger. Maybe I don't deserve to graduate. Sorry, I didn't mean to say that out loud. Don't worry, I won't let you down. My head just really hurts."

Kayla needed a few paces to let all that sink in. "You remember what Jason said when he went through all of her emails? It didn't look like she came here planning to sell secrets. If you'd caught her earlier, it would have been for something that she hadn't done yet. That would have been scary. But you caught her in the middle, before she did any real harm, but far enough in there was no doubt what she was doing."

"I think the pictures I showed you of that damaged knot guardian pushed her over the edge," Hannah muttered.

The toe of Kayla's shoe caught on the flat ground, but she shook off the stumble. "You couldn't have known she'd react that way. Those pictures helped convince me to try harder."

"I was so focused on you, I missed everything else."

"Congrats, you're human," Kayla said, repeating wisdom from her brother Noah and adding, "You're a Shadow, not a god." She raised a hand to pat Hannah on the back, but caught herself. Trying to cover up the moment, she added, "I'm starving. Hope there's something good for dinner."

Hannah's smile didn't reach her eyes. "Thanks. You're right."

Kayla grinned. She was tempted to pretend she hadn't heard, to make Hannah repeat that last part, but that would be childish.

"Something is still bothering you," Hannah said, her eyes insistent.

For a moment, Kayla thought it was the interrupted pat on the back. But the reason she'd wanted to avoid the dinner table slapped her in the face. She tried to keep in it, but the words spilled out. "Miranda acted like *I'm* the reason you figured out what Jade was doing! Which is stupid, because Jade is what changed, not us."

Hannah bit her lip and watched her footing for five or six steps. "You're right about Jade, of course."

Silence.

Kayla waited as long as she could stand. "And?"

Hannah shrugged. "Holding onto Nathan's arm probably would have worked almost as well."

Kayla threw her hands in the air. "Exactly as well. Or Jason's. He was right there. Miranda didn't need to have you drag me along." Feeling like a convenient battery would have been bad enough, a career of being tied to Hannah was worse.

"You're still not comfortable with the idea of us tying?" Hannah asked.

Kayla looked at her incredulously. *How can she spot a traitor in the computer lab, but not see that the two of us would drive each other mad if we had to spend years together?* "I don't want to be tied with anyone. Jason and Nick aren't. Why do I have to be?"

Hannah tapped a rhythm, only she could hear, against her leg before speaking. "Jason is a teacher, but he hasn't left Tidal Water. You watch. Soon he'll be tied, maybe to Zach, and move to the field. Nathan will take his turn as teacher. I feel bad for Nick, waiting for his brother to grow up. Being tied means having someone there who always has your back, who sees and understands you. A partner in this wild quest we're all on to save magic."

It sounded nice, but ideals were never the reality. Kayla had listened to more than enough of her friends complain about their romantic partners to know real life wasn't like the movies. Hannah's version of being tied was likely equally inaccurate.

"I hope you find your partner ASAP. I, however, am good just the way I am." Kayla shrugged.

They were almost to the east-side door before Hannah spoke again. "For someone as independent as you, I can see why that seems appealing. I respect you for not feeling the need for someone else. But it's a shallow version of the life you could be living. I'll ask

Miranda if the Tied Twins can stop by sometime. They're amazing together. I knew them as they became tied. It's such a beautiful thing. And the Shiner has gorgeous pink magic."

"You're welcome to be wistful out here with the sunset, but I want reality and food. Thank you very much." Kayla took the steps two at a time, but forced herself to stop at the top and hold the door for Hannah.

Hannah smiled serenely and walked through the doorway. "Thanks. I think I'm still going to ask Miranda about them giving a talk to the trainees."

Kayla gritted her teeth and marched down the hall, into the dining room, and straight for her seat.

Nathan smiled as they approached. "All hail the mighty heroes."

Kayla tucked her chin into her jacket.

"Congratulations, Hannah," Zach said. "I didn't see it until you already had it all in hand, but it's obvious now you saved us all a lot of trouble."

"Thanks," Hannah said, sounding surprised but gratified.

Zach gave a brief nod before dropping his gaze back to the napkin he was doodling on.

Luckily, the baked rosemary chicken, rice, and roasted vegetables were at the table, so Kayla could sit down and start helping to pass serving plates.

Nathan and Samantha had a lot of questions, and slowly Ben added his. Luckily, Hannah fielded them all. She was quick to highlight the evidence against Jade and underplay her role in seeing the shadows.

Zach was sketching a stormy sea as he ate. Kayla hadn't realized she'd been looking forward to a wink or a conspiratorial look from him, but she was a little jealous of the attention he was giving his drawing. *Has he forgotten he wanted to be friends?*

She started planning the route for an evening run. Good hard exercise would clear her head of this whole uncomfortable day.

Around her, the conversation shifted to alchemy and the highlights of the recent basketball games Ben had picked up while on the computer. That spiraled into a debate about what was a valid and safe use of computer time.

"You're rather quiet? Everything okay?" Zach asked.

Kayla looked up from the serving plate of chocolate chip cookies she'd been contemplating, but Zach wasn't looking at her. He was speaking to Ara.

"It was a lot today," Ara said.

Kayla took two cookies.

"It was awesome you had just the right potion for the situation!" Ben said. "I don't know what Miranda would have done otherwise."

Zach's frown deepened, and Hannah shifted uncomfortably in her seat.

"What?" Kayla's gaze flickered between them, landing on Hannah.

"Nothing. The potion was available. A bit of memory loss is a small price to pay for what Jade might have done to us otherwise," Hannah said, but her eyes stayed on her barely touched dinner.

"And if the potion wasn't available?" Ben asked, putting his finger on what was bothering Kayla about Hannah's tone.

"It was. So it doesn't matter. It's not like Miranda discusses strategy with me." Hannah pushed away her plate.

"The potion wasn't ready, though," Ara said. "It was my first attempt. It's dangerous magic to mess with someone's brain. Miranda and Jason took it off property to use, so I didn't even get to see how well it worked. There had to have been a better option!"

"Miranda made the call. It's not your fault if it doesn't erase her memory quite right," Ben said.

"Miranda will have fail-safes in place to keep Jade from hurting us," Nathan added.

"But how? She's not the police," Kayla said. She was comfortable that the evidence they'd found proved that Jade had betrayed them, but she had also gotten the impression, as the staff tore Jade's room apart, that if it hadn't, Miranda would have fabricated some. Kayla shivered.

"She kinda is, though," Nathan said. "We're going into a new, Wild West-like time. Magic back in the world is going to shift our broken power structures and change the world in ways we can only begin to guess at. Like many of our technological advancements, but this time it'll actually be for the better."

"Nathan's right. Miranda and the other leaders of Searcha are in charge. They'll do what they have to to keep us safe from the ignorant and cowardly as we free magic," Hannah said.

"Then that's a 'no' to checking how my basketball bracket is doing? I'm heartbroken," Ben said with a smile.

Most of the people around the table laughed.

"Bet Dahlia will check them for you," Samantha said.

"Nah, Captain Fitzroy, he's usually a stickler, but his bracket is leading. He'll be checking," Nathan said.

More laughter as Ara got up. "I'm on dish duty tonight." She brightened as Ben jumped up to join her.

Samantha made a face. "My turn too."

"Thanks!" Kayla said to the alchemists before turning to Hannah. "I'm going for a run. See ya later."

"Isn't it better to wait thirty minutes after eating?" Hannah asked, then caught herself. "Never mind. Have fun."

Ready for battle, Kayla blinked. "Thanks? You too." She left without looking back. Of course, she was going to walk for a while before running, but she wanted out now.

Stepping out into the brisk night cleared her head. The stars were endless and would only grow more beautiful as her eyes adjusted, but thoughts of the Wild West, dystopian future trailed her as she walked. Was that really the future she wanted to help bring about? But then again, Florida was supposed to be underwater in a few years, anyway, right? Plague, systemic racism, staggering income inequality, and broken political systems. The world was going to shit, anyway, right? What did it matter?

Kayla screeched through her teeth. Downward-spiraling thoughts weren't the company she wanted to keep. She reached for her phone, but of course it was in her room. Running wouldn't help without her music, and the camp was so small, she felt like she was going in circles.

Maybe Ben and the rest could be talked into a basketball game after they were done with the dishes. She should have stayed to help.

Movement caught her eye. Zach was walking towards the beach where she'd done tai chi with him. She jogged over.

"You know," she said, falling into step with him, "Hannah didn't see that stuff about Jade today because we're becoming tied or anything." She regretted the words as soon as they left her mouth, but she wanted him to know, in case that was why he'd barely spared her a glance all dinner.

Surprise flashed across his face. "I know." He smiled at her, and breathing was easier even as her stomach filled with butterflies.

Stupid, stupid crush! It sucked that anyone could have that much impact on her emotions. But she smiled back. "It's good to be out-side."

"Beautiful night for tai chi. Want to join?"

"Please."

He nodded. "How was your day before all the drama started?"

"Wow, that feels like days ago. Oh! I have a cool person for my latest profile report! Have you had to do one of those yet? Such a pain."

"But this time is different? You sound excited."

She grinned and gave him a summary of her findings.

"That sounds awesome. I've been to Jamestown, but I don't know much about Smith's early life. What else did you find out?"

Kayla needed no more invitation. By the time she was walking back towards home, not only had she discussed Smith and dissected her and Zach's favorite childhood movies, but she'd slid into the tai chi like a warm bath. Her mind was so in her body and so focused on the movements, her thoughts drained away. She danced with the breeze and felt at one with the star-filled sky, shimmering water, and her magic.

It was easy to believe she could master her power. She'd graduate in no time.

The last glow of her magic faded from her skin when she saw the living room light was still on and minor-key music floated out the open window. Hannah was waiting up, picking at her guitar, making sure her wayward roommate made it back alright. Kayla groaned and braced for an interrogation.

Seventeen

Zach
Day 6 of the Lockhouse Knot Leak
Wednesday, dawn
Tidal Water, MD

Window-rattling thunder from the night's storm wove into Zach's recurring nightmare of waves and teeth. Laying there in the dawn light, long after the clouds had quieted to a steady drizzle, it was too easy to imagine that the storm was the monster from the Lockhouse Knot, coming for its revenge.

Sitting up and switching on the bedside light, Zach tried to banish the fear writhing in his gut. His brain wasn't awake enough to battle it back to its corner. Shaking his head, he reached for his sketchpad, but it didn't help him untangle reality from the imagined.

He craved a check-in with Terra and Alexis. Not only would they have good ideas for getting the spellbook, but maybe they'd found another option. With computer time on hold, he couldn't check the motorcycle-repair message board where they were supposed to pass messages. Maybe he could break into the computer lab in the middle of the night, but if Hannah noticed even the idea of that in his shadow, it would risk his cover. There was the magic earbud in one of his hidden jacket pockets, but it was meant for more imminent danger, when Guard members would be close and monitoring the channel. Using it probably wouldn't be obvious in his shadow, unless Hannah was looking for it, but it was still a risk, and it probably wouldn't work. There were the burner phones in Nick's car, but driving off property for cell service would break the Tidal Water rules and get a car key confiscated.

He needed to get the book and get out, but the shadows wouldn't show him how. Frustration filled the page in front of him.

Something whispered through the air. *No. Through the shadows.* Like butterfly wings disturbing dust floating in the air. *Outside?* Curiosity surfaced on the tides of his frustration and fear. Zach put away his pad and pencils and left the room. Anything was better than thinking in circles with his sketchbook. Slipping by the kitchen, he grabbed a protein bar. That *something* in the shadows shimmered and pulsed.

Stepping outside, Zach paused under the porch's protection and took a deep breath of damp air. It was chilly, but not truly cold. Low clouds muted light and shadows, blurring magic, and wrapping the landscape in a gray blanket. Rain came down in a fine mist that danced around him, cooling his skin and settling in his hair. There was time before breakfast to explore what was calling in the shadows. Calling him towards the bay.

A calm break between shadow waves, too regular to be random, beckoned him across the patio and onto the squelching lawn. The bay, lost in the mist, lapped against the rocks guarding the shore. To his right a flicker of color and light, like a sunrise on the ocean, interrupted his attention.

Smiling, he looked up. Kayla was jogging down a footpath perpendicular to his invisible one. Her blonde hair was a shade darker from the rain, and tendrils that had escaped her braid curled around her face. A windbreaker open over her usual running outfit was the only nod she'd made to the rain.

Lifting a hand, Zach waved once.

Kayla beamed, leaving the muddy footpath to join him. "I guess I'm not the only one who can't keep inside."

"It's rather beautiful, isn't it?" He tried to look at their misty surroundings, but his eyes didn't want to leave her face.

She laughed. "I prefer sunshine, but this has its charms."

Something about Kayla not needing blue skies when she was sunlight incarnate was on Zach's tongue, but he couldn't quite work out the wording. *Just as well, spouting lines about her radiant energy won't help me build a platonic friendship.*

"Are you going to do tai chi?" Kaula asked, when Zach missed his cue to speak.

He hesitated. "I was following this path thing in the shadows." Zach waved a vague hand at the ground in front of him. "Want to join me?"

"Where does it go?"

"I don't know, but I'm curious. It's new to me."

Kayla grinned. "Well, now I'm curious."

Zach described the shifting solid points between the waves to her as he followed them along the shore, not in the technical terms he'd discussed with Alexis or the vague terms he used on his Shadow Report for Searcha, but in emotional words—how he felt them.

A pine tree, uprooted by the storm, lay in their way. Shivering, Zach stepped over the scaly brown trunk. Kayla hopped lightly over and slid her hand into his. Or maybe he reached for hers. He didn't quite notice until their fingers were interlaced. The path glowed brighter, as if the shadow waves had thinned and more sunlight filtered through. Zach led the way around a bend in the shoreline, where mist and low clouds blanketed the dark water.

"Wow," Kayla breathed.

Zach looked over, curious what she was seeing in the strands, but she wasn't looking at the ground.

Not thirty feet away, dapple gray and as magical as the mist shifting around them, the unicorn stood beside the rocks where the sand met the jetty. Her lightning-white horn seemed to glow in the low light. Her ears pricked forward as she watched them with dark eyes. The meandering shadow path ended at her cloven hooves.

Goosebumps prickled Zach's arms. "The path was her invitation here."

"She's so beautiful!" Kayla squeezed his hand tighter.

"She is." *How can I capture the way Storm looks in the mist?* Maybe he'd come close with charcoal or watercolors, but he wouldn't be able to fully express the magic of the moment. This was Storm's natural habitat; it was as if she was part of the landscape, not the physical aspect of a toxin that didn't belong in the world. "But why did she call?"

Brian, Alexis, and Nick had a connection to Storm, but Zach didn't.

Storm nickered and stepped forward.

"I'm glad she did." Kayla moved closer.

Elliot's warnings about magical creatures rang in Zach's memory, but she hadn't hurt anyone yet, and her ears were forward, curious, not murderous.

Storm trotted forward and stopped, just out of touching distance.

Zach searched the cloudy, muted shadows for danger. Storm snorted, as if reading Zach's mind and dismissing his fears as silly.

"You're beautiful," Kayla whispered, offering her free hand.

Zach held onto her other hand but didn't try to stop her.

Storm arched her neck forward. She sniffed and then bumped the offered hand with her nose.

"She's so soft!" The wonder in Kayla's voice loosened the tension between Zach's shoulder blades.

He stepped up beside her. Storm turned her dark eyes on him. Hesitating a beat more, he offered his hand. "Hello." It was anyone's guess if she understood human language, but Zach had no doubt she was intelligent.

Storm nickered, the sound of soft rain falling on water. She pushed her nose against his hand. Gratified, Zach patted the velvety fur.

"This is like a dream," Kayla murmured.

Storm lifted her head and looked them over.

"To what do I owe the honor of your invitation here? Because that's what that shadow path was, right?" Zach asked. *Not a passive reflection of the world around, but a magic ability of Storm's?*

Storm whinnied, like distant thunder and breaking waves, and pawed the sand with a large cloven hoof.

"I don't speak unicorn, do you?" Kayla asked.

Zach shook his head. "Would be a more useful skill than reading Latin."

Kayla chuckled. "Her shadow doesn't tell you why she's here?" She reached out and rubbed Storm's neck and shoulder; the unicorn leaned into her for more.

Zach was about to say he could see frustratingly little in this fog and light, but maybe he could use that to his advantage. "I'm not seeing what she wants, but I am getting an interesting image. Something from her past. She's in Baltimore?"

"That's where the Guard stopped a Searcha mission. It's a black eye on our record people only whisper about."

"Storm is afraid of a knot in Baltimore, doesn't want it cut. She's even helping the Guard members stop Searcha?" Zach tried to sound puzzled and curious.

Storm snorted, as if she knew very well what he was doing and didn't have time for it. She snagged the edge of his sleeve with her mouth and tugged.

Zach followed his sleeve without protest, grateful her teeth hadn't been aimed at his skin. "I'm coming."

She dropped his sleeve and kept walking up the beach.

"Where are we going?" Kayla asked.

He grinned. "No idea."

The breeze shifted from inland. Storm's head shot up like a startled deer. Snorting loudly, she stood for a moment, her whole body focused on something in the direction of camp. Then she gave Zach and Kayla an apologetic look before leaping back the way she'd come and cantering out of sight around the rocks.

"What the hell?" Kayla asked.

"No idea." Zach turned away from where the unicorn had vanished and looked towards whatever had sent her running. Someone was coming up over the hill.

"Kayla! Zach!" Jason called through the mist.

"Now that's weird. Couldn't have been Jason who scared her," Kayla said.

Sure. "What?" Zach called back, dismissing his nagging curiosity. *If it's important, she'll be back, right?*

"Miranda wants you," Jason shouted back.

"Coming," Kayla replied.

"I think Storm has a weird relationship with Searcha. Not sure we should mention seeing her?" Zach said softly to Kayla as they started walking towards Jason.

"Fine by me. Hannah will feel left out, but I hope Storm comes back."

"Me too." It was a risk to push, but time was short. "I heard you had a cool grimoire from your uncle. Might it have info about how to speak unicorn?"

"I wish. It's all written in gibberish. Besides, Ara has it secured somewhere."

Kayla raised her voice, missing the gut-punched expression Zach couldn't conceal. "What does Miranda want?"

Hell! He was wasting his time; he should have been focused on Ara. The alchemist had said she was reading it—he should've asked more questions. He'd let himself get distracted by Kayla.

Now you know. You can pivot. If he didn't like Kayla so much, he would have seen this sooner. From the moment he'd seen her and her light, he'd missed all the signs that anyone else had the grimoire.

Jason waited for them to reach him and fall into step towards the main camp before he answered. "We just got word from Richmond. The storm last night uncovered a sunken boat with magical artifacts. The Tied Twins are en route, but we're closer. Last week they were beaten to a find by the Guard. We don't want to risk that happening again. Zach, your college transcript says you took scuba diving?"

Icy fear washed away Zach's self-flagellation. His leather jacket wouldn't stop the Twins from recognizing his face. He forced himself to nod. "Two semesters of scuba."

"Good. Most of the wreck washed ashore, but some of it could still be in the water," Jason said.

"You have dive gear?" Zach asked, mentally crossing his fingers that they'd have to stop somewhere to pick it up, giving him more time to miraculously come up with a plan.

"Fitzroy has gear and a small tank he uses for boat stuff. He's letting you borrow it, after he assures himself you know what you're doing."

"Great." Zach was glad sarcasm was part of his persona, because he was screwed.

Eighteen

"You were looking for me, too?" Kayla asked, barely leashed excitement in her step as they approached Xander.

"You and Hannah aren't as strong as a tied team yet, but this one time, we're making an exception about not going into the field before graduation," Jason said, opening the east door for them.

Kayla almost squealed, but that wouldn't demonstrate she was professional enough to handle this. She did allow herself to skip up the stairs. *A chance to prove myself in the field and get off property!* She held the door at the top for the others. *Why is Zach slouching in his jacket again?* His gaze was focused on the ground in front of him, and he didn't notice when she tried to share her enthusiasm with a smile. Rolling her eyes, Kayla let him be.

Miranda was waiting in the entrance hall with Fitzroy. "About time. We're leaving in ten—make that nine minutes. Fitz, I expect Zach ready and in the van in eight. Kayla, come with me."

Anticipation fizzled through Kayla's blood as she followed Miranda through the common room. Kayla had dozens of questions, but Miranda's focused expression wasn't inviting.

Miranda stepped into her office, motioned Kayla in, and closed the door. "I just want to check in with how you're doing."

"I'm thrilled," Kayla said honestly, but not sure what answer Miranda was looking for.

Miranda smiled. "I'm glad you can join us on this mission." Then she turned serious. "I just . . . I hear you and Hannah have been having some friction?"

We're loading in minutes, and you want to talk about Hannah?! "We approach the world very differently," Kayla said, using her brother's diplomatic language instead of complaining about how Hannah had grilled her the night before for hanging out with Zach or how Kayla had left the house early to avoid her housemate.

"That's one of the best parts of a tied team, opposites who are stronger together. Approaching the world differently is an advantage, not a disadvantage. You are both going to play an important role in the magic revolution that is just starting."

Kayla opened her mouth to argue, but couldn't think of a single thing that didn't sound petty, stupid, or selfish in the face of the magical revolution. Looking down, she played with the end of her braid.

"I know it's been an adjustment. But you are both innate magic users and helping to change and heal the world. That's a lot of common ground. I'd really appreciate it if you'd work a little harder to get along with Hannah. Her heart really is in the right place."

Kayla nodded, her stomach queasy.

"Thank you, Kayla." Miranda put out her hand, and Kayla shook it, suddenly wondering if she'd agreed to more than trying a little harder to be nice.

Miranda opened the office door. "Time we hit the road."

A tad numb, Kayla followed her out. The white van had three rows of passenger seats, and the back was almost full of wooden boxes, rubber waders, and beachcombing equipment. Kayla's excitement bubbled up again as she helped Ben load the last of their gear.

Walking to the sliding door of the passenger van, Kayla saw that Hannah was buckled into the far seat on the closest bench, while Zach had climbed into the way back, his orange Hawaiian swim trunks looking absurd with his leather jacket. Kayla smiled at him, but he was busy being broody. Ara climbed into the middle row, and Kayla was about to join her, but one glance at Miranda's expression and Kayla sat next to Hannah instead. Ben jumped in last and joined Ara.

"That's everyone," Jason said, and slid the door closed. He took the shotgun seat, and Miranda drove.

"This is so exciting!" Ben whispered.

Kayla turned around in her seat to look at Ara. "Have you ever gotten to go on something like this before?"

"No, the teams from Richmond have always gone. Sometimes, if they're close enough, they drop what they find off with us, though, instead of risking taking it all the way south."

Miranda cleared her throat. Everyone gave her their full attention, except maybe Zach, who was spinning a pencil between his fingers.

"Now that we're all here, Jason, would you give us a rundown of what we know?"

Jason pulled out a folder. "The research division is still working, but what we have so far is there was a smallish wooden vessel named *Otis* that was wrecked in the Bay in the early 1900s. Last night's storm dislodged it from the bottom and washed some of its contents onto a marsh and beach area south of here. We believe the ship, boat . . ." Jason looked at Miranda for help.

"Vessel," she supplied.

"Vessel," Jason continued, "was carrying several magical artifacts, including a coded description of where to find more knots."

"What are the other artifacts?" Hannah asked.

"We think there's a magic compass, a gauge that monitors magic levels, and we're not sure what else. That's why there are two Shadows in our group. They can verify what parts of the debris from the wreck are magical, and what's just ship."

"Who owned the vessel?" Ben asked.

Jason looked through the handful of papers in his folder. "We don't have that information yet."

"Where'd you get a partial manifest, then?" Zach asked.

"Early information suggests it was a private collection from over a hundred years ago with connections to the Smithsonian, but this is all classified."

Miranda cleared her throat. "This entire mission is classified. We'll discuss on the drive back how much, if any, of it you can share with your fellow trainees. If we weren't so much closer than the agents, we wouldn't be here. The Twins and field alchemists are on their way. Our mission is to secure the site and see what we can salvage while we wait. But as soon as they arrive, we turn this over to them. Do you understand?"

Everyone murmured their agreement.

"Can you tell us about the site?" Hannah asked.

Jason looked at Miranda for confirmation before leafing through the papers. "It's a bit of beach and sandbar, surrounded by marsh, with a deepish channel running by it. Part of the wreckage is in the channel, part is on land."

"Smallish vessel, deepish channel? Very specific words you got there," Zach said, a smirk in his voice.

"The information is good, even if the source lacks specificity," Jason retorted.

Miranda shot him a look that clearly said, *Shut up*. Jason ducked his head and shuffled his notes.

Kayla bounced in her seat. If it didn't make her sound like a three-year-old, she would have asked how much longer.

"You okay?" Hannah asked.

"Excited." Kayla found a grin. "The location for more knots—plural! This could be huge!"

"I wonder how complicated of a code it might be," Ara said. Something about the alchemist's mood was off, Kayla realized, like her energy was folded inward. It was an impressive ability for someone with such loudly dyed hair.

"We'll figure out how to crack it, and then the Guard won't stand a chance at stopping us," Ben said. "But I have to admit, I'm just as excited about any magical equipment we might find."

"Hopefully, the code is easier than trying to translate the gibberish in Kayla's grimoire." Ara gave a self-deprecating smile. "You know I'm in trouble when the Russian is the only part I can figure out and only with a lot of work. I'm hoping I can find something that's written in a similar fashion, like a Rosetta Stone, to make translating it easier. Even if I could translate the symbols, the verses and lines aren't like anything I've ever seen."

"You'll figure it out," Ben said, nudging her with his shoulder. She smiled back.

They jumped into a discussion about esoteric aspects of alchemy. Kayla wasn't tempted to talk to Hannah, when she was probably the one who told Miranda they weren't getting along. Zach was too far away to start a conversation with. Kayla tried breathing into the uncomfortable feeling in her stomach, but she couldn't name it and it was, well, uncomfortable, and she didn't want to. Out of options, she asked Jason about the sports games that had happened lately. He had more access to the internet than she did and was happy to fill her in on the drama. At least until Miranda's disapproving glances silenced him.

Luckily it wasn't long after when Miranda parked the van on an isolated stretch of road by a marsh. "Does that look like an old dead tree with a Y branch and a boll in the middle?" she asked Jason quietly.

"I'd say so. I'm impressed the research team found it. Even with these other landmarks," Jason replied just as quietly.

"Okay, everyone," Miranda said, "let's secure the site."

Getting into waders was an awkward, stumbling process that made Kayla laugh. Trudging the equipment between the prickly plants and over the sulfurous mud was a slippy-slidy adventure.

Kayla went back to help with a second load. Zach and Ara were the only ones at the van, standing close to each other, talking. A pang of anger—no, jealousy—hit her. Kayla froze in her tracks. *Jealousy?* Now that was a weird emotion to feel. *What the hell purpose does that one serve?* Shrugging, Kayla tried to shake it off and walked over.

Ara started. "Kayla!"

"What's going on?" Kayla asked, trying to sound casual and friendly.

Ara glanced around. "I probably shouldn't say anything, but when Zach asked what was wrong, I couldn't hold it in any longer."

Concern chased away jealousy. "What? I won't tell."

"I need the internet to translate Russian, so I was able to get special permission. While I was on, I looked up what happened to Jade. Miranda made it look like a car accident. They used one of the spare vehicles that are usually parked at the maintenance building."

"They had to explain the memory loss somehow," Zach said gently.

Ara nodded. "I get that, but the enchantment . . . I told them it wasn't ready."

"It's not your fault," Zach said.

Ara swallowed hard.

Zach frowned. "Is there more?"

Kayla suddenly didn't want to know what she had to say. Another minute, and Kayla would have missed this conversation. Now she was too curious to walk away, even if she could find an excuse.

"She's in a coma," Ara blurted out. "The doctors don't know if she'll wake up. The article made it sound like they doubt it."

Zach staggered. Kayla caught his arm.

"It was an experimental potion. It shouldn't have been used," Ara pleaded.

"You told Miranda that," Kayla said firmly. "Zach's right. It's not your fault. She'll wake up."

"Kayla!" Miranda called.

All three of them jumped, but the Searcha leader was on the other side of the marsh.

"I'm bringing another load," Kayla shouted back, as if it wasn't obvious.

"Leave it for the alchemists," Miranda yelled. "I need you to lend your arm to Hannah, so she can start hunting for artifacts. Zach, get over here too."

Zach found his footing and saluted.

"And keep your eyes peeled for Guard interference," Miranda shouted, before turning back to the beach.

"Hope they're not in hearing range, or they'll know we're here," Ara muttered.

Zach gave an amused snort.

"That's why Miranda brought me along and not Nathan. I should have seen it coming. I'm just here to hold Hannah's hand," Kayla groaned.

"Better than asking you to do something that puts another person in a coma," Ara said.

Zach shouldered a silver tank and closed the door.. "Jade put all our lives at risk. That doesn't justify what Miranda did, but she was trying to protect us."

Kayla nodded in agreement, and the three started walking.

Ara said, "Thanks. That's a good point. Hey, Kayla, maybe you can find a use for your magic they aren't expecting."

"True, and at least I get to be here. It's pretty awesome to get to see what a mission looks like, and don't tell Hannah, but I'm kinda looking forward to meeting the Twins."

"They are pretty cool," Ara said.

The ground was tricky. Kayla had to watch her step and help the fully loaded Ara through the marsh.

They were getting close to the beach when Zach asked, "Was that the only one of those memory potions you had?"

"It was, but Miranda ordered me and Samantha to make more. The next one is almost ready. Hopefully I fixed it, but because I don't know what I did wrong, and I didn't see the enchantment in action, I can only hope." Ara shifted her load.

"Well, that should be the last traitor we'll have to deal with for a while, hopefully forever," Kayla said, with a reassuring smile.

"Fingers crossed," Ara said. "Better get to Hannah before Miranda gets annoyed."

"I got this," Kayla said. There had to be a way apart from enhancing Hannah's power she could use her magic to help show her worth. Thinking hard, Kayla tried to remember what she'd learned from Zach about the strands.

Nineteen

Zach fiddled with the scuba equipment longer than necessary, partially to fight his rising anxiety, but mostly to wait until Hannah was as far down the beach as possible. Thankfully, it was overcast, and Hannah was focused on figuring out Kayla's mood and finding artifacts, or she would have noticed something deeply wrong with his shadow. Then *he* would be the one bound and gagged with duct tape.

Thinking about Jade really wasn't helping.

"You almost ready?" Miranda asked.

Zach nodded, quadruple-checking the regulator. Hopefully, Miranda's paranoia meant the Guard was actually on their way. Though Zach had seen enough weapon potions in the trunk to know a confrontation would be bad, even if the Guard had invested any time in researching magical defenses, which they hadn't. Magic was supposed to have been locked safely away again by now.

"I have more information to help you look." Miranda opened the folder Jason had been carrying.

"Thanks," Zach said. Standing up to his full height, as if to give Miranda his attention, he could peek at the sheet she was studying. It looked like a photograph of a handwritten journal page. A modern one, judging from the lined, purple paper and the watercolor sword insignia around the page number at the bottom.

"A broken piece of wood shows the poor wrecked vessel's name, *Otis*." Miranda read aloud and then skimmed ahead. In her shadow, the words scrawled out on the sand in a modern hand that nodded at cursive but didn't quite take the leap.

The unicorn walks on the bottom beside me, but because it's a dream, we both can breathe. I hallucinate the unicorn often enough during the day. Why does she also have to visit me at night? Anyway. She points with her horn at something beside the shattered bit of boat.

Zach hadn't seen the handwriting before, but his gut said the author was a Shadow, visited in a dream the way Storm had once visited Alexis. Focusing on the shadow, he brought the author to the surface of the painted smudge at Miranda's feet. A dark-haired woman in forest-patterned PJs writing at a desk.

"Beside this wood," Miranda continued, "there is a box, rusted on the outside. Inside there is a whispered stream of nonsensical words that, once unraveled, will point the way to knots hidden deep." Miranda skipped to the next page. "Also close to a half-buried rubber tire is a glass orb, glowing softly, like a comb jelly."

Zach nodded slowly, his mind racing.

"Get both those things and anything else you can find down there."

Zach saluted, then squeezed himself into the wetsuit that was only a bit too big for him.

Miranda turned away to check in with Ara and Ben.

Hannah was at the far end of the beach, just before it turned back to marsh. *Now or never.* Zach slipped the magic earbud out of a secret pocket and slid it into his ear. He pulled on the equipment and carefully walked in his flippers to the water. The shore dropped off fast. He checked the regulator one last time before he let air out of the vest.

Slow, steady breathing came naturally, a habit drilled into him during his classes in the school pool. The ohhh-hhha of the regulator, the loudest thing under water, melted his fears and panic away. Practice. Lots and lots of practice. Panic made you run through your air faster. *Breathe, and never, ever hold your breath.* It helped that he wasn't going deep. As the muddy bottom dropped off, and the current picked up, he settled in about fifteen feet down.

The fins, a size too small, helped keep him from getting carried by the current.

The water was murky, visibility was like a night dive, which he'd only learned about in class. Fitzroy's diving flashlight helped some, but seeing only in a narrow beam of light was disconcerting, especially when his nightmares were filled with aquatic teeth coming for him.

His breathing got shallower shand irregular. As soon as he noticed, his training kicked in. Letting go of everything that wasn't important in the moment, he prioritized.

"*Testing, Testing,*" he mentally reached out. If the Guard was in DC, they wouldn't hear him, but if Miranda was right and they were closing in, they might be in range.

His breathing and the movement of the sediment shifting in the current were the only things that he could hear.

Letting out a long breath, Zach turned to searching. His bubbles would be visible from the surface, and Miranda would start wondering if he stayed in one place too long. The tire would be the best thing to look for first. He couldn't hand over anything that told where more knots were.

"*Testing?*" Brian's voice echoed.

"*You're in range!*" Tears welled up under Zach's mask. He hadn't realized how badly he needed to hear a member of the Guard.

"*Yep. We're headed to some out-of-the-way corner of marsh, something about important artifacts located there. I guess Searcha is already there.*"

"*Yes, and they've got enough magical firepower to be concerned. They'll fight you if you just roll up.*"

After a moment of silence, Alexis came on. "*Good to know. Is it safe to fill us in? It's so cloudy, I'm having trouble with the shadows.*"

With relief, Zach let his thoughts tumble out, trying to share everything with the team as quickly as possible, while also continuing his unnecessarily tight search grid. When he thought he'd finished, Alexis asked clarifying questions, helping him slow down and articulate the important information he'd missed.

"*Give us a minute to plan,*" Terra said.

Maybe they were going to get him out now. He hadn't gotten the spellbook, but maybe they'd figured out another way. Maybe he could take the box with the whispering words and run, or swim away, before Miranda and the others caught on. Before the Twins arrived and recognized him. Maybe he could sleep in his own bed tonight, safe, back in Guard HQ. A memory of Kayla dancing through tai chi forms, her skin glowing like a sunset in the starlight, came unbidden, but Zach shoved it brutally aside. At least he'd be able to remember her. If the Twins found him here, in the heart of a Searcha operation, he wouldn't even have that.

"*We're worried about your safety*," Terra said. "*It sounds like it's time to pull the plug.*"

Relief washed through Zach. "*You found another way to fix the knot!*"

The silence stretched; Zach's heart sank with each endless second.

"*Not yet.*"

"*You close?*" Zach swam over the same sunken tree a third time, dreading the answer.

"*No, we're losing ground, and we're running out of even the wild ideas.*"

Stomach twisting into knots, Zach answered, "*Then I have to stay.*"

"*If you're in a coma, you won't be able to help.*"

"*My cover is intact. If you can get whatever is inside this box to safety, if I can ever find it, and I can find a way to get out of here before the field agents show up, I'll be okay. Like Alexis said, this cloud cover is bad. They couldn't have picked a worse day to do this if they'd tried.*"

There was a long pause. Zach could picture Alexis, Brian, and Terra arguing.

The tire materialized in the flashlight's beam. Just past it, something glowed a soft, iridescent white.

"*Crap, found the globe thing.*" Zach poked it before picking it up. "*Looks like it shows magic levels, like some of Russel's tools. Searcha has some stuff like this. I don't think it's a dangerous find.*"

"*A bit of luck, good,*" Brian said.

"Take it to Searcha, and then go back to searching for the box. We've working on a plan," Terra said.

"Can do." Zach swam to shore, focusing on bringing his shadow back under control.

Kayla and Hannah were still at the far end of the beach, digging something up. Half a dozen crows were scolding them or egging them on from the roots of a washed-up tree. Zach couldn't worry about what they were doing now. He could only control his small part.

Miranda gave him one of her rare authentic smiles and accepted the globe.

"Any sign of our backup yet?" Zach asked.

"We're the backup," Miranda said. "But no, we're still on our own for now. Keep watch for the Guard."

Zach saluted. Miranda gave a nod of acknowledgement and moved to the pile of supplies in the center of the beach.

Zach checked his oxygen-tank levels: still enough air. Back down in the dark water, fear welled up, but he was prepared this time, and it faded faster. He almost stumbled onto the half-submerged chunk of boat. He would have found it sooner if he hadn't been following such a repetitive search pattern.

The weathered wood panels had peeling paint, with the name *Otis* barely visible under the muck, but the cloven hoofprints, as if a unicorn had walked across it, stood out. Storm really had been here. Beside it was the box.

"Found it," he said.

"That was fast," Terra replied.

"Sorry. I can keep my search pattern up. Buy us more time."

"We're almost ready. Can you try to open the box?"

Zach frowned. "*Might destroy whatever is in there.*"

"*That would make our lives easier.*"

Zach laughed through the regulator.

He swam down to the box, pushing air into his sinuses to adjust the pressure in his ears as he went. The ancient combination lock would be complicated for anyone who wasn't a Shadow. Zach didn't even have to force it open with the dive knife in his belt. After several spins of the dials to the locations the shadows showed, the box cracked open. Air escaped in bubbles, and water rushed in. There was a waterproof scroll made of animal hide inside. It wouldn't be destroyed fast enough for Zach to be able to safely take it to Miranda. He shared the info with his team, put the scroll back in the box, and hooked the box to his belt.

Keeping up his search pattern, he almost missed the slight glow of a magical artifact. He dropped down closer to get a look, but warning stripes of yellow, red, and black appeared in the surrounding shadows.

"*Crap, I found another one.*"

"*What is it?*" Terra asked.

Carefully, Zach swished water at the object. Murk dropped visibility before the current cleared his view. "*It looks like an unnaturally narrow, double-edged, bone-white blade, about five inches long, with backwards-facing serration. I'm getting warnings of venom, maybe, from the shadows. And—*" Zach concentrated and tried to keep his flashlight still. "*A ray?*"

"*Any chance it's an enchanted stingray barb?*" Russel asked. "*I've run across several reports of one that would fit the timeline.*"

Zach shrugged. "*Well, that would explain the shape.*"

"It is said to have been enchanted using the venom from a monster that resembled a stingray. But, of course, golems don't fossilize, so it would have been made from an actual stingray barb and then enchanted." Russel started asking questions to verify the theory, but Terra hushed him.

"I should be able to pick it up by the handle and not get hurt," Zach said. *"Do you want it? It wasn't on Searcha's list of things for me to look for, so they won't miss it, and I don't want to risk leaving it here for the Twins to find. The site is shallow enough that they can reach it with snorkel gear."*

The silence told him they were communicating without him. Zach swam back and forth, keeping the artifact in his line of vision.

"We have a plan. It's going to hurt and you can say no," Terra said.

Zach exhaled a long stream of bubbles. *"What is it?"*

"Do you think the venom from it will kill you? Normal stingrays don't. I just looked it up to be sure. The big problem is the wound can be deep or dirty. That's what kills a very tiny number of people, but if we give you a shallow cut, it'll hurt like crazy, but you should be fine. If this thing is on the same level."

Zach pulled his mask away from his face, letting it fill with water. Then he pressed the top of his mask against his forehead with one hand, ensuring the top seal and loosening the bottom. Breathing out his nose, he forced air into the mask, displacing the water until the mask was clear again.

"The pain," he answered, finally, *"will hide my shadow and maybe even get me out of here before a Searcha member who will recognize me gets here."*

"Mmph."

It was impressive that Terra could transmit such a dubious sound as a thought. She didn't like it, but she, they, were asking it anyway. They wouldn't do that if there was a better choice available.

Zach nodded. *"There's no skull and crossbones, just poison. Let's do it."*

"Then get the spellbook as fast as you can and get out of there."

"I'll do my best."

"Oh," Alexis added, *"I think we should call the golem forming from the Lockhouse Knot Chessie. It's vicious, like a female lion, so I'm going with female. And Chessie is the name of the imagined Chesapeake Bay sea monster, so I think it's fitting."*

Even without seeing their faces, Zach could tell the others thought it was a silly name. But it made the monster less terrifying. Zach carefully picked up the hilt end of the knife and waved it like he was knighting an invisible person. *"I like it. She is thus named Chessie."*

"It'll be good to have you home," Alexis said.

Zach couldn't agree more. He'd made some progress building trust with Ara that morning, even if it had damaged his peace of mind. Next step, find out where she was keeping the book.

Zach had added barely a dozen lines to his search grid when the beam of Russel's flashlight flickered through the water. Zach grinned at the sight of the spellcaster swimming his way.

Russel had a rebreather regulator, so there was no bubble trail. He gave Zach a wood tablet with a fake code on it that was gibberish but written in magical ink. If all went according to plan, it would have Searcha chasing their tails. As long as the tied team didn't see through it. Either way, Zach needed to be out of there.

Zach swapped out the scroll for the tablet and relocked the box.

Russel accepted the scroll and waited.

Right. The slash to his hand wasn't the worst part of the new plan. Zach pulled the earbud out of his ear and handed it to Russel. There couldn't be any trace on him or in the water that pointed to the Guard. But the loss of contact hurt in a way a knife couldn't. Switching to dive language, he gave Russel the okay hand signal. Russel returned it then swam away.

Zach clipped the box with the fake tablet back on his belt. Frowning at the stingray knife, Zach braced himself then sliced lightly into the pad of three fingers on his left hand. He'd say he got cut by prying the box loose.

Weird. There was only a mild stinging from the water as the current pulled a small cloud of his blood away. *Maybe I did it wrong?* His heart sped up. He stared dumbly at the knife.

The pain hit suddenly and built rapidly. Burning. Zach dropped the knife. It wouldn't hurt if Searcha found it, but no point in making it easy. Using his flippers, he kicked sediment over the knife, then focused on getting safely out of the water without hurting his eardrums or his lungs. He wasn't down deep enough to worry about the bends.

He staggered to shore with the box. *Yep, there really is an impressive amount of pain.*

"What happened?" Miranda asked.

Zach handed her the box and sank to his knees on the sand. "Hard to see down there. Water is too dark. Dug the box out and cut my hand on something. Something magical, I think. Wow, it hurts." He swayed, fighting to stay upright.

The pain completely blocked out his shadow. It blocked out most of his ability to think. He yanked the mask off his face and wiped at the tears welling up. He wasn't sad, just the pain leaking.

"Did you get the artifact that cut you?" Miranda asked.

Zach gave her his best are-you-a-moron look.

"I think he's poisoned." Hannah grabbed his arm and helped him to his towel.

"Any idea what kind? Or what we do about it?" Miranda asked.

Worry lining her face, Hannah put her hand out for Kayla, who immediately took it.

Huh? I must look as bad as I feel if Hannah is worried about me. The thought felt distant, as if someone else was thinking it.

"His fingers are turning blue!" Kayla warned.

"Should we start with cleaning the wound?" Ara asked.

"Should we suck it out like snake venom?" Ben asked.

Miranda waved him off. "That's an old wives' tale."

A half-dozen crows landed in the sand a safe distance away, adding their opinions in raucous caws no one understood.

The detached, distant part of Zach wanted to laugh at the farce, but he wasn't fully connected to his body. His hand was on fire and swelling. The burning, blinding pain was moving up his arms.

There was something about the crow's shadows. Puzzling over them was a welcome distraction. They had the same texture as the shadow hounds. *They could see magic!* Like some people, like Prince and Nobel. Searcha was too dense to have noticed.

The stupidity continued around Zach. There was no first-aid kit on the beach or in the van. That was something that the Guard hadn't accounted for when they were making the plan. Terra and Alexis leaving the house without one would be like a superhero without a secret identity. Wadding up his shirt in his hands stopped the bleeding, but it didn't help the pain.

Zach just sat there, cradling his hand, rocking back and forth. He couldn't care that the Tied Team was coming. There was nothing but blinding pain.

Twenty

Kayla
Day 6 of the Lockhouse Knot Leak
Wednesday morning
Eastern Shore, MD

It hurt to look at Zach, knees to his chest, clenching his injured hand. A sea of pain on the isolated splash of sand. Kayla couldn't stand it, but Hannah needed her magic, maybe even her focus. Kayla breathed into her discomfort and let Hannah's fingers dig into her arm. Kayla's brain cleared. *I can be here.*

While Kayla was focused on not fleeing, Hannah had figured out it was a stingray barb knife, and Miranda googled it on her phone.

"Captain John Smith was stung by a stingray, thought he was going to die," Kayla thought, then realized she'd done so out loud. *Really, Kayla? What an unhelpful thing to say.*

"He's not going to die," Miranda announced, then turned to the crows and flapped her folder at them. "Will you shut up?"

With angry caws, they returned to their broken tree.

"His fingers are really blue," Ben said.

"Or lose his fingers," Miranda said.

Relief, almost as powerful as the earlier pain, washed through Kayla. She edged back from the crowd, but Hannah still gripped her arm.

"How do we treat it?" Hannah asked.

"Clean the wound, and it'll heal in time," Miranda said. "He's young enough that he shouldn't get heart palpitations or anything, and it's just a scrape. He'll be fine."

"What about the pain?" Hannah pressed.

"Apparently, hot water helps. But he'll be fine. We need to keep this site secure until our agents get here."

Kayla had never seen Hannah look Miranda full in the face. "His shadow is bleeding pain. It's making it hard to read anything. Wouldn't it be helpful if Jason and Ben take him back to camp in the van while the rest of us protect the site? Help clear up the shadows? Then Jason could come back for us?" She presented the idea as if it were a question, but it wasn't one.

Miranda froze.

Hannah raised an eyebrow, let her eyes flick to Miranda's shadow, and then held her gaze.

Miranda's glower darkened before she collected herself and smiled warmly. "Great idea. Jason, Ben, take Zach to Tidal Water. Ben, you can stay and look after him. Jason, come back to get us."

Respect for Hannah warmed Kayla. She squeezed Hannah's trembling hand in support.

Hannah nodded to Miranda. "Shall Kayla and I go back to looking for artifacts?"

Again, it wasn't a question, but Miranda grabbed it and pushed forward. "Yes. And Ara, I want you tagging and bagging."

Kayla walked with Hannah down the beach, but couldn't turn her attention to looking for artifacts until Zach, supported by Jason and Ben, had disappeared towards the van.

"That was impressive," Kayla said when they were far enough down the beach.

Hannah let out a long, shuddering breath. "Miranda gets focused. She wasn't paying attention to how much pain Zach was in. She just needed a gentle reminder that we can stay on mission and ease suffering at the same time."

"You don't like Zach."

"I really don't, but no living thing should be in that kind of pain if it can be helped, and more importantly"—Hannah gave a shrug—"his pain was overpowering everything else in the shadows, making it impossible to do my job."

"Any sign of any more artifacts?" Miranda called.

"Not yet," Hannah called back, then dropped her voice. "We should focus."

"What did you see in Miranda's shadow?"

Hannah kicked at the muddy sand liberally sprinkled with crow footprints. "I was bluffing. She has normal stuff she'd rather keep to herself, insecurities and the like, but I've never figured out why she's so worried about it."

"Are you going to be in trouble with her?"

"Shouldn't be, this time. If I push her again, though, there will be consequences. And if we could find a spectacular artifact, that would help a lot."

"Let's see what we can find, then." Kayla smiled.

"This light is terrible for reading shadows. Maybe you could use your Shiner ability to help?" Hannah asked tentatively. "Artifacts should stand out against the debris."

"I'll try." Kayla had hoped her magic would come in handy, but so far, she hadn't been able to tap into it. If she was with Zach, maybe she'd have a chance. Taking a deep breath, Kayla tried to remember how she was connected to magic, to the world. Sinking into her feet. Feeling her body in space. The strands around her caught the low light. Or maybe it was easier because Hannah was holding her arm.

That was an uncomfortable thought; Kayla quickly buried it with a bounce. The strands faded. Sighing deeply, Kayla uncovered the thought and breathed into it. Hannah was a Shadow, Shadows enhanced a Shiner's abilities the way a Shiner enhanced theirs. No big deal. It didn't have to mean anything more.

The thought nagged at her again before dissolving in an exhale. The strands glowed into visibility. Kayla scanned them curiously, careful not to put too much pressure or edge towards desperation, she was just interested to see what they might show her.

"There!" The strands nestled around a glowing flat object mostly buried in the sand. One of the crows had been digging at it earlier.

Hannah let go of her so Kayla could race over and start digging it out. She had it almost free when Hannah caught up. "What is it?" Kayla asked, pulling out the slate slab with carvings of eyes and salamanders and bats and other assorted weirdness.

"I don't know," Hannah said, puzzled.

"You found a scale!" Ara said. "See, you put your ingredients in this square here, and a quartz crystal here, and the crystal will roll to the weight of your ingredient. I've been hoping we'd get one! The alchemists in Richmond have one. It's for measuring exact amounts for potion making! This will make our lives so much easier!"

"Great find," Miranda said to Kayla.

"It was a team effort."

Miranda's smile widened. "I'm glad to see you two working together so well."

Kayla wanted to bite her own tongue. She'd wanted to prove abilities, and this could have been her chance. Nope, Kayla would not take back her words. Hannah needed the support against Miranda after putting her neck out for Zach. There'd be other times for Kayla to prove herself.

"Here, Ara." Kayla handed her the slab, stood up, and dusted the sand off her leggings. She was going to add that they should encourage the crows, because they seemed to have a knack for finding magical things, but Miranda was shooing them off.

Rolling her eyes, Kayla said to Ara, "We're going to keep looking."

They had just finished uncovering a tarnished brass compass case that had Hannah hearing *Pocahontas* music when the agents arrived. Kayla guessed it was Captain John Smith's, but didn't have time to voice the thought.

Dressed in combat black, the agents were clearly the cool kids. Kayla was almost surprised there wasn't a natural wind fan blowing back their clothes and hair and making them look even more badass.

The Tied Twins were in the front. At first glance, Kayla didn't notice they were identical. The Shiner had her head up and chest out, no jacket over her black tank top, despite the chill in the air, showing off her glowing pink markings that matched the neon highlights in her hair. The Shadow looked like she was disappearing into her baggy black jacket, her gaze down and her hood pulled low, hiding her expression.

Alchemists flanked the Twins, like in a movie poster, their cargo pants and belts loaded with supplies.

"Subtle they are not," Kayla murmured to Hannah.

Hannah smiled slightly. "No. They're in uniform today. They go undercover when they risk drawing attention. Out here in the middle of nowhere, looking professional is the better call. People are less likely to call the cops. They'll assume they're SWAT or something."

"Fair." Kayla grinned. Though she suspected pink highlights weren't standard issue for SWAT.

"Thank you for holding down the site," the Shiner said, her voice carrying easily to the whole beach. "We'll take it from here."

The alchemists went straight for the bagged-and-tagged area. Ara clearly didn't want to hand over her new scale, but stepped back.

The Shiner walked up to Miranda; her Shadow hung back a half step. "Looks like you had an incident."

"One of our team cut themselves on a sharp, poisoned, magical object of some kind. It's been dealt with." Miranda said. "Though the object wasn't recovered."

The Shiner watched the water and waved an arm around. Kayla realized she was wrapping it around a strand. The narrow white knife flew out of the water. The Shiner caught it neatly by the handle.

"This object?" There was a light of scorn in her eyes.

Miranda inclined her head, almost low enough to be a shallow bow, and stepped back.

"Clear out your people and equipment. I want you ready to go when your transportation gets here."

Miranda nodded again.

The Twins turned away and walked towards Kayla and Hannah.

"I gather you two are the up-and-coming team we've been hearing about. Looks like you did a good job securing and scavenging the site. We're the Twins." The Shiner offered her hand to Kayla.

Kayla shook it. "Nice to meet you." She included the Shadow, but wasn't sure she should even look at her; it was as if the Shadow wasn't a full person. Kayla hesitated, but she really wanted to know. "How'd you do the knife thing?"

The Shiner glanced to her Shadow, as if giving her permission to speak.

"There is a large splatter of blood and pain on the beach. Like bleach, eating everything else away," the Shadow said, not lifting her eyes.

"It's tied to the knife," the Shiner said.

"I showed her where."

"Once I knew that, it was easy to pull on the other end of the strand," the Shiner finished.

Kayla shivered. "It was really cool."

The Shiner smiled faintly. "You'll be impressed with the extent of your abilities when you're fully tied. We look forward to seeing you in Richmond."

"We still have a ways to go," Kayla said.

"I wouldn't drag your feet," the Shadow said.

"Miranda does a decent job with the alchemists, but she's too afraid of Shadows and Shiners to help them reach their full potential," the Shiner said.

Kayla gaped.

"Those who can't do, teach," the Shiner said with a smirk. "You'll see what I mean when you get down to Richmond, where the real Searcha is."

"We're looking forward to it," Hannah said. Subtly, she nudged Kayla in the back to move.

"Great to meet you." Kayla nodded to each of them before heading to Ara to help haul the equipment back to the road.

Breathing into the trapped feeling in her chest was hard when her mind kept skipping around. Fully controlling her powers and graduating to agent was the plan. Securing protection for her family during the Unavoidable Upheaval was vital, but could she honestly get there without Hannah? Was she fooling herself? If Searcha was so much more than Tidal Water, how was she ever going to be strong enough on her own to swim in those waters? She couldn't imagine pulling an object she'd never touched or seen before off the bottom of the river.

"I'm proud of you," Hannah murmured, as they both picked their way through the marsh, their hands full of equipment. "You handled that well."

"Talking with the Twins?"

"Yes. You saw how the Shiner takes the lead. Just like you did. You didn't need to ask about the knife. I could have explained that to you later, but otherwise you did awesome."

Kayla tripped and slid several precarious steps before catching herself. She'd only done the talking because the Shiner had talked to her. Social cues weren't rocket science. Kayla hadn't been taking the lead. She'd just interacted like a human being. How was she supposed to know Hannah would have the answer about the knife?

It had been as much a compliment as a question. Kayla could talk to strangers without mucking it up.

Taking a deep breath, Kayla steadied herself. It was stupid to overreact, Hannah meant well. Kayla was sick and fed up with conscious breathing.

"I appreciate your support," Kayla said to Hannah, without looking at her, then jumped ahead. "Ara, want to see if we can get a basketball game together when we get back?"

Ara smiled. "I think we can do that. We deserve a break from work after all we accomplished today."

"We found some cool stuff. What do you think that box contains?" Kayla was happy to chat with Ara through the rest of the cleanup and all the way back to camp. For the moment at least, she could tune out her unwanted thoughts and emotions.

Twenty-One

Zach
Day 9 of the Lockhouse Knot Leak
Saturday afternoon
Tidal Water, MD

Zach waited all day for kitchen duty. Trying to find a moment, where Hannah wasn't watching, to maneuver Ara into giving him a tour of her lab and showing him where she was keeping the grimoire had proved challenging. Convincing Jason that an evening of food prep and dishwashing was just what was needed to knock some of the arrogance out of Zach had proved tricky, but doable. Finding out when Ara was on kitchen duty—and Hannah wasn't—was as simple as reading the posted schedule.

Zach's left hand was healing nicely, considering that three days ago he'd understood why Captain Smith had told his men to dig him a grave after being injured with the same venom. Kayla had blushed with embarrassment the night before when he'd reminded her she'd mentioned Smith on the beach. Laughing, he'd encouraged her to finish the story. After all, Smith hadn't needed that grave.

Spending time with Kayla was all too easy. Zach shouldn't have given her one of his sketches of Storm on the beach; she'd been so delighted. He should have figured out a way to discourage her from joining him for his morning tai chi and evening stretching by the water, but he told himself that he didn't want her getting suspicious and that his lusting for her in front of Hannah protected his cover.

It was tempting to wall himself off now to guard against the pain of walking away later, but he just tried to be grateful for the opportunity to get to know her—something that never would have happened if everything had gone according to plan at the lockhouse.

He needed that as a silver lining, because the trick with the knife had resulted in a consequence Alexis hadn't foreseen.

Nightmares of waves and teeth had woken him less than twenty-four hours after he'd cut his finger with the stingray barb. Drawing the shadows in the dawn light, he'd unraveled what they'd been warning his sleeping brain about. The scent of his blood in the water, magnified by magic venom, had floated down the bay. The sea monster golem, resembling a snakehead fish, paused while gutting a sturgeon five times her size to sniff the water. She'd tasted his blood before, when the magic that made her scalded him on the trail. Feeding was building her strength, strength she needed to hunt for her knot. It was slow going, but magical prey, Zach's Shadow flesh, would fuel her far more than mundane sea creatures.

His drawings showed that Chessie, growing in size and speed with each fish she devoured, was making good time. Zach estimated he had three, maybe four more days, before she crashed into Tidal Water to eat him.

It's fine. Zach tried to shake the fear. *Just moves up my timetable a bit.* He walked into the kitchen. "What are we making?"

Ara didn't look up from the three-ring binder. "The meal plan says tacos."

"Nice, sounds easy," Zach said.

"We had tacos last week, the cleanup was awful. So many dishes." Ben sighed.

Zach smiled. "At least there shouldn't be many pots."

"True. If we get the ground beef started now, we can clean it before dinner," Ara said. "Afterwards, we can just throw everything else in the dishwasher, which is good. Miranda has a presentation planned for tonight."

"What kind of presentation?" Zach asked.

Ara shrugged. "I don't know. Usually she delegates."

"Sounds interesting," Ben said.

Zach's brow furrowed. *One challenge at a time.* The terrible lighting in the kitchen meant the shadows offered no help with his mission.

"Ara, you're the head alchemist, and this looks like potion crafting to me. Want to run the show?" Zach asked, trying to use the truth to win brownie points.

She smiled and surveyed her troops. "Ben, you've been chopping all day, want a break?"

"Please," Ben said.

"You're in charge of cooking the ground beef, then. Zach, you're in charge of chopping, start with the guacamole ingredients. I'll start cleaning up the mess that's already here."

Zach nodded. Rushing would tip his hand. After the second cabinet he checked, Ara handed him the cutting board he was looking for.

"You do a lot of chopping in the lab?" Zach asked casually, as red onions stung his eyes.

"Not all the time, but today I was processing a big batch of clover root sent from Richmond, because they don't have the *time* to process their own potion ingredients." Ben rolled his eyes. "All those tiny roots and very detailed instructions. Took freakin' forever."

"I checked over your work before I left the lab. You did a good job," Ara said.

Ben huffed. "It was easy, just boring as hell."

"What is clover root used for?" Zach asked, rinsing a jalapeno.

Ben shrugged.

"Alchemy doesn't work like that." Ara said. "The ingredients are specific to the potion, not the other way around. Of course, they won't tell us what they want it for."

Barely stopping himself from calling bullshit, Zach focused on chopping until the jalapeno was added to the green plastic mixing bowl. Searcha must be missing the several volumes of spellcraft theory Sadie had meticulously translated. *Good to know, but not what I'm looking for.* Zach moved to washing the cilantro, before carefully picking his words.

"I thought alchemy was like cooking, but if the ingredients don't do certain things, how do they work?"

"Magic," Ara said with a laugh. "But I think it has more to do with how they are prepared. Occasionally the same ingredient prepared differently works, but more often than not, it blows up in your face."

"Literally, Ara has a potion blow up in her face like once a week," Ben teased.

Ara put her nose in the air. "Discovery takes risks. If, when, my current project works, it will be amazing."

"What does it do?" Zach asked, popping a piece of tomato in his mouth.

"Hatches a fire salamander."

Zach choked on tomato mush. Coughing, he got a glass of water. When he could breathe clearly again, he asked, "Like a living creature? Like the unicorn?" Elliot would argue that technically, Storm wasn't really alive, more a golem or magical robot, but that was a philosophical rabbit hole Zach was happy to leave for him and Alexis to hash out. To Searcha, it was all alive.

Ara smirked. "Yep. There's an entire section in Kayla's family's grimoire about creatures that can be hatched. I want to work my way up to a phoenix."

Zach gaped at her.

"How's the chopping going?" Ara teased.

Forcing himself to chuckle, Zach returned to dicing tomatoes. He shoved aside his horror at creating magical creatures and concentrated on circling back to the grimoire. "What are you going to do with a phoenix?"

"It'll keep me company in the lab."

"So cool, right?" Ben said. "Hopefully she can pull it off before I graduate—without blowing up something major."

Ara shoved him playfully, before turning back to Zach. "My goal is that one day there will be all sorts of mythological creatures running around Tidal Water. It'll be an oasis that will attract people all around the world to come here and train," Ara said.

"Sounds amazing," Zach said. He could see her point, if he pictured it like it would look in a graphic novel in which Searcha was as benevolent as it pretended. The colorful image in his head was devoured by the sea monster in the shadows. Sometimes his imagination was a killjoy.

Shaking himself, Zach tried to remember his goal and not cut his still tender fingers while he chopped. "What does alchemy actually look like in practice?" he asked.

Ara gave the Searcha textbook definition that Jason had given him, but Zach waved her off.

"I get, or actually, don't really get, the theory, but what does it look like? Do you stand in front of a big black cauldron stirring?"

Ben laughed. "More often than I'd think, but not normally. Why don't you come by the lab sometime, and I'll give you a tour?"

Zach forced a smile. *Wrong alchemist.* "That would be great."

"Just come early, less of a chance of something exploding," Ben stage-whispered.

Ara frowned, missing the affection in Ben's teasing. "Or you could come by tomorrow at one, and I'll show you around." Dropping her voice to give it a hint of suggestiveness, she said, "Give you the full tour."

Ben turned away, pretending to check the meat. The annoyance in his face was clearly what Ara had been going for. Couldn't she see it would push him away, not make him jealous enough to ask her out? Ben had written her off as out of his league as soon as he'd met her.

Zach gave his head a little shake and rolled his eyes at her. Ara put a hand on her hip and raised an eyebrow at Zach. She probably expected he could see in her shadow what she was doing.

Stop being an idiot, Zach scolded himself. Ara was giving him an in.

"I bet you give a great tour," Zach said, wincing internally. "I'm curious about this grimoire that tells you how to bring forth life."

Ara smiled. "It's kept behind locked doors, but I guess I could make an exception for you."

"I'd be grateful."

"Meat is simmering," Ben muttered. "I'll go set the tables."

Ara's eyes followed him as he took a stack of dishes to the dining room.

Zach wanted to throw his hands in the air, but focused on halving the avocados in silence. *Tomorrow, you'll see where the book is, analyze the security measures, sneak back in to retrieve it, and then get out.*

Kayla and Samantha arrived early to hangout and soon had Ben laughing. A game began involving setting the table and throwing a ball of used aluminum foil. Before long they had roped Ara in as well. Steeping in the aromas of taco seasoning, frying meat, and lemon soap, Zach enjoyed listening to them play and chat as he washed dishes. Searcha really had some good people working for them. He would miss them, he realized with surprise. Kayla of course, but he would miss the others too. Hannah walked in. *Well, most of them.* Zach bent his head to scrub a charred bit in the frying pain.

His invitation to case the lab secured, Zach's mind turned to contemplating what Miranda was going to say. Presentations after dinner were a regular thing; Ara had done one the night before on an enchantment-breaking powder. She'd doused three different magical flames with the glittering dust. Zach had taken careful mental notes, even as he'd kept his distance—a stray bit of powder could damage his mirage spell. *Miranda didn't do alchemy or have magic, though, so what could she have to present?*

After dinner, trainees and staff gathered in the main common area and settled into the furniture or on the floor. Zach leaned against the back wall, hands in his pockets, trying to project boredom that he didn't feel. There was little he could make out in Miranda's shadow, even before Jason dimmed the lights.

The room fell quiet as Miranda walked over to the empty area that functioned as a stage.

"Good evening," Miranda said.

Zach didn't bother parroting back with the others.

"I'm aware some of you were surprised by the speed and firmness with which I handled a traitor in our ranks." Miranda's eyes landed on Ara before moving on. "Magic is so wondrous we can forget sometimes that this isn't a game. I could go on and on about the theory behind that fact. But an illustration will serve us better. Would you like to know how I came to Searcha?"

There were enthusiastic calls from the group.

Curiosity burning brighter, Zach slouched deeper against the wall.

With the projector remote in her hand, Miranda brought up the first slide, an overhead photo of a jungle. "Just over a dozen years ago I was working for a company that was searching for rainforest plants and animals that could cure modern diseases. On a trip to South America to coordinate with our people onsite, I heard rumors about an indigenous tribe with extraordinary healing abilities. I introduced myself to the scientist who was going to investigate and accompanied him and his team."

Zach's breath caught as the rainforest dissolved into a group shot. Miranda looked nearly the same, just a bit younger. Beside her was a rangy, weathered man who looked like he'd spent his life trekking the globe. Next to him was a man who looked like a local guide and three students. It was the lanky students to the right that had Zach double-checking that Hannah wasn't watching his shadow. Seth, traitor to the Guard, looked like he was just out of high school. He was tanner than Zach had ever seen him and had a carefree grin that made him harder to recognize than his youth. Still, it was the man Zach had considered family until last fall.

Giving himself a hard mental shake, Zach tried to take careful note of the other people so he could sketch them later. A thoughtful-looking petite woman with brown hair, and a paunchy man with twinkling, dark eyes, both probably graduate students, rounded out the group.

"Dr. Beebe was a talented and visionary scientist. It took us two days through the jungle to reach the tribe." Miranda clicked to a slide of a smiling group of natives.

"The people of the village were happy, healthy, and in harmony with the natural world in a way I'd never seen before nor since. Birds would talk with them, bugs and snakes wouldn't bite them, and jungle cats didn't stalk them. The plants seem to unfurl and hand them food. They were magic users. There were only a few loose knots of magic in their corner of the wilderness, but they used them to their fullest potential.

"We had to earn their friendship before they explained what was happening and why it only worked in this place." She clicked to a slide of her sitting with a group of locals and scientists, all laughing and talking together. A small child was perched on Seth's lap, and more were gathered around; he seemed to be telling them a story. A young woman was showing Miranda how to weave a basket. Several more slides showed a thriving community. "It's a time in my life I look back and treasure," she said, but her shadow reflected a turbulent swirl of white light and angry flames.

"They told us their potions didn't work beyond their territory, but Dr. Beebe wanted to test the hypothesis. Magic had too many lifesaving applications for the rest of the world to ignore. We left." Miranda swallowed hard.

If it weren't for her shadow, Zach would have bought her heartbroken tone.

"It took us longer to return to the village than we'd hoped. Bad weather, local politics, and so on. When we finally trekked back . . ." The next slide showed the village in ruins. The people and children were gaunt and broken.

"We were too late to save them. The Guard had come, slain the unicorn guardian and tied the magic, taking it away. Now that the villagers could no longer protect themselves, the logging companies and cattle farmers were moving in. Starvation and disease were consuming the community. The villagers were going to retreat deeper into the jungle and look for a new source of magic, but they didn't expect to make it."

Outrage, horrified gasps, and murmurs erupted around the room. Zach struggled to understand what he was hearing. The Guard, his Guard, had never sent people there, not that he knew of, definitely not in his lifetime. There were other branches, in other places, distant cousin organizations, but they were supposed to be focused on buying and selling antiques, not believing in their power anymore.

"This is why I do what I do. I couldn't save those villagers back then. But now, with years of hard work and planning, we can save magic."

Zach gaped as the trainees cheered. *There has to be a flaw in Miranda's argument.* He tried to swallow, but his mouth was dry. Those villagers had to have been in jeopardy from magic. She must have misunderstood, even as her every word, every flicker of her shadow, pulsed with an absolute belief that what she was saying was right and true. Zach couldn't find the counterargument, the gaping logic hole that had to be in the middle of her belief. She couldn't be right.

"Magic weaves everything together in one harmonious whole," Miranda continued, her voice swelling with passion. "It's a fact I've felt, seen, and tasted. But the powerful, greedy, and careless have ignored this in favor of personal gain. Colonists and conquering armies decimated native cultures across the globe, tying their magic and doing untold damage to the planet. Those same bastards wrote the history books, trumpeting progress. One marvel of science after another, disconnected from that harmony, crushes the unfortunate in the wheels of progress while the planet dies beneath our feet.

"Every evil in our modern world stems from these broken connections with each other, the planet, and magic. Setting magic free will cause Unavoidable Upheaval as the selfish and small-minded cling to what they have, but the future will be ours again. Not some dystopian aftertimes, but a harmonious, glorious world worth fighting for!"

Hands trembling, Zach clapped with the rest of the cheering room, fighting for his cover as his mind scrambled to find footing.

Slowly the crowd quieted, and Miranda asked for questions.

"How did they take away the magic of the village?" Nathan asked.

"Once magic is knotted, caged, it can be taken anywhere." Miranda shook her head sadly, hiding her rage well. "There had been a push to get the natives to leave for a while, but it wasn't until a member of the Guard stepped in that the cattle ranchers could have their way. I'm sure Lewis, whatever his name was, was paid well for his services." Something dark and dangerous slipped onto her face. "It's not much consolation, but he didn't live long enough to enjoy his ill-gotten gains."

Zach's hands clenched into fists in his pockets. Lewis, all sunshine and fun, had died overseas when Zach was in elementary school. *Shit!* It had been South America. Heart attack had been the official cause, but Elliot had always believed magic was involved. If Miranda's attitude and shadow implied what he thought, Elliot had been right—Lewis was murdered because of magic.

Anger burned in Zach's chest, more comfortable than the questions Miranda's speech had raised. The camp leader hadn't been the one responsible, but she knew what happened and was glad. Miranda preached harmony, but agreed with murder, was that enough to invalidate her argument? Zach looked back up at the slide.

The sad faces of the natives stared at him. For once, maybe, the Guard hadn't been making the world a safer place. The child who'd been sitting happily with Seth looked down with sad, sunken eyes. The images were going to haunt his sketches and his nightmares tonight. What was so wrong with a tiny splash of magic in a distant corner of the world?

He could almost hear Elliot's gruff voice. *Maybe none of that magic was doing serious harm, but once it was discovered, dangerous artifacts could be brought into the contamination zone. Even a small spill is a crack in the world's protection. Just look what that little bit of magic caused. Clearly Miranda and the others hadn't been able to let it go. Because here we are today, with Searcha trying to tip the scales from that splash to a flood of toxic energy that would consume the world.*

Zach remembered the stomach-churning terrors in Baltimore last fall. Breathing out in relief, he unclenched his fists. *There. That's the gaping hole in Miranda's beliefs.* A little magic might be friendly enough, but like water behind a dam, each crack, each drip that slipped through, wasn't scary or dangerous on its own. However, it didn't take many cracks to bring the whole dam down. A wall of water would tumble out, drowning and destroying everything in its path. Magic would be worse than that; it wouldn't just be the towns downstream, it would be the entire world that would be lost to chaos and destruction.

Miranda was wrapping up questions. "When the Guard destroyed that little piece of paradise, they made a critical mistake, not only because those villagers were no threat to anyone, but also because Searcha was reborn that day. For over a dozen years we've been working towards bringing that connection and harmony back, not just to that patch of jungle, but to the world."

Samantha raised an uncertain hand.

Miranda acknowledged her with her eyebrows.

"Um, this is going to make me sound awful, but we're not going to have to live in huts without running water, are we?"

Miranda laughed with a delight she didn't feel. "No, of course not. Our version of living in harmony will look different. Connected to everything around us, we will be able to use science wisely, we'll be aware of the consequences of our actions in the bigger whole. I'm not proposing we give up our modern conveniences or technology, but we might find that, with magic, we'll be less reliant on the more superficial ones. We'll keep modern plumbing, though." Miranda smiled and people laughed. "As magic brings us so much closer to nature and each other, so much of the materialism, designed to make us feel inadequate and overwhelmed while the rich grow more powerful, will simply fall away.

"It will be difficult, challenging, and sometimes scary as the world shifts into balance. I will have to ask you to be brave time and time again, but I believe in each and every one of you.

"I can't describe what being in a place filled with magic feels like, to know how connected you are to the world and everything in it, but I can't wait to share it with each and every one of you."

The energy of the room was buoyant and excited. Zach worked to blend in or at least not draw attention. Miranda, standing at the head of the room in her designer clothes, made everything sound easy and right. It was all idealism with no plan apart from reintroducing magic. Even if everything Zach believed was wrong—even if the shadows had lied to him, and magic wasn't apocalyptically dangerous—she barely acknowledged the fallout that would result from power structures and economies breaking down. People pushing back, unable or unwilling to adapt to such rapid change. And mythological creatures wreaking untold damage on ecosystems that had long since moved on without them.

Miranda lifted her arms. "We spent the years gathering resources and preparing. Last fall was only our first move, but unlike chess, where each opponent takes turns, we're a boulder rolling down a steep hill. Magic, like gravity, is on our side. Soon we will pick up enough speed to be unstoppable. Only when the whole world is living in harmony with each other and with the planet will we rest."

The room cheered like a group ten times its size.

Zach was grateful the lighting was so poor. He didn't have a chance of hiding the fear in his shadow. But the child in the slide hollowed out a pit in Zach's stomach. Maybe catastrophe was the price that humanity would have to pay for living with such an obliviousness to the natural balance of the planet. Maybe magic didn't create that, it only illuminated it.

A serrated fin crested through the waves of the shadows, rising before falling away. That monster wasn't harmony, it was destruction incarnate. Maybe that small village in the jungle built a good relationship with magic, but clearly they hadn't been dealing with magic like the Lockhouse Knot or either of the knots locked in the Guard's vault.

Science, innovation, and hard work could repair the damage humanity had done to the planet and to society. It would take time, but like advancements in agriculture that had kept a growing world population from mass starvation in the mid-1900s, it would be done. It wasn't perfect. There would be consequences, but they'd be addressed. Magic wasn't the answer.

Pleased with that conclusion, Zach was glad the group was breaking up. He needed some fresh air, but he stopped in the doorway, looking back at the slide one last time. The pit gnawed at his gut, no matter how hard he tried to reason it away.

Twenty-Two

Kayla
Day 10 of the Lockhouse Knot Leak
Sunday afternoon
Tidal Water, MD

It was one of those glorious spring afternoons where no one should be inside writing dry reports on dusty history. The breeze, a perfect complement to the seventy-odd degrees of temperature, had sent Kayla's papers flying when she'd attempted to work on the porch. Spending her time wrangling paper wouldn't get her assignments done, so she'd relented and returned indoors. It was so unfair.

"You're right," Hannah said, coming through the front door.

"Huh?" Kayla looked up from the living room floor, where she was sitting in the middle of her spread-out notes. It didn't really help, but it looked cool, like she was solving a crime.

"You're right. It's too pretty to be indoors."

Kayla frowned, waiting for criticism to follow.

Hannah didn't seem to notice Kayla's annoyance. "It's Sunday, and you've been working hard. I talked Captain Fitz into letting us take the twenty-footer."

"Really?"

"Yes." Hannah smiled benevolently. "You deserve a break. Jason said you had a rough magic lesson this morning."

Kayla shook her head. The boat was tempting, but she was trying to avoid spending extra time with Hannah. *Besides, what is Jason doing gossiping about my lesson?* At least she hadn't blown anything up, like Ara. They'd heard today's explosion all the way from the grove of trees Jason had chosen for meditation practice. Making sure everyone was okay had been a needed break.

"You'll love this sailboat. Fitz just put it back in the water and rigged it up this morning," Hannah said.

"I'm supposed to have this stupid report done today." Kayla sighed. If she kept staring out the window, it was going to take all day and half the evening to finish.

"I got Jason to give you an extension. It really is beautiful out there."

Kayla had forgotten that sometimes Hannah could be cool. "Thanks!"

"No humidity and that warm sun. You should put on sunscreen before we go."

I'm not a child. It was on the tip of Kayla's tongue, but she bit it back. Hannah wasn't wrong. It was exactly the kind of spring day Kayla would wear a tank top for the first time and get burned.

Groaning, Kayla collected her papers. "I haven't sailed anything bigger than a sunfish. Can we get a group together?" More people would be a buffer between her and Hannah. *Does Zach enjoy sailing?*

"You'll pick it up fast enough. I have a really good feeling about this, but if you'd rather stay and work, I'll help you organize your notes and write your outline."

Kayla jumped up, shuffled her papers together, and headed towards her room. "Sailing sounds great. I'll get some sunscreen."

"Sunglasses too," Hannah called after her. "A hat if you have one. It's really bright on the water."

Kayla gritted her teeth. *Hannah is just being helpful.* Her jaw was still clenched when she joined Hannah with a baseball cap, sunglasses, spray sunscreen, and her water bottle.

"I've made us sandwiches," Hannah said, rinsing a plate and putting it on the dish rack. "Let's go."

"Thanks," Kayla said, though it would have been nice to have been asked first.

Less than half an hour later, Fitz was pushing them off from the dock. "I expect you and my boat back in one piece before sunset."

"Of course," Hannah said at the tiller.

The fumes from the little motor blew away in the stiff breeze as Kayla coiled the rope on the bow. Reluctantly, she moved back to the bench opposite Hannah's.

"We'll raise the sail when we get further out. Where do you want to go?" Hannah asked.

Kayla shrugged. "I figured you had a plan."

"You're welcome to pick. Here's the chart, take a look."

Unfolding the paper, Kayla blinked. It was strikingly similar to the map John Smith had made, which Kayla had a copy of in her notes. "Hey look, Stingray Point. That's where Smith was stung by the ray." Kayla pointed.

Hannah shook her head. "Too far away."

Kayla picked two more places of interest. One was too far, and the other the wind was wrong for. She was about to say that if Hannah had so many opinions, she should just pick, when a flock of crows caught her attention. "How about we go that direction for a while and see where it takes us?"

Hannah didn't look enthusiastic about the idea, but nodded. "Let's raise the sails." She turned the boat into the wind, put the motor in idle, and directed Kayla, even though Fitz had talked Kayla through everything before they left the dock. The two big white triangles of canvas flapped loudly and then quieted as they caught the wind. Hannah turned off the motor.

Kayla threw back her head and laughed with delight. The breeze tugged at her hair and clothes, making her want to take flight. The bow sliced through the low waves, like the start of a mighty adventure. The sunlight sparkled off the water, warming her skin even as the air whipped by, pulling the heat away.

"I thought you'd like it," Hannah said.

Doing her best to ignore the smug tone, Kayla said, "Way better than working on that report. Thanks."

Hannah beamed. "My best friend's family had a sailboat when I was growing up."

"Oh?" Kayla asked. It was worth encouraging any topic of conversation that didn't have to do with Tidal Water, training, or her apparently abysmal taste in music and film.

Hannah shared a story about sailing with her friend and then asked Kayla about her childhood. They talked about family trips and compared college experiences. Kayla relaxed, enjoying the conversation and the beautiful day. Hannah saw the world and experienced it differently than she did, which made the conversation more interesting, even if Kayla often couldn't understand how Hannah ended up somewhere or made a particular conclusion.

The water, land, marsh, and houses sliding by were all so interesting, Kayla didn't see the danger in swapping dating stories.

"What do you think of Zach?" Hannah asked, her tone overly casual.

Kayla sat up straighter and shrugged. *Has Hannah been working her way to that question since we left the dock?* "He seems to be settling in well."

"You've been spending a lot of time with him." Hannah didn't make it sound like a question or an accusation.

Tightening the port sheet an inch or two, though the sail's shape was fine, didn't keep Kayla's hands busy for long. "He's chill."

"You know it's against the rules to date him? Shadows and Shiners can't date."

Kayla hadn't realized the rule extended to dating, but it didn't matter. "We're just friends!"

Hannah scowled. "He wants in your pants."

Kayla laughed, blood flooding her cheeks. "Yeah, right." Part of her, the illogical, wild part that so often got her in trouble, wanted that to be true, but he'd been the one to push them towards friendship, and she was grateful. *Very grateful.*

"I'm serious. It's so uncomfortable trying to read his shadow. He's going to get himself in trouble and bring you down with him."

Bring me down with him? Kayla bit her lip and tried not to picture Zach laying her down on his jacket in the moonlight with kisses and exploring caresses. Warmth bloomed in her lower belly.

"Maybe you should respect his privacy and not try to read his shadow. Besides, we're just friends. He's not interested." *And I'm grateful*, Kayla lied to herself firmly. It was just her hormones that were ridiculously disappointed. *That's all.*

Hannah gave her a don't-be-an-idiot look. "I wouldn't be so concerned, except you like him back."

Hannah can't read my fantasies, can she? Looking away, Kayla scanned the tree-lined shore. Finally, she found her voice. "We're just friends, but that doesn't stop me from noticing how attractive he is. You're one to talk."

"What's that supposed to mean?"

"Jason." *Turnabout is fair play.* But Kayla was torn between anger and pity as Hannah tried to hide behind the brim of her sun hat. Hannah didn't have a simple crush on Jason that could be firmly ignored until it went away. Six months of knowing Jason and Hannah still looked up whenever he walked into a room.

"I'd never . . ."

"I know you wouldn't cross any lines. More's the pity. Probably do you both a lot of good."

Hannah looked genuinely horrified.

Relenting, Kayla pointed to the flock of crows. Some were circling, others were hopping around the tree tops. All were fussing loudly. "Wonder what has them so worked up?"

"You've turned the subject all around! My point is, you shouldn't be spending time with Zach."

"He's been teaching me tai chi, which helps me better understand my magic. Isn't that what everyone wants? Me to hurry up and learn magic?"

"He's newer to magic than you are. What does he know?" Hannah closed her eyes and dropped her head between her hands, as if she had a migraine. "What the hell is that music?!"

"What music?" Kayla asked before she realized Hannah was talking about the shadows.

Taking a deep breath, Hannah held it for a four count before letting it out slowly. She opened her eyes and hummed a few bars. "It's been playing on repeat since you picked this direction, but it keeps getting louder! Why won't it stop?"

Kayla listened more closely as Hannah hummed again. "It sounds like 'Just Around the Riverbend.' You know, from *Pocahontas*?"

"I don't like that movie," Hannah grumbled. "How am I supposed to know what it's trying to tell me?"

"But Captain Smith sailed this part of the Bay, just like we are. Maybe it's connected!" Kayla said with more enthusiasm than she felt—anything to push the conversation away from Zach.

"I don't give a shit about him either." Hannah put her hands over her ears, steering with her leg.

Kayla patted Hannah on the shoulder twice. "The shore is getting close." It was more than that. Something was tugging her towards land, like a rubber band attached to her gut. Kayla checked the distance again and froze. Between the gray trunks of a grove of trees was Storm.

Shaking Hannah's shoulder, Kayla pointed. "Look!"

Hannah dragged her head up, but they'd passed the grove and the unicorn was out of sight. "Yeah, the shore is close. We need to come about."

Kayla was almost positive Storm hadn't been a trick of her imagination. "Can we stop?"

"Stop?"

"Yes. That dock." It stuck out of a bit of forest, probably property of some mansion further back, but Kayla didn't care. "Just for a few minutes."

"We can't just—ow!" Hannah closed her eyes and held her head between her hands. "Fine. That dock better be in deep-enough water. If we run aground, I'm blaming you. But the shadows aren't going to give me any peace until you've done whatever you're supposed to."

Hannah started the engine, and Kayla lowered the sails. When they got close enough, Kayla jumped onto the dock and helped tie off the lines.

"Come on." Kayla started towards land.

Hannah double-checked the lines Kayla had tied before following.

Rolling her eyes, Kayla forced herself not to run, but if they missed Storm, Hannah would not be a fun companion on the sail back. "Come on!"

"Where are we going?"

Kayla ignored her. A creek too wide to jump blocked Kayla's way. No sign of Storm, but the sound of fussing crows gave her a direction, and her gut pulled her forward. Skipping a few strides to cover more ground, Kayla pulled ahead.

She skidded to a halt.

Storm stood among the silvery trunks of trees, as if waiting for her. The unicorn was as beautiful as she'd been in the mist. Her ears flickered, holding Kayla's gaze for a long moment. Eye contact broke when Storm turned her head and pawed the ground.

"What—" Hannah began as she caught up. Then she saw the unicorn.

Kayla shrugged. "I wasn't sure I'd actually seen her."

Storm nickered, like softly falling rain, in welcome.

Walking forward, Kayla offered her hand.

"Kayla?" Hannah said.

Brushing off her query like a mosquito, Kayla kept walking until Storm bumped her hand with her nose and let Kayla rub her neck. The smell of fresh summer rain clung to the unicorn's coat.

Storm nickered warmly, then lifted her head and looked Hannah over. The unicorn's nostrils flared, and she snorted.

Kayla wanted to say she totally understood how Storm felt, but resisted. "Storm, this is Hannah. Hannah, you remember Storm?" Catching herself, Kayla didn't add this wasn't the first time Storm had called. Better to not mention Zach again.

"Of course," Hannah muttered.

Storm sighed, then shook herself as if shaking off dust.

Kayla smirked at the dismissive greeting.

"She really is so beautiful," Hannah breathed.

Storm nickered again, like a small wave breaking on sand, and turned. Picking her way easily through the forest, she glanced back, as if to make sure Kayla was following.

"What's going on?" Hannah asked. "The shadows are like an orchestra, with rain and wind mixed among the strings and brass. It's incredible. But there is a thread that's off-step, as if it's trying to catch up, but it keeps tripping."

Storm snorted in impatience, or maybe agreement.

"Tidal Water should really teach a class on speaking unicorn." Wishing Zach was here, Kayla pushed a branch out of her face. "Come on, let's keep up."

Storm veered off the trail, towards the sound of the crows. Kayla smiled; she'd been right about the connection. Jumping over obstacles with the grace of a deer, Storm had to keep stopping for Kayla and Hannah to catch up.

Hannah tripped on the undergrowth, pinwheeling her arms to catch herself, and smacked her hand into a trunk. "Ow!"

Kayla sighed. The terrain wasn't that difficult. "You okay?"

"Yeah, fine. I don't like this. We're going to be late getting back if the wind changes. Or what if the owner of the dock takes the boat?"

Storm pawed the leafy ground.

Kayla hopped onto the trunk of a fallen tree. "You could go back and wait by the boat. I'll be back in a few."

"I'll get lost out here."

What is your magic good for then? She dug for patience. "Not much further. Didn't you say the shadows wanted us to go this way? So does Storm."

"I don't understand why she wants us to do anything. Nick's her person. He's the one who set her free."

Kayla shrugged. *Isn't Storm the guardian of the magic from her knot, not of any individual person?*

Ahead, a giant sycamore's root system had been undermined by the eroding creek and the tree had fallen, probably during the storm that had unearthed the *Otis*. Storm stood by the massive root ball and nickered over her shoulder at Kayla. Several crows took to the air. The rest watched with unnatural silence from the surrounding trees.

Holding onto a sapling for support, Kayla slid down the steep slope to the bank. "What is it, girl?"

Storm pawed at the tangle of roots, dirt, and rocks that was taller than Kayla. Sliding, Kayla picked her way to the unicorn's side and put a hand on the warm fur to steady herself. Storm pointed her horn at a twist of roots near the right side, about shoulder height. A warm prickle walked down Kayla's spine. There was something dark and tangled wedged between a piece of quartz and the root that had grown around the rock.

"Is there something there?" Hannah asked from the top of the slope. "The music is more insistent now, like it's begging for help."

Storm nickered, like the call of seabirds above the pounding surf. She reared slightly and pawed at the soil below the quartz, but the rock, root, and dark substance wedged between them stayed put.

Magic tingled up Kayla's arm from Storm, and the strands glowed into visibility. There was a cage of fine magic lines repelling Storm and holding the quartz in place.

"Let me see." Kayla picked up a sturdy stick, stepped on the end, and cracked it to give it a sharp edge. Carefully, she pulled away the weblike strands with her left hand and dug into the dirt with the stick in her right, trying to get leverage.

The hunk of quartz popped out. Kayla caught it before it hit the ground. White and clear, with a vein of rusty orange dancing through the middle, it was the size of a small apple. It glowed softly; a magical artifact.

Storm snorted at it and backed away, as if it might burn her.

Kayla pulled back her arm to throw it far away, but Storm whinnied. The crows cawed.

"You don't like it?" Kayla told her.

Storm tossed her head.

"But you don't want me throwing it away?" Shrugging, Kayla slid the rock into her pocket.

The unicorn blew out then pointed at the black tangle still wedged between the roots.

Hesitantly, half expecting the tangle to be alive, like some alien creature, Kayla peeled it loose. It was dark and glossy, the thickness of horsehair, and the size of a quarter. It was smooth and dry and . . . warm? Like a rock in the sun. Gently she turned it one way and then the other, and the sharp scent of tilled earth and freshly mowed grass brightened the air. The complex twist and tangle of strands begged to be untied.

Storm breathed a sigh that sounded very much like relief. The crows took to the air in a noisy flock. Sniffing the knot, Storm inspected it before butting Kayla affectionately with the side of her head.

"What happened?" Hannah asked.

With her horn, Storm pointed again at something. Kayla looked closer. A smooth piece of wood didn't fit with the roots. She slid out what might have been the blade of a paddle, with carvings on one side. Kayla brushed at the dirt. A carving of a tree stood out. *Is it growing out of a pile of bones?* But that didn't make any sense, so Kayla shrugged it off. The rest of the scrawl was indecipherable.

Her pockets weren't big enough. "Hannah, catch." Kayla tossed up the paddle piece.

Hannah retrieved the wood and turned it over in her hand. "What is going on?"

The unicorn gathered herself and jumped up the bank.

"Storm wanted me—us—to find something." Kayla slid the dark tangle into her other pocket and then scrambled back up the incline with considerably less grace than Storm. Hannah offered a hand when Kayla was almost at the top.

"Thanks," Kayla said, but made do with a root. "I'd rather not accidentally pull you down."

Hannah nodded, looking relieved when Kayla plopped onto solid ground.

Kayla pulled out the strand and showed it to Hannah. It almost hummed in her palm.

Hannah gasped. "It can't be?! It's a knot!"

Storm nickered in agreement.

"Oh . . . My . . . God. Oh, my God! I can't believe it!" Hannah squealed.

Storm nudged Kayla back the way they'd come.

"You're right," Hannah said to the unicorn. "We need to get this back to Tidal Water ASAP!" Hannah grabbed Kayla's free hand and dragged her towards the boat.

"Thank you," Kayla said over her shoulder to Storm.

The unicorn bowed as if to return the gratitude.

Reluctantly, Kayla turned back to the path and focused on keeping her footing as Hannah pulled her forward. The knot seemed to pulse in echo to Kayla's heart, each beat begging to be free.

Twenty-Three

Zach
Day 10 of the Lockhouse Knot Leak
Sunday evening
Tidal Water, MD

Ara's lab tour had given Zach everything he needed, but in his room afterward, an abrupt shift in magical energy interrupted his hurried note taking. The hairs on the back of his neck prickled as a shimmering, green glaze layered over the other colors in the shadows. Triple-checking that it had nothing to do with him or his impending grimoire heist, he finished his notes before leaving his room to find out what had changed. When he heard the rumors of an important meeting, his stomach knotted tighter.

Standing at the edge of the square, people murmuring and moonlit shadows rippling, he braced himself. It was eerily like the scene with Jade. Jason and Miranda stood in the middle, with Hannah and Kayla behind and to their right.

Not seeing his capture in the shadows was the only thing keeping him from edging towards Nick's car. It was just his imagination that had Jason dragging him forward and kicking him to his knees before Miranda. *It better just be my imagination.*

"Everyone here?" Jason's voice rang out clearly.

Zach shivered.

Captain Fitz nodded to indicate his head count was good. Dahlia, in an unusual display of public affection, was holding his hand.

Miranda triumphantly spread her arms wide to welcome them under the full moon. "Tonight is one of those moments the history books will remember. Kayla and Hannah's bond has grown so strong that the unicorn guardian has reached out to them and shown them something incredible."

Zach's eyes followed her wave of a hand to Kayla, standing stiffly beside Hannah. *Storm approached Kayla without me?* It shouldn't have hurt, but it prickled. At the same time, he didn't need to read the shadows around Kayla to know she wasn't happy with the camp leader's assessment of the situation.

Miranda continued. "Together, they discovered a treasure hidden by Captain John Smith in the early 1600s. From the inscription they found and the artifacts recovered from a shipwreck near here, we know Smith was a powerful and influential member of the Guard. He tied half a dozen knots during his time on the Chesapeake and countless more in his travels."

Zach put both hands on the rough wood railing, trying to shake the dark spots in his vision. His gut knew what was coming.

Miranda gave a laugh. "But I'm not here to talk about a man who paved the way for the colonial genocide of innumerable indigenous people by stripping them of their magic. I invited you here tonight because of what Kayla and Hannah found. It will leap us towards the harmonious world we're working so hard to build." Miranda held up a small but unmistakable tangle of dark strands. "We have the next knot!"

Zach ignored the splinters digging into his palms as he tightened his grip on the railing. *Can't let Miranda cut a knot!* Pushing his way to the front of the group would take time, though, and then what would he do? Try to wrestle it from her and run to the car?

As the crowd cheered, a distant part of his brain recognized he was going into fight-or-flight mode. Bad for clear thinking. Softening his gaze, he tried to take a deep breath. His chest hurt, but he pushed air in anyway.

The shadows! They weren't panicking. No gut punch of nausea. Zach's next breath was easier. There was none of the dread he'd felt when the Baltimore Knot had been found—or the Lockhouse Knot. There were happy flowers popping up in the moon-cast shadows, and even the ever-present waves were fading to the background. *Maybe she isn't cutting it today. Maybe they have to wait for a magical knife from their headquarters. Maybe the Guard already had a plan to intercept and capture the knot.*

Tension easing from his neck, Zach loosened his grip on the railing. The knot in Miranda's hand was small, too, less magic. Any additional drops in the world would be bad. Spells would be more powerful and more knots would be easier to find, but it could have been significantly worse. *Why did Storm help find this one when she helped stop the Baltimore Knot from being cut? Couldn't she see the difference between the Guard and Searcha?*

"Once upon a time, we would have had to untangle this knot to let the magic free, but now. . ." Miranda put out her right hand to Jason.

He placed a slim dagger, hilt first, on to it.

Air caught in Zach's throat.

Miranda crouched, dropping out of view. "Now, our alchemists have enchanted an entire supply of daggers. Let this be the daybreak of our new world!"

With a lightning-bright flash and a crack of air splitting, a rainbow of energy broke free, crashing around them in vivid contrast to the washed-out moonlight. It danced in white geometric designs across Miranda's face and lit the brightly colored markings on Kayla, Jason, and Nathan. For a heartbeat, the shadows around Zach were etched as if into metal. Mist boiled up where the light touched the ground.

Silence.

Silence, as if the universe was holding its breath.

His heartbeat in his ears, Zach blinked, trying to restore his night vision. Tension was a fist between his shoulder blades, and the shadows sharpened to a point as his adrenaline spiked.

Where is the knot's golem? Zach looked around for the monster. Miranda and the other senior members were scanning the field and sky too.

"Look." Hannah pointed to the center of the circular paving stone at the middle of the square, right where Miranda had cut the knot.

Zach leaned to the left and then the right, trying to see between shifting heads.

"Stand back, don't squish it," Miranda ordered.

"What is it?" Ben asked.

Zach shrugged. "I can't see it." If it was small, at least it wasn't likely to be a city-eating type. *Right?* The knot had been smaller than the First Knot, which had spawned Storm. *Did that mean a nice monster?* Zach doubted it; size like anything else could be deceiving. It would serve Miranda right if it bit her hand like a mad dog. But as much as he wanted Searcha stopped, he didn't want these people hurt. His job was to protect the world, even the idiot Searcha members, from magic. *Then why the hell am I not doing something? I should be trying to stop it. But how?*

The shadows still weren't freaking out. The green glaze faded and settled into the shadows, like a missing puzzle piece, adding depth and shimmering highlights to what was already there.

"For those of you who can't see, it's a plant. A magical plant?" Miranda added, feigning confidence.

A plant? An image of the monster from *The Little Shop of Horrors* came to Zach's mind, though he'd never seen the movie, a giant Venus flytrap-like monster. Or maybe it would be like Ents, the walking trees from the *Lord of the Rings*. He racked his brain for any mention of magical plant guardians in his research. There had been flora, but he'd not realized they were from knots. He'd assumed they were regular plants interacting with the magic.

"After you've seen it, step aside so other people can too," Jason said.

It was tempting for Zach to hang back. Anything coming out of a knot was dangerous, and he had no weapon on him, but he couldn't risk standing too far apart and letting his shadow be a silhouette. He wasn't sure his curiosity would be enough to overcome his wariness. He reached for the easiest masking option, his attraction to Kayla.

As he got closer, he realized Kayla was no longer uncomfortable. She didn't even seem to notice Hannah hovering protectively at her side. All of Kayla's attention was on the center of the square, awestruck.

Zach tore his eyes away from Kayla and gasped. About three feet tall, growing out of a newly formed crack in the stone, a tangled bush was topped by the most extraordinary flower he'd ever seen. It was moon white, about the size of the palm of his hand, reminiscent of a water lily. It glowed softly, as if each anther was made of a tiny star.

"It's beautiful!" Samantha breathed.

Zach nodded. The flower's shadow held a mossy glade, protected by an overgrown forest and glowing with incandescent wildflowers.

"How can it be a guardian if it doesn't move?" Jason muttered to Miranda.

"I don't know. Maybe it's not done growing?" Miranda sounded as baffled as Zach felt.

The flower smelled of earth and river water, with just a wisp of sulfur and jasmine. Shivering, Zach gave the group still around the flower a nod and retreated, hoping his shadow had told Hannah nothing. He glanced back and saw her focus was still divided between Kayla and the flower.

Mind churning, he tried to calculate how long it would take Russel's sensors to pick up the magic from the knot. He desperately wanted to speak with Alexis and Terra. Maybe Alexis could see more clearly why this knot was different from the others they'd encountered. *Why isn't it filling the shadows with apocalyptic imagery?* His questions would have to wait until he had the spellbook and could get back to HQ.

Storm! She must know this knot was different. Like *she* was. *But how, why?* A headache bloomed in Zach's skull.

He needed his sketchbook.

Swinging by his room, he took his pad to the beach. After a concentrated round of tai chi, which left him with a damp sweat and a calm brain, he sat with his back against a rock. Listening to his own breath and the soft lap of waves, he let the infinite overhead sink in.

In no mood to censor his drawings, Zach took his necklace off and uncapped the pen. There wouldn't have been enough light for graphite, but the iridescent, magical ink looked like molten obsidian on the page.

He didn't know what to draw, so he started shading in one corner of the page. In moments his pencil was dancing across the paper. The plant, with its beautiful flower under the full moon. The shadows, when the Baltimore Knot was a threat, bloody brambles spilling out from its shadows and pools of bubbling liquid—all that would have been left of the living if it was freed. Hannah, standing by Kayla. Storm, nose-to-petal with the magical plant, in harmony and balance except for the sharp edges lurking in the shadows.

Frowning, Zach filled another page with offshoots from the plant, which grew into dozens of different species. Its vines and trunks offered shelter for Storm and faceless people. It would have been cozy, except for the danger of the teeth in the unlit crevices.

The next page bloomed with an image of Storm lying in a magical garden. A woman Zach didn't recognize, with dark, wavy hair past her shoulders, leaned against the unicorn's side, pulling burrs from Storm's tail. Some of the burrs grew into flowers. Teeth and waves ate others, swamping the dark spaces.

Zach's pen froze. He did know the woman. He'd seen her in the shadows of her journal page. She was the Shadow Searcha had used to find the shipwreck. *Why am I seeing her in the shadows again?* No answers came to mind, so he shrugged and flipped the page.

The shadows of teeth and waves grew, coalescing into Chessie. She really did look like a snakehead. Unlike the invasive fish, though,

Chessie had snake fangs, in rows like the teeth of a shark. They were the cresting whitecaps of teeth that had haunted the shadows since the Lockhouse Knot was cut. The pattern of patches on her scales resembled a ball python's, but each patch was a lopsided hexagon. On her back was a long serrated fin that was reflected by a dorsal fin, which started a third of the way down her body, ending just before her blunt tail. Her pectoral fins were sturdy; Zach suspected she could use them to crawl on land, just like a young snakehead.

In the second-to-last drawing, Chessie dragged Kayla, Storm, and Guard HQ down into the depth of a whirlpool in the middle of a churning sea.

In the final sketch, Chessie looked forward, her snake eyes staring directly at Zach. Shaking, he dropped the pad. Still the monster stared back at him from the page. She was coming for him.

Swallowing hard, Zach closed the sketchbook and gazed unseeingly at the water. Mentally, he summed up what his drawing was telling him.

The plant knot wouldn't directly cause the end of the world. It was probably as benign as his drawings showed, but by releasing it, there was more magic in the world. More magic made Chessie stronger.

"She'll swim faster now," he whispered to the night. He checked his watch—it was late, but if he broke into the lab tonight … "Shit." Tonight was out. Ara was using the light of the full moon to help her brew a potion and stock up on ingredients. The knot being cut would only have pushed her timetable back an hour or so.

Tomorrow. Tension loosened in his chest. That gave him the day to tweak his plans and one last chance to recruit Kayla. If they could forgive Nick, surely the Guard could be convinced Kayla should join the team. But with or without her, Zach needed to be driving away from Tidal Water tomorrow night—with the book.

Something still nagged at him. He picked up his sketchpad one more time. The sea monster crashed like a wave onto the beach, where Zach sat now. He examined the positions of the moon and stars in the drawing, then compared them to the sky. She'd be there, looking for him and the magic plant, several hours before the next dawn. Tomorrow night was cutting it close; he'd have a margin of hours.

Zach's stomach twisted. If he couldn't get the book then, he'd have to leave without it. Terra and his parents would kill him if he got eaten, but after everything he'd done to get the book, he couldn't run now. Not when it was the last chance to stop Chessie. Taking a deep breath, Zach tried to let his panicky thoughts go with the exhale.

If Kayla didn't defect, she'd still be safe. Hannah would hear Chessie coming, and Searcha would evacuate. Zach wouldn't be leaving them in danger. They were on the wrong side of a fight to save the world, but they didn't know that. Hopefully, Kayla's book would have the answers the Guard needed to tie magic away before anyone got killed, on either side.

All Zach had to do was break into a high-security lab, steal a priceless grimoire, and get out before Miranda wiped his memory or the sea monster ate him.

"No problem," he muttered with a snort. Pushing himself off the ground, he headed for his room. Sleep, if it would come, was the best thing he could do for himself, the Guard, and the world.

Twenty-Four

Kayla
Day 11 of the Lockhouse Knot Leak
Monday afternoon
Tidal Water, MD

"Yikes! It's miserable out there!" Laughing, Kayla yanked the house door shut behind her and shook cold rain off her jacket. Working in the West Study with Ben and Samantha had been worth the trip. The dash home through the pelting drops had her blood flowing and mind ready for a last push on her report.

"I warned you it was going to rain," Hannah said, giving Kayla a once-over from behind her guitar.

The bounce in Kayla's step evaporated. She dragged herself over to the coat hooks. Water slid off her jacket, pattering on the tile floor. "I needed a change of scenery."

Hannah shrugged, picking away at a melancholy tune. "And now you've gotten mud on the floor."

Kayla turned her back so she could make a face as she pried off her sneakers. Pointing out that they were more wet than muddy wouldn't make Hannah happy. "I'm cleaning it up."

Hannah's guitar twanged with disapproval when Kayla pulled two sheets of paper towel off the roll. Kayla gritted her teeth. She'd heard the speech often enough. It might be a waste of trees to carelessly use paper towels, but she wasn't using her freshly washed towel, and apparently letting the floor air dry wasn't an option.

Kayla wanted to see if she could make the kitchen trash can from the welcome mat, but not enough to earn another disapproving look from Hannah. It was her own fault. If she'd worked at her desk after lunch, like Hannah had wanted, Hannah would be in a better mood. That was annoying as shit.

At least unearthing a knot seemed to have everyone believing she was well on her way to graduating. Jason had said in her lesson that morning that maybe her magic was more subtle than other Shiners, and she was clearly a lot further along than he'd thought. Kayla didn't care if he was right or not, as long as he believed it enough to graduate her.

The downside was everyone was convinced it was because she and Hannah were tying. *Maybe everyone is right.* Kayla shuddered. Hannah was a nice person and tried so hard. *I need to not be so sensitive and try to enjoy her more. Maybe this is what tying looks like.* It probably wasn't some amazing connection for someone like Kayla, who enjoyed people, but tended to take them for granted.

I'm the problem. I need to try harder. Next time she'd stay home and study with Hannah, she promised herself. For her family. When put into perspective, she was a selfish jerk. Kayla noticed the negative self-talk and tried to shake it off.

She dropped the damp paper towels into the trash. Maybe she'd see if Hannah wanted to watch an episode of one of the TV shows she liked after dinner. At least the cast was hot, especially the lead werewolf.

Kayla froze. Opening her mouth, she pointed at her desk, but no words came out. Her stacks of notes, reference material, half-written translation, and reports were nowhere in sight. The mint gum that helped her concentrate wasn't shoved to the right side, where her coffee mug should be. Headphones weren't dangling over the drawer knob. The only thing on her desk was a pencil holder Kayla had never seen, with one pencil, one pen, and one yellow highlighter.

She tried again. "Hannah? What happened to my stuff?"

"Oh." Hannah strumming a bright cord. "I organized your desk. There are now dividers in the drawers and file folders in the bottom one. I have no idea how you managed to work before, but it's going to be so much easier for you now."

Kayla tried to take a deep breath. She really did. "It's *my* stuff!"

Hannah stood up, set her guitar aside, and looked over the shadows in the room. Her face stiffened as it dawned on her that Kayla was the opposite of thrilled.

"It's in a common area, and it was a mess. No wonder you never want to work at home. Even seeing it from the other side of the room, it's been driving me crazy for days. I couldn't focus this afternoon, so I fixed it. You'll be a lot more comfortable once you get used to it."

"If it was bothering you, you should have said something. I could have cleaned it up." *Well, shoved it all in my room and closed the door.* Kayla opened a drawer. Her pens gazed heartbrokenly back, confined in a divider, segregated from the pencils. She wanted to scream but gritted her teeth instead. That was the other reason she chewed gum, so she wouldn't grind her teeth. Gum—she checked the next drawer. It wasn't there either.

"I was happy to. I don't mind cleaning up after you."

"I mind! I'm not a child!" *Though you do an artful job of making me feel like one.*

"Of course not," Hannah said, in a soothing tone that made blood pound in Kayla's ears. "But we're becoming tied. That means it's my job to look out for you."

"We are not tied!" Kayla clenched her fists at her side. Her jaw ached.

"Kay-la?" Hannah put a world of hurt into the two syllables.

Hannah's pain deflated Kayla's rage. She desperately reached for the logic she and her brother, Noah, had talked about before she started truly yelling. "I don't think we're going to be tied. We aren't a good fit. You worry when I go for a long run, even though I need to for my sanity. I don't understand your music, even though it's almost as important to you as magic, at least it was before I moved here from Xander. Your whole world is wrapped up in Searcha, mine isn't. Magic needs strong, compatible people to help it. You will be so much better off with someone who's a better fit for you." *If I have to be tied, is it too much to ask for someone who treats me like an equal?*

Hannah bowed her head and rubbed her temples. Dropping her arms, she looked up and spoke like she was explaining something obvious to a five-year-old. "Kayla, those are just excuses. Freeing magic is so much more important than making a few small compromises. This is being tied. I know the thought of being connected with someone in that way makes you feel trapped, but that's because your perception is inaccurate. Trust me, we'll be such a good team."

"We're not tied!" Kayla could barely hear above the blood raging in her ears.

"Not officially, but the unicorn came to us and led us to the knot. She's sanctioned our partnership."

Kayla screeched between her teeth.

Hannah's grating calm didn't waver. "You're going to enjoy being tied once you get used to it. As soon as your training is finished, we can leave Tidal Water. Richmond has an amazing music and food scene. You're going to love it. We'll have so much fun between missions. Our combined power is going to be invaluable in helping free magic. Imagine what amazing guardians we'll release next!"

You're not listening! Kayla couldn't get the words out. She would not spend her free time lounging around, eating artsy food and listening to music. She'd be doing something active and exciting or making trips up to DC to have adventures with Noah while he was still in grad school. Every muscle threatened to jump out of Kayla's body if she didn't start running.

"We'd drive each other nuts," Kayla managed to get out.

"No one is perfect, but our different strengths complement each other. A little friction is normal in a new partnership, but we'll smooth out the differences." Hannah's patient tone rubbed worse than sandpaper.

"A little friction! Are you blind?!"

"I am a Shadow," Hannah said, with precise enunciation. "I see things how they are. This is happening quickly for you. Your brain hasn't had time to catch up with your magic."

"It's not happening too fast, because it's not happening at all!"

"Grow up!" Hannah's patience splintered into brittle briskness. "Don't let your fear control you. We've been given a gift. We owe it to magic to use it."

Kayla hands clenched into fists at her sides. "Grow up? You're the one not listening!"

Hannah took a deep breath, then smiled warmly. "We're three-quarters of the way tied already. It's going to be an adjustment, but I'm here to help you through it if you'll just let me. There is no point in arguing, because it's already been decided."

"Who decided? Cuz it sure as hell wasn't me!"

"Magic. It brought us together for this purpose."

Furious energy lit Kayla's markings. "If magic is cruel enough to stick me with you for the rest of my career, I want nothing to do with it!"

Hannah gasped. Color drained from her face. "Kayla!"

Shaking with rage and magic, Kayla felt like a monster, but couldn't stop herself. "There's no way in hell I'm tying with you."

"I've been so patient." Hannah's voice broke. "I waited and waited for my Shiner to arrive. Then you finally get here, and you can't sit still. You're terrible at magic, you don't know a G major from an A minor, and I spend so much time looking out for you that I barely pick up my guitar anymore."

Kayla gestured that this was exactly what she was saying, but the tears threatening to spill down Hannah's cheeks silenced Kayla's words.

"But life isn't perfect." Hannah sniffed. "And you're what I've got, and we could make something of this if you put in the effort. I'm working so hard, and you won't even try." She burst into tears and fled the room, slamming the door behind her.

Kayla gaped after her. *I'm a selfish monster.*

Fury rescued her from self-flagellation, like a smear of tar over a wound that slowed the bleeding. Snatching her jacket and shoving her feet into wet sneakers, Kayla fled into the rain.

Flaming with rage, she barely noticed the cold and wet sinking through her already-saturated jacket. Hannah was an idiot. Miranda was blind for pushing them into tying. Storm was a monster for sanctioning their tying. *Or was Storm just showing me, and Hannah was along for the trip? Would Storm have shown me if I were with Zach or anyone else?* Probably. *I was an idiot for asking Hannah to stop when I saw Storm. I should have known this is where we'd end up.*

Kayla stopped in front of the plant. It glowed softly even in the downpour. She couldn't be sorry that it was free. If the Guard had found it first, they would lock it in a vault somewhere.

If she couldn't be mad that she'd rescued the knot, she could blame herself for sucking at magic. If she'd mastered her magic, she might have been able to ride Storm to the tree stump instead of needing Hannah to sail her there.

The color sapped from her markings, and she shivered. Wind-driven droplets pushed Kayla towards Xander, but she couldn't make herself go in. Company would get her out of her own head, but people would probably ask why she was soaked and shivering. She couldn't stand the idea of anyone telling her that she was overreacting and needed to just get over it and accept Hannah as her Shadow already. Those thoughts were loud enough in her own head.

"Looks like you could use an escape." Zach's wiry chuckle came from the far end of the porch.

"God, yes." A sob caught in Kayla's throat. She viciously swallowed it back.

Zach got up and slid his sketchbook into his bag. "I saw in the shadows that there is a hideaway key for Nick's car. Want to take it for a spin with me?"

"We're not allowed to leave property," Kayla said automatically, though his offer sounded like heaven.

Zach walked to a door and poked his head in. "Dahlia? Kayla is having a bad day. I can see it clear as high noon in the shadows. She needs some time away from camp. Can we please have permission to go for a harmless little drive? We'll be back later tonight."

Dahlia came to the door, her handmade earrings swinging and doubt written all over her face. "You should ask Miranda."

"She's at that big meeting in Richmond. We can't wait," Zach said earnestly. "Look at Kayla. She's going to explode. Magic and guts everywhere. Messy to clean up."

A surprised snort of laughter escaped Kayla.

Dahlia gave Zach a look that clearly said she wasn't buying his bullshit.

He shrugged a shoulder in acknowledgement, then gave her a devilish grin. "What's Miranda going to do? Kick us all out of Searcha?" His voice dropped. "Kayla needs this."

Dahlia pursed her lips. Her gaze softened when they fell on Kayla. "That bad of a day, huh?"

Tears welled up at the compassion in her voice. Kayla fought them back and nodded.

Dahlia heaved a great sigh before throwing her hands in the air. "Fine." Under her breath, she muttered, "I'd like to see Miranda do all the maintenance and mowing if she fires me."

"Thank you!" Kayla gasped.

"Come on." Zach led the way to the parking lot. The flashy black car looked powerful and defiant in the rain. Zach fished the key out of its hidden box.

"I was thinking about a real beach. I bet if you drove, we'd get there in less than an hour." He offered her the key.

"If I drove!" Kayla plucked the key out of his hand, no longer thinking about getting in trouble, Hannah's insanity, or if she'd ever get a grip on her magic. She peeled out of her sopping-wet jacket, shoved it in the back, and jumped in. The plush fabric hugged her damp clothes. The seat belt snapped into place as if she was a fighter pilot about to take off. She ignored Zach as he took shotgun.

The engine turned on with a satisfying purr. She had it in gear before Zach finished buckling in. Gravel flew as she sprang for freedom. As soon as they hit pavement, she gunned it down the straightaway.

Zach fiddled with the GPS on his phone, apparently unbothered by the speed. "Glad I downloaded a map to work offline. Left when we reach the road."

His calm should have bugged the hell out of her, but his acceptance of her reckless driving acted as a balm on her jagged anger. Her grip relaxed on the steering wheel. Kayla slowed to an only slightly dangerous speed. The roads were wet; it would be stupid to slide off and lose her escape.

The left took them onto a straight, flat road that divided freshly plowed fields. Kayla grinned, nudging the gas pedal even further down. The car growled its pleasure and cut smoothly through the rain, which was lightening to a drizzle.

"The next right," Zach said.

Kayla lifted off the gas. The car tires gripped without squealing through the turn. Pleased, she settled into driving. Escaping. But then she remembered why she needed to. The car's odometer edged up another ten miles per hour.

"Want to talk about it?" Zach asked, in his relaxed way.

"Can't you just *see*?" If one more Shadow told her what was best for her, she was going to scream.

Zach laughed brightly. "In this weather? I'm flattered you think I'm that powerful. I thought you could tell I was lying my ass off to Dahlia."

Kayla pulled her eyes from the road for a moment to glare at him.

Still grinning, he settled more comfortably into the seat.

She eased up on the gas a bit, even as her rage flared in her markings. "Hannah acts like we're already tied." *Crap, I do need to talk about it, or we're going to end up in a ditch.* Kayla let the car slow further. "Some of the time she's decent company, but she's condescending and micromanaging. What makes her think we're in any way compatible?! She 'organized' my desk today. I can't find anything!" Kayla gripped the steering wheel so hard the only color in her knuckles was from her markings. She had no idea why she was so angry, and that just made her more furious. "She says I'm not trying. I am! Does she think I don't care about my family? And when I tried to confront her about cleaning my desk, do you know what she does? In the middle of our fight! She burst into tears and runs away. Seriously?! I'm left as a monster and she's the martyr."

"Trust me, you're not a monster."

Kayla snorted. "But she's a martyr."

"I doubt you're asking her to be one," Zach said.

"I'm asking her *not* to be!" Kayla gave a blow-by-blow of the fight. "Why does she make me so angry? I can't stand losing my temper! It just makes everything worse."

"Your anger is your emotions' way of letting you know that something isn't okay." Zach shrugged. "It can be useful information."

"How is it useful?" Kayla scoffed. "She's trying to help me and magic. In helping me graduate, it ensures my friends and family will have protection during the Unavoidable Upheaval, whatever the hell that'll look like. Why can't I just be grateful?" At some point in the conversation, the car had slowed to a reasonable relationship with the speed limit.

"She might be trying, but she's failing spectacularly. She's gaslighting you. Probably not on purpose. But she's telling you what you think and feel isn't real."

That brought Kayla up short.

When she didn't reply, Zach continued. "Every time you let her convince you what you feel isn't right, or you compromise what you know is best for you, or you feel taken advantage of for being nice, or you let your boundaries slide, your anger tries to speak up louder, and the more that internal voice feels ignored, the louder and more reactive it gets until even the smallest compromise, which would have been perfectly okay before, sets it off like a volcano. It's like you're becoming allergic to her."

Something awful eased in Kayla's chest. "I'm not selfish or crazy?"

"Nope. Well, at least not about this."

Kayla smiled briefly, but Hannah was a Shadow. "Do my feelings even matter though? It's all in the shadows. Hannah and I will be tied." Kayla flinched at hearing the words out loud. The car swerved.

Zach gave her time to get the tires back in their lane before he spoke. "The future is hard to read in the shadows, even at the best of times, or the Guard and Searcha wouldn't still be fighting. Information about our own personal future is even harder to see. Besides, isn't being tied supposed to strengthen both of your abilities? If you're a bad fit, I imagine that would make you weaker, not stronger."

"Why can't Hannah see that?"

Kayla caught a sad sort of smile on Zach's face, but then he turned to look out his window. "When we want something as much as Hannah wants to be tied, it clouds a Shadow's vision. She's probably only speaking with authority because she's deluding herself or she wants to project more confidence than she feels to convince you."

"And Miranda and Jason are supporting her, which just makes it worse."

"Poor Jason."

"What?"

"I just feel so bad for the guy. Pushing Hannah into being tied with someone else is killing him."

Kayla gaped.

"Shit, you didn't know." Zach looked horrified. "Sorry. I thought it was obvious. I shouldn't have said that. Please don't share that! It's a huge breach of privacy. I just . . . it's so . . . well . . . obvious. He does everything he can not to directly look at her, but he's clearly so aware of her whenever they're in the same room. At first I thought he didn't like her, but then I put two and two together. I figure that is why Hannah is so unhappy, too, and taking it out on you."

Distracted by how cute he was when flustered, it took Kayla a moment for his words to sink in.

"Jason likes Hannah!"

"Seriously, it's not cool that I said that."

"I won't tell. It would be cruel to say anything, since nothing can come of it." Kayla's heart hurt for Hannah.

"Thanks. It doesn't excuse her behavior towards you, but yeah, it's a sad situation."

The last of Kayla's anger faded. "Then what do I do? How do I convince her I'm not the answer?"

"I don't know. If you continue to let her gaslight you and push past your boundaries, your anger is going to keep speaking up. If you set and maintain boundaries, she'll have to readjust her expectations, but she seems like the stubborn sort. For now, how about food?"

"What?"

"I've got granola bars, trail mix, some questionably old saltwater taffy, and"—he dug around in his bag—"a weird box of jelly beans I've been afraid to open."

Kayla blinked. At least the car stayed steady on the road.

Zach grinned. "We're going to miss dinner. Are you hungry yet?"

Now that he mentioned it, she could eat. "Weird jelly beans?" A big yawn loosened the ache in her jaw.

"From one of my sisters. She's got a questionable sense of humor."

Amusement battled with bafflement. "And you just happen to have them on you?"

"I always keep food in my bag."

"Why?" Kayla often tried to, but half the time she forgot it was there until it was crumbled in with the debris at the bottom, and the other half the time she'd forget to pack it.

"As a kid, if I wasn't at school, I was usually at a sports game or practice. Between my sisters, they played basically every team sport known to humankind. Since I'm the youngest and not team-sports inclined myself, I got dragged to all the games and a lot of practices. Having food and my sketchbook on hand was a must. It's still a handy habit." He unwrapped the wax paper on a pastel pink-and-yellow taffy. "We're making a right when the road T's up here," he said, before popping the candy into his mouth.

The thought of Hannah still frustrated her, but the thought of jelly beans and a young Zach sitting on metal bleachers with his sketchpad was much more interesting. "What do you draw? Besides that sketch of Storm you gave me."

Zach picked up the box of jelly beans and eyed them suspiciously before answering. "Oh, bit of this, bit of that. Sometimes I sketch what I see, sometimes imaginary stuff like comic heroes, and sometimes what's whispering through the shadows around me. Depends."

"Do you post on socials and stuff?"

"Nope, I just did it for me, until I gained magic. Now it feels more like a necessity—it's usually the only way I have a chance of deciphering what I'm seeing in the deeper shadows."

"Why'd you study chemistry instead of art?"

"Seemed like the prudent choice at the time." Zach shook the box of jelly beans like a wrapped package whose contents he was trying to guess at.

Curiosity nagged at Kayla. It seemed like there was something more there than simply a secure job, but he didn't appear inclined to elaborate.

She took her right hand off the wheel and held it palm up. "I'll try some jelly beans."

"Brave." Zach opened the box and poured a few into her hand.

Kayla let one roll between her index finger and thumb. Popping it into her mouth, she bit and then grinned. It took a moment to place the flavor. "Mango."

Zach gave her a suspicious look, as if she was attempting to lure him into an icy river by telling him it wasn't cold.

Kayla grinned and popped another candy into her mouth, giving him an I-dare-you look. "Apple." That wasn't exciting, though, so she added, "But not a green one, kinda red tasting." She missed the expression on Zach's face when he tried a jelly bean—driving had its downsides—but she heard him make a thoughtful sound. "So?"

"Strawberry smoothie," he announced.

"Seriously?" Kayla eyed him suspiciously.

He grinned mischievously. "That's what I tasted."

She brought her gaze firmly back to the road. "If you say so."

"Try another. Maybe you'll get the same one."

"Yick! Licorice!" Kayla swallowed it fast and held out her hand for more. "I need to get that taste out of my mouth." Carefully, she selected a light-colored one. "Coconut, weird."

"See! This is why I haven't opened the box. Who makes licorice or coconut-flavored jelly beans?" Zach sighed sadly and tried another. "Oh, much better, papaya."

Kayla laughed. The car purred happily over the road, and the sky opened up before them, leaving the drizzle behind. Feeling better than she had all day, she ate another jelly bean.

Twenty-Five

Zach
Day 11 of the Lockhouse Knot Leak
Monday, late afternoon
Assateague Island, MD

Zach hadn't been overly concerned that Kayla would crash the car—he'd gotten a brilliant, clear image of her running on the beach—but he breathed a long exhale of relief when she shifted into Park. People really shouldn't drive that angry.

The mostly empty parking lot at Assateague National Seashore was nestled among the dunes. Out the car window, he could see the wooden boardwalks beckoning them to the Atlantic, just out of sight.

"I'll race you to the water." Kayla jumped out of the car with a laugh before Zach could reply.

A blast of briny wind hit him in the face when he opened his door. Grinning, he jumped from the car, closed the door, and pushed into a run. With a burst of speed, he caught up with her graceful lope. She laughed and didn't pull ahead. Side by side, they ran down the long boardwalk. Pausing only long enough to tug off their shoes, they flew across the deep sand to the surf.

They played tag with the waves, Kayla laughing and beautiful in the golden light of the sunset. Zach laughed, too, as frigid water doused his feet and ankles. When conscious thought tried to interrupt, he let it go, choosing instead the taste of sea in the air, the feel of cool sand, and the joy of being there with Kayla.

"I don't want the sun to go," Kayla said wistfully, as they watched it sink behind the dunes.

The real world couldn't be kept at bay forever. "You still have energy? I bet you can run forever on this beach. I can get a flashlight and my sketchbook from the car, so I'll be happy here for hours."

Kayla hesitated. "I couldn't find my headphones and left my music at the house."

Zach pulled his music player out of one of his pockets. "Not sure it's anything you'll enjoy, but you might try the 'Take on the World' playlist."

"Really? Thanks!" She took it with a grin, then hesitated. "You really don't mind?"

"Not at all." In fact, he'd counted on her wanting a run. The minor deception nagged at him, but this much time undercover was making it easier to ignore. That bothered him even more.

Kayla flashed him a happy smile and tossed him the keys before taking off down the beach.

Zach let himself enjoy watching her until the curve of the shore took her out of sight. With long strides, he walked back to the car and slid into the passenger seat. Digging into the glove box, he pulled out the burner phone. Hannah's cleaning of Kayla's desk had solved several of Zach's problems at once.

Terra picked up before the second ring. "Yes?"

"It's me," Zach said.

"Are you okay? Can you talk?"

"I'm healthy and off property at the moment, so it's as safe as I can make it. Did your sensors pick up a knot being cut?"

"Yes, what happened?"

Zach summarized, finishing with, "The knot spawned a plant."

"A *plant*?" Terra's tone conveyed how insane it was.

A band of tension around his ribs eased. It *was* nuts.

"Yes." Zach filled in the few details he had. Pulling out his sketchbook, he flipped through the pages as he talked, to make sure he wasn't missing anything worth passing along to the Guard.

"The magic from this Plant Knot seems to be energizing the golem from the Lockhouse Knot," Terra said.

"That's what I'm seeing. And Chessie is coming for me. She got a taste of my magic when her magic spilled on me." Zach was careful to keep the horror of being torn apart and eaten out of his voice. Instead, he balanced the phone on his shoulders, interlaced his fingers, and stretched. "My plan is to finish my mission tonight and head your way before Chessie reaches Tidal Water, around dawn. I'm leaving with a friend, if possible. I think I can recruit her to our side." Zach scooped up the phone and switched it to his other ear, waiting out Terra's silence.

"The monster will be there that soon? Damn it. Yes, get out, but can you get a clear view if your recruitment will be a success?"

Zach hesitated. He'd spoken from experience when he told Kayla that Hannah was too close and cared too much to get a clear read.

Terra gently added, "We don't need more members. What we need is for you to get home safely with that book."

The idea of never seeing Kayla again, except maybe on opposite sides of a fight, or a battle, edged Zach towards panic. "Does Alexis see anything helpful?"

"She's been a little busy here. The box containing the Lockhouse Knot is cracking, and Searcha is aware it's leaking. We doubt it'll take them long to locate it. I stepped out of a meeting looking at our options when you called." Terra sighed.

A dripping gray watercolor flickered in the shadows for a moment, depicting Terra leaning her forehead against a wooden wall in HQ.

The Terra on the phone cleared her throat. "That monster has already attacked two swimmers. The press is saying 'shark attacks,' and no one has died yet, but . . . We ran out of viable ideas days ago, and now we're even running out of wild ideas. Zach, your safety should be our number-one priority, but we need that book. Both of those are far more important than recruiting anyone."

Zach massaged his aching forehead and batted away regrets that what had looked like a simple field mission had led them here.

"You still there?" Terra asked.

"Yes," Zach mumbled.

"I know part of your job was to build trust, and you are the kind of person who couldn't do that without making friends. If you can safely recruit your person without compromising your mission, then it's your call. I trust your judgment, but be very careful. We're losing ground in what is looking very much like war, not gaining it. If you can't get the book out, bring us everything you've learned. Maybe we can pull off a strike force. We've been throwing around ideas."

Images of Alexis, Brian, and Russel cowering behind the lab as Miranda blasted at them with a shotgun flickered through his imagination or maybe the shadows. The candy in Zach's stomach churned.

Swallowing hard, he tried to pull himself together. "Searcha will be evacuating Tidal Water before dawn, before Chessie arrives. Not much time to get a strike force in position, but I've got a plan to get the book tonight, quietly. I can do this." Zach hoped like hell he was right. If he was wrong, the book would end up who-knew-where during the evacuation, probably Searcha's main base in Richmond.

"Be careful. I'm moving a team closer to your location. Call when you're out."

"Be careful there. Sounds like I'm not the only one in danger."

"We'll be ready for Searcha if they launch a strike against HQ, but it sounds like they have their hands full for now," Terra said, finishing up the call.

Zach rubbed goosebumps on his arms, thinking of the weapon enchantments in the back of the Searcha van. This was just the training facility, not the main force. HQ was in a populated neighborhood. It was no place to start a war.

Returning the phone to the hiding spot in the glove box, he tried to settle his stomach with a swallow of water from his bottle. Grabbing his bag, he closed up the car and headed back towards the beach.

Turning Terra's words over in his head, it sank in that he would be back with the Guard by morning. *It'll be a relief to shed the leather jacket and all that goes with it. Won't it?* He'd enjoyed parts of it. Doing tai chi under the open sky by the water, many of the people he'd met, and being able to do translations anywhere on property, instead of in a sterile vault. But, it would be amazing to drop the lies, the watching his every step and word, to be done with hiding his shadow whenever Hannah might be watching. To be around people who saw the world the way he did. *Soon.*

Overhead, a few stars appeared in the violet sky. The rough wood, dusted with grit, supported him until it gave way to cool, loose sand that cushioned his heels and shifted between his toes. This beach, his existence, the entire Earth were all only a tiny part of a much larger whole. Waves crashed onto the shore, and the breeze danced across his face and ruffled his hair. Taking his time, he sat on a spot just above the high-tide line, leaning back on his elbows and breathing the salty air. More stars materialized as the sky grew navy and then dark.

There were things he would miss, but a lot of good things to get back to. He even missed Sadie's insane enthusiasm for spell crafting and Elliot's unyielding, uncompromising certainty magic was evil. Zach craved the simplicity of that belief, even if he could no longer fully share it, because it didn't matter. In the end, magic had to be locked away.

Zach pulled out his sketch pad, searching for ideas to convince Kayla to come with him. Instead, a tsunami of teeth rose about a city. Blinking, Zach saw he'd drawn DC's skyline. *Am I drawing it because it's familiar, or is it a possible future?* The stars overhead offered no guidance. Back on his sketch pad, the Washington Monument stood in the shadow of a gigantic wave. Pen to paper again, and Chessie filled a new page. An eighteen-wheeler-sized magical snakehead with a gigantic mouth thrashed and slithered its way through DC, searching for her knot. Goosebumps rose on his forearms. Death and destruction flowed in the monster's wake as she grew longer than the Reflecting Pool. If this future happened, Chessie would follow the leaking magic all the way to HQ, crashing into the lab to find it already evacuated and her knot moved. Furious, she would go on a directionless rampage until she could pick up the trail again.

DC and everyone living in it were in danger. Zach rubbed his arms, trying to fight a chill that wasn't from the salty breeze. The leaking Lockhouse Knot needed to be sealed before the image he'd drawn stopped being a possibility and became reality. He was tempted to go back to the car and warn Terra, but he'd see her soon enough if all went well, and if it didn't, Alexis would see the monster coming.

Zach itched to get back to Tidal Water and then to get the hell out. Once he got the spellbook to the Guard, they'd have what they needed to stop the possibilities on his sketchpad from happening. Ara had complained she didn't understand the book, but surely Sadie could decipher it. *If he could get it to her before dawn tomorrow, would she and Russel have enough time to craft a spell to stop the monster?*

Heartbeat in his ears, Zach closed his sketchbook and looked up. Rushing back now wouldn't help; Kayla was still out for a run, and it was too early to break into the lab. If he was at camp now, he'd have to be guarding his shadow from Hannah with everything he had. He was exactly where he needed to be in this moment.

He'd forgotten why he'd opened his sketchbook—ideas for how to safely recruit Kayla. Sitting up, he flipped to a fresh page. In a few lines, he captured Kayla laughing as she danced with the waves. Her rare stillness was harder to capture, but he showed her as she'd been earlier, taking in the setting sun, one with the moment like the sea birds behind her. A third sketch showed her grinning at him, gilded in light.

With a swish of pages, he flipped the book closed and shoved it back in his bag. He was lying to himself if he thought he wanted to recruit her for the Guard's sake. Terra was right, they didn't need another member, even if she was a Shiner with untapped potential. He was being selfish. *But did that mean it was the wrong choice?* Being aware that his judgment was warped was something, but every fiber of his being said he had to try.

Pulling his flashlight out of his bag, he turned it on and placed it on the sand, angling the beam to make it easy for Kayla to find him.

The moon was just peeking over the edge of the Atlantic, and Zach was thinking himself in useless circles, when Kayla plopped herself down beside him.

"It's a beautiful night." She sighed contentedly. "I needed that run, but I went further than I thought. I was worried I'd missed you until I saw the flashlight."

Reminding himself not to rush, Zach matched her smile. "Glad it was a good run. The music okay?"

Kayla grinned. "I've never heard half the songs on that playlist, but I really enjoyed them. So many kick-ass empowering ones. When it ran out, I switched to the pop music one, and that was great too."

Zach let himself enjoy talking music with her, savoring what might be some of his last easy moments with her, waiting for his opening.

"That moon is huge!" she said.

"It is." The moon was a day past full and just free of the horizon, massive and orange, bringing life to the dark sea.

"It's like it's calling to my magic." Kayla held up a hand, lit with her amber markings. "I can see the strands everywhere, more than I've ever been able to. Like I could almost reach out and pull the stars and the moon to us. I can feel how everything around us is all unique and individual and yet all part of the same whole, the same fabric of woven strands. My magic lessons have been so focused on using the strands to connect with individual things that this aspect slipped away from me.

"It's like the first time you taught me tai chi. I can feel how I'm an integral part of something so much bigger than me. How everything around me is, too." Kayla gave a self-conscious laugh. "Sorry, rambling."

"You're not. It's an amazing feeling." Zach swallowed hard.

"It's incredible." She touched the air as if strumming an invisible harp.

He could see the slight ripple in the shadows from the strands as she twanged. When she stroked one of the strands connecting them, his stomach flipped. Their eyes met. Zach wanted to lean in close and run far away at the same moment.

"Can you feel it?" Kayla whispered.

It took every shred of willpower for Zach to tear his gaze away. Focusing on the moonrise, he tried to slow his racing blood. Maybe, if he recruited her, he'd be able to kiss her. To explore the thrumming connection between them.

Purposely, he misunderstood her words. "I can see in the shadows what you can see in the strands. But I didn't need shadows to feel it. Looking at the sky can make me feel that way, or even my elementary teacher talking about the water cycle." He gave a self-deprecating laugh. "Magic is just icing on the cake. Lovely, but unnecessary."

Kayla leaned back on her elbows. "The icing is my favorite part of a cake. I think I'm actually going to enjoy being a Shiner. For a while there I was doubting it, but when I'm reminded what this feels like, I'm grateful for the gift."

Zach opened his mouth, but she wasn't done, so he waited.

"The run cleared my head about Hannah, too. I think you're right. If I stop beating myself up about being mad and taking the blame for Hannah's unhappiness, I can set better boundaries with her. If we both decide, after a few honest conversations, that being tied is truly the best way forward, we'll do it as equals or not at all. Easier said than done, but I think there's a path forward now."

"I'm glad," he lied.

Kayla gave a happy sigh.

"Doesn't it ever worry you that there might be a reason magic was locked away?" Zach was careful to keep his voice casual and his eyes on the rising moon.

Kayla shrugged. "Fear and hatred make people do stupid things and overreact all the time."

Zach rubbed the frown off his forehead. Searcha's argument that the Guard acted out of hatred irked him. Her statement was one he believed in, but for other people, bad people, about other things. Sure, it could be argued that Elliot was acting out of fear and hatred, but he had every reason to. A golem had killed people in the '70s, and this new golem would kill many more if left unchecked. Zach had pages and pages of drawings to support that fact.

"But surely," Zach said, "they're not afraid of a unicorn and a flower? All the work the Guard put into keeping magic locked away. What if there are some knots that are truly dangerous? Not just to humanity, but the world."

Kayla frowned. "Hannah showed me pictures from when my great-uncle tried to free magic. But that magic was only dangerous because it wasn't understood and was mistreated. You back anyone or any animal into a corner, and it can get mean. Why would magic be any different? Ugh. I'm sure Jason would enjoy debating you. I feel like I've heard him say something about small minds believing magic's ability to reshape the world for the better was dangerous."

Zach fought to find an argument that would be in character, in case Hannah saw the conversation in the shadows.

"Jason doesn't want to debate," Zach said. "He wants people to agree that Miranda is always, absolutely right. That irks me. There is an entire group of people that have been working so long and hard that they've altered the history books, and we're just supposed to believe they're scared idiots? I'm not saying Miranda isn't right, but there's no room for nuance."

"Scared, self-righteous haters aren't necessarily idiots. Many of them are even more dangerous because of their intelligence. Terrorists and violent extremists have done horrible damage to all sorts of different groups."

"What makes you think they are terrorists or extremists?" That label fit Searcha, not his people.

Kayla groaned. "They locked up defenseless entities and erased all knowledge of them. Of course they're evil. Why are we debating this?"

Zach forced himself to shrug casually, even while the sand felt like it was falling away beneath him. "Sorry. I don't like blindly accepting things. I find debating a useful way to explore a concept, but you're right. Jason would probably enjoy the argument if he doesn't get defensive. I'll try him sometime."

"Your funeral. Anyone who wants to lock away something as magnificent and kind as Storm doesn't have a leg to stand on."

"That's a fair point." *If that's all there is.* Zach itched to show her the other side of magic splashed across nearly every page of his sketchbook, but then Kayla would want a second opinion from Hannah, who hadn't been scalded by the Lockhouse Knot and clearly wasn't seeing what he and Alexis were. Hannah would go to Miranda, and Zach wouldn't be able to answer the awkward questions that would follow. He definitely didn't have the time for them.

Stretching his hands over his head, Zach played his last card. "If you don't want to be tied, you could always just walk away from Searcha."

"Believe me, I've thought about it." Kayla shrugged. "But I want Searcha's protection for my friends and family during the Unavoidable Upheaval."

"Have they ever given you a good explanation of what Unavoidable Upheaval even is?"

"The social and economic upheaval that comes with people adjusting to having magic in the world. I always figure it'll be like the chaos during the first year of Covid, only a bit bigger."

Zach rubbed his forehead. *Not even close.* "You could try moving them outside the range of magic."

Kayla shook her head. "Soon, magic will be everywhere. Besides, after seeing the magical plant bloom and feeling this connection to everything, how could I walk away? I don't want to miss what comes next! I'll graduate without tying, or I'll find a way to work it out with Hannah or the next female Shadow that's recruited. Who knows, maybe Storm will let me ride her someday. Or if Ara gets her potions perfected, a dragon."

Zach forced a smile, even as his heart cracked and collapsed inward. He couldn't risk pushing further. Kayla's belief in Searcha was clear, even in the watercolor dreamscape of the moonlight.

Giving himself a minute to watch the silver highlighted waves, as color faded from the moon, Zach tugged his leather jacket and his cover closer. When he was sure his voice would be light, he asked, "Would you like to make friends with a pocket-sized dragon or one big enough to ride?"

Kayla grinned. "Ride, of course. Can you imagine soaring through the air on its back?"

Smiling hurt deep inside, but he kept talking anyway. He had to find the strength to laugh and joke with her, because he had to hide any trace of his botched recruitment from her shadow. The drive back to Tidal Water would be his last chance to be her friend, and he would regret it later if he didn't savor it while he could; but the loss was already far more painful than he'd let himself anticipate. The sketchpad in his bag and the flicker of teeth-capped waves in the shadows were the only things reassuring him he was doing the right thing.

Twenty-Six

Kayla
Day 11 of the Lockhouse Knot Leak
Monday evening
Assateague Island, MD

It was hard to tell exactly when Zach drew inward, but on the walk back to the car, Kayla was sure it had happened. Maybe when he'd dug into his delightful bag and pulled out an unopened water bottle for her and granola bars for each of them. Maybe when she'd teased him about wanting to make friends with a pocket-sized dragon that would hang out on his sketchbook and get in the way while he tried to draw. Or maybe he had felt how romantic it was to watch the moon rise over the water together and started the debate about magic to distract them both.

Icy water from the foot-washing station broke through her contemplation. "Brr! This has been a perfect trip. Thanks for escaping with me."

Zach's smile didn't quite reach his eyes. "You're welcome. Thanks for not driving us into a tree."

Kayla laughed, though silently vowed never to drive that angry ever again. "Ugh. My shoes are still wet from the rain earlier." She eyed them unhappily.

"Brr is right." Zach said during his turn at the spigot. "A little sand won't hurt Nick's car. I won't tell him where it came from."

Giggling, Kayla carried her shoes to the car, picking up more sand on the bottoms of her feet as she walked.

"Want to drive back?" Zach tossed her the key.

"Is that a question?" Kayla said with a grin, but she sighed as she took one last look around. It was a shame to leave.

"We'd better get going before we get into any more trouble than we already are," Zach said gently.

"I hate logic and good sense."

Zach gave a bark of laughter, but there was a bitterness in his voice when he said, "I get that."

Kayla slid into the car, taking her time buckling up and starting the engine. She followed the park's brutally slow speed limit on the straight, empty road.

"Too bad we didn't get to see any wild horses," Zach remarked as the car crested the bridge back to the mainland.

"I guess we'll just have to come back after we finish training."

Zach grunted in what might have been agreement and dug into his bag again. "I'm feeling trail mix. Want some?"

Kayla sighed and held out her hand. They weren't even back at camp and her mood was sinking.

Music helped. Zach was able to find a pop station that played music from their youth, which led to singing and teasing each other about their respective taste in songs. Kayla nudged up the volume on a Taylor Swift song about asking to be remembered in a nice dress and sang along.

When the song ended and a bulletin started about shark attacks in the bay, Zach flipped through the channels. "When we go our separate ways, I'll remember you like you were tonight, laughing and playing tag with the waves. Classic Rock okay? Until the other station comes back?"

Kayla guided the car back to her side of the double yellow line. *What?* "Classic Rock is fine, better than Country."

"Some Pop Country can be entertaining, but if I listen to it for too long, it makes me want a drink."

Kayla laughed, but wanted to hear more about him remembering her. Zach *did* resemble the man in the Taylor Swift song they'd just listened to. He was tall and handsome as hell. But the rest of the song was bittersweet and romantic; Zach had kept them as just friends. *What had he meant?* She wasn't graduating yet.

"Who's your favorite Classic Rock singer or band?" Zach asked.

Kicking herself for chickening out and not just asking, Kayla tucked the comment away. There'd be time to overthink later. She dug up her limited Classic Rock knowledge instead.

When they pulled into the parking lot at Tidal Water, Miranda was sitting in a folding chair at the edge of the gravel, working on her laptop.

"Guess she's back from Richmond," Zach said, with a dry chuckle.

"I wonder how much trouble we're in," Kayla muttered, guiding the car back to its parking spot.

Zach offered his hand. Kayla slid hers in his, her magic tingling in response.

His eyes narrowed as he studied the moonlit shadows and puddles. "We asked permission. She's angry, but mostly because she's afraid we'll bond and is afraid she can't control me. She'll lecture me, but can't really do anything to punish me, which just makes her more angry." He shrugged. "I really don't give a crap, but best if you play apologetic and head straight for your house when she releases you. I'll stand through my lecture and be perfectly fine."

That raised Kayla's hackles, and she squeezed his hand tighter. "I should be in at least as much trouble as you. I won't let you take the blame."

His smile was bright and genuine, even in the dark interior of the car. "Thanks, but honestly, you defending me will only freak Miranda out more. I'd kiss your hand for your gallantry, but that'll really send her over the edge."

There was mischief in his eyes, but there was something deeper in his face. Sadness? A goodbye? *How much trouble is he in?*

"I don't regret a moment of time spent with you. Now come on. Let's get this over with." He squeezed her hand before letting go. Opening the car door, he got out without looking back.

Kayla put both hands on the wheel and heaved a huge, heartfelt sigh. Shaking herself, she slid out of the car, carrying her shoes. The gravel was rough, but manageable in bare feet.

"Hi, Miranda," Zach said, with an ironic tilt of his head.

With precise movements, Miranda closed her laptop, stood up, and placed it on the chair behind her. Crossing her arms, she looked her two trainees over.

Kayla wanted to edge closer to Zach, but that would only support Miranda's fears.

"Would you care to explain yourselves?" Miranda said, a light varnish of politeness covering a deep well of icy rage.

Zach shrugged and shoved his hands in his pockets.

Kayla rubbed her arms. "I've been running the same trails over and over since I got here. I needed somewhere new to run. It really helped clear my head. I feel much better. Ready for a good night's sleep and a full day of learning to master my magic tomorrow."

Miranda focused her hard gaze on Zach. "Did you go running with her?"

Zach gave a bark of humorless laughter. "Hell, no, I don't run. I stare off into space and contemplate the insignificance of human existence."

Relief and annoyance warred in Miranda's face before she collected herself. Her attention swung back to Kayla. "The rules exist for a reason. I've spoken with Dahlia. She now knows better than to give permission to leave property again. It's not safe outside for people who can use magic but haven't yet mastered it. Kayla, your training is almost complete. I expect you to make do with the trails on property until then."

"Of course," Kayla said quickly.

"Where did you get the keys for that car?" Miranda asked, putting her hand out for them.

Kayla handed them over.

"Hide-a-key in the wheel well. Clear as day in the shadows," Zach said.

"*You* are dismissed." Miranda gave Kayla a wave and turned her dark eyes on Zach.

Kayla glanced at him. Slouching arrogantly, he was only making things worse on himself. Every fiber of her being strained to stay and defend him, or shake him until he acted like a person, not a caricature of a bad boy. But he was a Shadow and far more aware than he acted. If he said she'd only make things worse by staying, he was probably right. Hands clenched at her sides, Kayla strode away as smoothly as she could, unable to make out Miranda's stream of angry words.

Clouds flirted with the moon, but there was enough light to walk back to the house. Kayla hesitated at the door to the cabin, wishing she could be anywhere else. It was tempting to sleep on the damp, rough porch rather than go in; well, at least in theory. Digging for courage, she slowly cracked the door open. Breathing quietly and shallowly, she peeked in. The light Hannah always left on if Kayla was out past bedtime lit the interior. Otherwise, the room showed no sign that Kayla had run off. She placed her shoes silently with the others, but winced when her jacket rustled as she slid out of it and hung it on the hook. Walking quickly by her desk, eyes averted from its baren surface, she turned out the light and slipped into her room. Kayla leaned against the closed door and breathed a sigh of relief.

A knock made Kayla jump. Shaking off the shivers, she bounded away from the door. "What?"

"Just making sure you're alive," Hannah called through the door.

"Yep. I'm alive." Kayla held her breath.

The silence stretched.

"I was worried." Hannah's voice held reproach and hurt.

Kayla inhaled through her teeth. A wave of anger saved her from apologizing for her actions. "I'm back." That made it easier to be compassionate. "I'm sorry you spent energy worrying when I was perfectly safe. Have a good night."

Hannah sighed sadly. "Good night."

Kayla waited a full five minutes after she heard Hannah's door close before she slipped to the bathroom to shower.

Sleep came so quickly and deeply she was disoriented when she woke. It was as if she'd been physically yanked awake, but she was alone in her room. The hunk of quartz she'd found with Smith's Knot glowed softly on her nightstand as she listened for what had disturbed her. She made another mental note to take the rock to Ara or Miranda.

Dream images floated through her mind. Surreal monsters made of waves chased her and Zach, pulling them apart, spinning and yanking her like a riptide. She'd been trapped beneath the water, the walls closing in on her. But it wasn't the nightmare that had woken her.

Worries about Zach being in trouble with Miranda and his odd mood on the drive home crowded into her mind. Something tugged at her gut. Kayla frowned. The tug came again. *Just like when Storm was on shore.* A strand was pulling her.

Her clock said it was too early to get up, but instinct told her it was important.

"I'm nuts," she muttered under her breath. But she was too awake and curious to go back to sleep. Slipping out of her room, she pulled her jacket over her brown flannel PJs and slid into her backup sneakers. The tread was worn flat, but they were dry. Careful not to let the screen door slam, she stepped out into the dew and moonlight washed night. Breezy, crisp air with traces of brackish bay soothed her warm skin.

The pull faded, so she skipped and twirled towards the bay, shaking off her nightmares. There was no sign of the unicorn, but the water was beautiful as the low, racing clouds gave the moon cover to play hide and seek. Hopping onto one of the boulders, she put her hands on her hips and surveyed the world before her. Grounding through her feet, the way tai chi had taught her, the tension drained out of her body. She yawned. Maybe she could go back to sleep after all.

The strands came alive around her. Almost as beautiful as they'd been on the beach with Zach. It had been such a magical moment. The yearning to kiss him, to let her mouth explore his and her hands explore his body had been almost overwhelming. Had he felt when she'd touched one of the strings of magic connecting them and ignored it, or was she alone in feeling something tangible between them?

A strand twanged at her attention.

Curious, Kayla traced the line of white light with her finger. Peace, warmth, and desire wrapped around her like a cozy blanket. The thread connected to Zach then. Frowning, she studied it. The magic line held its place, still and silent in the playful breeze. Kayla shrugged. *Maybe I imagined the twang?*

The strand shivered again, like a lightly plucked string.

"Well, that's new," Kayla muttered.

Letting the glowing strands fade, she shifted her focus fully to the real world. Nothing seemed out of the ordinary. Shrugging, she brought the strands back into focus and followed the bouncing string of light towards Xander.

She didn't see Zach at first, in black pants and his dark leather jacket, slipping through the shadows. She would have missed him altogether if it wasn't for the glowing thread running between them. *He can't sleep either?* She was about to wave and jog over to see if he wanted to practice tai chi, when he ducked behind a tree and snuck towards Newton.

"What in the world?" Kayla followed. Another strand shivered in the opposite direction, but she didn't have time to figure out what it connected to. Zach was moving fast. She picked up a light jog so she wouldn't lose sight of him.

Twenty-Seven

Waiting for a low cloud to cover the moon, Zach slipped through the open fields towards Newton. Despite the cool night breeze, Zach's hands were sweaty when he reached the stone building. He monitored every flicker of movement in the wave-tossed, moon-cast shadows. They were dreamy and surreal, but they'd do.

Not being able to recruit Kayla nagged at him like a buzzing mosquito. Earlier in the parking lot, the shadows had been clear as pen and ink. Having a Shiner close always helped his magic, but it felt like more with Kayla. Maybe Miranda's fears were correct, maybe he and Kayla were bonding. Maybe that's why he kept catching glimpses of her between the shadow waves.

"It doesn't matter," he scolded himself under his breath, following the stone around to the lab door. Kayla was staying with Searcha. Saving the world was more important than his crush on a bright-spirited enemy agent.

Newton was creepy at night in a way it wasn't in sunlight. A few spiderwebs, and it would be a convincing location in a horror movie.

Shaking off imaginary fears, he concentrated on looking for real ones. For a panicked moment he couldn't see the door code in the shadows. He encouraged his inhale to expand into all four corners of his torso. The shadows shifted and stilled. The moon broke free of a cloud. Numbers peeked through the shadow waves. Breathing into his whole body, he tried to cultivate curiosity instead of desperation.

The code he'd seen on Ara's tour had changed already. *There!* The entire code appeared just before a cloud muted the light. He punched it in. Silence for too many heartbeats. The light beeped green. The lock whirred open.

Zach glanced over his shoulder, but focused on the security in front of him. Rubbing away the itchy feeling on the back of his neck, he slipped into the dark interior.

The lock clicked into place behind him like a cocking gun. Zach shot it a dirty look. *Stupid, overactive imagination.* Keeping his head down, he ignored the security camera and pulled out his flashlight. He'd be long gone by the time anyone checked the footage. They'd be too busy dealing with Chessie arriving in the fading, predawn starlight.

The red setting on his flashlight cast harsh, shallow shadows, but it gave him enough to punch in the code for the second security door. The clouds shifted and moonlight poured into the courtyard. The net over the top, to keep the crows out, cast crisscrossed shadows he'd not noticed in the sunlight. Smoke from charcoal fires clung to the air. Turning off his flashlight and returning it to his pocket, he studied everything carefully, encouraging the shadows to shift through the past, present, and future.

The future was close. Zach staggered, putting his hand out on the stone wall to catch himself. As long as a pickup truck, Chessie would leap over the wall closest to the water and crash through the netting. Her powerful tail would knock down the wall to the lab supplies, and she would eat the spell ingredients, growing a foot as she consumed the magic stored there. Then she would wiggle and slam her way out, towards the plant golem, her stiff front fins allowing her to crawl as well as slither.

Shuddering, Zach tried to pull himself together. Should he call Tidal Water's landline when he got far enough away and warn them? *How the hell has Hannah not seen the monster coming yet?* How had the Shadow Twin not seen it? They'd not been scalded by its magic and weren't here, but Searcha was running out of time to notice.

Zach shook his head. If he didn't get that spellbook to the Guard, the damage to Searcha's facility would be the barest taste of the destruction to come.

Not seeing any other security measures, Zach strode across the courtyard to Ara's lab door. After several deep breaths, the code broke through the shadow waves. He punched in the numbers, swung the door out, but hesitated.

"It's too easy." He switched on his flashlight, bathing the neat room in red light. Lemon cleaning solution and an acrid bite of gunpowder wafted out at him. The shadows shivered, unnaturally still inside. Normally, still shadows would have been a blessing, a break from all the waves, but the hairs on the back of his neck were prickling.

Blinking to widen his narrowing vision, Zach searched for what was off about the room. Hints of chamomile and tea-tree oil underlaid the lemon cleaner.

Something skittered across the far corner. *A spider.* Newton would have spiderwebs then. Squinting, Zach tried to figure out what was off about the crawly critter. An ache bloomed in his forehead. He rubbed his damp palms on his pants. *It's not a real spider!* It was drawn in fine graphite lines. *A shadow.* Understanding one, dozens more peeked out, tucked into corners and against tables, bookshelves, and lab equipment, even climbing the walls.

Drawing back, Zach tried to see the big picture. His flashlight shimmered off paper-thin planes that reached from one side of the room to the other at random angles. Tilting his head, he frowned until the pain in his forehead intensified into a full-blown headache.

If Kayla was here, she would tease him about how furrowed his brow was and be tempted to ease the lines with her finger. She'd catch herself, but Zach would notice, like he had the other times he'd gotten lost in concentration in front of her.

A smile eased some of his tension.

The shadows shifted, the spectrum Zach could see widened, and several human-sized spiderwebs materialized. One was across the floor, a foot and a half off the ground, three others slanting at varying angles from ceiling to floor, and a fifth hung from one wall to its diagonal.

Zach put his hands on his hips. A magical version of a laser grid. *I'm kinda impressed.* Though this one probably wouldn't trip any alarms, it would leave him stuck until someone showed up in the morning. *No, Chessie would get me first.*

Rubbing away the goosebumps on his arms, Zach grinned. If the fate of the world wasn't resting on his shoulders, and the cost of losing didn't include being eaten, he would have traversed this room for fun.

As part of his mind tried to puzzle out how the spell was made, how they took it down during the day, and how the Guard might adapt it for their own uses, the other part tried to plot a course through the web. The spell was new and not perfected yet. The web was uneven, with large gaps in some places and a tight mesh in others. He itched to draw this as a scene from a comic book. Zach firmly pushed everything aside that didn't help him get across now.

He placed his flashlight on the ground, where it would give him the best light. Interlacing his fingers, he pressed them palms out, then shook himself loose.

There were no flips or cartwheels required to get to the far door, but every bit of his balance and control was needed. There were a lot of careful steps, ducking, and a short stretch of crawling on his stomach over the cold concrete floor.

An image of what he'd look like to someone who couldn't see the webs lit Zach's imagination. He gave a snort of muffled laughter.

His glance caught a web, and he stopped, foot midair. Mentally cursing, he set his foot down a good yard from where he'd almost gotten stuck. Reminding himself to stay in the moment, he made it the rest of the way across the room. He punched in the shadow-provided code and carefully opened the door. The scent of old books and cedarwood enveloped him.

The spellbook was on the bookshelf, exactly where Ara had shown him. Time itched at Zach to hurry, but he forced himself to triple-check for traps. It was more difficult now, with his flashlight on the other side of the room, but there was enough light to make it work.

He stepped into the room and looked the spellbook over one last time. Holding his breath, he picked it up.

Nothing happened. He checked for booby traps. None he could find.

Zach mentally counted to ten before he breathed out. Still, nothing happened. A huge grin eased his headache. He zipped the book into his inside breast pocket.

I did it! He wanted to do a victory dance, but the warning in his gut to hurry was making him nauseous. There were other interesting grimoires he could take, but nothing called to him. Nothing was important enough to risk more on.

He worked his way back through the webbed room. If he was going to make a careless mistake, it would be on the way out. Knowing that, he forced himself to take his time.

He didn't grin again until he stepped out of the lab building. *I actually did it!* Closing the door behind him, hearing the lock slide into place, he nearly whooped out loud. Chessie could be stopped. They were going to win.

He was no longer a supporting character in the Guard, but a hero. Terra and Sadie would be impressed. Even Elliot might be proud. Alexis would say she always knew he could do it. Brian would slap him on the back, and for once Zach would know he'd earned their praise. A contributing member of the Guard, not an extra piece that no one, especially Zach, was quite sure what to do with. He punched his fist into the air. Nick's car was packed and ready to go, the extra spare key in Zach's jacket pocket.

"We got you, you son of a bitch!" Hannah said.

Zach's stomach dropped like a rollercoaster.

Miranda stepped out of the shadows of the trees with a shotgun pointed directly at him. Hannah at her heels, triumph on her face. Looking confused and hurt at their side was Kayla.

"I'm sure he has a good reason for going into the lab," Kayla said, her eyes pleading with Zach to have one.

The shadows were clear enough. Kayla had seen him and followed. Hannah, monitoring Kayla with her magic, was awakened, and when the shadows showed Hannah what was going on, she'd gone for Miranda. Kayla had been trapped when Miranda and Hannah joined her, waiting for Zach to emerge from Newton. Zach had been too focused on his goal to recognize what the flashes of Kayla in the shadows had really meant. Mentally cursing himself, didn't make him less of an idiot.

"Hannah, search him," Miranda said. Raising her voice, she called, "Jason, he came out the door."

Zach sighed. *Of course, Jason was around back to catch me if I went over the wall.* He'd missed that detail in the shadows, too.

"I was just curious to see if I could get in. Test your security." Zach itched to run for the car, but Miranda would shoot him if he did. Emotionally, he couldn't believe it, but his blood was splattered red across the shadows. Desperately, he searched for another way out.

"Shut up and stand still," Miranda said.

Jason joined them, a taser in hand.

Zach swallowed back bile as Hannah searched his jacket pockets. With the help of the shadows, she sensed the spellbook in a moment, missing everything else. It took her a moment longer to locate the inside pocket and fish the book out.

"Got it!" Hannah held it up. "I told you, Kayla, he was just using you."

"My grimoire!" Kayla gasped. Her hurt knifed into Zach's stomach.

Brutally, he buried the pain. Getting the book to the Guard was all that mattered. There had to be a way.

"Like I said." Zach slouched into his jacket. "I was testing security. I have a few recommendations for improvements."

"Even I can tell he's lying. What do you see?" Miranda asked Hannah.

Hannah scowled and shoved the book into the waistband of her yoga pants. "I've struggled to read him since he got here. I thought it was my dislike clouding my magic, but if he's stealing grimoires, maybe it's something else?"

"I suspect he's using an enchantment to block you. Jason, will you do the honors?"

Jason clipped the stun gun to his belt and pulled out a small leather sack.

"What the hell?" At first Zach thought it was a memory wipe spell, but as he stumbled back, he saw that it was the spell-breaking powder Ara had demonstrated. He yanked the emergency button off the back of his jacket, and dropped it to the sidewalk. It rolled four inches before catching in a crack. Zach brought his heel down on it, hard, as Jason threw the glitter. Vinegar- and pine-scented flakes rained down on Zach. His skin cracked and itched like it was coated in a thick layer of drying sweat. The coating dissolved into sour mist.

Zach's eyes met Hannah's. He was all but naked as her gaze dropped to his shadow. Grinding the button under his heel, he hoped it had cracked in time. Reaching for anger, all he found was panic and soul-crushing failure.

"It worked," Hannah said slowly, as if she couldn't quite believe what she was seeing. "It broke whatever enchantment was obscuring his shadow. He's not being bribed by the Guard or a blogger to pass on information." Hannah gaped at him a moment before dropping her gaze back to the shadowy grass. "He was a member of the Guard before he got here. He's a spy!"

Zach could see Miranda connecting the dots to Nick. Zach had to obscure his own shadow before she started asking questions that would pull up answers Hannah could discern. He couldn't feel lust for Kayla when there was an ocean of hurt in her eyes. His anger against Searcha wasn't strong enough; he liked too many of them as people. Magic was dangerous, but he didn't hate it either. *Think! An emotion strong enough to hide my shadow.* His vision tunneled.

"A spy?" Kayla asked. "But then he'd have to have been lying to us the whole time?"

"Yes." Miranda was the only one who didn't look surprised. She emanated white-hot rage.

His death was clear in her shadow. He could taste it in the metallic tang in the air. Lightheaded, he struggled to keep his footing.

"Why?" Hannah shook his arm hard.

The jolt helped ground Zach. Miranda killing him was only one possible future. Chessie was another. A distant part of his brain noted that he was going to hyperventilate if he didn't get a grip.

"Why keep magic locked up?" Hannah pressed.

A panicked laugh escaped. "To save the world."

"Magic doesn't kill people. People kill people," Jason said.

Zach laughed again, ignoring how manic he sounded. "People killing each other with magic is the least of my worries, but you can't see the real threat." He turned to Hannah, anger helping him find his footing. "Why can't you, Shadow? Look around—"

Miranda jammed the butt of her gun into Zach's solar plexus. "Enough."

He doubled over, gasping for breath.

Miranda turned to the others. "Let's move. I'd rather interrogate him indoors."

"Interrogate?" Kayla asked.

Miranda yanked Zach upright and shoved the barrel of her gun into his back. "Move."

Zach wondered if he was fast enough to get the gun out of her hand, like an action hero, but she was a trained markswoman and he wasn't.

"Miranda?" Kayla pressed.

Miranda straightened. "It won't be like the movies. Now that the enchantment is lifted, Hannah will be able to read him." Her voice dropped, so only Zach could hear her. "Things shouldn't get too messy."

He could hear the smile in her voice, but didn't turn around to confirm. Red paint splattered into the shadows in front of Zach. Images of Nick getting ambushed and shot by Searcha agents. It would happen if Zach blew the man's cover. Then he shifted his gaze and saw DC being ravaged by a gigantic Chessie. The smell of rotting fish and metallic blood filled his nose. Zach tripped, landing on his hands and knees. He tried to keep the contents of his stomach down.

"Get up!" Miranda said.

Zach focused on his breathing. The ground beneath his sweaty, stinging palms was damp from the rain, not his heart's blood. There was nothing he could do about the bigger picture in this moment. Right now, he needed to manipulate his shadow to hide as much sensitive information as he could. To do that, he needed to be alive. He had to trust that the rest was being taken care of. He and the mud on his hands were made of the same stardust. He was one piece of a much bigger whole.

Fear helps nothing. Unless one needed a strong-enough emotion to hide one's shadow. A twisted smile touched his lips. He gave himself another breath to plan. The pain of his skinned hands added an idea.

Twenty-Eight

Kayla
Day 12 of the Lockhouse Knot Leak
Tuesday, deep in the night
Tidal Water, MD

Kayla looked from Zach to Hannah to Miranda, waiting for one of them to say, "Got you! Ha ha, you should have seen your face!" It was like when Dr. Caligo told Kayla the weird things happening to her meant she was magic; Kayla's brain couldn't keep up.

"You're all idiots!" Zach pulled himself to his feet. "There's a city-eating monster headed this way! And what? You just didn't notice?"

An uncomfortable laugh escaped Kayla. "You can't be serious." He couldn't be.

The look he gave her was dead serious, if a little manic. "Before dawn, it's going to destroy the lab on its way to eat your magical plant in the square. Then it'll head for DC."

Miranda again struck him in the gut with the butt of the shotgun. Kayla flinched.

On his hands and knees again, Zach wiped his mouth and then laughed. "That book is the only chance we have of stopping it."

Kayla's stomach twisted into knots. "Hannah would have seen it."

Zach spat on the grass as Jason hauled him to his feet. "It's clear as day. I've been seeing it since the Lockhouse Knot started leaking. It spawned from the initial ooze of knot coating that floated downriver and out to sea. It's been growing bigger and more dangerous in the Atlantic and is now coming back, attacking any swimmers it encounters on the way."

Kayla looked at Hannah and Miranda, waiting for them to laugh off this insanity.

"It's the guardian of the leaking knot?" Miranda said.

Zach nodded. "We call them monsters, but sure, in your vernacular."

Miranda looked at Hannah with a raised eyebrow.

"He's telling the truth as best I can tell. Or at least he believes it's the truth," Hannah said, before turning to Zach. "I've been getting bits of the *Jaws* theme music and other aquatic danger sounds, but how can you tell it's a sea monster or where it's going?"

"He and Kayla have been bonding," Miranda snapped.

Kayla opened her mouth to protest.

Zach guffawed. "Do you always jump to that conclusion? I was carrying the knot when one of your idiot alchemists nicked it with an enchanted blade. It leaked magic all over me. I'm more bonded with that monster than I am with Kayla."

Kayla flinched. She'd been ready to deny their bond, but hearing it from him? *Ouch!*

"You did the same thing when the knot started leaking." He scoffed. "Hannah figured out the grimoire existed because it holds the key to stopping the sea monster that was forming. Did you look back and see it happened at the same time the knot started leaking? It had nothing to do with Hannah and Kayla." He turned to Hannah. "They're teaching their Shadows not to trust their guts, afraid you'll not be able to stomach the true cost of magic."

Miranda shoved him forward with the barrel of her shotgun. "Move."

"Why would Kayla and I find the grimoire if it could be used to stop the sea monster?" Hannah kept pace at Zach's side. "Magic wants to be free."

Zach snorted. "It wants to be free, but also has a self-preservation instinct. Each knot is different. The unicorn and the plant are peaceful, the sea monster is, well, an enraged, bloodthirsty monster. Storm doesn't want to be eaten. That sea monster put multiple people in the hospital already. She will eat the plant when she gets here. Then she'll swim up the Potomac River to DC and tear the city apart, killing everyone in her path."

"Eat the plant? Kill people?" Kayla glanced at Miranda.

Zach looked back at Kayla, his eyes grave.

"It's coming for you next," Hannah gasped. "It wants to eat you."

Zach tilted his head respectfully to Hannah. "It does, and might, if Miranda here doesn't shoot me first."

Kayla gaped. He had to be joking. *Didn't he?* Miranda wouldn't actually kill him. Magic wouldn't hurt him.

"The monster wants to eat him?" Miranda asked. Her dark smile made Kayla shiver.

"Might want to let me go, see if it chases me. Might save you from having to evacuate," Zach said.

"Why do I keep hearing patriotic music?" Hannah asked, rubbing her temples.

"Like I said, it's going to DC after it comes here. I'm weirdly impressed you're willing to have that many deaths on your conscience. I get how you could live with mine, but the nation's capital? Three quarters of a million lives in jeopardy, and you're not going to use that book to save them?"

Kayla rubbed her arms, hugging herself against his words.

Jason cleared his throat. "The Navy Yard is right there. Surely, they'll stop a sea monster even if they do not know what it is."

Zach's manic laughter erupted again. "How? Bullets can't stop magical creatures. I doubt larger weapons could. They don't show up on cameras, but sure, they show up on sonar." His sarcastic tone sliced through Kayla like broken glass. "The sea monster will grow big enough to knock over buildings and sink ships, but no problem, we've got nothing to worry about."

Hannah flicked a nervous glance at Jason, then Miranda. "Zach, the sea creature is after its knot, right? It just wants to untie her, to be whole. That's why she's going to DC. That's where the Guard has the knot, right? Why don't they just give it to her? Save her from having to attack the city?"

"Because what the mid-Atlantic really needs is an angry, bloodthirsty magic raging free." Zach snorted. "That monster isn't going to settle down once it has its knot, like a good dog. Unlike Storm finding nice knots to let loose, it'll find the ones so dangerous the human psyche is still scarred from its prehistoric encounters with them. Can't you see the apocalypse that will cause? A million casualties would be a drop in the bucket."

Kayla looked at Miranda. Their leader finally seemed to notice the effect Zach's words were having on her people.

"He's exaggerating." Miranda waved a dismissive hand. "We've been getting intel. Nothing shows it as being methodical enough to kill everyone in DC. Not even hurricane power. More like a tornado."

Zach looked at her with a horrified fascination. "Let's just say it's the sea monster and nothing else. What's the acceptable body count? A quarter of a million? And sure, seeing a real life sea monster killing people won't cause panic or terrified people to do stupid and dangerous things."

Kayla shivered.

Miranda rolled her eyes. "So dramatic." She opened a door to the small building attached to the side of her house. Inside was a dirt-stained, moldy room with a concrete floor, cinder-block walls, and no windows. It looked like it had been a maintenance shed in a past life, but now it was stripped bare.

"You probably want to take his jacket," Hannah said. "It has a lot of pockets. He might have something useful in there."

Miranda put her hand out to Zach.

Zach crossed his arms over his chest. "Seriously? You disenchanted it, and it's kinda chilly in here."

"You can either hand it over, or I can tase you and take it off your twitching body," Miranda said.

"Now who's being dramatic?" Zach rolled his eyes, but slid out of his jacket and held it out.

Miranda, hands full with the gun, took it and passed it to Kayla.

Kayla clutched the leather to her chest like a shield.

All the sarcasm fell away from Zach. His fear and honesty were clear and even more frightening than his earlier words. "Please, we have *maybe* a day before that raging monster reaches DC. Please, something has to be done."

Miranda closed the door on him and locked it.

"We aren't really going to let a sea monster destroy DC?" Kayla asked, begging for reassurance.

The hardness drained away from Miranda. "Kayla, I know this is difficult. Hannah, was he lying? Is the Guard really so stupid as to not give the knot to its guardian and stop this?"

Hannah was pale. She shook her head. "He's not lying. He's dramatizing maybe, and his terror was overpowering a lot, but I didn't hear a whisper of a deception when he said the Guard fears that knot will cause an apocalypse. They'll let DC burn rather than hand over the knot."

Miranda nodded thoughtfully. "Those poor, short-sighted fools." She turned to Kayla. "Your brother is in DC, isn't he?"

"Oh, God!" Kayla hadn't thought that far ahead.

"Jason, get her a router thing so she can use WiFi to call. Kayla, tell him to get out as soon as possible. You can have him join us at our evacuation location. Then start packing your essentials."

Hands shaking, Kayla nodded. "But what about the other people?" She was in her freakin' PJs talking about people being killed by a sea monster.

"It's not after the people, and most will have the sense to get out of the way of a magical sea creature. The casualties really won't be that high. I'm sorry though. I know this is hard to wrap your head around. But this is part of the Unavoidable Upheaval. Hurricanes and earthquakes are natural—they kill people. This guardian sounds a lot like a tsunami, but smaller. Tipping the scales back to harmony will involve upheaval.

"If the Guard hadn't made things so out of whack, the corrections would be easier, kinder. But they're the real monsters. It's their fault this is happening. If we join them and try to stop the river today, we're just delaying the dam breaking down the road, and the casualties will be so much higher. I won't have that on my conscience. Now is really the only choice we have.

"Call your brother. Get him out of the city. Then focus on packing. We're going to need your help to evacuate Tidal Water."

"What are you going to do with Zach?" Kayla asked.

"Kayla," Miranda's voice was firm, but her face was kind, "focus on the people and parts deserving of your help."

Gently, Jason gripped her arm. "Come on."

Kayla went with him, every muscle in her body begging her to run. To be anywhere but there.

Twenty-Nine

"If you keep hitting him, I'm not going to be able to hear anything," Hannah said, her voice calm, but her shadow was disturbed. "His pain is making everything staticky."

Zach leaned into the pain caused by a third blow to his gut. *Glad my stupid plan is working.*

"You're having trouble hearing anything anyway," Miranda fumed.

"I don't think beating him to a pulp is going to make him any more cooperative," Jason said mildly from his place by the door, where he'd settled when he'd joined them a few minutes ago. "Not if you want the truth. Torture is highly unreliable."

Jason's shadow showed he pulled that fact out of his ass, well, out of a paranormal police procedural he liked. Zach might have chuckled, but he was too busy fighting nausea. Vomiting all over the converted tool shed might speed things along, but *yuck!*

"We could drive him to Richmond, dump him with the Twins," Hannah said.

Is she trying to save my life? Zach couldn't tell.

Miranda shook her head. "I want this dealt with now."

"Maybe if we got Kayla in here," Jason said.

"No. Kayla is too emotional and too naïve. She can't see the forest for the trees yet." Miranda tapped her index finger against the gun. "Jason, just hold Hannah's arm."

"I could get Nathan," Jason said quickly.

Miranda pointed at her watch.

Jason stepped away from the wall and placed a tentative hand on Hannah's shoulder.

Zach focused on Chessie gutting him. It wasn't pretty, but it overwhelmed subtler thoughts.

"Answer Miranda's question! Why did Nick bring you here?" Hannah's hand closed around his wrist. Magic crackled between them, pushing away like the north poles of two magnets.

Clarity in the shadows worked both directions. Hannah believed in magic. Believed everything wrong with the world stemmed from locking it away, that freeing it was the only way the planet would be peaceful and whole. But she was afraid she wasn't strong enough to do what Miranda thought was necessary. City-eating sea guardians and apocalypses didn't fit in a utopian future.

All of that, though, was overshadowed by a more immediate problem in her mind. She was deeply in love with Jason, and he had his hand on her shoulder.

Zach raised his eyebrow in a smirk.

Hannah paled. She was terrified Miranda would find out about her forbidden feelings, or worse, Jason.

A pang of sympathy for her surprised Zach.

"We're talking about Nick," Hannah growled.

Trusting her fear and conflicting feelings for Jason to cloud her magic, Zach focused on the version of Nick he hated. The man who'd started them down the road that led to this converted toolshed, who'd kidnapped children, and cut the First Knot. Zach recalled the absolute belief in the goodness of magic he'd seen in Nick's shadow when they'd approached Tidal Water.

Believing the lie with his whole body, Zach jerked his arm free and leaned into his fear. It was easy when his death was written in blood in the shadows on the walls. "Nick's totally on our side." He layered every doubt about Nick into his words and posture.

Frowning, Hannah studied him.

"Well?" Miranda asked, clearly not believing him, but wanting to be sure.

A flicker of relief warmed his chest, but as soon as he noticed it, he drowned it in the mind-numbing fear of being torn apart by the teeth that haunted him.

"I know you can hear the answer," Jason said.

Hannah's cheeks warmed with shame. She pulled away from Jason. He let his hand fall from her shoulder. His own pain and shame for his feelings were visible in his shadow. Hannah was too emotionally tangled to notice.

"Well?" Miranda repeated.

Hannah shook herself. "He hates Nick. Hates that Nick is the reason magic is back. There's no way they're working together. Nick thought he was bringing us a useful recruit," she said firmly, desperate to give Miranda an answer.

Zach could almost hear her think: *Seventy-five, eighty percent sure, that's good enough.* Zach couldn't blame her. Rarely were the shadows 100 percent clear about anything, but Miranda wanted certainty. He doused his relief with the image in Miranda's shadow of her shooting him, execution-style, and the Guard's disappointment in him.

They'd wanted him to come back alive. They'd needed him to bring the book. Alexis and Terra would get the Guard out of the city before Chessie got there, but what about the toddler next door, who liked to yell at the top of his lungs while playing in the yard? Or Sadie's girlfriend? Would Sadie follow protocol or protect her?

"Good," Miranda said. "Where is the Guard keeping the leaking knot?"

Hannah took a deep, frustrated breath.

Zach laughed, relief washing through him. "How the hell would I know? I'm sure they've moved it by now. I've been here." Searcha didn't have the same open communication the Guard did, making the truth even more believable.

"The shadows sound like he's telling the truth," Hannah said.

"You can't be more sure?" Miranda said.

"I'm not a lie detector," Hannah said.

"If you were better at your job, you would be."

"She's excellent at her job. You're the shitty one." Zach was rewarded with another blow to his gut. If he was going to die anyway, might as well not give up Guard secrets. From his hands and knees he groaned out, "You don't get how shadows work, and if you weren't so afraid of her—"

"Will you shut up!" Jason said.

Zach let himself sink to the ground and concentrated on not vomiting. As he got control of his stomach a twisted grin warmed his face. "I just figured out why you're so afraid of Shadows. Why you're so awful to Hannah. You're afraid she'll see what a failure you are."

Miranda kicked him.

Jason pulled her back.

"You were a Shiner," Zach said, pushing on. "When you tasted magic in that jungle you felt truly whole and safe for the first time in your life. You've never felt that way again. Even with magic back now, you can't find the connection, no matter how hard you look. You never will."

"Shut up," Miranda snarled.

"You're broken, unworthy, and old."

Miranda elbowed Jason, trying to get loose.

"He's goading us on purpose," Jason gasped. "He wants you to keep hitting him. He's using pain to hide his shadow. Hannah won't be able to do her job. He's pushing your buttons, not reading your shadow."

Miranda growled, but stopped fighting. Jason let her go.

"Not just a pretty face." Zach curled up in a ball. "No wonder your romantic feelings are returned. Too bad Searcha sucks, but you both have way more leverage than you think."

"What is he gibbering about?" Miranda snarled.

"He's just hoping I'll kick him," Jason lied, yanking Zach upright and shoving him against the wall.

"I'm really glad I'm a member of the Guard. We're nicer," Zach muttered. *And way more honest with each other.*

"How long have you been a member?" Miranda demanded.

Zach slouched against the wall. That wasn't a dangerous question, as far as he could tell. Playing defeated, he let the answer rise to the surface of his mind. Time was on his side. All he had to do was stay in control a bit longer.

"He was born into the Guard." Hannah sounded relieved the answer had come easily.

"Okay." Miranda started down her mental list of questions, but Chessie would be here soon.

Thirty

Kayla
Day 12 of the Lockhouse Knot Leak
Tuesday, sometime before dawn
Tidal Water, MD

Kayla put her knee on her duffle bag, forcing the zipper to close, but her attention was on her phone. "Pick up, pick up, pick up!"

Her brother's voicemail. Again. Tears rolling down her cheeks, she hung up and called again. Noah was going to freak when he turned on his phone and saw fifty-odd missed calls in the middle of the night.

She'd realized a dozen calls in that he'd warned her that he'd fallen behind in several important classes and was going to turn off his phone, social media, and regular email for the next few days to reduce distractions. He probably still had his school email, but she didn't know it.

His voicemail beeped at her. Kayla ended the call before it recorded her screech of frustration. It took everything she had not to throw her cell across the room.

"What the hell am I supposed to do?" *Call the school?* He lived off campus. *Mom probably has his school email.* But if Kayla called in the state she was in, her mom would want to know what was going on. Kayla couldn't outright lie to her. *What could I say?* If Kayla hadn't seen the conviction in Zach's and the others' eyes, she wouldn't believe any of this insanity either.

"Absolute, batshit insanity." Kayla sank to the ground by the bed, curling in on herself. Shaking and sobbing, she gasped for breath. Fear and helplessness consumed her as they worked their way through her body. *This isn't helping!* Anger only made the sobs wrench her gut.

Maybe it has value? It was something Zach would say to her. Pain knifed her chest. Gasping for breath, her body shook harder. Trying to lean in, instead of pushing away, like an uncomfortable point in a run, when if she just stayed with it a little longer, Kayla would feel the shift.

Zach's betrayal rose to the surface of her thoughts. Bewilderment slowed her tears for two breaths. *Was it all a lie? Is that why he never kissed me? Because he never cared about me?* She contorted into great, gulping sobs. *The pain will never end!* Her body worked through emotions that were too big for her brain to process.

She tried to stay present. Her nose was too stuffy. Distracted, her body and mind quieted. With a whine, she got up and dug for tissues. They weren't a necessity, so she had ignored them when they'd fallen behind her nightstand. Blowing her nose made everything a bit better.

Wrung out, but calmer, she padded to the bathroom. Splashing cool water on her face steadied her. One more blow of her nose and air flowed smoothly through it.

Back in her room, her phone sat on the bed, taunting her. Tears welled up. She batted them away with the back of her hand and had to blow her nose again.

Stretching her jaw and rubbing the sides of her head soothed some of the headache. *Water will help.* Going to the kitchen and draining a full glass made her feel more in control and reminded her it was the middle of the night. Even if Noah hadn't turned his phone off, he'd be sleeping. There was still time to reach her brother. *Maybe there is a point to this stupid feeling-emotions thing.*

Hannah opened the door and stepped in, flinching when the screen slammed behind her.

Kayla's calm slipped. "I can't get ahold of Noah!"

Hannah looked drained and exhausted. "I'm sorry."

Something in her voice made Kayla look harder. Filling a second glass with water, as the knots her tears had loosened reformed in her chest, she offered it to Hannah.

"Thanks," Hannah muttered, taking the glass.

"Sorry because my brother isn't picking up the freakin' phone or something else?"

Hannah looked away, but for once didn't seem to be reading shadows. "We got everything out of Zach we could, given the time constraints."

"What the hell does that mean?" He deserved to be squashed like a bug, not tortured. Kayla shook her head, trying to clear the jumbled emotions surging through her.

"He's been a Guard member his whole life, because his family is, but he's low ranking and doesn't know any of the inner-circle stuff. He's here as a last resort, to get your grimoire if they couldn't stop the leaking knot and sea guardian another way. Apparently there's not. They only chose him for the mission because he messed up, and the leaking knot spilled on him, and they didn't have anyone else to send. If they'd found another way, he would have just left with all the secrets he'd learned."

Kayla shrugged, attempting indifference, but anger surged through her. "Congrats. You were right. I shouldn't have trusted him."

Hannah sank into a chair. "If it's any consolation, he's right about the guardian. Unchecked, it'll reach DC tomorrow night, well, technically tonight. Maybe twenty, twenty-three hours from now."

Kayla turned away to see if any of her belongings had rolled under the couch.

Hannah finished her water and set the glass in the sink, then moved Kayla's there too. "Three quarters of a million people is probably an exaggeration, but, unchecked, it will kill people, and when it gets to its knot and unties it . . . the damage is going to be beyond anything I can comprehend."

Kayla couldn't grasp that scale. It was too insane. But her brother wasn't the only person she knew in the DC area. She had several old high school friends and some college friends that had moved there. The idea of a rampaging sea monster hurting any of them made Kayla shudder.

"So Miranda is going to find a way to fix it, right? That is way more than Unavoidable Upheaval, right? Just because living things didn't deserve to be locked away doesn't give them the right to go around massacring cities. That's the opposite of harmony." Kayla realized her words were making perfect sense. She didn't need to be freaking out about her brother. Murder, let alone mass murder, was unacceptable. Of course, Miranda would see that.

"Magic isn't just one thing. I've learned today that lumping them together is like saying Gandhi, Mother Teresa, and Hitler are all the same and would have deserved the same freedom and treatment, because they were all human," Hannah picked her glass back out of the sink, filled it, and downed it again, like a college guy guzzling a beer to impress his friends.

"Exactly!" Kayla breathed a sigh of relief. "We're all on the same page."

Hannah shook her head. "Miranda only sees in absolutes. I'm a Shadow, all I hear is nuance and unknowns. Miranda and Searcha are fighting against the Guard, who believe that locking an entire group of beings away forever is the only answer for a few dangerous individuals. Miranda is fighting for all the beauty, all that life, all that peace and magic that is there, and if she has to allow a few deadly individuals free to make that happen, then so be it."

"You're not talking about a few deadly individuals. You said we're talking about mass murder?" Kayla walked back to her room for her phone. She forced herself to pocket it when it went to voicemail instead of throwing it against the wall.

Hannah followed Kayla. "I believe in Searcha's mission, but maybe this one time, Miranda might be a hair too committed to freeing magic."

Kayla gaped at her.

"Yeah, don't tell her I said that. She'd brand me as a traitor for even thinking it." Hannah gave a half shrug. She picked up Zach's jacket from the back of Kayla's chair. "This was part of his disguise. He's not as angry or as combative as he played."

Kayla shrugged; she could have told Hannah that. He'd never been that way when it was just the two of them. She kneeled to check under the bed. Smith's rock glowed softly from where it had fallen during her packing. When she picked it up, it hummed softly against her skin.

"Take it with you. Storm wanted you to have it," Hannah said.

Kayla shrugged and pocketed it.

"I probably shouldn't say anything." Hannah let out a long breath. "But Miranda and Jason are zip-tying Zach to the dock. They're leaving him for the guardian, the sea monster."

Kayla gasped and jumped to her feet. "It'll kill him?"

"As surely as if Miranda had shot him with her gun. It's a shame. Now that I know what he was hiding, I can almost respect the guy. He really does care about you. Saving the world might come first, but that doesn't make his feelings any less real." Hannah shrugged. "He could have told Miranda how I feel about Jason, but he didn't. I was sharing every secret of his I could hear, yet he didn't lash out to hurt me with mine. He did take a metaphorical bite out of Miranda though." A twisted smile touched Hannah's lips before she shook it off. Setting down the jacket, Hannah retreated to her room to pack.

Too many thoughts warred in Kayla's brain for her to even start thinking through what Hannah had said. Panic choked her chest, and she wanted to cry again, but there wasn't time.

"Oh," Hannah called from her room, "if you can't get ahold of your brother in time, Miranda won't do anything to help him. Nothing personal, she's just got her priorities."

Hands shaking, Kayla looked at her phone. By the time her brother turned his on, it would be too late. If Miranda wouldn't help, who would? Zach's sketch of Storm on the beach caught her attention.

Filling her lungs and settling into her feet the way she did in tai chi helped clear her head and still her hands.

There was that time in college when she'd gone to a restaurant advertising free pizza. By the time she thought to ask why they needed so much information to give her a pizza, she was three-quarters of the way through the sign-up process for a credit card. In her opinion, she'd taken too long filling out paperwork to leave without her pizza, so she'd ended up with the card. When she'd gone to Noah to help her figure out how to pay off the debt and cancel the card, he'd explained the sunk-cost fallacy. Kayla swore never again to use getting in too deep as an excuse not to walk away from a bad situation.

Searcha reminded her of that pizza deal.

Kayla was totally on board with Storm, the magical plant, and the ability to feel how everything around her was connected and interwoven in a way that made her feel safe, a sense of belonging, and intrinsically valuable. But putting Jade in a coma, even accidentally, was highly questionable. Leaving an enemy to die at the teeth of a sea monster was something a cheesy supervillain might do. Not only allowing the destruction of a city, but impeding the saving of it . . .

"Screw this!" Kayla's gaze landed on the leather jacket.

Zach was a spy, and he'd betrayed her, but at this point he and his Guard were her brother's best chance, and he'd given her the keys to a fast car once. Maybe he could see where Miranda put them, and Kayla could use her magic to pull them to her. She yanked his sketch off the wall, tucked it into her duffle, and then tugged on his jacket. It smelled of sea breeze, moonlight, and his masculine body. It wrapped warmly around her, and the flat shape of one of his sketchbooks rested against her heart.

Kayla grabbed her duffle bag, propped her plastic bin on her hip, and took one last look around her room. It was *so* time to walk away.

She was halfway to the front door when Hannah stuck her head out of her room. "Take my scissors. Zip ties are a bitch."

"You knew I was going?"

Hannah shrugged. "I can only hear possible futures. You have to decide which one you'll choose."

"Thank you!" Kayla smiled and meant it. She snagged the scissors out of the pencil holder on Hannah's desk.

Hannah nodded. "Be careful, and good luck with the guardian, but the war has started. Once you step out that door, we'll be on opposite sides. I'll do almost anything to free the rest of magic."

Kayla hesitated on the threshold. "Searcha's rules about tying are stupid. Jason would be damn lucky to be your Shiner. Just saying, might be an argument worth having. Searcha would be foolish to stand in your way."

Surprise flashed across Hannah's face. "Thanks. Seriously, good luck."

"Thanks. You too." *I'm going to need it.* Kayla didn't look back again. She raced towards the dock, watching for anyone who might stop her.

Thirty-One

Zach
Day 12 of the Lockhouse Knot Leak
Tuesday, sometime before dawn
Tidal Water, MD

"If I was a comic book character, I would have a spare knife hidden in the sole of my boot," Zach muttered to the dark bay. Rubbing his wrists raw wouldn't help anything. It would cause his blood to drip on the sand and into the water, making it that much easier for Chessie to find him.

He was standing at the edge of the surf, under the dock, with his wrists zip-tied behind his back and around a piling. The wood was rough and weathered, but there weren't any barnacles or other sharp bits that might break through the plastic, which was cutting off circulation to his hands.

Reaching out for the invisible threads connecting him to Brian and Alexis, he tried to see if they were close enough to help, if they'd sensed his distress signal or seen what was happening to him. But the fear that he'd leaned into earlier and the choppy surface of the wave-tossed shadows blocked everything else out.

Tasting the brine in the air, Zach battled against his racing heart and shallow breathing, trying to allow calm back in. He couldn't feel his connection to the universe around him. Anger at himself for getting caught and at Searcha for their shortsightedness blocked some of his fear, but pushed his connection to his magic further away.

He should have helped Terra and the others come up with a better plan. He'd been an idiot to volunteer for a main character job. Secondary character energy, that's where he should have stayed.

That's not helping!

Think, think, think! There has to be something!

The waves lapped peacefully, no help at all.

"I will not be offered up to a sea monster like some virgin princess," he growled.

Soft laughter reaching his ears, he turned.

Kayla grinned at him in the moonlight. Zach's heart lurched. Face full of laughter, she was wearing his jacket. The shadow waves calmed around her, letting her reflection sparkle off them in warm tones of impressionist sunlight. A crow with a few white feathers hopped along beside her.

"At least you're not tied to a cliff," she teased, but her smile faded.

He tried to joke back. "Would that make you Perseus? If that crow is supposed to be Pegasus, he's got some growing to do."

A hint of a smile lit her eyes, but she shook it off.

Zach's eyes dropped to the ground. Shame washed over him, but that was his problem, not hers. He forced himself to look back up at her. "I'm truly, truly sorry I hurt you. Most of my lies to you were lies of omission, but that's absolutely no excuse. They still hurt you."

His head sank. "I can't regret trying to infiltrate Searcha. There's just too much at stake. But I'm really sorry for my actions that hurt you."

"I get why you were trying to get the grimoire. The sea monster sounds like it needs to be stopped," she said. "Sorry I accidentally led Hannah to you."

The crow cawed in agreement.

It wasn't quite an acceptance of his apology, but it was more than he expected. Probably all he'd get at this point. He glanced at the water. Chessie was going to close the distance in less than an hour.

"Wait! Why are you here? Shouldn't you be evacuating? You need to get as far away as you can before the monster gets here."

Kayla grinned. "You're tied up and trying to protect *me*?"

"Why are you here? Not that I'm not happy to see you," he added hastily.

"Seriously, are you that dense?" She walked behind him. "I was just starting to get the hang of magic, but that doesn't mean it's worth a crap ton of lives. Plus, after I get you out of here and back to your people, I kinda need to borrow your car."

With a snap Zach's wrists came free. He pulled her into a hug, holding on as if she was the only safe place in the entire world. There was no time to go to pieces, but he let himself have the moment, swallowing hard.

She held him back just as tightly.

The crow cawed at them.

Zach forced himself to step back. The shadows cleared a bit. "Jason's coming, we need to go." Zach hesitated. "Maybe leave the scissors?"

With a shrug, Kayla dropped them to the sand.

The crow hopped over and pecked the plastic handle.

"All yours, Munin," she told the crow. "I'll miss you."

"Nice name. Come on," Zach said. The stars almost matched his drawing.

The crow cawed and took to the air, circling them.

Kayla snagged her belongings, which she'd left a few feet away. Zach felt more useful when she let him carry her duffle bag.

Jogging, they looped around to avoid Jason and headed for the parking lot. The crow glided along beside them.

"Any ideas of how we can get the key?" Kayla asked.

"Miranda confiscated the one, but the second is in the inside right zip pocket." *Thank you, Nick.* Two keys weren't overkill.

"Right, your jacket."

Zach shot her a sideways glance. "I'd complain, but it looks good on you."

She smiled, tugging on the lapels. "I think I'll keep it."

"You earned it."

Munin cawed, changed directions, and landed on the fence lining one side of the square.

"Does he want us to go that way?" Kayla asked.

Zach definitely didn't want to go that way. They'd be out in the open, and anyone in the main house or Miranda's could look out and see them.

At least the training facility was in full-blown evacuation mode, with everyone following their compartmentalized jobs. If anyone besides the people who'd detained Zach saw him, they'd assume he was busy doing his part.

Munin cawed louder and more insistently.

"Stupid bird is going to call attention to us," Zach muttered, but there was a path leading through the shadows towards the square, like the one Storm had made for him. "Fine."

"The plant is so beautiful," Kayla murmured.

Shadow waves parted enough to show Zach a possible future. "It's a shame the monster is going to eat it."

"Can't something be done?" Kayla whispered.

The crow landed by it and cawed at her.

Zach shook his head. "We've got to go."

Kayla reached out to touch the leaves.

The plant reached out to her with its vines.

Kayla drew back.

"Wait." Zach frowned, trying to puzzle out what he was seeing. "I think it wants to come with you." It was a terrible idea, but the magical plant, golem, whatever, didn't want to be torn apart and eaten any more than Zach did.

Kayla hesitated, then offered her left arm. The plant tentatively reached out again. It looped around her arm, then the part with the flower grew until it rested on her shoulder. Shedding small branches and leaves, the rest of the plant followed. Its smooth trunk slithered like a snake up her arms, with branches like a dozen sloth-slow insect limbs. Then it tugged its roots free of the patio tiles and pulled them into a root ball, like a lobster curling its tail. The plant shifted around Kayla's arm and settled.

Zach let out a breath, very, very grateful it didn't want to strangle Kayla.

"Wow," Kayla whispered.

Munin gave an impatient caw.

"Yeah, thank you. I hear you. We got to go." Zach led the way to the shadows of Xander and paused. Ara and Ben were loading the van with alchemy supplies and enchantments.

Zach pointed at the plant. "Can you drive with that thing?"

Kayla frowned.

The plant shifted as if lifted by a breeze and reached half a dozen tendrils out to Zach, like an alien baby asking to be held. Zach frowned, but Kayla was the better choice of drivers. He reached out. The tendrils wrapped around his arm and then seemed to pull itself slowly over to him. It was light for its size, but the trunk was solid, and the roots tickled.

Ara and Ben headed back to the lab for another load.

"That's our chance, let's go," Zach said.

He helped stow her belongings in the trunk next to his. The crow took off to join the flock boiling in the air above the lab, unnerving in the dark sky.

Sliding into the shotgun seat, Zach buckled up.

"Where to?" Kayla spun the tires, tossing gravel behind them.

Zach dug the burner cell out of the glove box and turned it on. "Main road first." He picked up a signal as soon as they were off property.

Terra picked up on the first ring. "Hello?"

"I'm leaving the training facility now."

"Merlin's wisdom! Are you okay?"

"Yeah, I'm okay." Zach sank back into the plush seat, tension draining from him. He was back with the Guard. Home. The plant unwrapped from his arm and settled in his lap like a sleepy cat.

Terra's sigh of relief was audible. "We got your distress signal and were in the middle of trying to come up with a rescue plan. We were very determined, but it wasn't going well. Glad you didn't need us."

A hint of a smile touched Zach's face. Terra could be so matter of fact. His humor evaporated as he remembered his mission. He pushed past the shame that threatened to choke his voice. "I didn't get the spellbook."

"Well, that sucks. I'll divert the rescue planning back to working on the Chessie problem. It'll be good to have your help when you join us. We really need a fresh perspective. Besides," Terra added, "there's no guarantee the repair for the 1979 magic breach is there or that we could recreate it in such a short amount of time. You, however, are irreplaceable."

Zach fought back tears. "Thanks." Most of him could believe her. He did his best to let go of the part of him that wanted to argue.

"How are you leaving the facility?" Terra asked.

"Nick's car."

"I assume his cover is blown, then? Wait, you're driving? It doesn't sound like you're on speaker."

Zach had to chuckle. With everything going on, it was driving while talking on a cell phone that really worried Terra.

"No." Zach sent a smile to Kayla. "I made a friend. She saved my life and is driving." He couldn't quite believe she was actually leaving Searcha with him, after all.

Kayla waved a hand at the road, indicating she would need directions soon.

"Where should we head?" Zach asked. "You do know Chessie is headed for DC?"

"Yes. Russel is working to model the monster's movements. If she turned now and headed up the Potomac, we think we'd have about ten to thirteen hours until she reaches DC, but she hasn't turned yet. We're at a temporary safehouse near St. Michaels. I'll give you instructions when you get closer."

"Thanks. Apt place to fight a monster."

"Get here safe."

"Will do." Zach realized he'd skipped answering the question about Nick. "Oh, and his cover should be fine. I'm as sure as I can be that they believed my lies. I shared a bit more about the Guard during my interrogation than I wanted. I'll go through it all with you to be sure, but I don't think I gave away much they didn't already know."

"Great job. We need all the good news we can get. Call when you get to a gas station or something, and I'll give you the rest of the directions."

"Okay." Zach couldn't blame Terra for wanting to talk with him out of earshot of Kayla, so she could confirm all was well before sharing her exact location.

Call ended, Zach pulled up the GPS on his cell, which had been in his messenger bag, already packed in the car when he'd been captured.

Kayla tapped her index finger on the wheel as he relayed directions, but otherwise, she looked relaxed.

"I think I forgot to say it earlier," Zach said. "Thank you for saving my life."

Kayla shrugged. "Miranda is batshit. It wasn't a hard call. Even Hannah pitched in by offering her scissors. I'm just sorry I couldn't come up with a way to grab the grimoire. You'll be able to stop the guardian, won't you?"

The leather seat was suddenly uncomfortable. "Eventually, I expect, but I'm not sure how long it'll take. I recreated all the pages from the book I saw during the tour Ara gave me. Sketched them out as best I could. Might help." He'd forgotten to mention that to Terra.

"The longer it takes, the more people will get hurt? Die?"

Zach nodded. A thought tugged at him. "Wait! Your brother is in DC, isn't he?"

White lipped, Kayla nodded. "I can't get ahold of him. He turned off all distractions to study. After I drop you off with your people in DC—" She swallowed hard. "Like I said, I'd like to borrow the car. Is that okay? I have to find him. In case you can't stop the guardian in time."

"We're not being directed to DC yet, but it's in the right direction. Of course you can use the car." A cavern of sadness opened up inside Zach, but he did his best to think logically about her leaving. "We still have time before you need to go, though. Maybe you should rest first. Did you get any sleep last night?"

Kayla looked surprised. "Last night?"

"First light. Technically, it's morning." He nodded to where dawn was softening the darkness in the east.

She shook her head. "A little, what feels like days ago."

"You'll be a lot safer driving all the way to DC if you get a nap first." And that would give him and the Guard time to find another way. He couldn't tell if it was his fear or his intuition talking, but he was afraid that if she dropped him off, he'd never see her again. "Maybe I'm just being selfish. My brain is so melted."

Kayla's hand dropped gently on his arm for a moment. "Well, to be fair to your brain, it has had to deal with a lot. Being interrogated as a spy and almost being eaten by a sea monster is a lot."

Zach chuckled despite himself, despite the shadows filled with teeth and waves, devoid of any answers. He'd escaped from Chessie, for now at least. She was still headed for Tidal Water, away from DC. Russel's equipment would notify him when she changed directions, when their ten-to-thirteen-hour clock started ticking down to mass destruction.

Kayla heaved a sigh. "You've got a point about falling asleep at the wheel, though. You won't change your mind about the car?"

"I won't. The rest of the Guard will back me up. We value family." Brian and Alexis would have it no other way.

"What about the plant?"

Zach shrugged. "Storm helped save Guard lives last fall. That's a helpful precedent. For now at least, we have much bigger problems than a tiny plant golem."

"But the Guard is against all magic. Or did Miranda and Jason lie about that?"

Rubbing the smooth bark on the trunk of the plant with his index finger, Zach tried to figure out how to explain the truth without denying what he'd learned. The plant rustled happily, sounding like a summer breeze through a forest, and cuddled more comfortably in his lap.

"They weren't. The Guard is against having any magic in the world, because a little magic always leads to more." Zach pulled his sketchpad out of the bag at his feet and flipped through it. "Apart from the fact that loose magic is changing the fabric of reality, Storm and this plant don't seem to be a threat, and I don't think they are. Some Guard members will argue otherwise, but I'm starting to think that's just to make what has to be done easier on their consciences." Elliot could return the magic that had spawned Storm to her knot without any of the doubts and regrets Zach was going to have to face and push through. Shoving the thought aside, Zach tried to stay on track.

"Each knot that is cut and each artifact that is found, is like a crack in the dam keeping monsters like the one heading for DC at bay. The knot in Baltimore that was almost cut last fall was just as terrible. We have another one in our vault that makes me nauseous anytime I get near it. Those types of magics are what the Guard is trying to protect the world from."

Kayla rubbed her jaw. "But if there was magic in the world, then there wouldn't be a dam to break, it would just be a river."

"Probably, but a river full of monsters."

"My great-uncle, whose notebook you tried to take, he freed a magic that was only angry because it was separated from its knot. It would have been amazing otherwise."

Zach weighed racing to the safe house against pushing his argument, then said, "If you pull off up here and stop the car for a moment, I'd like to show you something."

Kayla pulled into the parking lot of a closed real-estate office. "Show me what?"

Zach opened his sketchbook to the first page he'd marked with his fingers and used his enchanted pen to make the magic ink visible.

The plant screeched like a squeaky door and tried to hide behind Zach's calves and the seat.

"Easy," Zach said, soothing it with his free hand. "It's just a picture."

The plant shivered against him.

"I can see why she doesn't like it. What is it?" Kayla frowned. "Wait, is that the guardian of the knot my great-uncle tried to free?"

"It's what the shadows show me when Elliot talks about what happened in 1979. He was there when the knot was damaged, too."

"Was he involved in murdering my great-uncle?"

"Yerik Gause? No, the monster killed him. Its knot is the one in our vault that makes me nauseous. I'm grateful it's locked safely away. Eight people would have been a drop in the bucket as far as casualties went if Gause hadn't sacrificed himself to help stop it."

"What?"

They compared the versions of events they'd been told, but Zach didn't want to get in the weeds trying to figure out whose story was more accurate. His point still stood; the guardian and its magic were dangerous.

He tapped the next image he'd marked. "This is what I saw in the shadows when the future held a high chance of the Baltimore Knot being cut. It's metaphorical, I think, but I could smell death when I saw it."

"That looks like some kind of apocalyptic future." Kayla frowned.

The plant gave another door squeak and wrapped several branches around Zach's legs.

Juggling the sketchbook with one hand, Zach rubbed the plant reassuringly and brought forth the last picture he'd marked.

Kayla gasped. "That's DC."

The waves of teeth and the snakehead-shaped monster overshadowing the skyline.

Zach winced as the plant tightened its grip on his leg, but he stayed focused on Kayla. "This is why the Guard was tasked to keep all magic out of the world." He flipped the page and tapped his magical pen to make pictures of Storm and the Plant come into focus. "Yes, it's far from perfect. With no magic in the world, there's no way to prove that it exists, much less that the knots and artifacts are worth collecting, and messes like what happened in 1979 always have the potential to happen, but it's the best we can do."

"That is a sucky choice."

"If you can come up with a better solution, I'd be happy to hear it."

The plant peeked out and climbed up, chirping, apparently at the drawing. It was hard to tell, since it didn't have a clear head or face. It traced a branch end along the lines of Storm, then curled up on top of the sketchbook.

"It really is like a cat," Zach muttered.

A laugh escaped Kayla. "I think it needs a name."

Zach nodded thoughtfully as Kayla put the car back in gear. "Well, there is a hypothesis that all guardians are female, so maybe a female name?"

"I like that. Something sweet and innocent sounding, too."

They batted a few names back and forth before Zach remembered she spawned under a full moon.

"What about Luna?" he offered.

The plant rustled like a cat purr.

Kayla grinned. "Sounds like a yes."

Luna folded up her flower and tucked it under her rootball tail and gave every appearance of going back to sleep.

Zach patted Luna's trunk, not noticing the silence had stretched on too long until Kayla brought up his cover. With painstaking honesty, he answered all Kayla's questions about what had been real and what had been lies.

As he talked, Zach slid the sketchbook out from under Luna when she started rustling softly; apparently the plant equivalent of snoring. With a graphite pencil, he traced the magical lines he'd made of the spellbook so he could take a picture and send it to Terra.

When they found an open gas station, they stopped. Kayla used some of the cash stashed in the glove box to pay for gas and get snacks, while Zach left the plant in the car and called Terra.

She had a bit of good news. Chessie was still moving toward Tidal Water. The monster's commitment to hunting for Zach and Luna on the Eastern Shore would buy the Guard needed time.

As Zach expected, Terra had questions about Kayla and security, but she trusted Zach, even after he admitted he couldn't see anything useful about her in the shadows. Alexis, on speaker, supported bringing Kayla to the safehouse. Zach sent the pictures he'd copied so far and added that they were bringing the plant golem with him.

"Good thing Elliot is still in DC, preparing for evacuation," was all Terra had to say about that.

They ended the call. He walked back to where Kayla was filling the car, feeling lighter and more grounded. The waves in the shadows around calmed marginally.

"Duh!" He slapped his forehead and called Terra back. "Kayla's got a brother in DC she can't reach. He goes to the same college as Sadie's girlfriend."

After he explained what he knew, Terra asked to speak to Kayla.

Zach handed her the phone and took over the gas pump. He smiled as he listened to Kayla fill Terra in on how to find her brother and sent Terra some pictures of him. It felt good to have a way to help.

He checked the car for trackers, though Searcha had bigger things to deal with at the moment. Satisfied, he slid back in.

"You said Hannah gave you her scissors to cut me loose?" he asked.

"Yeah, she was annoyed that, other than being a member of the Guard, you're a decent person." Kayla guided the car back to the main road.

"But I'm still Guard. Why help me?"

"Freeing good magic is very different from murder and homicidal monsters."

"I hate the idea of owing Hannah anything. I wonder if that's why Jason was coming out to the dock—to set me free, too? If that's why the shadows told me to leave the scissors. So the two of them can finally say to each other what they've both been hiding?"

"If that's true, then she'll owe you, too." Kayla smiled.

Zach shrugged. It would also mean he'd have helped two powerful members of Searcha tie. Helping Hannah and Jason understand each other better was like the plant curled up in his lap—it didn't feel as wrong as it should have. It was past time he got back to the Guard.

Thirty-Two

Kayla was grateful for the flat, straight route. The car would be a blast to drive on a busy highway or twisting mountain roads, but her attention span wasn't up for the challenge. Knowing Zach's people were helping find her brother lightened the pressure that had been keeping her sharp. She yawned. Zach was right about her needing a nap before driving to DC.

The conversation had slowed after they'd stopped at the gas station, and the silence wasn't helping her stay awake. The thought that had been bugging her during their conversation about his cover popped out of her mouth.

"Hannah complained you were lusting after me, but you said you just wanted to be friends?" Kayla put a hand over her mouth, but she'd already said it.

"Um." Zach scrubbed his face in his hands. He looked as tired as she felt. "Anger worked pretty well to hide a lot in my shadow, but it wasn't enough, so I leaned into other base emotions when needed. My attraction to you was an easy one to lean into."

"Was? Like it wasn't real?"

"Oh, it's real. The past tense was leaning into it to hide my shadow. It's a relief to be away from Tidal Water."

Her exhausted self-control couldn't keep up with her mouth. "You said you just wanted to be friends, though."

Zach gave a frustrated sigh. "I couldn't lie to you and then kiss us both senseless. I was already betraying you."

Kayla blinked. Warmth spread through her at the image painted in her mind. She swallowed hard, then spoke before she could overthink. "Well, you're not lying to me now."

Zach choked on air. Spluttering and coughing, he tried to pull himself together.

Feeling mischievous and feminine, Kayla relaxed as she waited him out.

Finally he cleared his throat and asked softly. "Does that mean you forgive me?"

Her amusement flitted away. His honesty deserved the same from her, but hard thinking was making her eyelids heavy. "I think so, but I'm also stupid tired at the moment." Just because she understood why he'd lied didn't mean she'd emotionally worked through it.

"Fair. Maybe sleep on it? Plus, I can't ask you out until this whole sea-monster thing is dealt with. We'd risk ending up with a hungry third wheel."

Kayla laughed. "If that was a graphic novel, how would it go?"

Brightening, Zach started a silly tale of their imaginary first date. Passing the story back and forth, they added a goofy shark sidekick, who always managed to interrupt just before they could eat. The characters chose a string of increasingly absurd places to get away.

The GPS announced they were arriving just as the imaginary Kayla and Zach were trying to eat meatball subs while hang gliding. The real Kayla couldn't stop giggling.

The unassuming two-story house was blue with white trim and shutters and had a small porch. A splash of yard separated it from its neighbors. An old Corolla and a pollen-coated Ford pickup were parked in the narrow driveway, so Kayla parked on the street.

Kayla glanced in the rearview mirror and smoothed the fly-aways from her braid. She looked like she'd been cramming for finals. *Great, time to meet the bigoted, uptight, magic-can't-be-any-thing-but-evil, Guard.* Her rumpled appearance was the least of her problems.

Zach sighed.

"You okay?" Kayla asked.

"Yeah. I just royally screwed up my mission, and they're going to be kind." He gently scooped the sleepy plant off his lap and into his messenger bag. "It's all good. Just bracing myself. Come on, let's get our stuff." He swung the car door open and stepped out.

A tall, stocky, thirty-something woman with brown hair opened the screen door. Her faded Camp Cattail T-shirt and blue jeans had Kayla double checking the house number.

"You made good time!" The woman raced down the stairs and bundled Zach into a big hug. "Alexis had us all worried with what she was seeing in the shadows."

Kayla stood awkwardly to the side, shifting from foot to foot as the motherly hug lasted several times longer than she expected.

"It's good to be home," Zach said as they pulled back. "Terra, Kayla. Kayla, Terra."

Terra offered her hand. "It's good to meet you in person. I'm the coordinator and paperwork wrangler. We haven't had any luck locating your brother yet, but I expect another update in four hours."

Kayla shook her hand, blinking back tears. This stranger understood how much Kayla needed any answer about her brother, even if it was that they didn't know anything yet. "It's good to meet you."

"Where's the plant golem?" Terra asked.

Zach held up his bag. Several leafy branches were sticking out. "We've named her Luna."

"Merlin, help us." Terra shook her head. "Let's get you inside. There's food and beds, for whichever order you prefer." Helping with the bags, Terra led the way up the porch and inside the house.

A twenty-something man, with a pencil behind his ear, looked up from the dining room table he was standing beside. His flannel had a light splatter of paint and grease stains, and his smile was warm.

"Zach! Glad you're here. Come see if my mapping of Chessie's movements looks accurate. My equipment is having trouble with her abrupt changes in direction." He gestured at the charts, maps, and papers scattered over the table. "Kayla, nice to meet you. I'm Russel." He waved.

Kayla gave a wave back, standing uncertainly in the entryway.

Zach dropped his duffle at the side of the stairs and moved to the table. Russel slapped him warmly on the back, then started pointing out dots on the chart.

Kayla realized why the hug earlier had thrown her. *They don't keep their distance from Zach!* Did they not take him seriously as a Shadow?

"I can see your problem." Zach gave a ghost of a laugh and pointed. "That's where she picked up my scent—from my blood mixed with her magic at the shipwreck—and here's where she caught my scent leading towards Tidal Water."

"Since you didn't get eaten, I'd call it a win. Her detour is buying us time," Russel said. "She's just reaching the camp. When she realizes you and the plant are gone we expect she'll turn towards DC. I'm still estimating it'll take her ten to thirteen hours to make that swim."

"Kayla," Terra said. "Do you want to eat or sleep first?"

Kayla didn't have to think about it. "Sleep."

"Peter?" Terra said.

A teenage boy with pale blond hair and blue eyes that looked old for his age slid off a stool at the bar between the kitchen and dining room. He was gangly, like he'd grown a foot overnight. He looked familiar, though Kayla was sure they'd never met.

"Peter?" Zach asked Terra.

"A precaution," Terra said. "I'm glad it wasn't necessary."

Kayla looked on curiously, but reminded herself it was none of her business. She wasn't Guard. Wasn't sure she could get on board with their absolutely-no-magic philosophy, even if they were a lot warmer, so far, than she'd expected.

"Where are Alexis and Brian?" Zach asked.

"Out walking Prince, they'll be back soon," Terra said. "We were all thinking ourselves in circles so I called a mandatory break."

Zach nodded and returned to the chart.

"Peter, will you show Kayla the sunrise bedroom?" Terra said. "And make sure she has everything she needs? Kayla, would you like me to wake you if I get word on your brother?"

"Yes, please. If you can't find him, I'm going to drive to DC and get him myself."

"Zach told me. I don't see how you'll have any more luck than my people, but logic isn't always helpful in situations like this. If you're not up in time to make the drive, I'll wake you."

Kayla blinked. Unless she was reading the situation wrong, Terra didn't like the plan, but was deferring to Zach. She'd done it with the plant, too. *Isn't Terra the Guard equivalent of Miranda?* Apparently not.

Kayla was too tired for that much brain spinning.

"Come on," Peter said. When they reached the top of the stairs, he added, "Don't take it personally. They don't include me either. They're like a tight-knit family and are cautious of outsiders."

"But I thought Zach was low ranking?" Kayla tried to remember exactly what Hannah had said after the interrogation.

Peter snorted. "They don't really do ranks. But Shadows see truth, so of course everyone listens to their input."

"Wait, you're not Guard?"

He shook his head. "Hopefully, one day. Here you go. Bathroom is on the right. Anything you need?"

"I'm good, thanks." Kayla stepped into the peach-colored room.

Peter nodded and headed back.

Kayla dropped her duffle bag and tub on the ground, shrugged out of the jacket, kicked off her shoes, and crawled onto the soft mattress. *I need to relax, so I can sleep, so I can hurry up and get up and get to DC.* She was sound asleep before she even started to even out her breathing.

Thirty-Three

"My calculations indicate Chessie's speed is increasing with her size. By preventing her from eating the plant, you've slowed her growth," Russel said. "We're going to need every second of time we can buy."

Zach nodded, but it was taking everything he had to follow. Running on adrenaline, fear, caffeine, and gas-station snacks was catching up to him.

"We haven't had any luck with the copied pages of the spellbook you sent. Sadie recognizes some Russian, but can't figure out what the other symbols are," Terra said.

"Searcha's alchemists couldn't figure them out either. Here are the last of the pages I found." Zach tried to pull his pad out of his bag, but Luna was in the way. With some encouragement, she moved up his arm and hung from his neck and around his torso like a monkey. Zach handed the pad to Russel.

"I'm so glad Elliot isn't here," Terra muttered. "Getting her out of Tidal Water was a good move, but what are we going to do with her?"

"I don't know," Zach said. "She's drooping. Maybe she needs sunshine?"

Terra sighed. "Have you given her water?"

"Um, nope," he said.

"I'll get it." Terra squeezed his shoulder before walking to the kitchen.

Zach sank into a chair; his legs were grateful to be done.

Terra filled a bowl, and came back and set it on the floor.

Luna reached out a branch, tapped the water, and then slowly uncurled her root ball and sank into the bowl.

"Good call, thanks," Zach said.

The door opened. Alexis, Brian, and Prince filled the space with energy and sound.

Zach heaved himself to his feet to receive his hugs and dog licks.

Prince greeted him and sniffed Luna and her water bowl before going off in search of his own drink.

"Where's Noble?" Zach asked.

Russel sighed. "With Elliot, helping guard HQ."

Alexis fussed over Zach and was about to send him off to bed, when Peter's quiet voice caught their attention.

"Do you have the rest of this proof?"

"What?" Terra asked.

"Sorry," Peter muttered.

"Wait. It's a page from a spellbook. A proof of what?" Alexis asked lightly, but her eyes were drinking in the shadows.

"Like a mathematical proof?" Zach asked. "It does kind of look like a proof or a chemical reaction. You know, one line changing into another into another down the page. The two sides could be balanced. Though it's all gibberish."

"I assume there is a key somewhere," Peter said in a small voice. "Looks like a fun puzzle to solve."

"Doesn't look like any math I've ever seen," Brian said with a chuckle.

"This part kinda looks like a calculus problem." Peter pointed at the lines that, indeed, seemed to explain the symbol that was a cross between a Celtic knot and a magnetic field.

Russel tilted his head sideways. "I think I can see what you mean."

"That would explain the vague math equations I'm getting in the shadows around it, like a chalkboard in a movie with a crazy scientist," Alexis said.

"Math can explain or model everything in the universe," Zach said, more because it sounded good than because it was helpful. He should really take Alexis's advice and get some sleep. "But I thought magic broke the laws of nature."

"Yes, but from what we've observed so far, magic functions with its own rules," Russel said. "How do you think I do my estimations and projections?"

"Gause was a scientist at Fort Meade in 1979. It's his journal. Maybe math is how he approached magic, too." Terra pulled out her phone. "Let's loop Sadie in and see what she thinks."

"But spells are all about language choice," Sadie said on the video call when she'd heard the new idea. "Isn't that the opposite of math?"

"Searcha's alchemists were doing spells without any of the theory we've discovered, but they still work," Zach said. "I wouldn't be surprised if there are plenty of other levels or perspectives we haven't explored yet that also work."

"But you can't just pull math out of thin air," Sadie said. "I've never seen it in a book before."

"The equal sign wasn't invented until the fifteen hundreds," Peter said. "Math hasn't always looked the way you're used to. Could you have run across it before and not recognized it?" He looked like he wanted to hide under the table when everyone looked at him. Instead, he crossed his arms, looking very much like his brother.

"You solved math problems in the hospital for fun," Alexis said.

"They are problems that can be solved, at least until you get into the really high-level theoretical stuff," Peter said.

Terra looked around at her team.

Alexis nodded, Russel shrugged one shoulder, and Zach tossed his hands up.

"Would you mind looking at what we have then and seeing if you can find a pattern?" Terra asked Peter.

"Really?" Peter brightened.

"Yes, please."

"Sure!"

"Here, take this too." Russel passed Peter a spiral notebook. "It's a guide to what we know of spell theory so far. If the math explains the underlying logic, it might line up somehow."

"Thanks!" Peter took the spellbook pages and the notebook to the counter.

Alexis turned on Zach, her hands on her hips. "Now, Zach, seriously, bed."

Out the window the sky was showing the hints of a red sunrise.

Sighing, Zach pulled himself to his feet. "You're right. Thanks. Wake me if you need me."

Brian let Zach manage his shoulder bag, but carried the rest of his stuff up to a room on the second floor. Zach thanked him and then, partially for fun, partially because he was safe, and mostly because he really couldn't deal, he fell face-first on the bed. His shoes still on, sleep took him.

Thirty-Four

Kayla woke slowly, groggy and disoriented.

Noah! The bedside table said she'd slept just over five hours. Terra hadn't woken her, so that would mean there was no news. If she could trust Terra. Kayla shook her head. Zach trusted Terra, and so did Kayla's gut. Closing her eyes, Kayla let her head fall back to the pillow.

Bit by bit, she mentally reconstructed where she was and what'd happened. Pulling herself out of bed was slightly easier. Digging her hairbrush out of her bag, she let the past few days float around her mind like clouds, observing, but not trying to hold on to them. Unbraiding her hair, Kayla took her time untangling the long fine strands and reached out for the strings of magic. They glowed softly into her visible range. The web connecting her to Zach pulsed softly.

Kayla blinked. He was asleep—she could tell by the quality of energy she felt through the strand. *That's new.*

Intellectually, she wasn't sure she liked being that aware of another person, that connected. Emotionally, though, it was reassuring.

Weaving her hair into a fresh French braid, Kayla reached for the bigger sense of connectedness. It was there. She knew it, but couldn't quite cross the threshold into feeling it. Looping a blonde hair band around the end of her braid, she let go of her magic and turned her attention to the day ahead.

She frowned as she dug through her duffle for a change of clothes that spoke to her. Going downstairs without Zach was daunting. The Guard members had been weirdly nice, but Peter hit the nail on the head; she was an outsider.

Even dragging her feet, it wasn't long before Kayla returned from the bathroom and put her toothbrush away. Standing in the center of the room, she tapped her toe impatiently. Nothing to do gave her too much time to worry about Noah. Her stomach growled. Zach was still sound asleep, but she was pretty sure if she kept fidgeting, she'd wake him up. *Annoying.* She should be able to fidget in her own room and not bother anyone.

She tugged on his jacket. It had been his armor around Searcha. Maybe it could be her armor around the Guard. The stiffness of the notebook in the inside breast pocket caught her attention. He'd shown her a few of the pictures in his sketchbook, but they couldn't all be of monsters. Guilt tugged at her, but Zach had told her she could keep the jacket. She found the zipper and freed the slim orange volume.

Kayla gasped. "How the hell?" she muttered, turning her great-uncle's notebook over in her hands. Baffled, she mentally retraced her steps. *Hannah!* The Shadow was the last one she'd seen with the book—she'd picked up Zach's jacket just before Kayla left.

Kayla stared at the faded book a long minute more. Hannah had said it was up to Kayla to make her choices. Maybe she knew that Kayla wouldn't find it right away, and that would give her more time to make the decision? Maybe she thought she'd give the jacket back to Zach, and he'd find it? Maybe it was just to obscure the fact that Hannah had given away a prized Searcha possession so Miranda wouldn't find out.

I'll never understand her. Hugging the jacket closer, Kayla left her room and headed for the stairs. This was more important than waiting for Zach.

Actually, he was awake now. In a mood, but awake.

Kayla backtracked and tapped on his door.

"Yeah," Zach said.

Kayla wasn't sure if that was an invitation or not, so she said as quietly as she could, "Guess what I found in the jacket?"

Zach answered the door, shirtless and in tight jeans. His hair was tousled, because he'd literally just gotten out of bed.

Kayla swallowed and tried not to stare. His athletic routine clearly worked for him.

"Is that the spellbook?" He gaped at her.

Kayla nodded.

"That's awesome." He sounded like he was really trying to mean it.

"Yeah. You okay?"

Rubbing his forehead with the palm of his hand, he sighed. "Just all catching up to me a bit. Are you going to take that downstairs?"

Kayla nodded.

"Thank you."

She gave a half shrug.

"I'm going to give myself a bit to get my head on straight, and I'll be down."

"Looks like there's enough room in there for one to do tai chi, but not two." Kayla heaved a sigh, but smiled. "I'm here if you need me." She twanged one of the strands between them.

Warmth brightened the darkness in his face. He touched the air where her fingers had plucked the strand.

So, he can feel that. A shiver of awareness raced up her spine. She sensed he didn't need her flirting with him now though. "See ya downstairs when you're ready."

"Thank you," he said with sincerity, then closed the door.

Reminding herself that sometimes she just needed a run, and it was only fair Zach needed time, too, she turned towards the stairs, trying not to picture him doing tai chi shirtless.

An enormous beast that probably was a dog, woofed once from the rug under the table, wagged his tail, and then returned his head to his massive paws. Luna was curled up against his side.

"Morning," Terra said from a seat at the table. "No word on your brother yet. But Chessie was at Tidal Water until approximately nine a.m., so there is still time to find him."

"Thank you," Kayla said.

A pretty brunette Kayla hadn't met yet left the table to greet her with a handshake.

"I'm Alexis. Great to meet you. Thank you for rescuing Zach. I was horrified I couldn't see a way to save him in time."

Kayla bristled. Zach had shared a lot about his real life, but had he forgotten to mention a girlfriend? It took her a second longer than it should have to recognize the fizzle, like a carbonated beverage up her arm and tingling across her skin. *Shadow.* That's what she'd meant about not seeing a way to save him.

Kayla stepped back and held her breath, waiting to hear what Alexis would say about what she'd read.

"Coffee or tea?" Alexis asked.

"Huh?" *Great, classy.* Kayla adjusted her stance a little wider, trying to find her balance.

"Figured you could use some caffeine. There's a fresh pot of coffee or . . ."

"Oh, yes, coffee, please."

Alexis tilted her head and walked towards the kitchen. "This way."

The smell of rich, aromatic fuel wafted over Kayla as Alexis poured a cup and showed her where to find the cream and sugar. Kayla downed the glass of water Alexis handed her first and then wrapped her hands around the hot mug.

"Pizza should be here soon. Brian, my boyfriend and Shiner, went out to get it."

Kayla blushed. So her pang of jealousy had been visible. *Great.*

Alexis continued as if that was the way she always referred to Brian. "There are a few pastries and muffins around, if you'd prefer something more closely resembling breakfast food."

"Pizza is totally a breakfast food."

Alexis grinned. "See, Russel. I told you pizza was better than Mexican."

Kayla blinked. They'd thought about her when choosing food?

Russel didn't look up from the notes he was taking. "Not my fault the new girl slept until lunch."

"It's barely eleven." Alexis threw a crumpled up napkin at him. It bounced off his head. He ignored it.

"Not that there is any pressure for you to join us," Terra said. "We get that leaving Searcha and joining our side aren't the same thing."

Kayla sank into the empty seat at the far end of the table. "Thank you for understanding."

Terra shrugged. "Plus, we haven't been able to do a full vet of you yet."

"Like you vetted Mia?" Alexis laughed and turned to Kayla. "She's the one doing the vetting. Some members are a bit uptight about security. Like a computer search tells us more than a hand-shake with a Shadow." Alexis rolled her eyes. "Not that that is fool-proof either, but that's exactly my point."

Kayla had nothing to say to that, so she sipped her coffee. It was just shy of scalding. Even the smell made her more alert.

"Oh, right." Kayla pulled her great-uncle's book from under her arm and offered it to Alexis. "Found this after I woke up."

"The spellbook!" Alexis handed it to Russel, who pulled it open and started poring over it. Peter moved closer to read over his shoul-der.

"That jacket is really clinging to that mirage spell," Alexis mut-tered. "Plus, I was too busy trying to read you. Still. I missed it."

"You can't see everything all at once. Your brain would probably explode," Terra said. "Kayla, you found it?"

Kayla explained Hannah's perspective that not all magical strands were the same. Alexis headed off the others before they could re-peat the same arguments Zach had given Kayla on the drive. Terra stepped out with a call.

"That's the key we need," Peter said, pointing to a page.

"You were spot-on about it being math," Russel said. "One of these formulas must be for repairing damaged knots."

"Thank you," Alexis said to Kayla.

Kayla shrugged. She was handing it over to stop the sea monster, not to help the Guard.

"Kayla." Terra poked her head in from the back door. "Sadie found your brother, but she can't get him to take her seriously. Would you mind getting on the phone with him?"

Kayla bolted up before Terra finished speaking. "Of course!"

Terra held her hand over the mouthpiece as she explained the nonmagic version of events they'd concocted to persuade Noah to go with Sadie and abandon his studying. Kayla nodded and accepted the phone. She sank onto the back steps, relief washing through her when she heard Noah's voice. Tears welled up. She filled him in, as best she could, given Terra's version. She'd sound crazy if she tried explaining the truth. Her words probably didn't make much sense, but her fear and gut-wrenching relief came through clear enough to get her brother to agree to leave the city with Sadie.

Kayla hung up, hands still shaky. Noah was safe. She didn't have to race to DC. With that weight off her shoulders, it was remarkable she didn't just float away. Kayla snorted at the absurd thought. Her mind cleared of the panic she hadn't realized was clouding it. It was time to find out how she could help save everyone else in the city.

Thirty-Five

Zach
Day 12 of the Lockhouse Knot Leak
Tuesday morning
Guard Safehouse, between St. Michaels and Easton MD

Zach woke slowly, trying to detangle himself from his clothes, shoes, and a nightmare about zombie attacks. In his dream, he'd been at college. His alarm hadn't gone off, and he'd missed his organic chem exam, and while he was rushing to explain to his professor, zombies had shown up and it had turned into a quest for survival. Then it started raining, and soon he and random classmates and people from his life were fighting rising water and the flesh-eating dead. Even awake, his brain was trying to solve how they were going to make sandbags out of material from the civil-engineering lab.

A knock on the bedroom door dragged him into full wakefulness. He pulled himself together enough to speak with Kayla, but as soon as he closed the door, he stumbled back to the bed. At least he sat on the edge, instead of crawling under the covers. His mind and body hurt. Tai chi was a great idea, but he couldn't make himself do it, even knowing it would make him feel better.

He buried his head in his hands, trying to banish his nightmare problems and focus on the real-life ones, like a city-eating sea monster.

A chuckle vibrated in Zach's chest. Fear and tears welled up just behind it. He was safe here. As safe as he could be. He was with the Guard. Kayla was safe with the Guard too and they would help her. No one needed him to be strong just this minute. There was a bit of time to feel the tide of emotions.

His most vicious insecurities, which had been battling for his attention since he'd been caught by Miranda, saw a gaping fissure in his defense and poured into his awareness. Their lies grounded with tiny grains of truth tried to overwhelm him. Zach battled to ride the waves of thoughts and emotions without drowning in them.

Kayla and Hannah got the spell book to the Guard, no thanks to me. Even Nick's extra keys and car played a role. Zach'd been busy getting caught. *Would have been eaten without help. The Guard would have been better off sending anyone else. I shouldn't have volunteered. Should have left space for someone else to take the mission.*

Rage at Searcha's blindness tried to shelter him from the pain and terror at seeing his death by Miranda's shotgun, so vivid in the shadows he could feel the blood soaking through his boots, making them squelch with each step he took.

Every emotion he'd managed to push down to keep going rose like a riptide, pulling him under. Breathing as best he could through the pain and tears, he tried to stay with the current.

It felt like an eternity.

When the current let go, it had passed by much faster than seemed possible with so much to feel.

More at peace, or at least wrung out, Zach could unfold himself and stand up. Kayla was right, there was enough room to do tai chi. He slid into the habit like it was a cool lake on a summer day. Tension melted and his mind cleared.

When he was done, he sat on the floor, his back against the bed, and reached for his sketchpad. By the nightstand was his full art set. Alexis must have brought them from HQ for him, and he'd been too tired to notice when he'd arrived. Brian and Terra were brilliant for bringing her to the Guard.

He flipped through the wooden case and found his markers. Without the fear of Searcha looking at his art, Zach let loose. Images in loud colors filled pages as he took apart and examined all the major events since volunteering to join the field team.

Thank you for trying to protect me, he thought to the gremlins in his mind. *But I can handle it.* Digging into the things he wanted to shy away from, dark thoughts, his mistakes, he drew with bold, bright lines. His thoughts were just thoughts, not facts. His breath hitched when he realized he was angry at his friends, too.

Logically, he shouldn't be mad for the stingray venom cut or being sent on a mission that nearly killed him or for not finding an alternative answer to stopping Chessie. *Shouldn't* wasn't a word that helped, though. It was what he was feeling. The anger was protecting him from fear and hurt. Breathing into it, Zach rode the waves of pain. Slowly he pulled apart the thoughts that triggered the emotions, acknowledged the flaws in the logic, and worked his way through.

When his hand finally stilled on his pad, his anger and pain had washed away. His friends were human and had done an amazing job under the circumstances. Miranda and the people that followed her were doing what they believed best. The hardest was to forgive himself. *I'm human, and I did the best I could at any given moment under those exact circumstances.*

Something awful lifted off his chest and he could see he did things right, too. He'd been strong and made some good decisions under crazy pressure. He started sketching and found a long list. The most relevant at the moment, his honest friendship with Kayla and his not ratting out Hannah's feelings for Jason to Miranda were two of the reasons the spell book was here with the Guard. His mission was a success, thanks to him. He was intrinsically worthy of all the help he was given.

I was right to volunteer, I am the main character. He chuckled at the internal voice, but it had a point. He could see himself now as a vital part of an ensemble cast, not a mere supporting character.

Zach smiled, even as he acknowledged he would have to revise versions of these revelations over and over again as they surfaced with different facades to make the connections in his brain stronger. But it was a marvelous start.

At the moment it was easy to see Chessie's rage wasn't about him. She was just a monster, doing what monsters did best. When put like that, he could find no anger for her. He just had to help stop her.

The shadows around him crystalized into clarity.

"Well, shit." Zach muttered as goosebumps stung his skin. Tilting his head, he tried to get a better perspective. "Woulda been helpful to see that sooner." With a flip of his pad, he closed it. Exiting his room, he started down the stairs, grateful he'd had the chance to ground himself. It was time to volunteer again.

Thirty-Six

Kayla
Day 12 of the Lockhouse Knot Leak
Tuesday, midday
Guard Safehouse, between St. Michaels and Easton MD

Zach came down the stairs. Kayla knew he took one look at her and understood Noah was safe. He walked straight to her and wrapped her in a big hug. She leaned into him. Grateful about Noah, and grateful Zach had found his footing again.

"Any luck with the spellbook?" Zach asked, letting her go and accepting the glass of water and cup of coffee Alexis brought him.

"The math used is fascinating," Russel said, checking something on one of his three wristwatches. "We think we've found the spell we need."

Terra's phone rang. She squeezed Zach's shoulder before taking the call outside.

"This symbol isn't in the key." Peter pointed at something in the grimoire. "Maybe it's a Russian word?"

"I'll send a picture to Sadie. Hopefully, she can translate it quickly." Russel pulled out his phone.

"What if you hold it up"—Zach tilted his head—"to the light coming in through the window."

"Brilliant!" A smile lit Alexis's face. "Focus on the symbol you want translated. The shadows will help."

Kayla watched in amazement as the four of them worked on puzzling out the formula. There was no separation between the magic types, no rules about a Shadow standing three feet away from everyone else. Alexis squeezed Peter's shoulder affectionately when he solved an important piece. Zach fist bumped with Russel when they said the same answer at the same moment. Zach and Peter had a better grasp of the math than the others, Russel was better at visualizing the mechanical aspects and the outcome, and Alexis was the stronger Shadow. They all leaned in close, heads almost touching over the top of the table, notes and spellbook between them.

Luna crawled over and climbed in Kayla's lap. Kayla rubbed its trunk between the branches. The dog got up and put his head on her knee.

"Feeling left out?" Kayla murmured to him.

He sighed. She rubbed his head. His tail whacked happily against the floor. The plant investigated Kayla's mug, but turned her tendril up at the dark liquid.

Kayla giggled.

Zach looked up from the spell work, his smile warm and intimate.

"How'd you get the plant to do that?" Alexis asked curiously.

Kayla shrugged. "Luna seems to enjoy sitting on laps." Kayla picked her up and offered her to Alexis. "Want to try?"

Alexis looked surprised, but put out her arms. The plant poked at her hands and arms a few thoughtful times, then leapt right over.

"She's kinda like an alien bug baby," Kayla observed.

"And even cuter!" Alexis said. Luna examined her, then curled up like a sleepy cat.

The dog jumped up with a deep woof, tail wagging furiously.

"Pizza's here," a dark-haired, green-eyed guy announced, coming through the front door, balancing five pizza boxes. "Down, Prince."

The dog stopped jumping, but tangled around his legs instead.

"Brian! We've found a spell that should work!" Alexis said.

"Awesome!" Brian slid the pizza onto the table in front of Kayla, the only spot not covered in papers, and kissed Alexis. "Nice lap plant?"

"Hopefully she doesn't grow as big as Prince and think she can still sit on laps." Alexis grinned.

"Or we find a way to retie them all before that happens." Brian turned to Kayla and introduced himself.

"Retie who?" Kayla asked.

"The knots," Brian said. "It's shitty," he added with feeling, correctly reading her expression. "Storm saved my life and helped save my family, but she'll understand. Her predecessor helped Merlin tie her knot back in the Dark Ages."

Brian turned back to the group. "You said you found a spell?"

Kayla frowned at him. Focused on his fellow Guard members, Brian didn't notice.

"It's a big net," Russel said, "using the same technology the magic earbuds use. It'll take a lot of magic clay, but if you can collect it, it'll be a lot faster than anything we can craft with spellcaster magic."

Kayla frowned at Zach.

He tilted his head in acknowledgement of her feelings and let his own sadness over the plan show on his face, but then gestured to the image from his sketchbook that was on the table. The ugly, gigantic fish attacking DC.

Kayla gave a one shoulder shrug. She didn't like it, but they could all agree that the sea monster had to be stopped. If Hannah and Jason could be convinced that some magic was too dangerous to be free, maybe she could, with time, convince the Guard to let Luna and Storm be. It might be a long shot, but it gave her another reason to stay.

Serving herself a piece of veggie pizza, she realized she'd missed something important in the conversation.

Brian and Zach were glaring at each other.

Thirty-Seven

Kayla's one shoulder shrug was reluctant, but Zach was glad she didn't start a fight about Luna's eventual fate. If they lost this fight with Chessie, then reining in *any* magic might be beyond them.

"How much clay do you need?" Brian asked, accepting a plate of pizza from Alexis.

"Estimating the size of the net needed, plus extra for safety . . ." Russel frowned at his paper. Absentmindedly, he nodded thanks to Alexis as she served him.

"Fifty-five," Peter said. "If they're approximately the diameter of a dime. More if they're smaller."

Russel scratched at the paper with his pencil and nodded. "Sounds right. Peter is rocking this math."

Peter beamed and accepted his plate.

"That's going to take a bit, how much time do we have?" Brian asked.

Russel scribbled on one of his notepads. "With our estimates of Chessie's speed, our driving time, planning to cut her off before she reaches DC, and adding in a safety margin . . . say four hours."

"I better get started." Brian looked sadly at his uneaten slices.

"I think it's better if I go after Chessie and you and Alexis take point on protecting the knot," Zach said with as much confidence as he could.

Brian waved a hand. "She wants to eat you. Better you are as far away from her as possible."

"True, but if you go, she'll eat you both. She's hunting me because she got a taste already, but she'll devour anything with magic she can get her teeth in."

Brian glared. "That's only one possibility. You're in more danger."

Zach glared back. There was no best person for the job, there were just bad options, but his gut told him it was time he faced Chessie.

"It'll chase Zach. If Alexis and Brian fail, we'll need you to help lead it away from the populated areas," Terra said.

Zach hadn't heard her return, but was glad she had. "You can use the leaking knot for that. Chessie wants it way more than she wants me."

"The clay on the net won't have time to dry. It'll have to be held by the strands. Only a Shiner can do that," Russel said.

"If you go, she will kill you both. I can see it. I drew this just before I came down." He flipped his sketchbook to the last thing he'd drawn—Brian and Alexis being pulled into the depths by the monster. It was only a possible future, but it felt very real to Zach.

"I'm so jealous you can show what you see," Alexis commented mildly. "I can see the shadows so clearly and I know exactly how

I'd capture them with my camera, but of course they don't photograph."

"I'll go with Zach," Kayla said. "Net a sea monster. Sounds like fun."

Zach's stomach twisted as the others turned to look at her.

"It's going to be really dangerous," he warned.

"So I gather." Kayla grinned before taking a bite of pizza.

"I wish I could be selfish and say you should stay safe, but too many lives are at risk. Thank you." Zach was glad she'd volunteered before he could work up the courage to ask.

Her smile was infectious. "I love a good adrenaline rush."

"You're not tied," Terra said. "Which means your magic isn't as strong as Brian and Alexis's."

"It's not about bulk strength, not if they work together. I wish it was, so I could argue harder," Alexis said pensively. "I can't see the shadows clearly about Brian and me. Not about this." Frustration built in her voice. "I can see it'll be really dangerous, Zach and Kayla, if you go. There is something missing. A piece I can't see."

"We're never going to see it all. Wish it wasn't true, but we're not gods," Zach said.

"I know." Alexis rolled her shoulders and sat taller. "I wish there was a third option. Something brilliant and easy that cleans up this mess with a nice bow, but this is what we've got."

"Honestly. I think Kayla and me netting Chessie is the third option. I'm sorry it doesn't include a bow."

Brief amusement brightened the atmosphere.

Terra facilitated a detailed discussion of the plan and the creation of several desperate back ups, before leaning back.

"I don't like it, but at least Zach and Kayla aren't ditching us and trying to do it on their own," Terra concluded, humor in her face.

"Hey!" Brian protested, but laughed. "We weren't trying to ditch *you*, we were trying to ditch Elliot."

Alexis swatted him on the arm, a grin ruining her scold.

Zach's shoulder tensed at the reminder; the shadows could withhold key information.

"Alright." Brian leaped up. "Fifty-five magic marbles to collect. How much time?"

"If you make the net on the drive there? Let's aim for two hours, but three at the most," Terra said.

Brian opened a pizza box. "You got it. Come on, Kayla, we've got our work cut out for us."

Alexis dug a reusable bag out of her backpack and handed it to Brian, as he piled half-a-pizza worth of slices on a paper towel.

Kayla grinned and followed his lead with nearly as many slippery slices.

"Take a pair of magic earbuds to practice with. Kayla should know how to use them," Terra said.

Brian nodded and fished the Ziplock bag with the green magic earbuds out of the supplies on the table.

"Maybe get a few extra marbles for safety margins. We should have a mold made for them by the time you get back," Russel said.

Brian saluted, whistled for Prince to follow, and headed out the front door with Kayla.

"You two are cute together," Alexis said.

Zach blushed; he'd been staring at the door after it closed behind Kayla. "I didn't find her. You all sent me to steal her book."

"Mmph. That spellbook could have belonged to anyone at that camp and you'd still have connected with her."

Zach wanted to protest for form's sake, but she had a point. Ara was the one who'd been keeping the spellbook, after all. He shuffled through the papers in front of him without seeing them. "Can you see? Will she stay? If we survive, that is."

Alexis squeezed his arm. "I think that's a question you ought to ask her, don't you?"

Zach snorted. "Very diplomatic. Being a Shadow is a pain in the ass sometimes, isn't it?"

Alexis grinned like she knew what was in his Christmas present but couldn't tell him. "Yep."

"Sea monster first," Zach said. "How are we going to catch that thing in a net?"

"We're going to need a bigger boat," Russel said.

"That's not funny," Terra said, but Zach and Alexis laughed.

"What?" Peter asked.

"It's from the movie *Jaws*."

"Ah. At least she's not a shark," Peter said.

Zach thought Chessie probably had as many teeth, but said, "I'll take all the silver linings I can get."

Smiles faded, replaced by frowns of concentration as they dug into the challenge of how they were going to get Chessie into the net. They debated throwing it from a bridge over the Potomac, but they wouldn't make the 301 bridge in time, and as Russel pointed out, you could see the monuments from the bridge on 495. Alexis could see that motorboats would scare off—or worse, anger—Chessie, but luckily Zach remembered Kayla could sail. Russel checked to make sure there'd be enough wind.

They were deep in prep for net making when Terra wrapped up a call with a friend who could lend them a sailboat and rejoined the table.

"Does this look right?" Peter said, using a compass to check an angle on the rudimentary tool he and Russel had made out of a scrap block of magic-conducting wood Russel had in his trunk.

Russel double-checked it. "Best I can tell. Zach, let us show you how it works."

Zach moved closer.

"The directions say you fold and squish the clay five times, then shape it into a hexagon. This wood should allow you to mold it. Then you use this part to push it in, that will give the three grooves. Kayla will then need to weave the strands into it." Russel frowned. "If it doesn't work, you can mold it by hand, but the angles of the strands are the most important part."

"Thanks." Zach caught a flicker in the shadows as they blossomed with vibrant color. He smiled and turned towards the door.

Kayla, Brian, and Prince bounced in.

"Got them all." She held up the reusable bag.

"Good job," Terra said.

"They're beautiful," Zach breathed. Gingerly, he reached into the bag, ready in case they shocked him. The bead of magic he lifted out was soft and light, like foam clay. Pulling it up to the light, it was the same red/amber as Kayla's magic. As he squished it, the smell of sunbaked earth and the tang of raspberries wafted up.

After five folds, he placed the magic clay carefully in the mold. It resisted, but Zach concentrated and imagined warming the wood with his energy, trying to make it an extension of his hand. The clay cooperated, sliding into the hexagonal shape. Then he squished the lid on, like a garlic press. Gently, he opened it, turned it upside down over Kayla's hand, and shook. A knot piece of the net fell out. It held solid in her hand.

"Perfect!" Russel said, holding Kayla's hand to examine it without touching the clay. He let go. "So if you weave the strands through it . . ."

"Which strands do I use?" Kayla asked.

"Umm?" Russel said.

"Try the ones between you and Zach. So the net is connected to both of you," Alexis said.

Kayla did, and then held both ends of the strands; the bead hung in the air.

Zach met her grin. She had come so far with her magic. Her smile brightened when she saw the pride in his face.

"Looks perfect," Brian said.

"Nicely done," Terra said. "Can we be out of here in fifteen?"

Everyone nodded.

"Let's do it."

Thirty-Eight

Kayla was hauling her duffle down the stairs when Prince started barking at the front door.

Terra looked up from the table where she was boxing up papers. "What?"

Stomp, stomp, came from outside.

Prince jumped at the door, tail wagging frantically.

Terra opened the door as Kayla reached the landing.

Storm was standing on the porch, sides heaving.

"Alexis!" Terra called. "We've got company."

Kayla dropped her bag and hurried out to the unicorn.

Blowing, head up, ears flicking nervously, Storm ignored the dog winding between her legs.

"What's wrong?" Kayla asked, not that she expected an answer. She put a tentative hand on Storm's sweaty shoulder, while Alexis patted the unicorn's cheek.

"It's the sea monster. She's afraid to be this close," Zach said, coming up beside Kayla and placing a reassuring hand on the small of her back.

Storm backed down the steps onto the grass, whinnying like a downpour hitting a pond.

"Why is she here, then?" Terra asked.

"She wants something." Alexis frowned at the shadows. "I'm getting a reminder of a rock? Like a hunk of quartz?"

"Oh, this?" Kayla pulled the Smith rock out of her pocket.

Storm reared and backed up, her whinny like a crack of thunder.

Kayla shoved the rock back into her pocket.

"That's it, but I don't understand." Alexis said.

"In the shadow, the spell in the quartz looks like a large shield," Zach said.

Understanding dawned on Kayla "We can use it to protect us from Chessie. Thank you, Storm."

The unicorn gave a half bow, but popped right back up, dancing in place and whinnied again.

"She wants something else?" Zach said.

"The plant!" Alexis ducked inside and came out with Luna.

Storm quieted a bit, but she was still breathing hard.

Luna extended a curious tendril towards the unicorn and then reached with all of her branches.

Alexis looked to Terra.

"Well, I wasn't exactly thrilled about bringing her back to HQ. Will they be okay together?" Terra said.

"Yes, as long as we stop Chessie. Storm wants to look out for her," Alexis said.

Zach nodded.

Alexis held Luna out, and Storm moved closer. Luna wrapped her branches around Storm's neck and settled on her withers. Then she reached two branches around Storm's belly, like the girth of a saddle.

"I'll miss you," Kayla said to Luna.

Luna rustled her leaves mournfully.

Storm whinnied in gratitude, then whirled and galloped off.

"Never a good sign when Storm is scared," Brian remarked.

"I want us pulling out of here in five," Terra said.

"So, we're going to go *towards* the sea monster that the unicorn is afraid of?" Kayla muttered to Zach.

"Yep. I hope you're still up for it?"

"While we were hunting for magic clay, Brian showed me how to feel strands connecting me with more people in DC than I can count. Not only do they need our help, but I'm not missing this adventure." She slid her hand into Zach's. Brian had also casually shared about his experience of being tied and how much joy it was bringing him. Not only was he clearly head over heels for Alexis, but he confided that the structure she added to his life helped tame the mundane, so there was more freedom for them to be spontaneous. She'd tucked away his words to think about later.

"Zach, Kayla," Russel called. "I've got a gear belt for you."

"Thanks!" Zach said, accepting one of the black webbing belts with pouches and dangling things. "A small dive tank. Nice!"

Luckily hers was smaller and less cumbersome.

"The tank won't give you much time, but a bit," Russel said. "Five minutes if you're breathing hard, longer if you're calm. Kayla, have you used one before?"

Kayla shook her head.

"I'll walk her through it on the drive," Zach said.

Russel nodded. "At least the Potomac isn't deep where you'll be."

Kayla shifted, trying to find her balance. She pulled the rock out of her pocket. "Zach, can you take this? It's more than I want to carry with the belt."

"But Storm gave that to you to protect yourself."

"And I'm giving it to you," Kayla said. "Chessie is focused on you."

Zach stared at the rock. After a thoughtful silence, he nodded. "Thank you." He tucked the stone into a pouch with a zipper.

"It's so hot that you can be smart rather than prideful or macho," she murmured to him.

Zach gave a startled laugh. "I'm glad you think so."

They finished loading the vehicles. Brian and Alexis got to take the Porsche. Russel and Prince loaded in the pickup. Kayla slid into the back seat of the Corolla with Zach; Terra drove and Peter rode shotgun.

"I'm going to miss that car," Kayla remarked, watching Brian and Alexis zoom away.

"Where is Nick?" Zach pulled out the bag of magic marbles and mushed together a handful.

"Reaching out to every contact he has in DC," Terra said. "Trying to get the city evacuated while being vague about the why and not burn through all of his capital in case we're able to stop Chessie in time."

Wait, Nick is working with the Guard? Kayla felt dense for not realizing that sooner.

Zach pulled off a section of clay and put it into the mold. "Has he had any luck?"

Terra sighed. "A lot of the wealthy and connected are finding excuses to get out, and I think the president is taking a last-minute trip to Camp David, but the average person has no idea they should evacuate. At least we won't have a ton of government instability if things go sideways. It's not much, but mass panic won't help anyone. No matter how I look at it, I can't come up with a workable plan."

"You're doing an amazing job," Zach said. "I can't imagine juggling all the variables you're working with. Besides, if Chessie manages to get by Kayla and me, Brian and Alexis will divert her before she gets to DC."

"Which would have her tromping through several other cities and heavily populated areas." Terra took a deep, steadying breath. "Sorry. We got this. We're doing the best we can at this moment with what we have. And you two are building that net which *will* work."

Zach's hands stilled. "You know if something happens to us, it's not your fault, right?"

Terra swallowed hard. Kayla's heart hurt for her.

"If you tried to stop us, we'd go behind your back and go anyway," Zach teased before returning to seriousness. "This is a good plan. Might we, in retrospect, see another that could have worked better? Sure, but this is the best option we have now with everything we know here and with every bit of clarity we can give ourselves.

"I mean, the other option is to move to the middle of nowhere, live off the grid, and prep for the end of the world. Could be fun, but Brian's sisters would stage a revolt."

Terra burst out laughing. Wiping away tears with one hand, while still keeping the car steady with the other.

When she'd collected herself, she spoke again. "You know that advice applies to you just as much as it does to me?"

Zach frowned.

Kayla slid her hand into his. His fingers, warm and large, closed around hers.

"You're right," Zach said. "Easier to give advice than take it, but I'm trying." He squeezed Kayla's hand before letting go to mold more clay.

"All we can do." Terra grinned again. "Speaking of Brian's sisters, Vicky sent me another email yesterday, begging to help. Guess what I did?" Terra said.

"What?" Zach asked.

Kayla pulled strands into her physical plane, choosing ones to build the net with, while enjoying listening to them talk.

"Do you remember that journal translation you were doing before you left?" Terra asked.

Zach seemed to have to think about it a minute. "You mean the cross between Orcish and pig Latin?"

Terra laughed. "Sadie picked it up after you left on your mission. She apologizes, by the way. She had no idea how awful it was when she assigned it. She called it a desecration of the Latin language. I never thought I'd see the day when she'd complain about doing a translation. Anyway, I sent it to Vicky. Told her if she wanted to be helpful, she could start there."

Zach hooted with laughter. "That's fantastic!!"

Terra grinned. She turned her attention to Peter, asking about his language classes in school.

Still grinning, Zach filled Kayla in on Brian's family and his little sisters' deep frustration that they weren't allowed to join the adventures at HQ.

Kayla asked questions and laughed at his anecdotes as she wove the net with the strands that webbed between them.

When he was sure he'd have left over clay, Zach made earbuds and Kayla used a strand to connect them. It was as natural as talking to share their thoughts, though she was grateful for the practice with Brian earlier. The more relaxed she got, the more she was distracted by his hands as he molded the clay, his shoulder brushing against hers when the car went around a bend, and his eyes, a warm amber which looked at her, not her shadow, and yet still seemed to see deep into her. She blushed the first few times an errant thought slipped through, but Zach smiled warmly back, making her feel safe and free to be fully herself.

Kayla liked that he saw Terra's fears and tried to help, even though she was the one acting as leader. She liked the way he was kind when he joked about the younger members of the Guard. And she enjoyed making up stories with him about what their life would be like if they were in a graphic novel. When he was done molding the clay, he even sketched out a few of the panels, adding her ideas as they went.

"I understand that you're not ready to be tied to anyone," he said softly in her mind. *"But, if you are at some point."* He blew out a breath. *"Um, well, I'd be happy to be tied with you, if you wanted to be. I mean, we've got Chessie to deal with and all that first of course, but just thought I'd throw that out there."*

Kayla's mind went blank. *He likes me, but that much?*

Zach fiddled with his pencil. "Sorry," he muttered. "*Stupid ear-buds. They don't give me enough space to think before I share, but still, I should have been more careful.*"

Kayla very much wanted to lean over and kiss him. "You're over-thinking," she murmured instead.

"*I am? I didn't overstep?*"

"*You just surprised me.*" Kayla leaned her head against his shoulder. Hiding her face it was easier to admit, "*I have a silly fear. What if we find one day that we're bored with each other's company, but we're stuck cuz we're tied?*"

Zach rested his head on hers. "*That isn't a silly fear for you,*" he said matter-of-factly. "*Boredom scares you.*"

"*But it's not like it's life threatening or anything. It's not a sea monster.*"

"*More of an everyday challenge, which in some ways is worse, because you can't risk your life to net it once and be done with it. Boredom leaves you with nowhere to hide from uncomfortable feelings and thoughts.*"

Shit, he's right. "*Unbearable ones, which is stupid. And weak of me. Because nothing seriously bad has ever happened to me.*"

"*It's not stupid or weak. For someone who's afraid of heights, twenty feet off the ground can be as bad as a hundred. And you've already been exploring the adventure of feeling your feelings. With practice it'll continue to be easier to manage the scary.*" He hesitated.

"*And?*" she asked.

"*And life can be like tai chi—if it becomes too routine, easy to do since it's the same series of movements every time, we can stop paying attention, and it can become boring.*"

Kayla sat up to look at him. *"But it's not routine, there's always something to pay attention to. Every little movement, every subtle shift of weight, the way the air feels, everything."*

He grinned.

"Oh. I sometimes feel the same way when I'm running or partic-ipating in a sport, fully in the moment." Kayla leaned back against the seat with a bit of awe in her chest and let that sink in. *"You're saying I can apply that to the boring parts of life?! That's the freakin' mindfulness Jason and Dahlia wouldn't shut up about!"*

Zach laughed. *"The look of annoyance on your face."*

"It was torture! All that meditating and conceptual crap!" But his amusement was contagious, and she couldn't keep the grin off her face.

"Heads up, we're almost there," Terra said.

Straightening up, Kayla finished tying off the net, folded it care-fully, then stored it in an empty pouch on her utility belt.

She slid her free hand into Zach's. *"I'm here now."*

He smiled at her. *"As am I."*

If they both survived, she'd think about what came next then.

Thirty-Nine

Zach
Day 12 of the Lockhouse Knot Leak
Tuesday evening
Just south of DC

DC traffic was on their side, and Terra's friend's directions for accessing her marina and boat were clear and direct. The overcast sky reflected the city lights as Kayla double-checked that she understood how the unfamiliar model of sailboat worked, and Zach tied a spell rock to the bow that would obscure magical activity from the view of regular people. *Instead of putting their time into crafting weapons, the Guard puts their time into protecting humanity.* Zach smiled with pride, dusted his hands off, and stood.

Terra and Peter helped push them off, but stayed on land, where they'd be ready to enact plan W or X or something if the current plan went wrong. In the meanwhile, Terra could continue coordinating Guard activities.

Using the glow from her Shiner markings to light her way, Kayla and Zach hoisted the sails. A smile stretched across Zach's face at Kayla's whoop of glee as the wind caught. Beside her, he leaned back on the high side, water splashing by. Yellow lights shone from houses between the trees, and red and green lights from a distant motor boat moving away.

Zach whooped as the boat tipped further, but his focus was on the shadows.

Kayla shifted the bow closer to the wind, easing the tilt. "Any sign of Chessie?"

He shook his head. "Not yet."

As they zig-zagged back and forth they didn't talk about what would happen if their calculations were off, if the monster had swum past before they arrived.

"What's that?" Zach pointed at the sky downstream. A dark, boiling cloud stood out against the light-polluted night sky.

"Are those birds? Crows from camp?"

Just visible between the waves was the long, dark shape of the sea monster in the shadows.

"They're harassing Chessie like they would a hawk."

"We're in time! We can cut her off up there and net her." Kayla pointed towards the far side of the channel.

Nodding, Zach prepared himself to take the tiller. He just had to keep the boat steady long enough for Kayla to manage the net.

The crows turned sharply upwards.

Chessie arched into the air. As long as a bus, she snapped her huge, teeth-filled mouth at the birds. Her sharp dorsal fin reflected the skyglow in oily rainbows. When her snub tail pulled free of the water, she turned like a whale and crashed back down. Waves splashed into the air, almost reaching the crows.

"Can you tighten the sheet?" Kayla called.

Fingers numb, Zach fumbled with the line.

Waves from the monster's impact rushed towards them. Kayla yanked the tiller. The boat bounced, but the bow cut through the waves. The wind hit from the other side.

"Jibe!" Kayla shouted.

Zach ducked. The boom missed his head by inches as it whipped over. He yanked the sheet free, jumping to the other side to pull the front sail over.

"What the hell! We're coming about?" Kayla fought with the tiller. The boom shifted to the other side. The boat lurched forward. Before Zach could fix the front sail, the wind shifted behind. He stayed low as the boom banged over.

"The wind is circling us!" Icy dread clawed at Zach's chest. "She knows we're here."

Kayla yanked the mainsail tight. The boom couldn't swing, but the erratic wind pushed them harder. "The sea monster can control wind?!"

"You got a better explanation?"

A line of waves hit them broadside. The boat tipped wildly.

Zach pointed at the murder of crows moving directly towards them. "She's coming this way."

Kayla gave up with the tiller and reached for the canvas bag on her belt. "At least we don't need to intercept her."

"I appreciate the optimism." A small internal smile battled the tightness in his chest. Zach frowned at the shadows. *The net! The boat!* "Shit! Keep the net in the bag until the last possible minute."

"Zach?!"

The crows were almost overhead.

"I'll try to distract her," Zach called, then gulped air.

The boat flipped. Dark water closed over his head. The teeth of his nightmares sank into his left leg, pulling him down.

Forty

Kayla
Day 12 of the Lockhouse Knot Leak
Tuesday evening
In the Potomac

Kayla's PFD popped her to the calm surface. The boat lay on its side, close by. Cawing crows flapped overhead, circling in the still air.

"Zach," she called.

Silence. Even the crows quieted for a moment. Baby waves sloshed against the boat.

"Zach!"

The crows seemed to echo her call.

She flailed in a circle, looking for any sign of him. The foam jacket kept her from choking on water.

The crooked-toe crow, Hugin, landed on the boat. Urgency lanced his caw.

Kayla shook herself and swam towards the boat. "Right, the net. But distracting her better not involve getting eaten," she muttered.

Kayla efficiently righted the boat the same way she would a sunfish. Breathing gently through the tightness in her chest, she felt the fiberglass under her fingers, then the metal ladder on the back of the boat. The net's bag was secure on her belt.

The flock of crows looked like buzzards overhead.

There was no breeze. No way to drop one side of the net then sail over the monster and drop the other side.

Alexis had strictly warned against using the motor.

Is he already dead? Mentally, she reached for the strands that connected her to Zach.

He wasn't there.

A stitch bit into her side.

There were no strands anywhere.

My magic is gone!

Her vision darkened around the edges.

Woop woop. Munin landed on the railing and looked at her with dark, intelligent eyes.

"My magic's not gone. I'm panicking," Kayla said out loud.

It didn't fix it, but acknowledging it helped. Every part of her wanted to run from what she was feeling, shut it down and bury it. But that would bury her magic.

"I don't have time to breathe!" she yelled at the bird.

Woop woop.

If she didn't take a moment, there was nothing she could do.

Kayla breathed into her panic. Into the slicing pain in her leg. No. Not her leg. Zach's leg.

"He's alive!" She welcomed the pain, because he was still there to feel it. Breathing into her fears and doubts, she let it be. Letting it all float to the top of her mind, she reached for her net bag. Strands bloomed around her. *There!* Just to her right. The outline of

Chessie, like a bioluminescent spiderweb exoskeleton, glowing near the bottom.

With shaking fingers, Kayla pulled the edge of the net free.

She reached out mentally. "*Zach*?"

Forty-One

Zach
Day 12 of the Lockhouse Knot Leak
Tuesday evening
In the Potomac

Teeth dug deeper into Zach's leg, pulling him down, rolling him against the mud and debris of the bottom like an alligator's death roll.

He kicked her with his free foot, but her scales were boulder hard.

Lungs screaming for oxygen, Zach reached for the last thing the shadows had shown him. Fumbling with the zipper pocket, his hand closed around the hunk of quartz, and he yanked it free.

With a bone-aching screech, Chessie spat him out.

Zach kicked towards what he hoped was the surface.

The water didn't stir.

Every cell in his body was panicking for oxygen. He remembered the regulator on his belt just before he inhaled water. After clearing it with his last gasp of air, Zach carefully breathed in. More firmly, he cleared it again.

The ohh-ahh of his breathing through the regulator cleared his mind.

Still, Chessie didn't attack.

Keeping the rock out in front of him, he loosened the mask from his belt with one hand, put it on, and cleared it.

The crystal in his hand glowed white in the murky water. He hovered just above the mud. The PFD hugged his body, but didn't pull him up, as if it was a scuba vest at neutral buoyancy. Kicking for the surface, he tried again, but his arms and legs moved without resistance, like he was swimming in air, not water.

The surrounding sediment began coalescing into clumps that settled out of the water like snowflakes. Chessie swam just outside the bubble of still water, pacing back and forth. *Shit. I'm in a magical snow globe.* Smith's rock was keeping her out, but her magic could still alter the water around him.

The crystal in his hand flickered, just for a second, but it dimmed a fraction of a degree.

Chessie smiled with her wide mouth. Wicked teeth glittered in the white light.

"*Zach?*" Kayla's thoughts filled his head with warmth.

His earbud was still in.

Evil joy lurked in Chessie's fish eyes, and something else.

Zach concentrated on replying to Kayla. "*I'm alive. In a bit of a standoff. You okay?*"

"*Yeah, I've still got the net.*"

"*Good.*" The rock flickered again. "*I don't know how long I can hold her off.*"

"*Stop that!*"

"*What?*"

"Sorry, the crows keep playing with the net as I'm trying to untangle it."

"Okay," Zach said, but most of his attention was on the dark-green eyes glowering at him. *Is my air tank going to run out of air before or after the rock dies?*

"Are you mad?" Kayla asked.

"What?" Was I thinking loudly? "More resigned and curious."

"Why am I feeling rage?"

"Oh. Chessie. You're probably picking up her emotions." Zach said.

"I wonder what all that anger is protecting her from?" Kayla joked.

Zach smashed himself on the forehead, hitting his mask. It dug into his face. He cleared out the water that slipped in.

"Shit, you're right!" Chessie wasn't just a destructive tidal wave of teeth. There was intelligence in her eyes. Like Storm or Luna. If she was a person, it would have been one of his first questions. His belief that magic was more like a nuclear weapon than a living thing had blinded him.

"Zach?"

"It's more than just anger at her knot being withheld from her." The rage was even deeper than that. The rock's protecting light flickered and dimmed. *"Ah, we're running out of time. I'll stop distracting you."*

"Tell me later."

"Sure." If he survived.

Chessie screeched at him, trying to bite down on his protective bubble. The light flickered but held. An image bloomed like squid ink shifting into an India-ink painting on the side of the bubble—Zach's leg being torn off. It shifted into Chessie digging into his stomach and his intestine being caught in the current.

Zach swallowed back vomit before it could reach his mouth.

He was supposed to be stalling, and she was trying to communicate. Even if it was ghastly, it was an opportunity.

His magic pen was still around his neck. *Why not?* Luna had reacted to his drawings. He uncapped it and tried drawing on the water. The still molecules held the ink, and the magic of Smith's rock shined through, projecting the image on the edge of the bubble. He drew the knot and her going back into it. Reunited with her strand.

She screeched, making his teeth ache.

With a swish of a pectoral fin, the ink she'd painted on the side of the bubble shifted into a beautiful stingray with bioluminescent magic swirling down her back, like a Shiner's markings. Zach's chest ached. She could be so beautiful if he loosed her knot.

The image shifted again: the ray betrayed and netted by a man with red hair and a beard.

Captain John Smith, Zach realized. Her pain sliced into him. The stingray barb knife he'd found diving was Smith's. The explorer had enchanted it from Chessie's predecessor's barb after he'd attacked her and she'd stung him. The plant knot wasn't the only knot Smith had tied.

The image changed. She leaked out of the knot into a polluted river and there was no food. Images of bioluminescent tipped crabs and brightly colored mollusks bloomed. Zach could feel her confusion.

Where are they?

Was she being fanciful? No, they were magical creatures. He tried to show they were also in knots.

She screeched again. Zach touched his ears to see if they were bleeding. *Not yet.*

She turned to leave.

"Wait!" The regulator muffled the word. If she got away now, they'd never catch her in time. He drew her, breaking through his bubble of protection.

She swished her tail. The net was coming, and she knew it.

With fumbling fingers, he tried to show her the best place for her was back in her knot. There was nothing here for her. No food. No home.

Chessie screeched. Zach's head pounded. Her next image was clear. If she couldn't eat her preferred food, she'd settle for humans and magical creatures, starting with him.

His light sputtered like a dying flashlight. "*Kayla!*"

Forty-Two

"Kayla! The spell is running out of juice." Zach's thoughts were laced with acrid panic.

"I'm trying!" The strands of the net glowed brighter as Kayla spread it across the cockpit. "If I can hook the strands to the parts connecting to the sea monster or under her, I could pull it over her," she muttered. She'd seen movies where fishermen threw nets and they fanned out into a big circle, but she suspected it was more difficult than it looked. She couldn't risk messing it up and spooking Chessie.

Munin cawed at her from the railing.

"I said, go away."

Caw caw.

"The net is not food."

He pecked at it.

"I said, stop that."

Picking up the strand with his beak, he pulled.

"What are you—" Kayla bounced in glee. It was a crazy, insane idea, but . . . "You want to help?"

Munin dropped the net and turned away. Kayla scolded herself for being silly.

Hugin and the rest of the flock returned his caw. A dozen crows landed on the deck, and each picked up a section. Kayla took her edge to the bow. The birds ascended in unison, lifting the net high.

Horror hit her like a high-speed soccer ball to the solar plexus.

Zach was too close to the monster. He'd be caught too.

Looping the drawstring of the net around one arm, the way she was never supposed to do with a real rope, Kayla reached for every strand connecting her to Zach. Their need to stop Chessie. The laughter and stories they'd shared. The wild car ride to the ocean. The tai chi lessons. His acceptance and validation when she was furious, fidgety, or silly, and even as he helped her understand Hannah's perspective. His love and loyalty for the Guard echoed hers for her family.

The strands stretched like an endless rubber band.

Kayla reached for more. She wove in her hurt when he'd betrayed her. Her fears of falling even harder for him and then losing him. Her fears of being that vulnerable with another person. Every uncomfortable feeling Kayla could find, she wove into the rope with the happy ones.

His fear and pain crashed down on her. Kayla stood her ground. Her stomach knotted. Her chest tightened. Her hands clenched. All of it washed through her, but didn't make her crumble.

Just a little more.

Below the thoughts and emotions, she pulled up that constant, distracting simmer of attraction.

There was no way she was going to let him get eaten by a sea monster. She needed to kiss him. Needed his hands in her hair, his lean, powerful body against hers, their mouths exploring.

The strands condensed to the density of a bungee cord. Kayla put her foot on the rail and heaved. Using her body weight and every ounce of strength, she leaned back. The boat rail dipped closer to the water, but the line didn't budge. The crows dropped the net.

Kayla's muscles strained.

The line slackened. Kayla fell back. Pain jarred her as she hit the deck. The boat rocked back to equilibrium.

Zach popped up by the railing, his life jacket holding him afloat.

The net's drawstring slid down Kayla's arm. Wrapping her hand around it before it could escape, Kayla held it fast. On her back, she braced her feet against the railing and started hauling.

The crows cawed, and the flock boiled.

Chessie thrashed. Wind and waves rocked the boat.

Hand over hand, Kayla fought to bring the drawstring towards her.

Zach climbed into the boat.

Waves jostled. The line yanked Kayla to her feet, almost off the boat.

Zach wrapped his arms around her waist from behind, which allowed her to brace both feet against the railing.

Ear-splitting, jaw-rattling screeches rent the air.

Kayla's arms shook from exertion.

Slowly, the wind eased. Tension melted out of the line. Soft waves bumped against the hull. Blood was thundering in her ears. Her and Zach's uneven breathing was loud in the quiet.

She leaned back in his solid embrace, as hand over hand the net came closer. The strands and beads of clay woven together were no bigger than the size of a coin purse when it broke the water. Kayla pulled it to her and carefully loosened the top to peek inside; murky, gelatinous glop glowed ever so slightly in the darkness.

The crows quieted and veered towards shore.

"Did it work?" Kayla frowned. *The enormous sea monster is now that?*

Zach let go of her and sighed. He leaned down to pick up his fallen scuba gear. "Yes. She's gone. What's left will coat the knot and keep it sealed. If the knot is ever cut again, the next version will rise from it."

Kayla triple-tied the sack closed, added a lopsided bow as a joke, then stowed it in a pouch on her belt. "Are you sorry?" She wrapped an arm around his waist.

He relaxed into her and put his arm around her shoulder.

"No." He shook his head, shaking out water and thoughts. "No. She was set on destruction and vengeance. But under different circumstances, in a different world, she could have been beautiful." He smiled at Kayla. "Thanks for saving me, again."

She was about to tell him about not letting him die because she wanted a kiss, but a splash of red caught her attention.

There was blood pooling in the boat.

Kayla helped him sit. "You're hurt."

"It looks worse than it is. The teeth were more like needles than daggers."

"You mean like those needles they use to inject adrenaline straight into the heart? I'm glad it's not worse." Kayla's stomach turned at the metallic scent and the sight of blood oozing from his torn pant leg. "Tell me about what happened. It'll help distract us both."

Zach shared how he'd used his magic pen to communicate with Chessie while Kayla helped him wrap up his leg with a roll of gauze from the first-aid kit. Kayla couldn't quite share his sympathy with the sea monster, since it had tried to eat him, Luna, and everyone in DC, but she did treat the bag of goo with more consideration. Leg and story sorted, she lowered the sails and started the motor.

Zach leaned his head on her shoulder. "I heard something interesting right before you pulled me free. Something about not letting me die because we haven't kissed?"

Kayla twanged one of the strands connecting them. Desire sizzled through her—or through him? Through both of them.

A blush warmed her cheeks, but she didn't look away from his amber eyes. "You heard right."

His smile made her insides melt. She reached up and put her hands through his hair. Her energy flared, lighting her markings.

Their lips met, and it was even better than Kayla had imagined. Even better than she'd dreamed.

Reluctantly, Zach pulled back so she didn't run the boat aground. Trying to catch her breath, Kayla stayed cuddled against his side and managed the tiller with one hand.

Zach cleared his throat twice before he found his hesitant question. "Does this mean you're staying?"

Kayla blinked. "I guess I haven't thought ahead. But this is the Guard's job, right? Stopping Searcha's Unavoidable Upheaval?" Her thoughts crystalized as she spoke. "There are more monsters out there, and Searcha members like Miranda won't hesitate to release them, but you and the rest of the Guard will risk your lives to stop them."

"Yes." Zach's eyes stayed on her face, never dipping to her shadow.

"I don't believe all magic is evil."

"I'm no longer sure any magic knot is truly evil, but that doesn't mean I'm going to allow them to rampage with death and destruction."

"Sounds like a lot of exciting adventures. I'd better stay."

The warmth in Zach's smile, his entire face, took Kayla's breath away. She didn't bother to catch it as he kissed her again.

Forty-Three

Zach
Day 14 days since the Lockhouse Knot Leak was repaired
Tuesday evening
Camp Cattail, MD

Zach lounged on the porch stairs of Terra's house, out of reach of the heat of the bonfire. In the two weeks since netting Chessie, his leg had healed well. Twilight dusted the sky with stars, while wood smoke and laughter wrapped him in a warm blanket of contentment. Off to the side, savoring the moment, he was fully part of the festivities.

Kayla, Alexis, and Alexis's BFF, Mia, were setting up a s'mores station. Sadie and her girlfriend were on a walk to the bay. Elliot and Camilia, a Guard member who checked in on HQ regularly, were swapping stories in chairs by the fire, while Mia's boyfriend, Eric, listened with rapt attention. Brian and Russel were in the kitchen, doing up the few dishes from the cookout. Zach had offered to help, but didn't mind when he was waved off because the kitchen was too small.

Terra sat down beside him, and Prince rested his head on her knee. "Beer?"

"Thanks." He accepted the icy can and clicked it to hers. "I'm glad I was outvoted when I didn't want to do this party. I'm worried about what Searcha will do next, but we need this."

"We do. Camilia's usually right," Terra said.

"I'm sorry you have to give this place up."

Terra's resignation from camp had been the final push towards a party. Magic was still a threat, and she couldn't organize the Guard and work summer camp. She was practically living full-time at HQ since the breach anyway, but at the end of the week it would be official.

"I'll miss it, but life comes in stages and phases." She shrugged. "I'm glad we got one last hurrah, though."

"Kayla will be talking about how much fun the zipline and climbing tower are for weeks to come." Zach grinned before sipping. The beer was citrusy and foamy on his tongue.

"Fun watching her and Mia bond over it," Terra said, but her mind seemed to be far away. Something in her shadow tugged at his attention, but it was easier to ask.

"What's up?"

Terra sighed. "Sadie and Russel are working on a way to modify the blueprint for the net we used to capture Chessie. They think we'll be able to use a version of it to catch the other knot golems."

The beer slipped in Zach's hand. The metal dented under his fingers as he stopped it from falling.

Terra continued. "We still need to figure out how to turn the airborne magic back to strands that can be tied, but now we know how to seal knots, once we do."

Laughter bloomed by the fire. Kayla had accidentally lit her marshmallow on fire. She blew it out, met Zach's eyes, and grinned.

He tried to smile back. Not fully succeeding, he turned to Terra. "That's what we've been working towards."

"It has. It's for the good of the entire planet, but I don't want to paint us as the absolute good. There are hard choices we're going to have to make, and they need to be hard." Terra played with the tab on her beer. "Turning Storm and Luna into goo isn't going to be easy on most of us."

Zach shuddered. "It really won't."

"I think we should have the discussions, look for alternatives, test our beliefs, but if, in the end, that is our only choice, I need us to be able to follow through and still live with it."

Something uncomfortable loosened in Zach's chest, but he hesitated. "Elliot won't like us debating it."

"His perspective is understandable, important, and based on experience, but it's not the only one. He hasn't met Luna."

Zach smiled. "She is special."

Terra nodded, but her frown deepened. "And as special as she is, if tying her knot is the only way to make the world safe from magic, we need to net her."

"I know. I've seen the consequences."

"That's why I'm going to ask. Would you make some drawings for HQ, maybe a graphic novel or two, that we can send to those outside the contamination zone? Show what we're up against, what the stakes are. The horror and the joy of magic."

"Don't we know that?" Zach asked.

Terra downed the last of her beer. "Saying magic is more dangerous than the climate crisis and nuclear war combined doesn't have the same impact as seeing the individual lives it'll destroy or connecting it to a human level and seeing Storm play with Prince."

He nodded slowly. "You tell people an entire village needs to be saved, or you show them the picture of one child that needs help. The child gets the charity over the village." Like the impact of the slides in Miranda's presentation. "You're asking for the truth as I see it in the shadows, not the Guard's historically absolutist views?"

"Yes, and to talk to Alexis and get her feedback, help show the truths she sees, too. That's what your magic is supposed to do after all, show truth. Only the afraid ignore facts when they can be obtained. It'll make the decisions harder, but hopefully better."

There were dozens of sketches that jumped to mind. "Yes. I can do that."

"Thank you." Terra got up and squeezed his shoulder before she walked over to join the s'mores crafting.

Zach pulled his sketch pad out and started flipping through it. The LED string on the railing gave off enough light.

Brian and Russel came out of the house.

"S'mores?" Brian asked.

Zach waved him away. "In a bit."

They joined the group by the fire.

Zach was contemplating a sketch of Chessie pulling everyone into the deep when he felt a tug at his sternum.

Kayla was holding up a roasting stick.

Zach shook his head.

She held up a s'more.

He smiled and gave a giving-in shrug.

She bounced over and sat beside him, offering him the s'more.

"Thanks. I guess I should join in." The graham crackers cracked as he took a bite. The marshmallow was warm and sweet, and the chocolate was a bit cold. His smile grew.

"All the s'more sticks are in use. You have a minute. That felt like a serious conversation, but you're excited?"

Zach filled her in, not sure when her hand and his had intertwined, but he hoped he'd never take for granted how right it felt.

"That's awesome!" Her smile was so infectious. "Do you know what you want to draw first?"

"That's what I was trying to decide." Zach flipped through a few more pages.

"Wait, go back. Who's that?"

A woman with dark hair was tucked against Storm's side. "Searcha's secret Shadow. You know, the one I told you about, whose journal described the boat wreck."

Kayla's hand went cold in his. "I think I recognize her."

"Oh?" Zach said mildly, even as his heartbeat increased.

"I met her. In Dr. Caligo's office, the psychiatrist who diagnosed me as a Shiner. I thought she—Gwen, that's her name—was a patient. She was talking nonsense, only it wasn't nonsense. She told me I'd meet you. Tall and handsome, with eyes the color of magic." Kayla gaped at him.

"What else did she say?"

"She asked me to help her. I didn't do anything. I didn't believe her."

"She probably knew that. If she saw us meeting, then maybe she knew this day was a possibility. Did you get a last name?"

"Gwen . . ." Kayla frowned. "Gwen, short for Gwyneth . . . Webb. That's it."

"Mia and Eric will find her. Terra will organize the rescue mission. Without her, Searcha will lose their edge." Zach made to get up, but Kayla pulled him back.

"You know I'm staying, right? With the Guard. With you. If you want me to."

"I want you to be happy. If that's staying, then absolutely yes, I want you to, but you said you would while hopped up on the high of saving the world from a sea monster. Not a great time to make major life decisions. And there's this." Zach kissed her until his breathing hitched and his blood heated. Leaning back, he smiled. "Also not helpful for clear thinking."

Kayla gave a grin that was only a little loopy. "And that thoughtfulness is just one more reason I'm staying."

Zach thought about asking again if she was sure, but by his estimation, that would go from being thoughtful to being an overprotective idiot. He kissed her again.

Prince put a paw on each of their shoulders and whined in their faces.

Chuckling, Zach pulled back. "The shadows show Elliot is getting ready to dump the water jug over our heads if we keep up. Thanks, boy." He ruffled the dog's ears.

Kayla laughed. "We should join the fire. I'm not roasting you a second marshmallow."

Zach laced his fingers with her. "Our wrists!" The amber knots and swirl tattoo laced across both their wrists.

"You're surprised?" Kayla teased.

"You were so against it."

"Because I hadn't thought I could be tied with you."

Zach raised an eyebrow at the cliche.

Kayla rolled her eyes. "I'm not as afraid anymore. I still have a lot to learn about being present, but I trust now that I will continue to improve. And you don't make me feel tied down or trapped. You make me feel like I have even more room to be myself, even the best version of myself. Being tied with you will be a boatload of adventures I'm so looking forward to exploring. And with you, even the boring and hard parts will have a spark of fun. Come on, before they eat all the marshmallows."

Grinning, Zach let her pull him forward. "If this was a graphic novel, I'd draw it exactly how it is."

Kayla risked the water jug and kissed him again.

ACKNOWLEDGEMENTS

Wow! I can't quite believe it; the final details of *Tide of Shadows* are wrapping up and it's time to write the acknowledgements. For those of you who have been waiting for this book, thank you so much for your patience and kind check-ins! Special shoutout to Walter, who's been asking for a copy by the 4th of July for months and helped give me a final deadline, even though I won't quite be able to get him a paperback in hand for his trip, it's been a tremendous help pushing me to reach the finish line. The adage that the second book is more difficult than the first was more applicable to me than I'd hoped, but it has really helped knowing you all were looking forward to reading it.

I couldn't have done it without my awesome Beta Readers and Critique Partners. Telling the story to myself isn't the same as sharing it with others. Whether they helped me work on the first few, very stubborn chapters, or the whole manuscript, their feedback and support has been invaluable! And bonus: Jenna asked if Kayla has ADHD. Kayla is her own character and she's not felt the need to share with me if she was ever diagnosed, but the question started me on a fascinating journey of discovery about my own neurospiciness. So many of my life choices are making way more sense; I love it!

My editors Emily Rapoport, Ginni Smith, Christopher Hoffmann worked very hard to make the manuscript stronger and, in the process, helped me become a stronger writer. I so appreciated all their feedback and suggestions, even the ones I chose to ignore. Any errors in the book are mine.

Proof Readers Sharon, Barbara, and Lauren used their truly magical ability to find errors.

Lauren is my location scouting buddy and our brainstorming and philosophical conversations help me untangle thorny story brambles.

Mom supplied tons of support, enthusiasm, and fresh eyes for reading what, at least to me, felt like endless drafts and revisions. Dad believes in my story telling abilities and reminds me that someone else can always help with the spelling and grammar. And to those talented people a sincere thank you.

And there are so many others. A story, at least for me, doesn't form in isolation, but through the influences and support of so many people over years and decades. I'm so grateful to them all.

Thank you to everyone who's read, shared, and reviewed *Tangled Shadows*: It means so much! I hear over and over again in this industry that friends and family will never read an author's book and if they do they are even less likely to enjoy it. I never take for granted that y'all have proven the exception to the rule.

Last but not least, thank *You* for reading *Tide of Shadows*!

About the Author

Christina Crothers has been writing stories almost as long as she's been reading them. Besides fiction, she enjoys exploring forests, practicing yoga, and spending time with family and friends. She lives in Virginia with her cat, who is a daily reminder she's not ready for a dog.

Nick and Gwen's story will complete the trilogy next in *Truth in Shadows*. For more information and updates check out Christina Crothers.com

www.ingramcontent.com/pod-product-compliance
Lightning Source LLC
Chambersburg PA
CBHW020329010826
48973CB00005B/1195